The Girls

The Girls

A NOVEL

ELAINE KAGAN

ALFRED A. KNOPF

New York   1994

THIS IS A BORZOI BOOK
PUBLISHED BY ALFRED A. KNOPF, INC.

Library of Congress Cataloging-in-Publication Data
Kagan, Elaine.
  The girls / by Elaine Kagan.—1st ed.
  p.   cm.
  ISBN 0-679-43395-3
  1. Women—Missouri—Kansas City—Fiction. 2. Man-woman
relationships—Missouri—Kansas City—Fiction. 3. Friendship—
Missouri—Kansas City—Fiction. 4. Marriage—Missouri—Kansas
City—Fiction. 5. Kansas City (Mo.)—Fiction.   I. Title.
PS3561.A3629G57 1994
813'.54—dc20   93-42402
                                                      CIP

Manufactured in the United States of America
First Edition

This is for my girls:

My mother, Milly Zeff
My daughter, Eve Kagan

Acknowledgments

With a full heart and enormous gratitude for their gifts to me, thank you to Jeremy Kagan,

Carole Smith, David Freeman, Denise Worrell, Gena Rowlands, Tim Rutten, Jean Vallely,

Jack A. Thorpe, Tom Edmonds, Bambi Loomis, Greg L. Burnetta, Michael P. Smollen, Richard Solomon of the Police and Fire departments of Beverly Hills, California, and Prairie Village, Kansas,

Milly Zeff, Isadore Zeff, Anita Blackman, Sherry Shafton, Fran Glazer, Sis Kagan, Eve Kagan, Ron Rifkin, Iva Rifkin, Carole Isenberg,

Charlotte Zolotow,

John Cassavetes,

Tonto,

and, of course, Bob Gottlieb.

Ellen

WELL, IT WAS JUST a regular Tuesday morning, Frances, ordinary . . . just the same old same old. Tom left at the crack to open the store—he and his partners take turns opening —and I got up when he did: I wanted to get an early start with the shopping before it got too hot. But then Stevie was late for school and his car wouldn't turn over, so first I had to drop him off; he's driving that old clunker of Mama's and it's always acting up. Tom wanted to replace it but I said no, he's going away to college in September, he can just make do till then.

Oh, aren't you funny, Frances—of course it's a Buick; Mama always drove Buicks. Of course, you can't tell to look at it, you can't tell what any car is now. Remember her Buick I drove in high school, how beautiful it was? Like a big, long, two-toned green boat with ventiports and all that leather inside . . . and you had your daddy's two-door blue Pontiac Chieftain and . . .

Ventiports, Frances, the chrome holes on the sides that were half closed that looked like portholes on a ship.

You don't remember those? Well, they were a Buick trademark. Of course, that was then, when each car looked different. A Ford was like two boxes and you knew it was a Ford when you looked at it, and a Chevy was more rounded. . . . Now they don't care. Now you stand there in the parking lot and you don't have the slightest idea which one is yours; they all look alike and you feel like a moron because you don't know where yours is.

Of course, you don't have to worry about that, do you, Frances, living in New York and all—you just stand there and yell "Taxi!" and you're on your way.

Well, anyway, Stevie's car wouldn't start, so I had to take him. You'd think with it being the last week of school he'd be up on time, but he's just like me with being late, Frances—the older boys are just like Tom but Stevie's just like me.

I mean, look how late I was to get you, and you know I know how to go to the airport and even if I didn't Tom had it all written out for me on a paper I had right next to me on the seat, and then look what happened—I got all turned around at that interchange and was going south instead of north and I didn't even know. I thought I knew but I just wasn't sure. I kept looking for clues. You know, something familiar. But it was only grass and signs for fried chicken places that I'd never been to and then a Pontiac dealer that I thought sounded right but . . .

Oh, I know . . . I know you don't, Frances, but it makes me feel like a moron to think I can't get to the airport without a helper or something.

I know you aren't . . . I know.

Well, anyway . . . it was just a regular Tuesday.

I dropped Stevie off and then I went to get the wagon filled at the Mobil on Ninety-fifth and Mission. And then I did the shopping. You know I have to go all the way out to Pawnee's now that Hopkins closed. I mean, if I want really good homegrowns, not those plastic things they try to pass off as tomatoes at the Price Whackers. Did you know Hopkins closed? You know, sometimes I forget how long you're gone, Frances. . . . I forget what's the same and what's all changed. Isn't that awful—that I forget? I think it's awful.

I'd lugged all the bags up and into the kitchen. I tell Tom all the time, Someday I'm gonna have a garage where you drive in and there's a door right there leading into your kitchen. Those steps are gonna kill me, I'll tell you.

I was putting away the groceries and I got to thinking about how this summer would be the last. I mean, how it's all gonna change. Stevie going off to college in September and Adam staying in Syracuse till grad school and Ben all the way out there in Idaho doing God-knows-what. All my babies gone, Frances. Soon it'll just be Tom and me. It's like the time just slipped right by me while my back was turned. Here I was so busy driving car pool and wiping noses and taking on and off galoshes, and then the boys were all grown up. I don't know how it happened.

There were times when I thought I couldn't make it till they'd be gone and I could be alone in the house with Tom. But now when I think about it—you know what happens, Frances? I get afraid. Isn't that awful? I don't know what I'm afraid of. It surely couldn't be Tom. I've always loved him. I loved him from the start, I don't have to tell you. But I think, Maybe I won't know how to do it, maybe I won't remember how to be alone with him, maybe all I know is how to do Little League and sew mittens on the ends of people's sleeves.

Oh, I know, Frances. I know. I'm just being silly. I couldn't be afraid, it must be something else—I just don't know the word.

Anyway, I was sitting there thinking about it all and the dog got his head stuck in a grocery bag. He was trying to get it off with his paw, tap dancing all around the kitchen floor, crashing into cabinets, and I was helping him and laughing, trying not to let the Fudgsicle drip all over me. I know it was only ten-thirty in the morning, but it was hot already and I just needed a little taste of sweet like you do sometimes. And the doorbell rang.

I just opened the door right up. I didn't look through the peephole or anything. Of course, even if I would've, I would've let her right in, considering. Well, you know.

She was real white. I noticed that right off. Like all the color had been drained out of her or like she was wearing that makeup those Japanese women wear, you know, that looks like chalk dust. She was white all over, but especially her face.

And she was barefoot. Not that that's unusual—I mean, she was always going around barefoot. You remember that time when they saved up and left the kids with Grady and spent a week at that fancy lodge in Colorado in the snow and she got frostbite in a couple of toes? Can you imagine being so dumb as to run around a place barefoot in below zero? Well, anyway, she was barefoot, which meant she had walked up from Ninety-first like that. I couldn't have done it, I'll tell you. I can't even stand the feel of sand under my toes, much less pebbles and what-have-you from the street. Never could. It makes me nervous.

And what's more, she had on a robe. She was walking around our neighborhood in a short white terry-cloth robe. I guess people could have thought she had a bathing suit on underneath, that she was off somewhere for a swim, but it certainly didn't seem right to me, running around in a robe. Her little legs were as white as the robe. That's when I realized I hadn't seen Jessie's legs for a very long time. You know how she's always covering them up, wearing pants instead of a dress. Even when we were girls she said she was too fleshy in the legs—remember when we spent practically the whole summer down at the lake, she had those pretty wrap things that she'd pop on as soon as she got out of the water, to hide her legs. Her aunt Jewel got them for her in New York, I think. They kind of wrapped all around and were long to the ankle and thin like bandage gauze, remember?

You know, Frances, it's the funniest thing but if I get even the tiniest whiff of Coppertone, why, I can just see that whole summer in front of my eyes. The six of us—you and me and Tee . . . Jessie, Anne, and Anita—all of us riding out to Latawanna every chance we got, drifting the days away sitting in those fat old inner tubes from Billy's daddy's store or slamming back and forth over our own waves in Nat Glazer's motorboat . . . remember? You had a green bathing suit, lime green with skinny little straps and a ruffled skirt, and I had a white Jantzen with that little swimmer embroidered on down by the leg—and Jessie had black. A black bathing suit. I thought that was so sophisticated, so daring. Nobody else had black. I thought she was surely the one—I mean, of all of us, I thought Jessie'd be the one to go off to New York or someplace real exciting, marry somebody real important, and be famous, you know? I thought it would be Jessie. I mean, I was sure it wouldn't be Anne. She might have been the oldest of all of us, but I never thought she'd have the courage to go anywhere; I couldn't believe she even went all the way to Texas to school. And Anita was too set in her ways. I don't think she ever got used to living here after Tupelo, much less go anywhere else, and especially not after she got all turned around by Neil. And I hope you don't mind my saying this, Frances, but I didn't think it would be you either. Not that you weren't talented and all, even back then, being in *Carousel* and *As You Like It* and everything, but I just never thought it could really happen, you know, someone from Kansas City making it as a real actress in New York in the theater and all. And, anyway, all you wanted to do then was be with George. Of course, it could have been Tee since she was the smartest, but look what happened there, all her plans just went up in smoke when she got pregnant and had to marry Billy, didn't they?

Oh, Lord, look what I said, Frances—I wasn't even thinking about Billy being a fireman when I said that, it just popped right out of my mouth.

Well, anyway, of the six of us, I thought Jessie would be the one. She was always such a handful. Daddy used to say she was full of piss and vinegar—that little girl is full of "p and v" he'd say to Mama and me.

Of course, I knew it wouldn't be me, Frances. I never wanted to do anything. I just wanted to stay right here and marry Tom and have his babies and get a house on the Kansas side and fix it up real cute and go to the club and play cards and read recipe books and make interesting things, you know. I just wanted to be . . . well . . .

We were young. Young and . . . Lord, were we foolish? That's what the song said, didn't it? Mama used to sing that. I don't think we were foolish. I think we were brave. And sweet. Tom always laughs when he catches me remembering.

"You thinking about that summer again, Ellen?" he asks, and winks at me. That was the summer . . . well, you know . . . that was the summer when we all grew up, wasn't it? Except, I don't know, sometimes I don't think we ever grew up—until now, of course. . . . Now we'll have to, won't we? Well . . .

She was smoking a cigarette, which riles me up, you know. I mean, what right does a woman with three children have to smoke? And I thought, Well, she certainly knows how I feel about that— why is she standing on my front steps at ten-thirty in the morning, smoking, when she knows it's just gonna set me off? Well, before I had a chance to even breathe, she just rushed right in past me, slammed the door with all her strength—I swear all the pictures in the front room tilted—and she said in this real quiet voice with her teeth gritted, "Don't let him in, Ellen. Don't open the door."

Well, my Lord, what could I say? I must have still had the Fudgsicle in my hand. I know I hadn't finished it. And you know, I never have found the stick. I promise you I looked everywhere for it, but I never found it. I bet the dog ate it.

She sat down on one of my dining-room chairs and put her

face in her hands. She kind of crumpled into the chair really, like
a dead balloon. That's when the phone started to ring, but I didn't
make a move. Something about her face just fixed me to the
ground. I hadn't really seen her since one night two years ago last
March at the Thornes', when she got so drunk and Pete made such
a fuss over RC's new wife. I told you—he had her all backed up
against Marlene's refrigerator, practically drooling on her, in front
of everybody. Said she had the blondest blond hair he ever saw or
some piece of hooey like that. I know 'cause I went in to get a piece
of ice and he had his hands on her and she got all red-in-the-face
embarrassed when she saw me. But Pete didn't. Looked right at
me as if he was standing on a corner. Natural as can be.

And Jessie got drunk on those iced-tea things that Jack
was making . . . New York iced tea—*Long Island* iced tea; that's
right—you know all those fancy things now, don't you, Frances?

Anyway, it's been since then. I mean, I've seen her but we
haven't talked. I should never have tried to talk to her that night.
I should have known better. I didn't realize she was drunk. She
always did fool me about how much liquor she'd had. I mean, up
until she'd get all loud and passionate about some point she was
making or she'd turn real quiet and stare off into space as if
somebody had died or something—then I'd know. Tom could
always spot it early. He'd say, "Look out, Ellen, Jessie's on her way."
But I never could tell. Never. Of course, I never was as close to
her as you were.

Anyway, that was the night I picked to talk to her outside in
the Thornes' backyard about getting a divorce. I mean, how many
years can you live with a man fooling around right in front of your
nose? It's just degrading. Beneath her, I said. I mean, I swear,
Frances, I'm practically the only woman left in Kansas City he
didn't have. I don't mean you, of course, but you know . . . I mean,
after all, he even had Anne. You knew that, didn't you? That's why
she doesn't come home anymore. . . . That's why she stopped. It
was two summers after you and George moved to New York. Or
was it three? Wait a minute. . . . You see? I can't remember anything
anymore. . . . No, it was two. Anita had just had Mary. And Ben
came down with chicken pox right after the Fourth of July barbecue.
I mean, the very next morning he was covered, just covered . . . I
remember now—July . . . two summers after you left. Anne was in

from Dallas, like she used to do twice a year. But without Joe that time; she was by herself. Pete had her over at Miller's one afternoon. Nobody had to tell me; I knew. You could just feel it. Jessie had to live with that. Her very own sister . . . Well . . .

That night at the Thornes' was the night that ended our friendship. Jessie just didn't want to hear a word of what I had to say and she got furious and threw that whole New York drink all over my green silk dress. I was beside myself. I never thought they'd get the stains out. She marched back inside the house and left me standing there with my high heels stuck in the grass. Just like that.

Well, we hadn't said a word to each other since that night. I mean, we did nod and give a hello when we ran into each other, and she did leave me her kids once when her mama was so bad at the end and the three of them were practically living over at the hospital. But other than that, not a word had we spoken. I promise you. Even at her mama's funeral. I mean, I cried my heart out and all since I knew Mrs. Connell my entire life—I mean, even though I didn't like her, Lord knows—but Jessie and I just didn't talk anymore, didn't really say anything to each other since that night, and now here she was sitting in my dining room.

It seemed to me like I stood there staring at her for maybe two whole minutes. Like we were a photograph. The phone had finally stopped ringing. It was so quiet. I mean, you could hear the birds and somebody's lawn mower buzzing and Melba's little one pulling his wagon and just jabbering away to himself in their backyard. I felt like we were frozen.

And then this long sob broke out of her and the moment was over and I moved a little closer and said, "Jessie?" and she turned and looked at me. There was something sticky and mashed all over her hair and across her forehead. I couldn't believe I hadn't noticed it when she first came in, but maybe it was 'cause she'd passed by me so fast and all. Anyway, I just stood there staring at her and then I could smell it and I realized what it was—it was banana, smashed banana. Her hand reached up and touched at her hair, at those little wispy ends that always curl so sweet around her face, you know, and they were all pasted down to her forehead and cheeks with the banana, and she looked at me and then this laugh came out of her. It wasn't her regular laugh, let me tell you. It was much higher pitched and kind of strange, like from one of those horror movies the kids all love. And then she started to cry.

"Lord sakes, Jessie, what's the matter?" I said, and I couldn't help but touch her, you know. I put my hand on her shoulder and she just kind of fell forward into me, burrowed her face right into my stomach, and these sobs just tore all through her. And that's when the doorbell rang.

And I thought, Well, my Lord, if this isn't some Tuesday morning, and before I could even move she pulled her head back, stared up at me with her eyes all big in her face, and said, "Ellen, don't let him in." And she got up and just flew up the stairs.

Well, I tell you, I felt so funny. Something about the whole thing just spooked me—I mean, like I didn't know her or something. Like it wasn't Jessie. I mean, we were Brownies . . . well, I certainly don't have to tell you. All these years since Border Star . . . like Mama used to say, "A lot of water under the bridge." And after all that, here she was with banana squooshed all over her face, barefoot, with wild eyes and a funny laugh, hiding in my bedroom. I don't know. I just felt creepy all through me, like when you know you're coming down with something and you can't do anything to stop it. And the doorbell rang again.

I wiped my hands on my slacks and walked to the front door. I looked through the little opening in the door and, of course, it was Pete. All smiles, looking at me, smiling with his teeth showing.

"Mornin', Ellie, got a cuppa coffee for your old buddy?" Real sweet like. Never lost that drawl, not in all these years. He and Anita both, they still have it.

And you know, I was thinking, Why is it that I let Pete call me Ellie? I hate that name. Even Tom wouldn't dare. From the very first day he turned up in Spanish class and Miss Meuser said our names out loud to him and then in the hall right after he asked me to point him to old Marble's class and he called me Ellie and I never said a word. I never corrected him. Isn't that strange? Pete's called me Ellie all these years. And I never minded.

I said, "What's goin' on, Pete?"

"Whatcha mean, babe?" he asked, real innocent . . . and he grinned at me.

We were talking to each other through my peephole. I couldn't believe it.

"Aren't you gonna let me in?" he asked.

"No," I said, "I'm not."

"She's here, isn't she . . . my Jessie?"

"She is," I said, "and what is goin' on? I don't like any of this."

"It's nothin', Ellie," he said, "just a little squabble. You know . . . nothin'." He looked real sheepish, his eyes all blue, smiling at me.

I stood there a second. I kind of felt a little better, just seeing him and all.

"You look like a baby with your hair like that," he said.

"What?"

"Up in a ponytail like that, you look like you did in high school. With your face all washed and scrubbed, you look like a baby today."

"Oh, cut it out, Pete, you know how old I am—I'm the same age as you."

"You don't need all that stuff, Ellie. I been tellin' you that for years."

"I like makeup. And, anyway, you don't know anything about it—I know how I look best."

He grinned at me. "Okay," he said, "I don't know a thing—you look god-awful to me."

Standing there smiling at me. Well, I couldn't help but smile back. You know Pete, the way he could get to you.

"Stop flirting with me. I'm not a moron, you know."

"Okay, we won't talk about your looks. Let's talk about the weather. You think it'll rain today?"

"Pete . . ."

"What?"

"This is ridiculous."

"Well, it wasn't my idea. You're the one who won't open the door."

"Well, Jessie asked me not to."

"Oh. Well, then, what are we gonna do?"

I looked at him. "You two could make a person nuts, you know?"

"Oh, come on, Ellie, how 'bout a cuppa coffee?" he asked, and he put his hand up to that little opening and tried to touch my nose with his finger. "I sure as hell could use a cup," he said, real soft. I moved a ways back from the door. I remember I thought, Don't you start with me, Pete Chickery.

"Well, so could I, Pete," I said, "so could I after this lovely morning I've been having, let me tell you. But you're gonna have to go get your coffee someplace else, because Jessie asked me not to let you in."

"Why?"

"How the Lord should I know?" I was getting angry. I mean, really, if they want to act up it's their business, but I'm surely not interested in watching.

"Let me in, Ellie," he said. "Come on, I'll talk to her. I'll fix it."

"Listen," I said, "I don't know what you did and I don't want to know, but I don't think it's gonna be so easy to fix. I think you had just better run on home. Okay?"

"Come on," he said. "Open the door, Ellie."

Telling me what to do like I belonged to him, like I was Jessie or one of their kids.

"Listen, Pete, you're making me angry. Now go on home and she'll be home when she's calmed down. I don't want to be in the middle of this."

And then his face changed. I can't explain but it was like it wasn't him, like it wasn't Pete.

"I asked you to open the damn door, Ellie. You remember I asked you that nice and easy, didn't I?"

Cold. That's what it was, Frances. Icy cold. Like he didn't know me. Like he was talking to a stranger.

"Did you hear me?" he said.

I've heard the stories, you know. How he's mean to her, how he pushes her around. Only when no one can see him do it. I know you and Tee don't tell me what you know, but I hear, Frances. I hear plenty. I even heard once years back that he hit her, but I never saw any signs of that, so I was sure it was a lie. Just some gossip that had gotten out of hand, you know, like it can. I mean, I can't imagine Pete hitting anyone. Really.

"Ellie!"

He was yelling at me. I couldn't say a word. I just couldn't. It was all going too fast. Pete and me, looking at each other through my peephole, talking words to each other that I didn't understand, and my heart was beating too fast and I just said, "Now look here,

Pete, I've had just about enough of this. Now you go on home!"

I slammed the little opening shut and turned around, my back up against the door, my heart racing. I swear, Frances, I put my hand across my breasts and it was thumping away so hard my skin was moving. I couldn't believe it. I was scared of Pete. Me. Scared. I felt this drop of sweat just slide right down my front from under my breasts to the waistband of my slacks and I realized I was dripping wet all over.

I just stood there trying to gather my wits for a minute, you know. I thought I'd better call Tom down at the store, when suddenly the dog started barking up a storm and before I could move even a step, there was Pete looking at me from inside my very own kitchen. Frances, he'd broken through the back screen door and was standing by the stove. I couldn't move. I was absolutely rooted to the ground.

He had on a light-blue cotton shirt with short sleeves and his left arm was more tan than his right from all that driving and sticking it out the window. He shouldn't be on the road so much, I thought. Maybe they'd be better off if he was home more.

I knew I was gonna cry. I was angry with myself but I couldn't help it, I was just so confused.

"Pete," I said, "you're out of bounds, absolutely out of bounds, and you know it. Why, I'm scared—you've actually scared me right here in my own house. Why are you acting like this? Have you gone crazy?"

I was yelling, Frances. My voice echoed off the walls like from a loudspeaker or something. The whole thing was just so ridiculous. I mean, Pete Chickery jumping our back fence, busting through our screen door, breaking into our house . . . I mean, I know him since I'm fifteen years old, Frances. We watched each other grow up. It just didn't make sense.

"Now you just get out of here right this second!" I screamed at him like he was a little boy, pointing my finger toward the back door, crying by then so that I could hardly see, and Rusty had his lip all curled up like he was gonna bite Pete and I yelled at him to stop it. And right then Pete moved out of the kitchen and through my dining room, past me like I wasn't even standing there.

"Where is she?" he asked, real quiet like. "Upstairs?"

I didn't answer. I was about to say I'm not telling, but something just said to me, Why, that's absurd; we're not children anymore, we're all grown up. He had reached the first step in the hall and had his hand on the wood banister, about to take them three at a time, and I screamed at him.

"Pete Chickery, you go up those steps and I swear to God I'll never speak another word to you as long as I live." I was shaking, I was so furious.

You could hear Jessie upstairs. She was trying to push Tom's big mahogany chest of drawers up against our bedroom door. There's no key to lock that door. I always had a thing about closed doors. Remember? Remember when your brother locked us in your bathroom when we were trying to sneak bleach on our hair and I got terrified that we'd never get out? Well, there wasn't a key for that door when we moved in and I never had one made.

I could hear things falling off the chest of drawers as she scraped it across the wood floor. That little blue china shoe that Mama had saved from the World's Fair fell and smashed. I mean, it's not important, but I always did think of Mama when I held it, you know. See her face. Smell her. The way she used to be, you know, not the way she is now. I mean, she doesn't even know who I am when I go to visit her. Isn't that amazing? Doesn't even know her only child. Anyway. He stopped when he heard the chest scrape the floor. He stopped dead in his tracks on the steps, looked up and laughed. It was a quiet laugh but it was ugly, let me tell you. Mean and ugly. Tee's grandma used to say, "God don't like ugly." And I thought of that right then. And I felt terrible all over. Terrible. Like right before that tornado hit when we were in the first grade. Remember, the sky all funny green-yellow and dead still, nothing moving, and I knew we were gonna get hit. I knew it with all my heart, with my head under my little desk and Miss Coleman standing at the blackboard, one hand holding her breasts and the other one gripping the eraser, her face frozen white in a terrified smile while she yelled, "Take cover, children, take cover!" Oh, I knew it, all right.

And he looked up at the ceiling and he said real quiet like to himself—I mean, she couldn't possibly have heard him, he said it so low—"You can't hide from me, Jessie . . . you're mine." And he flew up those steps, just flew.

I felt my knees buckle out from under me. Like I was Jell-O, orange Jell-O all over my dining-room rug. And I heard him call her name. He must have been at the door by then. Pushing it.

Rusty was licking my face. Poor puppy, he gets so concerned if I'm upset, just as if he was a person. I was crying and I wanted him to stop but I couldn't move. And then I was just staring at my yellow-rose rug and I didn't know how long I had been sitting there. Like sometimes when I'm driving, I suddenly realize that I'm driving—like I've been unconscious for blocks and it all jams into focus and there I am sitting behind the wheel driving and it's such a shock to me. Does that happen to you? Well, there I was sitting on my dining-room rug and I knew I had to get up and phone Tom so he could come home and try to settle this whole thing and I pushed Rusty away and put my hand behind me to push myself up. I felt like I couldn't stand on my own two feet, Frances. It was then that it happened. Right at that moment.

The shot filled the whole house with sound. The most awful sound I ever heard. Loud. So awful and loud. And I swear to you I didn't breathe. Not a breath. Nothing moved. I could see the dust caught in the stripes of sunlight coming through my lace curtains. I could see this little spider trying to make his way around the corner of the dining-room table. I could see my hands. My wedding ring.

I never did want that gun in the house, Frances. Tom and I fought over it years ago. I was so afraid the boys would find it in the closet when they were little. I remember how I cried for him to take it back. But he said no. He said we needed it. Just in case. That's what he said. "Just in case, Ellen. We need it, just in case." All these years that gun has been sitting in the closet behind my shoes. I mean, I don't even see it anymore when I hang up my things. Years and years . . . it's like it just isn't there.

I heard the fall. Upstairs someone fell. And I couldn't move.

I could see Pete the night of our senior prom. See him standing in my mama's living room with his white tux and a pale-blue cummerbund that matched his eyes, just perfect, so blue. And he was holding out this plastic box at me with this big purple orchid inside. There were little drops on the inside of the box along the top, little dewdrops, and there were marks on the outside, sweat marks where his fingers had stuck to the plastic. And he handed it to me and he grinned and said, "You look real nice, Ellie." I blushed, I was so nervous. They were all three standing there. We were a double date—me and Pete with Ronnie Green and Jessie. Jessie was all pink tulle around her shoulders, pink slipper shoes, and Ronnie Green gave her a pink baby-rose corsage that she tied to her wrist. And Mama said, "Why, Jessie, you look just like a cone of cotton candy standing here in my house." And my daddy laughed. Ronnie Green's hair was all slicked down and his ears stuck out. I can see us just as plain as if it was yesterday. Me looking at Pete and Pete looking at Jessie as if he'd just seen her for the first time.

That's the night it started with them. That very night when he had a date with me, that's the night he fell in love with Jessie. Of course, we didn't have a real date, he only took me to the prom because Tom couldn't get home from Missouri because of finals so he asked Pete to take me, but I remember how sweet Pete was. Dancing all the dances with me, holding me close but not too close because of Tom, but not too far away like I was something awful, you know? And he listened to me. I told him how I didn't want to go to college one bit, that it didn't matter to me except to be closer to Tom, that that's why I was going. Not because I wanted to learn how to be anything. I told him I didn't give a hoot about learning how to be anything. Pete looked at me real serious, Frances, and he said I didn't have to learn how to be *anything*, that I was already *something*. That's what he said. Isn't that sweet? I thought it was so sweet. And he leaned forward and kissed me on the nose. Soft and dear like butterfly wings, Frances, on the very tip of my nose. Pete's hand was pressed into the small of my back and he raised my face and kissed me just like that. I never forgot. The next morning I stayed in bed forever thinking about it, and you know, for a minute I forgot who it was I loved. It was just for a minute but I did, Frances, I forgot. Mama was in the hall, vacuuming up a storm, making noise so I'd wake up and tell her about the dance, but I lay there real quiet with my eyes closed so I could keep thinking about Pete. Of course, Tom called and then I remembered. I mean, I wasn't confused anymore after he called, you know, about who I was supposed to be with. Besides, could you imagine me with Pete Chickery? Lord, what a laugh. Why, I never could have put up with him and his lies. Not in a million years. Besides, he always loved Jessie. From that summer on. Pete and Jessie, me and Tom. That's the way it was supposed to be. I always knew that.

Rusty whined. That's the next thing I remember. And I looked at him. His tongue was out, panting, and I thought, Poor puppy, you don't understand. I thought I'd said it to myself, but when he cocked his head over to the side like he does, I knew I'd said it right out loud. I was so shocked at myself.

I had to move. I pulled myself up by the table legs. Rusty jumped all over me like it was a game. I had to yell at him to stay.

And then, halfway up the steps, I could hear her—Jessie, sobbing Pete's name over and over. And I knew right then.

I sat down. Halfway up and halfway down. I sat there holding on to the banister. It was just like people say, Frances—a dream, an awful nightmare in the daytime that just won't go away. I don't know what I was staring at, where I was looking. . . . I just know there was no sound but the sound of Jessie crying Pete's name. No other sound in the world. Everything else had stopped.

And then this terrible thing happened, Frances. I should be too embarrassed to tell even you . . . I should. I haven't told one soul, not even Tom, but I . . . I thought about the blood, Frances . . . that there would be blood on the floor and that I had to get it out before Stevie got home from school. Lord forgive me, that's what I was thinking. Like a cold woman. I couldn't remember what took blood out of a hardwood floor, and this panic overtook me about how would I find out, who would I call—that Mama would know, but her mind's so gone now that she couldn't tell me even if I paid her. Why couldn't I remember? That's what I was thinking, Frances, bloodstains on a hardwood floor. That's what was on my mind. Like a cold woman. Like it wasn't Pete up there. Like it wasn't Pete and Jessie. Like it wasn't us.

They must have been ringing the bell and knocking and Rusty must have been barking his fool head off, but I didn't hear a thing. Not a sound. All I remember is two policemen standing in my living room at the foot of my steps, looking up at me. Two policemen with their mouths moving, looking wrong and out of place, big gray uniforms in my yellow living room. I wanted to tell them to go away, that it was a mistake, an awful mistake. . . .

The one with the mustache, the young one, was coming up the stairs. He was saying something serious—I could tell 'cause he had little frown lines all squinched up in between his eyes, like my Ben used to look when he played cops and robbers—stalking up my steps like a big cat, trying to scare me. Black shiny boots coming up one step at a time. A gun in his hand, an awful black gun getting bigger and bigger as he got closer. I felt a knot of crazy laughter jumping around inside me. . . . I thought he was going to shoot me, Frances.

"I said we received a call that there were shots fired, ma'am. Do you have a gun in the house?"

I heard him. I heard him call me ma'am like I was my mother. Like I was old.

I felt like I was underwater. Everything looked big and wobbly, like from inside a scuba mask. The gun, his hands on the gun, his fingernails, a little torn place where he'd been picking on his cuticle, his face, brown hairs in his mustache, brown eyes locked into mine . . . I could see everything . . . everything.

He blinked and took a breath. His body stayed straight but his eyes were flickering up the steps and back down. He tried to speak, then his voice caught, he had to clear his throat.

"Is there anyone else in the house with you, ma'am?" he asked real soft.

Why, he's scared, I thought. My Lord in heaven, he's scared. And that's when I realized what had happened. It was at that precise moment, Frances. That's when my heart broke and the pain set in on me. Slow and deliberate, like honey sliding down the side of the jar.

"Ma'am?" he asked again, looking at me.

So young. Lord, he was so young, that policeman. Young and strong. Just like we used to be, Frances, and that's when I knew. And I said to myself, Pete Chickery is dead, Ellen. The first of us is dead.

And I couldn't say a word.

Tee

*O*H, COME ON, FRANCES, I don't give a flying fuck if it's only noon. Pete is dead and I'm having a drink. You want one or not?

How long did you have to wait for Ellen? Come on, I know she was late. She's been late her whole life. She was late for the fucking third grade. God, I'm tired. Billy keeps watching me. No, it's true; I see him. He's got his eyes on me, watching, like I'm gonna explode or something. He already called home maybe eighteen times this morning before you got here. He's only gonna be at work for six fucking hours. I told him, What can you do here? There's nothing you can do, nothing. Pete's dead. Go to the fucking station and put out somebody's fire, for crissakes. I mean, what's he gonna do—sit and look at me? Sit with me in the bathtub and hold my hand? That's all I do, you know—take baths and cry. I must have taken a hundred baths since Tuesday. This morning I discovered myself sitting in a tub of fucking *ice* water—God knows for how long; I can't remember—and I snapped to, like right out of a dream, snapped awake. And I realized that the whole time I was sitting there turning into a prune, the whole fucking time, I was trying to visualize Jessie with the gun in her hands. You know, like in a western, like in *Gunsmoke* or something, with smoke coming out of the tip. Jesus. What a thought.

Of course, Billy's done everything since it happened, I haven't done a thing. Billy and Ellen and Tom. The police called Tom down at the drugstore and he called Billy at the station to come home. Of course, I knew before he got here. And Tom was the one who called everybody. And Billy did the airport run except for you, Frances, since Ellen had a fit about nobody but her picking you up, but Billy picked up everybody else.

And Billy and Tom are the ones who told Amy, Frances. They went to the school. Those two lugs. Not me. Not Ellen. Or Anita. Billy and Tom. They're the ones who had to sit there and tell Amy her daddy was dead. I just couldn't. I wanted to go with them, but I couldn't get my clothes on. I really couldn't, Frances. I couldn't figure how to get my arms and legs through all the holes. I can only take baths. That's what I'm in charge of—bath-taking and walking around. I must have done a hundred miles in this house since Tuesday. I have a route. Around the dining-room table and into the kitchen, then back through the living room and up and down the stairs. I promise you, Frances, that's all I do.

Ellen went to Jessie's house the afternoon it happened and made supper so that when Tom and Billy brought Amy home from school there would be food. You know Ellen and her goddamn food. She even sent Billy home with supper for me. And it was good, Frances, that's what killed me, it was good. And I was hungry. I couldn't believe I could be hungry. I couldn't get my clothes on and Ellen was making soup. And she and Tom spent the night there to be with Amy until the boys got in. She and Tom slept there. Of course, I'm sure nobody slept. Who can sleep? I sure as hell can't.

God, look at me. I don't know why I have a mirror in the kitchen. My fucking mother has a mirror in her kitchen too. It figures, huh? She keeps coming over to see if I need anything. Let me tell you something—if I needed anything, she sure wouldn't be the one I'd ask. I know what she's really up to with all this newfound fucking "interest"—she's watching me too. Her and Billy, my two watchdogs. Waiting to see how this is gonna hit me, how I'm gonna react, if I'm gonna go off my rocker again. What do they think—I don't see them? The assholes.

Billy keeps following me around the house. I swear to God, it's like a fucking ball game. I go into the kitchen, he goes into the kitchen. I go upstairs, he goes upstairs. Yesterday he was so close behind me on the stairs that I turned around real fast and slammed right into him. It's like a fucking cartoon, I swear to God. He's trying to act real cool, like he can handle it. But I see. I see plenty. Yesterday I caught him looking at the pictures. Last year I stuffed all the pictures into two drawers in the family room. I was gonna put them into albums—you know, chronologically—but I just never could. I bought the albums and everything; they're still there, all wrapped up in the plastic. I bought them but I just couldn't do it—I couldn't sit there and watch it all pass before me like a bad movie. Yesterday I walked into the family room and Billy was looking at the pictures. Him and Pete and Tom and all of us at Harrison . . . David White and Patash . . . everybody in their letter sweaters, and mugging for the camera at our wedding . . . I know what's in that drawer. He tried to make like he was looking for something, for a coaster or something, but I saw him stuffing the pictures back in the drawer. Then he went out. All of a sudden he had to get the car washed. Shit. And then last night I heard him crying in the bathroom. He thought I was asleep, because he had called Knelman and got a prescription for something to help me sleep; he thought I took it, I guess, but I heard him. He was sobbing, Frances, sobbing like a baby.

Billy and Pete. Shit. What a duo, huh? Billy following me around the halls of Harrison and me following Pete. The wrong person fell for the wrong person. What a fucking mess. Remember how I made you and Anne take turns driving me around and around his block, up and down past Pete's house. His mother must have thought we were nuts. If Jenn knew, she'd laugh herself silly, huh? To think her own mother could have ever made a fool of herself over a boy. All my notebooks with his name scribbled on the pages: Pete Chickery. Mrs. Peter Chickery. Mr. and Mrs. Peter Chickery invite you to lunch. Tee and Peter Chickery request your presence for cocktails at the club, Sunday the seventeenth of August, six o'clock . . . Shit.

You know, I spent maybe two hours yesterday sitting upstairs just staring at my face in the mirror. I don't know how this happened. Look at this. These aren't wrinkles, sweetheart, they're fucking crevices. I look like the surface of the moon, for crissakes. The astronauts could plant a flag on me.

Did Ellen tell you how I heard? She only told you about herself, huh? It figures. You know, you wouldn't believe how she's changed. I'm telling you, she's turning into a fucking dimwit. An absolute dimwit. I'm not kidding. She lost her car last month. No, *lost* it. She went down to the plaza to buy shoes for this dance at the club; you know Ellen, she's got to make sure she's making the right choice. Frances, believe me, she could make you crazy. She'd already been to Ward Parkway twice and to Prairie Village; she even dragged me all the way downtown. She knew what she wanted; she just had to convince herself. A prom—can you fucking believe it? A bunch of fifty-year-olds at a prom. Jesus, spare me.

Anyway, she buys the shoes at last and she's ready to leave, but she can't find the car. She can't remember where she put it, she says. "It just went right out of my head," she told me. So she took the bus home. Took the bus to wait for Tom to get home so he could take her back down to look for the car. Anyway—listen to this, Frances; this is the best part—she remembered. I mean, before he got home she remembered. So she gets back on the fucking bus . . . she's gonna go back to the plaza, get the car, drive home, and not tell anybody, right? And the bus breaks down. No, I'm not kidding. The fucking bus breaks down and everybody has to get out to wait for the next one. No, on Wornall. Wait a minute, Frances . . . listen. So she's standing with the rest of the people from the bus, the cleaning ladies and what-have-you, and they're waiting there . . . no, on Gregory and Wornall . . . and who do you think she sees? No; she sees Tom on his way home. Do you love this? Now Tom's on his way home and she can't get down to the fucking plaza to get the car to go home 'cause she's waiting for the goddamn bus. You could die from her, right? No . . . no, she called me. I'm telling you, Frances, I nearly peed in my pants, I laughed so hard. No . . . you know Ellen. I'm driving and she's sitting next to me with a straight face telling me the story and she keeps saying to me, "There's really no reason to laugh like that, Tee. It really isn't that funny, you know." Frances, I nearly fell out of the fucking car—I was hysterical. Jesus, she makes me laugh. . . . Anyway, she didn't tell you, huh? I mean, how I heard.

It was noon, maybe one o'clock, and I was standing right here looking at a heap of wet chicken on the sink. It must have been one, I guess—I don't know. Billy had called to say he'd be home by seven, seven-thirty the latest. Jenn was gonna eat with a bunch of kids and go to the ball game, and it dawned on me that Billy and I would be alone in the house until maybe ten, ten-thirty. I was thinking, I could give it a shot. You know, try . . . I mean, I could try, you know? Take out the black nightgown, candles, music, you know . . . make it romantic, maybe we'd do it on the kitchen floor, on the sink, on the fucking stove, for crissakes . . . something. Anyway, I thought I'd make the chicken special . . . fancy. Surprise him. It was lunchtime and I was happy, looking at cookbooks, having a beer. The soaps were on TV, but I wasn't really watching. I was looking at the recipes. I had this whole perfect day in front of me, right? Put the chicken into a slow oven, go to Marlene's and play mahj all afternoon—God, just like my fucking mother. What happened to me, Frances? I was the one who was gonna do it all, wasn't I? Be a somebody, a real somebody. A real joke, huh?

You know, I found them all the other day—all my certificates, my awards—all crunched up and stuffed into a box with Jenn's kindergarten drawings: purple Crayola houses with pink smoke curling out of the chimneys . . . yellow stick figures of people too big to fit in the houses. Well, shit, that's right. Isn't it?

Oh, shit, it's okay, Frances. I know, I know, I'm terrific . . . sure I am . . . sure. Where was I anyway? . . . Oh, yeah, olives . . . I was reading this recipe for chicken with olives—Billy loves olives—and I'm trying to see if I can figure it out, if it's too complicated for me. I mean, I have trouble with fucking toast, right? Anyway, the TV was on—I said that, didn't I? And all of a sudden out of the corner of my eye I see this woman on TV, she's standing in her driveway falling apart crying and somebody is holding her, a cop, two cops, and then they put her in this squad car and drive her away, and I'm thinking, Hey, this ain't All My Fucking Children, it's the news. And the guy, the announcer, is saying, "In Mission Hills this morning, on the corner of Belinder Road . . . ," and I'm standing here with a wet chicken leg in my hand and like a fucking ass I say, "Oh, well, sure, that's Ellen's driveway, that's Ellen crying on TV . . . no wonder it looks familiar, it's Ellen. Well, she certainly looks god-awful; she could have at least put on some lipstick. . . ." I mean, it took me a full minute before it hit. I mean, that it was really her. By then I couldn't hear a damn thing the news guy was saying. I guess I screamed or something, I don't know. I didn't know it was Pete. Not till later. I didn't hear a word the guy said after that.

Frances, if you cry I'll kill you. Have a beer, it'll make you feel better. Okay, it'll make me feel better. Thank you. Make me another gin, will you? Shit, I'm tired.

Were you guys still here when I nearly burned the house down? You weren't, were you? I tell you my mind is going—I can't remember dick; I'm turning into Ellen. I'll lose my fucking car next. Then they can put us all away with Jessie, all locked up together, the six of us. Just like the old days, huh? Wait a minute. I must have known it was Pete—I mean, the guy must have said it. That must have been when I lost it, I guess. I don't know. I don't remember anything except realizing that it was Ellen. After that, I don't know. . . . Cute how the mind can shut down, huh? Just stop when it wants.

Since Tuesday it's like I'm in a dream. I'm telling you, Frances. I was making Jennifer a sandwich yesterday, I'm standing right here slicing fat off the roast—God forbid my daughter should touch fat—and smack in front of the fucking refrigerator, where Jenn's standing talking to me, suddenly I don't see her, I see us. The six of us on the steps of Harrison . . . I mean, I see us clear—I remember everything—dyed-to-match Bernard Altmans, stitched-down pleats, Weejuns, our socks rolled down. Clear, I see us, and in color, living color—orange-and-black pep club sweaters and white god-awful gym suits and dressed up for the Redskin Revels—like flash cards flipping in front of my face. Pete and Billy washing Shapiro's old Ford in our driveway . . . Anne nearly collapsing 'cause she was with me when I swiped a Milkmaid lipstick out of Katz's Drugstore . . . I could have reached out and touched your fucking ponytail, it was so real, and then I hear, "Mom? Mom?" and it fades and Jenn is standing there with her hands on her hips, staring at me funny. She actually looked like me. She looked just like me for a whole minute. So what do you think, Frances? I'm dreaming standing up. Since Tuesday. I keep falling out and snapping back—bing, bong, in, out. Cute, huh? Don't tell Billy. He's already talking about how I should go see Knelman and talk to him about my feelings. That Knelman, what an asshole. The whole time I went to him I never told him my feelings. None of his fucking business. He was the fucking shrink, for crissakes. . . . Let him figure it out.

Oh, come on, Frances, don't be a jerk. I know what I'm doing. Wasn't I the fucking Class Genius? Miss Most Intelligent and Miss Most Humorous . . . why, I'm a double fucking whammy, Frances, a real funny smarty. You want to know a secret? Yesterday I locked myself in the bathroom and made a list. A list of memories. All the good stuff. I figured I could carry it around with me and take it out when I couldn't bear any more of this shit, you know? No way. I'm not going to read it to you, Frances. No way. No fucking way. Oh, shit, don't even try it. It won't work . . . absolutely won't work. Frances . . . Frances . . . yes, yes, I know that . . . I know you do. All right . . . oh, shut up, Frances. *Okay, I'll read it to you. Okay,* for crissakes.

God, I miss you. I miss everything about you—especially your brains and that crazy laugh. Shit, I wish you hadn't moved. What's New York got that we ain't got? I know, I know. *The theater.* Let's not talk about this, okay? I'll fall apart. . . . Let's talk about it later, tomorrow or something, okay? Okay. Shit. What were we talking about? Oh, right, my list. So—what'll you give me if I read it to you? Okay, okay . . . shit, I was only kidding. I folded it down into postage-stamp size so Billy wouldn't notice it in my pocket. You ready?

One. When Anita got that god-awful sunburn and we were at LaPizza and we made the waitress bring us a bowl of vinegar 'cause Jessie read in *Seventeen* that vinegar took the sting out, so we soaked our paper napkins in vinegar and took turns putting them all over Anita's back and arms till she stunk like a leftover salad. Remember that? Remember all the mugs hanging on the wall? Remember? Shit.

Two. When Ellen announced to us that she was gonna have a baby and Anne got so excited she fainted in Winstead's parking lot. I knew you'd like it. Oh, shit, I forgot that part. Stop it, Frances. If I laugh anymore I'm gonna . . . Stop already. I'm gonna hit you. Where was I? Oh, yeah . . .

Three. When I got hives from the sausage at Girl Scout camp and then was allergic to the calamine lotion on top of it and they had to bring a doctor out with my fucking mother because they thought I was gonna die. Well, I know it's not funny, you ditz . . . they don't have to be funny. They're memories, that's all. How could you not remember? That was the same summer you nearly drowned in the fucking lake. You did, too. Oh, come on, Frances, they were pumping water out of you, for crissakes. Well, then, don't put it on your list—this is my list. I will not. Fuck you.

Okay, four. No, come on, you'll love four, it's great. Okay, when Neil kissed Anita at the altar and turned around and walked back down the aisle by himself and left her standing there all alone clutching her bouquet, pale as the candles. Talk about a sign from above! She should have had the priest declare an annulment before she got one step outside Good Shepherd. Well, it's not like we didn't all tell her, Frances. Neil Finnegan was drunk from seventh grade on, she just thought she could change him. Hell, she thought she was Mother Teresa or something. Of course, even I didn't think old Neil would take a powder and leave her flat with two babies. That was charming, wasn't it? What a creep.

What was that—four?

Right, four. So, five . . .

Five. Hey, you know what? You're the only other person in the world besides me who knows number five. I never told another soul. Never. You ready? When Pete took me to that dance at the Tune Shop and danced me right outside into the parking lot and kissed me. Remember, Frances? Smack up against the wrought-iron fence and those honeysuckle bushes. Jesus. I was sixteen.

I keep playing it all back, like movies in my head, trying to figure it all out. How this could have happened. I sit here and I can see Jessie the day she got the fucking training wheels off her two-wheeler. I can see you in that green bathing suit. You know, the one with the skirt you had that summer. Remember? That was the stupidest bathing suit I ever saw. Oh, yes it was. You looked like a pickle in it—a chubby little sweet pickle. God, how could it be so long ago and only a moment ago? I can hear you telling us you were gonna marry George, all those tears slopping down your face. God, Frances. You know, Saturday I was sitting in the car waiting for Billy—he went back in to check the stove or the windows or something; he's always checking some goddamn thing—and while I'm waiting, I close my eyes and I'm necking with Saulie Rifkin in his father's Pontiac in the driveway of our house on Seventy-ninth. Remember that car? Old Pontiac's head smack in the middle of the steering wheel. I learned to drive looking at that fucking Indian. I could taste Saulie's mouth, Frances, just like he was really here, like it was really happening—like I was seventeen—and then Billy got in the car and it all vanished.

How could we just be seventeen and now there's crevices in our faces and we drink too much and Pete's dead? Jesus, I hate this. Wasn't I telling you something? No, before the list . . . I was telling you something, I remember, something about Pete. . . . Oh, the fire, that's what it was. I was telling you about the fire, when I tried to burn the house down. Shit, it's a joke, Frances. A joke, for crissakes.

I was "a little funny" after Jennifer was born? No kidding. Who told you that? She did, huh? Well, that's how much she knows. I was a *lot* funny. I was a fucking maniac is what I was. But they didn't know. You're not the only fucking actress in the group—I should have gone to New York too. Anyway, not one of them knew I was nuts. Even Billy the brain didn't notice. He thought I was postpartum—that's what that fucking asshole Knelman told him. Postpartum? I was post-bananas. Waiting all those years to get pregnant again after the first one, all those rotten years after that baby disintegrated inside of me, that awful baby that made me have to marry Billy in the first place and then had the goddamn nerve to fall out of me in bloody pieces and clots in my underwear, scaring the shit out of him and me. And then finally getting pregnant again after all those years and actually having her, actually holding on to her and not knowing what to do with her, not knowing what to do or where to go. Postpartum, my ass, Frances. Every time one of them said postpartum I wanted to run my fingernails down somebody's face. I used to scream in the shower, Frances. I did. Scream. And wring my hands. I was the Madwoman of Chaillot. They should have called you—you could have flown in to see me. I was a fucking lounge act. But I spited myself—is that a word? I mean, secretly I think I wanted you to come in . . . I mean, under the madness, I wanted you to come in and save me, but I did such a great job of acting that these fuckers didn't know I was in trouble, so none of them called you. Anyway, I'm gonna tell you this story, Frances, so stop interrupting me, okay? Get another beer, why don't you?

All right . . . all right. Pete was coming over to pick up Billy's clubs. I don't know where the fuck his own clubs were or why he needed Billy's, but he was coming over to get them. It was morning and the house was quiet. I had just put Jenn down. I felt okay, I remember that, I felt pretty good that day. Not totally in control or anything, but I wasn't about to be taken away to Osawatamee just yet.

I was boiling up nipples in this pot on the stove and listening to the radio. They wanted me to make Jenn take a bottle once in a while, you know, so that Billy could help me out in the night. I was so fucking tired all the time. Anyway, I had opened up the packages and dumped all the nipples into this big pot and I was boiling them. And Jenn woke up. I don't know why; she'd practically just gone down. But she woke up and cried and I ran upstairs to get her. I was always running to her, afraid to ever let her cry—I couldn't take it, her crying. It ripped me up, like a hole right through me.

I took her out of the crib—God, she was sweet; she wasn't even wet—and I took her into my arms and sat down in the rocker. She nuzzled right up to me. That was the only time I felt okay, you know? The only time . . . When I was feeding her, when she was attached to me—then I knew I could handle it. I mean, the mother stuff. I knew I was okay. But the rest of the time . . . well, fuck. Anyway, she took a little drink and then she stopped and looked at me. And she smiled. It was the first time. I mean, a real smile, not a gas bubble or anything, a real smile. I'll never forget it. She just popped her little mouth right off my nipple, looked up at me, and smiled. Right at me. I nearly fell off the fucking chair. It was perfect.

Anyway, that's when the smoke started billowing up the staircase. I couldn't believe it. I mean, Jesus, I'm the one married to the fucking fireman. Talk about embarrassing. Of all people to leave a pot cooking on the stove, huh? I ran downstairs with her and put her into that plastic thing—you know, those chair things we carried them around in. What the fuck do you call them? An infant seat—right. God, I hated those things. I put her in it, propped the front door open with her and the seat, and ran into the kitchen to see what was happening. The curtains were flaming real good by then and the wall was going up. God knows how long I was upstairs, rocking. Anyway, for some reason, I felt if I could get the curtains down it would stop the wall . . . , Shit, I don't know. I pulled over a kitchen chair and the next thing you know, I'm stuck to the fucking curtain rod. Jesus, so stupid, my fingers held on to that son-of-a-bitch rod like Krazy Glue. Jennifer was screaming. I could hear her and I'm freaking 'cause I can't get to her. The wall is flaming, I'm attached to the damn curtain rod, but

I'm yelling, "I'm coming, sweetheart, Mommy's coming." And all of a sudden, there's Pete. He's all over the place, slamming everything with the throw rug from the front hall and prying my fingers off the rod, one by one, and that's when the firemen got here. Firemen all over the place. They took me to K.U. and bandaged up my hands. Jesus. What a fucking mess. You'd think it would have been Billy to save me, huh? Billy and not Pete. Jesus. Pete, of all people.

I was still gaga over him then. I was too, Frances. I never could believe he didn't notice me. I never could believe he could love Jessie and not me. He went out with me first. I loved him first. But he only had eyes for Jessie. Little did I know . . . You want another beer, Frances? I know I'm having another drink—I haven't lost my mind yet, not totally anyway. Okay . . . okay, I'll have a half, but only if you make it. I can't move. I'm suddenly unable to move. No, use the other bread; that one's stale.

You look real good, Frances. No, you really do. You look nearly the same. You the most of all of us. It must be the fucking water in New York, huh? I'm kidding, for crissakes, I'm kidding. Okay, it's you, you're gorgeous. You're a star, for crissakes. It's in your genes. Look at your mother—she looks fifty, for crissakes. My mother looks a hundred and two. God, I hate her. I do. I hate her. She never lets me forget that I didn't amount to what she expected. She's made a career out of making sure I never forget. A fucking career.

God, I wish you still lived here. I don't have anybody to talk to. I don't, it's the truth.

Are you kidding? I can't talk to Ellen, she's worse than when we were twelve—she goes over everything a million times until you want to smack her in the face. Like how they took her to the police station—she's told me the whole thing at least thirty times, in infinitesimal detail. How they took her in the squad car, what the room looked like where they interviewed her, how they recorded everything she said, what the detective asked her, how he was wearing cowboy boots . . . Oh, she didn't tell you that? Well, the detective, who had gray hair and gray eyes, and whose name was Bob, by the way—you know Ellen, she's already calling him Bob; she's probably having him and his wife over for dinner next week— anyway, Bob the detective was wearing gray lizard cowboy boots and a striped shirt, blue and purple, to match his purple tie. Just ask me, Frances, I know it all by heart. And then the tape . . . she went on ad nauseam about the yellow tape: how they'd roped off the whole area, you know, where Pete had gone in the house—in the back door and up the front steps and into her bedroom, you know, they'd taped it off, and they wouldn't let her near there when they brought her home, so she couldn't go upstairs and she couldn't take a shower or whatever the hell she wanted to do until they were finished. They made her sit in the kitchen. She went on and on about the tape, Frances, how she was sure it would make marks on her walls. Like the marks were more important than what had happened.

Oh, I know it's just her way, Frances. It's just that sometimes I can't take it, sometimes she makes me want to scream. It's like she's turned into one of those women in that movie—remember, where they were all zombies, all those housewives, walking around the grocery aisles pushing their wagons and grinning at each other while the Muzak . . . Remember? Yeah, *The Stepford Wives* . . . that's what Ellen is. Well, you don't fucking know, you're not here. I swear to God, she could spend two hours discussing how to get the black out of the bottom of a pot, you know, when it discolors. She could give you all the different theories: boil it with baking soda, soak it in lemon and salt . . . I mean, what the fuck? Throw the fucking pot out and buy a new one if it bothers you. Shit, I can't talk to her sometimes.

Oh, come on, Frances, you know Anita. She can't take too much of me. She can't take my language, she hates it when I drink—she doesn't say anything, she just looks at me, but it's a loud look. It's like she's rattling her rosary at me. Let's face it, if Anne wouldn't have brought Anita in with us, Anita and I never would have been friends. Anne needed somebody from her own grade and Anita was the new girl from Tupelo and didn't know a soul. She was perfect for Anne, a pair of goody-two-shoes. Of course, they're not close like they were in high school, something went on between them, but I sure as hell don't know what it was, and furthermore, I don't give a shit. The older Anita gets the more tight-ass she becomes. It's all that Catholic crap, Frances. Remember what Pete used to say, "When you dance with my sister you can't get too close, you got to leave room for the Holy Ghost." Anyway, I hardly ever see Anita.

Well, no, I do talk to Anne. Sometimes.

Well, she's way the hell out in L.A.

I know it's the same distance away as you are, Frances, but it's different. You know we were never tight. I always scared the shit out of her. Of course, a stiff wind could scare Anne, her fucking mother saw to that. God, what a piece of work old lady Connell was.

Anyway, I was never close to Anne or Anita like I was with you or Jess, or even like I was with Ellen. I mean, I can razz the hell out of Ellen, but I still love her and I can still talk to her sometimes when she's not being a zombie. The other two make me feel like I have to watch what I say; it's like having a muffler in my mouth.

Okay. Okay, so I'm exaggerating a little. Okay, Frances.

Well, sure there's Jessie, but Jessie and I haven't really talked in years. Well, we just haven't. No, nothing happened. I don't know, it just changed. . . . Oh, shit, Frances, I don't want to get into it. Frances, I really don't, okay? No, Billy's gonna be home; he'll walk in right in the middle and then I won't . . . Oh, come on, Frances, leave it be, why don't you? No, we didn't fight. I told you that. We didn't do anything. No. Frances, I promise you, I can't do this now. I really can't. Okay? Okay.

Did you ever feel like your life is passing you by like the dates on the tops of yogurt cartons? Did you? That's what I think about—yogurt tops and milk cartons. Someday I'll expire like an old date on a milk carton. I'll just go sour and they can throw me out. What a relief that'll be.

Oh, shit. I can't stand this. Well, I'm not answering it—let it ring. It's Billy, I promise you. All right, you answer it. See? I told you. No, tell him I'm fine. Tell him I'm in the can. I'm fine and I'm in the can and we don't need him. Yeah, tell him to take his time. Yeah, perfect, tell him to pick up ribs. Ribs—tell him to go to Gates—and coleslaw. Tell him not to forget coleslaw. And sweet potato pie . . . God. I knew it was Billy.

Oh, come on. I don't want to talk about me and Jessie. It wasn't me and Jessie anyway. . . . Frances, you're gonna piss me off. . . . Jesus, Frances. Okay . . . okay already. *I'll tell you!* What the fuck is the difference if I tell you? Who cares now? Nobody, I'm sure. It's sixteen fucking years ago—who the fuck cares? But you gotta make me a drink. And you gotta have one with me. A real drink. No more beer. Good girl.

Okay, let's see. Well, it was after the fire . . . So we'll eat the sandwich *and* we'll have the ribs, who cares? It'll be good for us. It'll fill us up. It was after the fire—actually, it was the day they took the bandages off. I should write a book, you know? I could call it "The Year of the Fire." Whatcha think? It could be an exposé on postpartum. Shit, Frances, don't make me laugh. I'll throw this fucking sandwich at you. Shut up. Frances, shut the fuck up.

Anyway, I was at the Muehlbach. I went down to get a room for me and Billy. Cute, huh? It was Ellen's idea. Well, I had been having a really hard time. No, not just with that. With sex. I hadn't let Billy even touch me since Jenn had been born. I couldn't even think about it—it made me sick. And I told Ellen. I don't know what the fuck possessed me to tell Ellen, of all people . . . talk about a weak moment. Anyway, her brilliant idea was I should book a room in a hotel and she would take care of Jenn for the night. She said that after three baby boys she could certainly handle one tiny baby girl. She said that way I'd be in new surroundings, I wouldn't be at home, I wouldn't be thinking about Jenn, it would be like when Billy and I were dating or first got married or something . . . I don't know. Anyway, I decided to go along with it. I told you I was crazy.

So I was standing at the desk of the Muehlbach, waiting for the clerk to look at me, when suddenly someone puts their hands over my eyes. "Guess who?" he says. Guess who? I knew who it was from the smell of his hands. I knew that smell since the honeysuckle bushes. So we do a little chitchat in the lobby and he tells me that it's Market Week and all the stores are in town and he's showing his blouses in some room upstairs. He's telling me all about who bought what. I don't know, I wasn't really paying much attention to what he was saying. I was just looking at him. I mean, in all the years that all of us have been together, all the years we've been friends, this was probably the only time I'd ever been alone with Pete since the kiss—except for the fire, of course. So I was just looking at him and being . . . you know, just standing there. Jesus.

So he says, "Let's have a drink, Tee. Let's go into the bar and have a drink." Well, why the fuck not? We're good friends, we're grown-ups, right? So we go into the Tiki Room and sit at the bar and have a drink, two drinks, and we're talking. Shit, I don't know, we're talking like we always talk—about the baby, his kids, the job,

Billy, regular stuff. We're there forty-five minutes, maybe an hour. And then— Did I say we were at the bar? Right. Well, we're sitting there and my hands are on top of the bar and there's this little lull in the conversation, you know, like you do sometimes, kind of stop talking both at once, and he smiles at me and picks my hands up and holds them in his. And he looks at the fingertips. The bandages had just come off and they were all red and tender, you know, new. And he holds my fingers and moves my hands to his lips. And then he kisses each one of my fingertips, Frances. Slowly. Kisses each one of them and says, "I figure I should be the first to kiss these, since I'm the one who pulled them off the curtain rod, right?" And he looks at me. I mean, he *looks* at me. "Right, Tallulah?" he says. Frances, he called me fucking Tallulah. You know, nobody but my father ever dared call me Tallulah; I hadn't even heard the word since that rat bastard left. I couldn't fucking believe it. "Right?" he said again. And I said, "Right, Pete."

I could hardly breathe. That's when I realized my pants were wet. I swear to God. Here I thought my libido had up and died, and it hadn't died at all, it was just sleeping, waiting for Prince Charming. . . . Jesus. My legs were shaking so hard that I had to hook my heels around the bottom of the barstool to stay on. He's got my fingertips pressed to his lips and I'm looking at the gin and tonic 'cause I know if I look at him I'm gonna do a swan dive off the barstool and be face-to-face with that god-awful carpet they have in the Tiki Room. I swear, Frances, my whole body went into shock. Then he put my hands back down on the bar, real gentle, like I was his little girl or something, and we just sat there for a minute, you know, not moving, not saying anything.

Then he took a gulp of his drink, glanced at his watch, and said, "Hey, Tee, look at the time. Don't you have to make old Billy his supper? We better get a move on." I'm telling you, Frances, I could hardly walk. I felt like I had made the whole thing up. I mean, my pants are wet, I want him so bad I hurt, and he's talking to me about Billy's supper. He walked me to the car and I rolled down the window to talk to him; I was gonna ask him if he was out of his fucking mind or something—I mean, I might have been crazy but I wasn't that crazy. I know a pass. But before I could say a word, he bent down on his haunches and looked at me through the open window. "Tee," he said, "I'm gonna tell you somethin' and I don't want you to say anythin'. I don't want you to answer me. I just want you to drive home and think about it. Okay? Will you promise me that? That you'll listen and not say anythin'?"

"Okay," I said. I couldn't imagine what was coming.

"Tee," he said, "I want to make love to you. I want to make love to you over and over until you beg me to stop. That's all I want. I'll arrange where and when, I'll call you, I'll do everythin'. All you have to do is show up. Show up and let me love you. I want to love you, Tallulah. I want to feel you from the inside out. I want to touch every inch of you. I want to hear you come. Do you understand?"

Frances, I nearly died. I couldn't answer him. I couldn't fucking speak. I spent practically my whole life dreaming this would happen. I just shook my head yes. He reached inside and touched my cheek with his finger and then locked my car door. "Be careful goin' home," he said. "Pay attention." And he smiled and turned around and walked away. And I drove home. I don't know how, but I did. I didn't know whether to laugh or cry. I kept hearing what he said, over and over. I couldn't get it out of my mind. I was a fucking wreck.

He called three weeks later. It was a Monday morning; I'll never forget. Jennifer was lying on a quilt on the kitchen floor; she was trying to eat the quilt, actually, and I was watching her. That's all I was doing—watching her and trying to figure out how to make the day go faster. And the phone rang.

That's how it started. I met him at this place on the Kansas side—The Red Roof Inn. You probably drove past it a million times and never even saw it. Right off Mission and Ninety-fifth. I met him twenty-two times, Frances. You know, if you keep on looking at me like that one more minute your face is gonna freeze. You're the one who wanted to hear this fucking story, right? You're the one who wanted to hear this. Well, then, close your mouth. Drink your drink, for crissakes.

Anyway, I made these little dots on my calendar. Little red dots down at the bottom of the page whenever we met. Twenty-two wonderful little red dots. If you looked at my calendar for that year—Jesus, it's sixteen years ago, Frances—anyway, if you looked you'd see the little red dots.

That's why I don't talk to Jessie anymore. It's since then. You see why, right? It was so fucking crazy. Everything else stayed the same. Billy and Pete still played golf every Saturday, the four of us went to the movies every other week, Jess and I went shopping. . . . It was fucking crazy. I was like two people, Frances. I was the regular me—dust the living room, change the baby, make supper—and then I was that other person, the one who met Pete and fucked her brains out. And you know what else was crazy? In that room I was beautiful, Frances. Pete made me beautiful. My breasts weren't too big. I wasn't short-waisted. I wasn't dumpy. My hair wasn't too curly. My eyes weren't too big. I was beautiful, Frances. And I knew it. And it wasn't what he said, not just what he said. It was when he looked at me, that's when I knew. When Pete looked at me, I was beautiful.

Hard to believe, huh?

Oh, come on, Frances, I know what I look like. I never kidded myself about how I look, that's for damn sure. But in that room I did. In that room, I was beautiful.

And you know what else? I was better. I mean, inside me, about the baby. I was calmer. I wasn't so crazy. And it was because of Pete. He got me through that time, Frances. It was Pete who got me through. He said I was just scared and he said every woman was scared when they had a baby, they just didn't say it out loud. He said it was the best-kept secret among women. He said all I had to do was love her, that's all there was to motherhood.

"You just love her, Tallulah, and all the rest'll be fine. You already know how to love, darlin', you're way ahead of the game."

Simple, huh? Well, nobody else told me that. Nobody else who'd had a baby ever said that to me. I was falling apart all alone. Not getting out of my bathrobe, carrying her around with me in that fucking infant seat, afraid to even take a shower, afraid that she would cry . . . Jesus Christ, Frances—talk about crazy. But after he said it, I just stopped worrying. Worrying that I couldn't do it, worrying that I'd do it wrong, that I'd fuck her up . . . I just stopped worrying about everything. Hell, Frances, I was even better with Billy. Talk about crazy. I remember once we all went to the club. It was Jack and Marlene's anniversary and we went for dinner, all of us, and Pete and I ended up sitting next to each other. We had just left each other not two hours before. We had been doing it practically upside down in a fucking shower, screaming and laughing and doing it, and then we were sitting next to each other all dressed up, smiling politely, cutting the chicken, passing the bread, and talking about shock absorbers or some shit. My hair was still wet, Frances, and I was talking to Pete about shock absorbers.

Well, Pete would call, he'd say hello, and the way he'd say hello I'd know he could meet the next day, and the way I'd answer he'd know if I could get away. We had it all worked out . . . like fucking spies, Frances. Two fucking spies, that's what we were. *Fucking* spies. What a wit. See, I'm still the Most Humorous. Anyway, I thought my dreams had come true. Here I was pining for Pete Chickery all these years, sure that he'd made a mistake marrying Jessie, sure that he'd see the light someday, see *me*, look at me and really *see me* and know that I was the one. And now it had come true. I had waited and now it had happened. Here we were together. And he understood me. He saw who I really was. And he loved me. I was sure. He loved me now just as I had loved him all those years.

Some joke, huh? Some big fucking joke on the class Most Humorous. Well, I'm gonna tell you what I mean, Frances. I'm gonna tell you. Competition. See, I thought I was the only one. I mean, I knew there was Jessie, for crissakes, but I was sure that she was it. Me and Jessie. Well, Frances, that's where my problem was. I wasn't counting correctly. You see, there wasn't just me and Jessie: there was McGraw. McGraw, Frances. Susy Mae. Don't tell me you don't remember McGraw. No, she was divorced by then. Shit, Frances, I know. *You* were crazy about her? *I* was crazy about her. We used to have some good times, me and Susy Mae. Good taste the motherfucker had, didn't he? Pete always had good taste.

Well, it wasn't too spectacular. I was in the Jones Store, trying on bathing suits. They were having the after-the-Fourth sales and I wanted a new suit that would make me look half decent. I was in one of those stupid cubicles, sweating and looking at myself in all the mirrors, trying to see myself from the back and the side—shit— and there were two girls squeezed into the cubicle next to me, trying on suits together. You know how crowded it is when they have sales. And they're laughing. And I can hear them, you know. I mean, they're in the same room with me—there's only a panel separating us—and one is telling the other one this story about her and this guy that she sees. It's pretty graphic, this story—I mean, she's telling it in detail—and I'm listening. I actually laughed a couple of times too. And then she said "Pete." She said "me and Pete." And I got quiet. I got real quiet. And before I took a breath, she said something about Jessie. She said "Jessie," Frances, and then I knew. The bottom fucking dropped right out. "Jessie and Pete," she said. That's when I placed the voice—when she said "Jessie." It was the way she said it. That's how I knew it was McGraw. McGraw always hated Jessie.

I was standing there in that cubicle, Frances, naked. I was looking at myself in all those mirrors, naked. I saw myself sit down on that little ledge where they put the pins when they're making a hem. I just sat there and looked at myself, I don't know for how long. And then I cried. After they left. Shit, did I cry. I don't know how the fuck I got out of there.

And then I confronted him. It was on our twenty-second little red dot. I told him what I knew. God, I was like an outraged wife. Jessie would have been proud of me. I mean, I was so fucking in love with him, you would have thought I was the wife. I said I knew about him and McGraw. And get this, Frances . . . he said, "Yes, there are others." *Others*, Frances, he said *others*. I nearly shit when he said "others." He was looking right at me. I had just gotten to the room. He already had his shirt off, and his shoes and socks. He was sitting on the edge of the bed in his pants, with his belt unbuckled. I wanted to touch him so badly. I'll never forget. And he stood up and said, "Why? Does it make a difference?" Just like that. "Does it make a difference?"

And I said, "Yes, Pete, it makes a difference to me." And he said, "Are you sure, Tallulah? Because if you're sure, then we'll never see each other again like this."

He was staring at me. With those eyes of his, those fucking blue eyes. And I looked right back at him, that fuck. I looked right in his eyes. My insides were about to fall on the floor, I was dying inside, dying, but I looked right back at him—I made myself—and I said, "I'm sure, Pete." And I picked up my purse and walked out of that room and shut the door.

And that's what happened, Frances. I closed the door and I drove home. I cried all the way. I cried on and off for days—shit, for weeks. Just like I'm crying now. Shit, look at me . . . what a fucking mess. What a stupid fucking dishonorable mess I am. I could have ruined my whole life on that shithead. My whole life. If Billy ever knew! I mean, he'd have died, Frances. He'd have curled up and died. He thought Pete was everything. Shit, he thought Pete was his best friend. Jesus. Some best friend, huh? Give me another Kleenex, will you? This one's all fucked up. . . . I can't believe this. That's what I've been trying to figure out since Tuesday. Why am I crying? Am I crying for Pete? Is that why I'm crying? For which Pete, Frances? The Pete from the honeysuckle bushes that made my sixteenth year so important that I never gave him up? Or the Pete who did all those things to me at the Red Roof Inn? Because, Frances, he never looked at me again. In all these fucking years—ball games, picnics, poker, kids' birthday parties, their house, our house—he never ever looked at me again, not once, never said anything that would indicate that it had happened . . . *nothing*. Like I made it up. Like it was all a dream. He just moved on. Like I meant nothing to him.

He probably had a second-stringer just waiting to go in all along, huh, Frances? Probably some cunt who went to Shawnee Mission. A blond with long legs and feet with arches, a cheerleader. Don't you think, Frances? Someone all of us would hate.

Oh, shit, that's Billy's car. Shit, I gotta wash my face. Just let me wash my face and get my breath, okay? You talk to him a minute—okay, Frances? Will you?

I'll be right back, I promise. God, I love you, Frances. You just don't know how much I fucking love you. I'll be right back, I promise. I'm starving. You watch. I'm gonna eat two whole slabs all by myself.

Anne

I DON'T THINK I can bear any of this, Frances. It was all I could do to get myself on the airplane. I wanted to run the other way as fast as I could and never look back.

And then I had a wretched dream while I was flying. I couldn't make the last non-stop from L.A. I had to drive home after Tom called me at work and I couldn't figure out what to bring with me. I kept crying all over everything and sitting down and then standing up and rushing, so I had to take the one that stops in Phoenix and I was squeezed in between two people, trying not to cry, trying not to think about it, but I couldn't stop thinking about it, going over it again and again in my head, what Tom had told me on the telephone. Trying to understand how it could be true. And then I fell into this horrible drugged sleep. Grady was standing by my crib. I was a little tiny baby but she was holding out a pink bundle at me and talking to me as if I was older.

"Here's your baby sister, Anne pie; here's Jessie. . . . Isn't she just the sweetest baby you ever did see?" And then she took the pink bundle and hung it from a big hook that was on the ceiling over my crib. As if the baby Jessie was a mobile—her little face spinning around and around in the air above my head, her sweet arms flying out, tiny fingers clutching at nothing. Oh, it was horrible. I woke up flushed and confused, and the stewardess was standing over me holding trays in her hands, asking me: Well, did I want the Salisbury steak or the smothered chicken? Her lips were pressed together white and tight, the way Mother used to do. She must have been asking me while I was dreaming, but I didn't hear her. I started to cry, Frances. I just didn't know what to say to her. I didn't know where I was or what to say. Everything just rushed in on me and I was beside myself. You know how I hate flying. I hate being up there loose, with nothing to hold on to. I just hate it. That was always the only bad thing about coming home. I always meant to take the train, but somehow I'd forget and then it would be too late. I'd be up there choking.

I used to come home twice a year. Remember? Twice a year no matter what . . . like clockwork. Always Christmas. To see the lights on the plaza. And once during the summer. I'd try to outsmart the humidity, to pick the month when it wouldn't be so unbearable. I never won. Even if it was only June. I'd walk out the airport door and the heat would smother me. I'd always planned so carefully what I was going to wear on the plane—something lovely that Mother would see me in and think I looked wonderful. Something that would please her. I guess that was silly, considering I was grown and already married, but it didn't matter anyway . . . the awful hot air would hit me and I'd be sticky all over, my outfit would be wrinkled and my whole plan would be ruined. Mother would press her lips and look at me as if I'd done it on purpose, gotten all wrinkled on purpose. Isn't that silly?

Of course, I was home. That part of it was wonderful. Always. You know the way our sky is just so big, it just goes on and on, way out in front of you and way far behind you. Wherever you look. It's not like that out there. The sky is chopped off by mountains and there are lots of edges. Edges where if you stand on top of them and look over, you know your feet will slip. Or you're in a car and somebody else is driving and in your mind you see the car slip off, just skid and fly out into the air. Sometimes I don't know why I live there.

Anyway, I haven't flown in a long time. I haven't gone anywhere. And I haven't come home. Except for emergencies, Mother and Daddy and all, I haven't been home since a particular time after you and George were gone. A time I had with Pete. I would have told you about that time, Frances, if you'd still been here, but you were gone and it was never something I could have written about in a letter or said in a phone call. Never. I just couldn't. I never told anybody. I'm sure they all gossiped about it, because it had to do with me and Pete and an afternoon we spent. You know how everybody always jumped at a chance to tell another bad story about Pete, my bad brother-in-law. I'm sure they gossiped plenty, but I didn't care, because no matter what they thought, they didn't know. None of them knew what happened with us. They'd never guess. Not in a trillion years.

I was home for two weeks. Like always. Joe hadn't come with me. He said the only time he really liked it here was that one Christmas right before you and George moved to New York. You were all packed up and there was nothing in the living room but the tree and all those boxes. And we each brought you ornaments. Remember? It was so beautiful. No lights and all those candles burning everywhere. Tee said the house was gonna go up like a giant sparkler. That made me a little nervous, but it was so beautiful.

Anyway, Joe didn't come with me that July. He never really liked it here. No, I don't mean that. He liked it but he never felt comfortable, like he fit in. We'd all known each other for so long and everything about each other, and Joe always said he felt lonely in the middle of us. Isn't that silly? A big guy like that. I understood. Really I did. He always asked me if I wanted him to, because if I did he would. But I knew that he didn't want to. I never wanted to push him. Mother always said not to push a man.

So I was here and it was July. Of course, the humidity had waited for me to arrive. By eleven in the morning you could hardly get your breath. The longer I live away, the harder it is to take when I come back—the heat, I mean. I was staying with Mother and Daddy, in my old room. They were still good then. At least he was. She was starting to get a little funny, she'd forget things. She'd tell me something twice and I'd say, "Mother, you told me that yesterday," and she'd look at me. As if I was teasing, as if it couldn't be true, that I'd made a mistake. She was always so perfect, so organized, running everything, doing everything. So . . . perfect. It was shocking to her. She'd get angry and go upstairs and sit in her room by the window with her hands clutching the arms of the chair, just sit there and stare. She couldn't believe she had told me something twice. Couldn't believe it. Of course, that was only the beginning.

Grady knew. She told me as soon as I got home that time. Came in my room before I'd opened my bags. "There's somethin' wrong with your mama's head," she said. "I knows it, but your daddy won't pay me no mind when I point it out to him. He just don't wanna listen; whisks me away like I was dust on a table. You keep your eyes on her, Anne pie, and you'll see Grady's right. You hear me, baby?"

She *was* right, of course. It was the beginning of Mother's deterioration. If only we had . . . well, it doesn't matter now, does it? She's gone.

I know it's awful to say, Frances, but if Mother were here she couldn't take this. It's true. She'd never believe that Jessie could have done this. Never. Jessie was her favorite. Always. I knew it, I could tell. Even when I was real little I could tell. Her eyes would sparkle when Jessie would come into the room. Mother's eyes, they would just light up whenever she looked at Jessie. Not for me. I mean, she loved me, but not like Jessie. Jessie was beautiful. Her white skin and her black hair and her brown eyes. I used to want so to look like her. Not anymore, of course, but then I did. I used to wish on the evening star. Isn't that silly? I'd say, Oh, please, when I wake up, let me look like Jessie. It never worked—I always looked like me. Anyway, I understood. I mean, that she was the favorite and all. I would have loved her the most, too, if she had been my little girl. Really.

Well, anyway, it was July and I was home. Seeing everybody. Going out to dinner at Romanelli's and the Wishbone, listening to all the news. What had happened since Christmas. Jessie and Ellen and I shopped on the plaza and lay out by the side of the pool at the club and sat for hours at Winstead's drinking vanilla Cokes, eating french fries, and talking. Just like when we were kids.

Anita had Mary that summer; such a precious baby—pink, with all that orange hair. She was shocking to look at, so beautiful. We had a shower for her at Tee's. Tee was drinking too much—you know how she does. I guess everything else was pretty normal. It was hot, of course. Terribly hot. There hadn't been any rain and everybody was talking drought.

Of course, you guys were gone. That was so hard for me to get used to. I went by your house a lot, sat in front with the motor running. I kept thinking you'd pop out and we'd go down to

Harzfeld's and try on shoes. I missed you, Frances. They had painted your house yellow. Bright yellow with brown trim. I thought it looked terrible, but I didn't say anything.

Anyway, the Thornes gave a giant barbecue for the Fourth. You know Jack—he had all these ribs and this barbecue thing set up in the back, and the boys were standing out there basting them with sauce and beer for hours and hours in the hot sun. And he had cases of wine that somebody's grandmother made in her basement. Big glass jugs with no labels, and that little place on the side of the bottle where you could hook your finger. You know? It was awful. It made my teeth purple, and my gums. But we were all drinking it. I think I had a whole jug just by myself. I did. I carried it around with me all day. Can you imagine?

We played softball. Everybody. Pete hit a home run and we had to stop the game to find the ball. And we didn't let Anita touch the baby the whole day—we each took turns holding her and everything. So sweet. Tiny little toes and fingers. All that orange hair. And she smelled like powder. Maybe they all do—I wouldn't know. Before it got too dark we took a walk—me and Jess, Ellen, Anita, Tee—just us in the twilight. You were the only one missing. We walked right down the middle of the street as if nothing could stop us. Tee had on those dumb loafers she loves, with no socks. Her big breasts and her skinny legs in those loafers kicking at rocks in the street like a little kid. Wearing Billy's shirt. She had it open and you could see her bra. You could. She said it was too hot to wear clothes, she said we should all be naked. She was walking with a drink in her hand, laughing. And then when we got back, Jack had put this big floor right down on top of the grass and we danced. Ellen's little Ben and his friends had made up a band. They were so cute with their hair all slicked and trying to act grown up like they were a real rock band. It was sweet. There were babies sleeping all over Marlene's house, on top of crumpled baseball jackets, tucked in corners of stuffed chairs with pillows blocking them from toppling off.

I felt good. Like nothing could happen to us. Ever. Like time could stop. If we could just keep eating barbecue, we could stay the same forever and nothing bad could happen. Like *Brigadoon*, remember? I know it was silly of me, but that's how I felt. I danced a lot with Tom. Ellen never liked to dance much, did she? He's really good. And I danced with RC. We did all the old stuff. The kids weren't really too together as a band but that didn't matter. And when they got tired, Marlene turned the stereo way up and put the speakers in the windows facing outside. I felt wonderful. Safe.

Joe and I were a little better than when I had been home the Christmas before. At least I thought so. It was hard to accept that we weren't going to have any children. I mean, that I couldn't have children. That it was me. After all those awful tests and everything. I don't know, I felt like I had done something wrong or something. Me. Can you imagine? I never did anything. Everybody ran around but me. Why, I was a virgin when Joe married me. I was. An old virgin. It was silly to feel guilty, but I couldn't help it. I kept thinking, What did I do? I always tried to do the right thing. You know I did. Well. He wouldn't discuss adoption—wouldn't even talk about it. Really. The doctor tried. His mother even came in from Lubbock and told him he was a fool—that we could raise a baby and it would be our own. Love is what makes a baby yours, she said. Love. But he said he couldn't deal with it, it just wasn't for him. So. What could I do? I just had to learn to live with it, about myself. That it was me and all. Silly, isn't it? Jessie with three kids, and none for me. I always thought . . . well, it doesn't matter. Jessie tried to be really sweet to me about it. She flew in to Dallas and spent two days with me and we talked, but really, what could she say? She couldn't know how I felt, could she? Of course not. I know you could understand, Frances, but you never really wanted children like I did. We all know that. You said you never pictured yourself with a baby, and I always did. Anyway, I thought I had made my peace with it by summer. I thought so. Of course, Mother said that's what started all the trouble between Joe and me—my not being able to have a baby, I mean. She said he didn't feel the same way because of that. I don't think she was right, but Joe always did confuse me. I loved him so much, but I never really felt comfortable. He was so big. And always laughing, always happy and loud. He was like Texas. He was, I mean it. Big, and just like Texas. He could step into a room full of strangers like at one of those conventions and he'd just walk right up to people he didn't even know and say hello. And they would want to talk to him. I couldn't do that. I'd die. Really I would. He was sweet to me. He took care of me as if I was his baby. He used to rub my feet. This big guy would stand on his feet all day and then come home and put my feet in his lap and rub them. He was always doing things like that. He used to carry me around the apartment sometimes. But then he could freeze up. Like about the baby—that we couldn't have one. I mean, that I couldn't. He'd just clam up. I don't think it had anything to do with why he stopped loving me. Mother thought so but I don't. He said it wasn't.

Well, it was real late by the time we left the barbecue. Jessie and Pete drove me home to Mother's. I was drunk. I was. Actually, we all were. We were singing in the car. Loud. I'm sure Mother and Daddy could hear us. I wonder what she thought. I mean, me—drunk. I never even got drunk in high school, did I? We were singing old songs and Pete was doing all the dee dums and dee doos, the bass part, you know, like he was all four guys in a quartet. And Jess and I were singing the chorus, the melody part. Oh, we were laughing, it was so funny. We sounded like one of those groups.

Anyway, they asked me what I was gonna do the next day. I only had two days left. And I said I didn't know. I wanted to go out to Miller's but I didn't know if I could take Daddy's car. I thought he had to go downtown. And Pete said he'd take me. He said he had to call on two customers right off of Forty and it would be great for him because he would have company on the road. I said I didn't know and Jessie said that I should because she had to lug the kids to the doctor for shots and it would take her forever and if I didn't go with Pete I wouldn't get there at all this trip. So I said okay. I wanted to put flowers on the graves. Grandmother Wood's and Daddy Long's and everybody. And just be there for a little while by myself. To say hello, goodbye . . . I don't know. I always went when I was home. I'd go to the cemetery and visit the graves and then I'd go to Miller's and have a few beers with Sally and Gene and come back home. I went every summer. Always. I know it pleased Mother. She always wanted to know how Grandmother Wood's ivy was, if they were keeping it up properly. She told me over and over: "I paid for perpetual care, and that's what I want. If the ivy isn't decent around Mother's stone, then you just find the man and tell him." She told me every time as if I wouldn't remember. Even before she started to act funny, before she started to forget what she said, she still told me every time. "Do you understand, Anne?" she'd say, with her lips pursed up. "Just find the man and tell him."

"Yes, ma'am," I'd say. I never did tell her about the ivy. It was there but it certainly wasn't healthy. I don't think they fed it or fertilized it or whatever they were supposed to do. It was kind of yellow at the tips. I always weeded all around the stone and tried to make it pretty, the way I thought she would want it. Mother didn't go anymore. She stopped when I could drive there by myself. She kind of gave me the chore, passed it on. Well, I don't mean chore. I didn't mind. After all, it is my family. And I am the oldest. I know it's silly, Mother having Jessie and me only a year apart and all, but I always thought of myself as much older. I think Mother did too. She always spoke differently to me. I don't mean without love in her voice or anything; just differently. More strict, more serious. I don't know. But not the way she talked to Jessie. I'm sure it was because I was the oldest.

Pete picked me up right before lunch. He said if we had gone any earlier we would still have been drunk. Pete always made me laugh. From the first time I saw him. Your brother and Tip Rutten and Pete were riding through Meyer Circle on their bikes. Right through the fountain with all their clothes and shoes on. Can you imagine? They were drenched. That was the first time I saw him. I thought, Who is that boy with those blue eyes? He'd just come from Tupelo with Anita and their mother. And Ellen said, "That's Pete Chickery—isn't he cute?"

The whole time Pete snuck around with Jessie he made me laugh. He was always sending me presents—she'd bring them home with her. Silly things like a button off his shirt or a stick of gum. Once he sent me a ribbon, a purple satin ribbon. I kept it for a long time. Even after I was married. That was when he started calling me Serious Face Anne, the summer he started dating Jessie. Right to my face. Then he decided that in front of people he'd say SFA, and then he shortened it to SF. He's called me that all these years. SF. I remember once when Aunt Jewel sent me something from New York from Saks Fifth Avenue and it said SFA right on the box. I thought it was so funny. My initials. Serious Face Anne.

He had on a blue shirt. It matched his eyes. Pale blue. Tee said he was vain about his eyes and that's why he always wore blue. I thought he looked nice.

I had sandwiches and we ate them in the car while we drove. Bologna with kid's mustard. Mother still bought kid's mustard even though Jessie and I were both grown up and gone. I sent her some of the French mustard once after I had moved to California, but she said it made her head hurt. She said Daddy didn't like it either and why did I waste my money on fancy things that nobody understood. She said she threw the whole jar in the trash. Isn't that silly? She could have given it to somebody—to Jessie, to Grady even.

We ate the sandwiches and I had peaches. Big fat ones off somebody's tree. I can't remember whose. They were ripe and some of the juice got on the front of my dress. And we stopped for Cokes on the road. There really was going to be a drought, you could see it. So much corn was ruined, brown and finished before its time. Everything so dry, and it was only July.

Pete talked about his job. About how he believed in Ship 'n Shore and that's why he didn't mind being away on the road so much. He covered five states then. He said they made a good blouse and he could sell it. He said it was quality merchandise, that the buttonholes and seams were done properly. He said it was a damn good product for the money. He talked to me just like I was a store. I could see why they bought from him. He certainly convinced me. And he said they had a nice pension plan for their salesmen and he was putting some away out of every paycheck. For him and Jessie in their old age, he said. I laughed. I couldn't imagine either of them old.

And he said he was happy. I never asked him about the women. I know you all thought he was awful. Everybody did. But I really could never believe all those stories. And Pete was good to me always and I didn't think it was any of my business. After all, what could I say to him anyway? Pete, why do you have to cheat on my sister? I couldn't say that. It would be silly. So I didn't say anything about the women. Not that trip. Not ever.

We had fun in the car. He told me jokes, terrible ones about traveling salesmen—you know, dirty ones. I was all red in the face from laughing and Pete said if I kept it up he'd have to change my nickname.

He could always make me laugh, you know, and he was always interested in me, Frances, in what I had to say.

We talked about when he and Anita moved here and all of us

growing up—me and you and Jessie, Ellen, Tee—you know, how good we all were and how bad he was. He told me stories about the Sons of Rest and what they did at the Rainbow Tap Room, smuggling Country Club malt liquor into the Leawood Drive-In, the time when he and Shapiro made that riot outside the north door over the game with East and Pete hit Larry Yord in the nose. Remember?

And he told me about Bill England. That Bill had been shot down over Vietnam. I mean, I didn't know that, Frances. Nobody had written me or called to tell me that. He'd gone to Vietnam, he was a navigator, and they'd shot him down in a C-130. I couldn't believe it. Peachy's big brother. He was the sweetest boy, Frances. I mean, we never went out or anything because he was older and all—he was a senior when I was just a freshman—but he never treated me like I was a baby, you know how some boys could do. I still have a picture of him, Frances. He's wearing a suit and a white shirt and he's sitting on a chair on your mother's screened-in porch on Seventy-third. I don't even remember why I have it or what he was doing there. Maybe he was going out with your brother, doubling or something, or maybe Peachy gave it to me. I don't know why I still have it; it's in a box of photographs I was going through before I came. I told Pete about an afternoon a million years ago when Bill England and I hung crepe paper streamers all around the gym together for the Bowery Ball and somebody had a record player on and Buddy Holly was singing "Maybe Baby" and the record got stuck and it played over and over all after-noon—nobody ever fixed the needle. "Maybe Baby," over and over. Pete said, well, Bill England was up in heaven now with old Buddy Holly and the Big Bopper and Ritchie Valens. I had this picture of them in my mind—all of them sitting together on a big pink cloud playing their guitars and Bill singing away, wearing his army uniform with his hat on and all these medals across his chest. . . . Maybe that's why Pete went with me to the cemetery. I mean, because I was crying. He'd said at first that he was gonna drop me off and then pick me up after he made his calls, but he changed his mind. Maybe because I was crying. I don't know. Anyway, he said he'd go with me to visit the dead—that's what he said—if I'd go with him to visit the "near-dead," and I said okay.

He called on one store in Fulton and one in Mexico City. It

didn't take long. I waited in the car. He'd go in with his blouse cases and I'd read this old *Redbook* I found in his car and then he'd come out smiling. He said we'd go to the cemetery and see everybody and then we'd swing by Miller's, see Sally and Gene, and get shitfaced. He was trying to make me laugh, you know how he did.

When we got to the cemetery the gates were locked. I couldn't believe it because it was still light, but it was after six and I guess they just lock it up at five or six. I was so disappointed. I really wanted to see everybody. And Pete said, "Don't worry, SF, we'll just break in."

I couldn't believe he meant it, but you know Pete. Before I could even say a word he was making a kind of step with his hands and he told me to take off my shoes and stockings and he boosted me up and there I was, bare-legged, straddling the stone fence of the cemetery. Can you imagine if Mother had known? It was probably sacrilegious. I'm sure it was. Pete kind of climbed up and over and held out his arms for me. And I jumped. And we were in. Just like that. I was laughing. Bare-legged and barefoot in a cemetery. Like little kids doing something wrong. I don't know how I did it—I guess being with him made me brave.

He said we had to split up. I always know exactly where everybody is in there, but that's when I drive through the gate, and I got so confused with the jumping in and everything that I couldn't get my bearings. So Pete said we'd split up and search. Like detectives, he said. I went one way and he went the other and we yelled back and forth to each other. We did. He would yell, "Hey, SF, here's McGraw's dad. Did you know that bastard died?" And he'd yell, "There's a stone over here that's bigger than the memorial downtown for the dead soldiers." And things like that. I know it was disrespectful, but I was laughing so hard, I thought I was gonna collapse right there.

Anyway, I found Grandmother Wood first. And he found Daddy Long, and then I got straightened out and I knew where the rest were. I fixed up the ivy and pulled weeds the way I always do and just said a little something to each one, like a little prayer, sort of. Pete smoked a cigarette and sat on somebody's stone. He did. I said, "Pete, you shouldn't." But he said he had picked somebody that was probably related to his uncle Ned, so it didn't matter. And then we were ready to go. We were walking back to the car and it was starting to get dark and I guess we made a wrong turn. And there we were, at the baby part of the cemetery. I don't know if you've ever seen it. It's awful. All these little stones lined up in rows. And they have a tiny white picket fence around the area, just like you would around a dream house. I don't know why they did that. It's so awful. And I walked in. I don't know why. Pete said, "Don't go in there, SF; we don't have anybody in there." But I couldn't stop myself.

I opened the white gate and went in. I read all the names. I did. All their little names and the dates. And some said things, you know, like prayers or poems or a special thing that their mother or daddy wanted to say. I guess they felt they just had to carve something right in the stone to make sure, so they'd know, in stone, that their baby was really gone. That God had done that. It was so awful. All those babies.

And then I don't know what happened. I just fell apart. I started to cry and I got sick. I did. I threw up the bologna sandwich and the peaches and everything. Right in the grass. It was awful, just awful. Pete was there and he held my head. He was touching my arm, saying, "C'mon, SF, let's get you out of here. It's okay, honey. Come on. Let me help you out of here. Take my arm."

And he was trying to pick me up. But I couldn't move. I felt like they were my babies. All my babies that I was never gonna have. Like they had died, died before I even got to hold them or anything—touch their little toes, hear them cry or laugh or anything. It was so unfair. I couldn't understand what I had done that God decided I couldn't have any. And I was crying and crying. I felt like my heart had broken. Like I was just gonna die right there—right there—on top of the grass, on top of all those babies. Like I should. Like I belonged there with them. And Pete tried to pick me up and I was yelling at him to stop, to leave me there, that it was where I belonged, that I wasn't any good, that I wasn't allowed to have any babies because I wasn't any good. And I was hitting at him to put me down. Oh, it was awful. He had to carry me, half drag me away from there, and I don't know how he did it but we got back to the fence. And over it. He sat me down in the grass by the side of his car and got a rag from the trunk or somewhere and tried to wipe me off and I was crying and crying.

I couldn't stop. And Pete kept saying it was all right. "It's all right, SF, don't worry, darlin'. You're with me. You're with Pete."

And then . . . I don't know. I felt so empty. I reached out for him. I did. It was me. I reached out for Pete and he held me. He held me and he kept saying it would be all right, over and over. "You'll be all right, SF, we'll get you home and you'll be fine." And he kissed my face where I was crying.

"Stop cryin', honey," he said, "stop cryin' now. I'm gonna take you home. You're gonna be fine, darlin'."

But I knew I wouldn't be. I held on to him tight because I knew I was gonna disappear. I knew if I didn't hold on I'd be gone. I'd fly right out into the sky, like I was on one of those edges. I'd topple right out into the sky, right off the edge, and I'd never get back. And no one would hear me scream. And then Pete was saying he was gonna put me in the car. Help me up and put me in the car, I think he said, but I could hardly hear him anymore. It was true. I was already toppling. Soon I would be over the edge. No more Anne. All gone. Who would have missed me? Jessie? Mother? No one. Not really. I was never important to anybody. There weren't any babies waiting for me to hold them or give them supper or lullaby them to sleep. Nobody needed me.

Even Joe didn't need me. Not really. He'd miss me for a little while, but he'd get used to it and he'd be happier. He could have more fun. I always spoiled the fun. I could never stand up with the rest of you. The rest of you were always pushing at me to catch up. It was always, "Come on, Anne, have one beer. It won't kill you."

"Anne, come on, we're going to the lake. Oh, come on with us. Oh, don't be such a stick-in-the-mud."

"Anne, he's sweet. . . . There's nothing wrong with kissing a sweet boy. Oh, Anne, you're such a prude. Anne, you're a sissy. Anne, have a little backbone. Come on, Anne, come on, Anne. . . ."

I always spoiled the fun. I probably spoiled Mother's fun. That's probably why she never loved me. Because I was her first and I spoiled all her fun. That's why her eyes didn't light up. Suddenly I understood everything. It was all clear to me. I put my hand in Pete's back pocket and I grabbed his pocketknife—the one Daddy gave him when he married Jessie, the one he always carried, with the mother-of-pearl on the outside and his initials. "What are you doin', SF? Hey, give me that . . . what are you doin'?" Pete was yelling at me and trying to take the knife out of my hand; I was trying to get it open, the blade out, and he was grabbing at my hands.

I didn't want him to stop me. I wanted it to be over. I wanted it to be finished right there. Just finished. All of it—Joe not talking and Mother not remembering and me knowing now that it was me, always me, who made everything terrible. I wanted to be gone.

I cut him with the knife. I didn't mean to, but he was in my way. I swung my arm to push him away and I cut him, his blue shirt ripped, the fabric split and blood was seeping across the front, a stain running down his shirt in lines. I was trying to cut my wrist. I wanted to slice it through, and he pushed my hand and I cut my arm, only my arm, the side of my arm. I was crying. There was blood on my dress. I couldn't see, I was crying so hard, and Pete was yelling something. The knife caught him by the eye. I screamed. I thought I'd cut his eye, blood down his face by his nose, his mouth. He grabbed at my hand and he slapped me. He slapped my face and I lost my balance. I tried to run, but he tripped me and I fell in the grass. He was pulling my dress, rolling over in the grass, grabbing for my arm. He was everywhere. I kicked him, I kicked him in the face. He was pulling my leg—he wouldn't let go of my leg—and then he threw himself on top of me. I couldn't get out from under him. I spit at him. "Stop it, SF!" I could see his lips moving. I couldn't hear him. He had my hand, squeezing my fingers so tight it hurt. I couldn't hold on to the knife; he was shaking my hand, shaking my fingers to drop it. Squeezing. And he got it. He got the knife away from me. I was choking and crying. I wanted to get up. I was hitting at him to get him off me. He grabbed my hands and pushed my arms down to my sides with his hands. He was yelling something. He was straddling me and then he was on top of me. All of him right down on top of me, pinning my arms to my sides, yelling in my face. I was trying to turn my head away. He was hurting me. Yelling. He said he loved me. I thought he said he loved me. I was pulling my head away from him. I couldn't get my head . . .

"Never again. You can't do anythin' like that ever again. Do you hear me?" he was yelling at me. "You can't hurt yourself." I was crying. I wanted him to go away, leave me alone. He wouldn't leave me alone.

"Answer me! Goddamn it, answer me!" I heard him. I was crying, but I heard him. I remember that. I could hear Pete.

"Look at me, SF. Don't turn your head away—look at me. I'm your family, do you hear me? I'm your family and you're my family and you can't do that. You can't hurt yourself. I won't allow it. Do you hear me?"

I stared at him. All I could see were his eyes, Pete's blue eyes.

"I need you. I will always need you. You're important to me. Do you understand?"

My ears were wet. The tears were running down my cheeks into my ears, just like in that silly song, Frances. His hands pressed hard against the sides of my head, his fingers holding my head. I was crying.

"I love you. Answer me, goddamn it!" He was heavy, yelling, he wouldn't stop. And I tried to shake my head yes. "I love you," he said, "you're my family. I need you. I'll always need you, SF, do you understand?"

I closed my eyes and shook my head yes. His fingers were so tight. He kissed my face. "Important to me. You will always be important to me." Over and over. He kept saying it over and over. That I was important. That he needed me.

And then he made me promise. Promise that I wouldn't ever try to hurt myself again. He said that he couldn't bear it. That I was his family and he couldn't bear it. He said he needed me. Pete needed me.

I don't know how long we were there, in the grass beside his car by the cemetery gates. I don't know. He picked me up and put me in the car and he said I didn't have to talk. I didn't have to do anything. That he was going to take care of everything. And he did. That I was his sister too. That's what he said.

We stopped by the side of the road. There was a Conoco with a little restaurant attached. The bathrooms were inside. I remember I stopped him. He was holding on to my arm and we were about to walk in and I stopped short. If there were people inside, they would see me. I didn't say the words, but Pete knew what I was thinking. He said, "It doesn't matter, darlin'. It doesn't matter how you look. I'll fix it. Just walk right through. Go ahead, darlin', I gotcha . . . just walk."

He opened the screen door and held on to my arm as we walked all the way back past the counter and the pinballs to the

ladies' room. There was just one man sitting at the counter. I think
he was the only person there except for the waitress and the cook.
I didn't see anyone else. He looked right at me. He was eating
berry pie; purple berries had made a stain around his mouth. He
looked up at me and then real fast back down at his pie.

Pete came into the ladies' room. He didn't even look to see if
somebody was in there. He just walked right in with me and shut
the door. He washed my dress in the sink. He did. My dress and
his shirt. I lifted up my arms and he took my dress off, slid it up
my arms and over my head like I was a little girl. He took paper
towels and soaked them in the sink and cleaned my face and my
arms and put Band-Aids on the cuts. He got them from the waitress.
He told her it was an accident, that we had an accident. I remember
that. And he brought me milk, warm milk in a coffee cup. He made
her heat it up and he brought it in to me. He said I had to drink
it all. I sat on the toilet seat in my bra and panties and Pete watched
me drink it. I was so tired. He put our clothes back on us wet.
Dripping wet. Stuck my arms through the sleeves. He buttoned me
up into a wet dress. It stuck to me all over.

"It's okay, SF," he said. "It doesn't matter, darlin'."

I didn't speak. I never said a word.

We rode all the way back with the windows rolled down and
that awful hot air blew us both dry. My dress and his shirt. As if it
never happened, we were dry. And he took me home to Mother's
and walked me to the door. And when I went inside he nodded
his head yes at me through the screen door and smiled like
everything was fine.

And that was it, Frances. That was what happened. I'm sure
everybody thought something else. I'm sure they thought we were
bad. That Pete had me like they talked about him having all those
women. Like I was one of them, the women in the stories. But Pete
wasn't like that, Frances, I know he wasn't.

I went back to Texas, back to Joe, and I haven't been home a
lot since. Except for emergencies, like I said . . . for Mother and
Daddy. I really don't know why. I didn't have anything to be
ashamed of. I didn't do anything. I just didn't want anybody to say
anything, to ask me. Jessie never said a word. She never asked me
what happened that day at the cemetery or why we never got to
Miller's. Nothing. Not a word.

And Pete called me once a week. From then on. Always. Even after Joe and I split up and I moved all the way to California. When they offered me that job in Los Angeles and I was afraid to go, it was Pete who encouraged me to do it.

"It's just a transfer, darlin'. You already know how to do that job; you'll just be doin' it with palm trees outside your door."

I was sitting there in Dallas with the map spread out in front of me on my coffee table talking to him on the telephone, trying to figure out where Pasadena was, since that's where IBM wanted to move me.

"Well, what does it look like?" he was asking, and I was measuring it with a pencil flat on the map and telling him.

"Well, that's just an erasure away, darlin'. It's just like drivin' to Lawrence is all it is."

That's why I took the transfer after Joe left me, because IBM had room for me out there and not in Kansas City, and Pete said in a new place I wouldn't have old memories and I should go.

Did you know that all these years he's called me once a week? He's never missed, Frances. Once a week I'd pick up the phone and he'd be there just like I did last Monday morning, it was about seven-thirty, right before I left for work.

"Hello, SF," he said. "How you doin', darlin'?"

And I always told him. He's the only one I've ever told how I feel about anything. The only one.

And now he's gone.

Anita

PETE WAS BAD. Just like Daddy.

You all think I'm a terrible person to say such a thing about my very own brother, but I know more than any of you about who he really was, Frances—underneath his smile, behind those blue eyes. I'm the only one who knows. I thank Jesus I'm the only Chickery left to see what's happened in this family. I'll pray for Daddy and I'll pray for Pete, but I won't cry for them and I won't forgive. I'm not like Mother. I don't make allowances. I've learned not to.

Pete was just like Daddy even from the start. Looked like him. The very same but for the hair color. Pete's was yellow and Daddy's was fire red-orange. All the rest—eyes, face, the stance, that strut of a walk—like looking at Daddy all over again. Like looking at Daddy reborn.

When I was little, I thought Daddy was fine, just fine. I didn't know about evil close up; only what they told us in church, the nuns and all. I'd never seen it in the flesh. But the rest of them, they all knew, both sides. My aunt Hazel never even said his name out loud. The same like they did with cancer, wouldn't say it right out because if it was heard, it would exist. It was like my daddy didn't exist. They had to deal with him only because Alice Maude had lost her head and married him. He wasn't a Catholic. He might have come from good people, but he wasn't a Catholic boy. And he was wild. Even his own people admitted that. He was beneath her and a disgrace. Gagee stood up for him, but he was her son, she couldn't help herself. Even Poppa said his boy was a disappointment. I heard him say it in my aunt Eula's house, but they all acted like I made it up, like Poppa hadn't really said that at all.

Before Daddy married my mother he stole Gagee's savings. Took her bonds right out of her pocketbook, forged her name, and cashed them in. He did that to his own mother. But she wouldn't hear of it, wouldn't let any of them discuss it around her. She made allowances for her boy, said he was the firstborn, so they were too hard on him, hadn't disciplined him proper—like it was her fault. Whatever the excuse, she was on his side. And so was my mother. They both cried over him plenty. A string of women crying over Daddy and Pete. A string of foolish women.

He looked like he stepped right out of the sun, my daddy. Red-orange hair and that smile, just like the light. When my Mary was born, that was the very first part of her I saw, the top of her little head sticking out, bright red-orange, just like Daddy. I had forgotten. That's when I started to cry, when I saw that hair. "Look at this child's hair," the doctor was saying in the delivery room. "It's like a flame of fire." I knew that hair. I was lying on that steel table and I was already afraid for her. Afraid she'd be like him.

Daddy was flash. All the stuff that covers up what's the real man underneath. He prided himself on his abilities: telling a joke right, making a perfect omelet, reading Shakespeare out loud. He could barely feed his family, but he looked like he stepped right out of a magazine, perfect and fine. He could hardly make a living, but he prided himself on being the best dancer in the county. As if those were the important things, as if those were the things you strive to achieve in your lifetime.

At night he'd dance Mother round the kitchen. Hold out her chair, she'd fold up into him and they'd dance round me and Pete sitting at the table finishing supper. He said they had their own imaginary music that only they could hear; they didn't need a radio. Used to make Pete mad.

"I can hear it," he'd say. "Hey, Daddy, I can hear that music. I can."

"No, you can't, boy," Daddy'd say, not looking at Pete, never taking his eyes off my mother.

Daddy said they weren't in our kitchen in Tupelo, they were on the starlight roof of some New York fancy hotel. Told her what she was wearing, what they had for dinner—wouldn't call it supper, like we did then; called it dinner. He said they had fine things to eat like duck under glass, things that Pete and I didn't understand.

Pete would get furious. "I wouldn't eat duck in a glass even if you'd let me. I wouldn't! I hate duck in a glass! It's worse than okra, it's worse than eyeballs!"

They didn't listen. They only heard their music and only saw each other. I watched how she'd look at him. He'd dance her all round that yellow linoleum and we'd finish supper. Left out.

Then maybe the very next day he'd be gone. You never knew when. He didn't give away any signs like getting angry at her for no reason or acting bored or looking trapped. No signs. He'd just be gone.

She'd take Pete and me with her to Saint Theresa's. Sit us down in front of a statue of the Holy Mother and she'd pray and pray. For hours. As if she was doing penance, as if she was the one who was bad. Pete would get terribly fidgety, like boys do, but he knew he had to stay put. He'd rock back and forth, and I'd think, I'm gonna scream, Lord, please don't let me scream in church. When Pete was about to explode, Mother'd kiss her rosary, put it back in her purse, light a candle, and we'd leave.

She never said a bad word about Daddy's going and she'd never answer about where he was or when he'd be back. She'd say the same thing no matter how many times a day me or Pete would ask her. "Your daddy will be back just as soon as he can." As if it was all right, his walking in and out of her life like that. As if it was right and proper.

I found out, though. I was walking home from school and I told this boy that my daddy was away "on business," this fancy story I had made up to tell, and he laughed at me.

"Business?" he said, his face all scrunched up. "Your daddy ain't got no business. Your daddy ain't nothin' but trash. He's gone to Columbus so's he can get drunk."

"He did not!" I screamed, my face red and hot, my heart pounding.

"You're just stupid, Nita," he said. "You don't know nothin'. You're just a stupid shitty girl."

"I'm not allowed to hear cussin', Mark Dee. Don't you dare say cuss words at me!"

It seems he knew all about the comings and goings of Jimmy Chickery because his uncle Albert was Daddy's buddy. It seems those two made a lot of "business" trips to the 45 Club in Columbus. Mark's mother knew plenty about her brother Albert and about my daddy. I held on to the information for some three hours and then I finally burst and told Pete. He ran out of the house looking for Mark, found him in the vacant lot next to Brucie Bahm's house, playing ball, and busted his lip in two places 'cause he called Daddy trash. Pete was a whole foot shorter than Mark Dee but it didn't matter, he still busted him. I felt bad Mark got hurt, 'cause I liked him. His hair was always falling down across his forehead and into his eyes, soft gray sweet eyes. But I felt good about knowing where Daddy was. When you're little you feel better knowing information. It's when you're older that it hurts your heart when you know too much.

I didn't understand why Daddy had to go so far to drink, why he just couldn't do it at home. I was too little to understand it wasn't about drinking, it was about leaving. I'm surprised he didn't have a bottle in the house, but he didn't. The house was hers. The only liquor that ever came through the door was in the rum balls Aunt Eula brought over Christmas, and my mother never so much as touched one with her fingertip, much less ate one. She said they were poison.

When he was gone she would watch the door. I'd see her, her shoulders perched up in the air like she'd been surprised, never settling back down until he was home. Sometimes he'd disappear for just one night, sometimes it'd be for days. I would practice how I was gonna be when he'd return. I wasn't gonna talk to him. I was gonna stay mad, turn my back, and not say a word. But I couldn't. He'd hold out his arms to me and I couldn't.

I was sure they never discussed his leaving. I was sure that once he was back she'd just pray it wouldn't happen again. Mother wasn't one to discuss personal things, ever. But I was wrong. I'd been sent home from school with a temperature and a sore throat and I heard him talking before I opened the back door. He was promising her. He wouldn't do it again, he didn't know what came over him. Why, she was his whole life, he said, and he didn't mean to do those things, he just couldn't stop himself when one of those urges overtook him.

"But not ever again, Alice Maude, I promise you. I'm finished with it now. It's all out of my system, I swear to you." He was slumped on a kitchen chair, crying like a little boy, his head buried in my mother's breasts as she held him. I stood there in the doorway with the note from Sister Catherine Angelica in my hand and watched her stroke his beautiful red-orange hair and tell him she forgave him.

She forgave him every time. And then it would be all right. He'd go to Lane's every day, kiss us goodbye in the mornings, go make coffee tables, and come home five-thirty, natural, like nothing happened. For a time.

And then it would be something. Maybe he'd find money she'd tried to hide from him. He'd take it and bet it. Didn't matter on what, he wasn't particular. A ball game of two teams up North even, or a dog race, or cards . . . it didn't matter. He would take the money and lose it. I'd lie in bed and hear her crying in the bathroom with the door shut. Hear him walking back and forth in the kitchen. Daddy never gave my mother any peace. He never gave her anything—just imaginary music and lies. That was the whole of it.

The last time he left was two years before we came here. Pete was thirteen and I was fourteen. It was my birthday. Gagee was making me a party, with everything pink. She got the idea from a magazine: the food, the decorations—all pink. She said I could have any cake I wanted. I picked coconut, my favorite, with lemon cream in between the layers and coconut sprinkled all round. It turned out like a big pink snowball. I was a very young fourteen to be so pleased by something so simple; a pink coconut cake wouldn't please a fourteen-year-old nowadays, would it? Well, don't I know it. But it was different then. Or maybe it was different there. Tupelo. Maybe.

Daddy was the one bad thing about my birthday. He picked that day to leave for the last time. I've lived with that fact all my life—one of his evil urges was more important to him than his own daughter's birthday. I shed my tears long ago over it. Not anymore.

It was the very last time any of us saw him. I was already dressed and waiting for my friends to arrive. It was a luncheon of only girls, six girls. Mother had made chicken à la king on crisp patty shells. That was what you called it. It was Mrs. Esther Smith's recipe from some fancy restaurant in Atlanta. The table was all set with pink paper everything. There were little baskets next to each setting, filled with salted nuts, and I was standing in the kitchen in a pink dress, looking at the table, touching everything, so excited I couldn't sit down. Mother was in the bathroom, changing. Pete was outside, throwing the ball up against the side of the house, furious because I hadn't invited him. I saw Daddy go to the back door.

"Where you goin', Daddy? You have to take the pictures when the girls come. You promised."

"Missy," he said, "I've got me twenty-two minutes before this gala starts, and I'm gonna get me a breath of air and be back before your mother's dry from her bath. I assure you. Okay, baby?"

He was smiling that smile at me. He had his hand on the doorknob and something made me nervous in the pit of my stomach, but I thought it was the party and all.

"Daddy, please, please don't be late. I want a picture of June Unger's face the very second she sees my dress. Okay? She's gonna be just green. Okay?"

I should have known he'd promise and I should have been an older fourteen and known his promises didn't matter. But I wasn't. I believed him.

When I was little he told me that if I wished on my rosary when I was falling asleep and didn't finish it, then the angels would come to finish it for me and grant me my wish. That's what I did every night after he left. Wished for him to come home. Wished for the angels to bring him home. It took three nights. They brought him home. The same way my brother Pete came home from Ellen's house. Dead.

The foreman came from Lane's to tell my mother. And some other man. They had on suits. They knocked on the kitchen door, not the front-room door, but they had on suits. Mother went to the door. It was early; she was making our lunch sandwiches and she had the knife still in her hand, peanut butter stuck to the tip.

Yellow curtains blew right next to her hair. Yellow curtains with little red flowers as she opened the door. Those two men standing there. One of them took off his hat and I knew.

Pete did too. He said, "Oh, shit!" right out loud. Mother didn't even turn round about him saying a cuss word. My spoon slipped and oatmeal made this warm plop in the lap of my uniform and I started to cry. I knew Daddy was dead.

You know, I called McConnell's because I wanted magnolias for Pete's coffin. But they can't get them. They just don't exist in Kansas City right now. No magnolias. I never thought of that happening.

There were magnolias at Daddy's funeral. That's what I remember. The smell of magnolias and the sound of my mother. And Gagee. And Pete. Even Poppa Chickery was crying. All of them. But not me. I didn't cry even when Mother fell forward on Daddy's casket, sobbing for Jesus to take her too. Making a fool of herself. Gagee and Poppa were trying to stop her and Pete was pulling at her dress, crying. My mother screaming, "Oh, Jimmy, please, don't leave me here alone with these children. . . . Don't leave me . . . Jimmy, Jimmy . . . please don't leave me." Sobbing and yelling like she had become someone else. A stranger with her face all distorted and her hair flying. I just stood there.

I had cried all my tears the night he left. Waiting for him to come home, waiting till long after it was dark, standing at that kitchen door making wishes in my head, praying for him to just please come home. He must have known all along when he went out that door that he wasn't coming back for my party. Even the fact that it was my birthday didn't matter to him. I didn't matter to him. I cried myself to sleep long after that pink coconut cake was gone.

By the time we buried him I had no tears left and I had figured it out. I knew my daddy had made a choice to run from his family. A choice to be a drunk and a gambler and do anything he could that was evil. A choice to drive into that tree and die. He even made a choice to do it on my birthday so I could remember it every year. And I knew I would never forgive him for it.

They told my mother that there wasn't another car on the road when he hit that tree, nothing in his way, like he hit it for no reason. They told her he died fast. "Didn't know what hit him, Mrs. Chickery," the man said, twisting his hat round and round in his fingers. As if that would matter. All that mattered to her was he was gone. She was thirty-four years old. It would have been a lot easier for me if Neil had smashed into a tree when I was thirty-four. A whole lot easier than the way it was. Him leaving me with two babies, never to be heard from again. All those years, Frances. If I could have only found him, I could have tried to get an annulment. It broke my heart to have to marry Leonard outside the church. So good, my Leonard, to take me in with both my girls and in the eyes of the Lord and the church I'm still married to Neil. I'll never be able to forgive Neil for that. People stay what they are, Frances, no matter how much you try. You can't change them. No matter how much I loved Neil, he couldn't change. And look at my brother. No matter how much Jessie loved him, it didn't matter. And Daddy was the same. No matter how much my mother loved him, it wasn't enough to make him change his ways.

I assume Daddy had other women, just like Pete, but I don't know for sure. No one ever told me. What I do know is he was alone in the car when he died. He wasn't with a woman. At least Mother had that.

Mother told me and Pete that we weren't to question the ways of the Lord. We were to accept. Sister Anne Pierre said Jesus needed Daddy for something special. I told Pete Jesus probably had some big crap game going on up in the sky, that's what he needed Daddy for. Pete slapped me right across my face. I had to hide the whole afternoon so Mother wouldn't see the finger marks. Pete loved Daddy—he wouldn't hear a bad word about him ever.

After Daddy was dead, Pete's mouth got worse and worse. He was always in trouble. More and more Mother looked the other way. I thought it was 'cause he was little and so angry about Daddy being taken and all. Later I figured it out—she was doing just what Gagee did, making allowances for her boy. I thank Jesus I had girls. I never made allowances for Mary or for Charlotte. None.

The day we left Tupelo was the very last time my brother set foot in a church except for when I married Neil. All dressed up to step on the train, Mother suddenly insisted Poppa turn the car round; we had to go back to Saint Theresa's to take Communion before we left. Gagee said not to worry, it would be fine, just fine, we had lots of time. I shot Pete a look in the car. I knew he couldn't take Communion; he hadn't been to confession. He'd already lied to Mother all that year about going to church. When she decided we really had to leave Tupelo, that she couldn't make it and we had to go to Kansas City, that's when he told me. "I'm not goin' to church anymore, Nita. That's it." I laughed at him. "Mother'll never let you," I said, "never."

"Oh, really?" He smirked. "You watch."

I was already nervous enough about leaving home. I wasn't about to get mixed up in his lies. Poppa pulled up right in front of Saint Theresa's. Pete glared at me when I got out. He stayed put in the back seat, said he wasn't going in, told Mother she'd have to drag him, 'cause he wasn't going. Gagee tried to get herself in the middle, but Mother said, "Step aside, Ethel Mary, I'll tend to this myself." Poppa lit a cigarette and looked off up and down the street like he didn't know us. Mother bent her head into the back of the car. "You're goin' in that church with me, son. You're goin' in and you're gonna kneel right next to me or I'll take a strap to you myself. You hear me?" I'd never heard Mother talk like that. Neither had Pete. She grabbed his hand and yanked him right out of Poppa's car and into church.

Father Vincent put the wafer on Pete's tongue and Pete let it fall on the floor. Right out of his mouth and onto the floor. It got deathly quiet. Father Vincent blanched and then got bright red. He leaned over and whispered, but it was like he was spitting, his teeth were so tight.

"You've dropped the body of Christ, my son."

Pete stood up from the rail right next to my mother, he stood up and said, "That's not the body of Christ, you old fart, it's a fuckin' cracker." And he spun round and left the church. I was holding on to my mother. She didn't faint but she could hardly stand up. Father Vincent had to help me get her out to the car.

The three of us got more than halfway to Kansas City on that train with nobody saying a word. I threw up, I was so upset. And when we got here, right before we got off the train, he said, "Mother, don't ever ask me to go into a church again. I'm sorry for what I said and did but don't ever ask me, because I won't go." Fifteen years old, skinny and still short, but he said it strong, like he was all grown up. Like he knew what he was talking about and she better listen. Mother didn't say a word, just stared at him. The sound of the train on the tracks filled the space between them. I held my breath. Then she turned her head away and watched out the window as the South flew by in the dark. The discussion was over. That was the whole of it.

I was probably the only one who knew that was why he and

Jessie got married at the club. He said he wouldn't get married in a church. He only walked me down the aisle when I married Neil because I cried for weeks that who would walk me if he didn't, because by then Poppa was gone, so he said he would. "But that's it," he said, "no prayers and no kneelin', just walk you down and that's it. You hear me, Nita? That's it."

He hated the Church, everything about it. When he had his first Communion at six years old he sold the rosary the nuns gave him to Lesly Kopit for a quarter. He fought Mother always about going. He said Daddy didn't go, so why did he have to? Of course, she wouldn't discuss it—he had to go. But Pete went out of his way to rebel. When we passed Saint Theresa's we were to cross ourselves; he refused. He made it his business to eat some kind of meat on a Friday and to make sure he told me so I could be upset. I was always scared he was surely gonna be punished for being wicked. He got dismissed from being an altar boy 'cause he and Brucie Bahm were laughing during Mass. And we were supposed to try to get to special seven a.m. Mass before school the first Friday of each month because Sister Annunciata said if you did nine in a row, then surely God would have someone hear your confession before you died, but Pete said he didn't give a rat's ass about who heard his stupid confession. Said by the time he died he would've done so many bad things it would take weeks to confess it all.

From the day we came to Kansas City Pete got worse and worse. You all thought he was funny—the whole lot of you couldn't wait to see what he was up to next. Pete Chickery was always up to something. He nearly destroyed Mother with his pranks and lying . . . what was left of her after she buried Daddy, 'cause she was never the same.

She begged Uncle Ned to help discipline him, but Ned laughed. "Hell, he'll outgrow it, Alice Maude. He's a boy—that's what boys do." Whenever Uncle Ned would cuss, Mother's lips would pull tight but she wouldn't say anything. After all, if it wasn't for Uncle Ned we would've been starving in Tupelo most likely. If it wasn't for Uncle Ned we would've stayed in Tupelo, which I know now would have been best for everyone, Uncle Ned especially. He offered her the little house off Wornall where we lived and a job down at his place as a bookkeeper. I didn't even know my mother had schooling to be such a thing, but she did it. She got on the bus every day and went to work wearing a hat and gloves like she was going to a tea, not to that filthy store. My mother always stayed a Southern lady. The Midwest never touched her. She wouldn't like it that there aren't magnolias for Pete's coffin, she wouldn't like it one bit. I thank Jesus she's not here to see it.

Uncle Ned was Daddy's first brother, the oldest. He was successful. I knew. I'd heard about him all my life. He had three big Chickery Auto Parts stores in Kansas City alone. He didn't look anything like Daddy or like Pete. Thin, pale-yellow hair like old straw, and a little belly hanging down over his belt. He lifted me up at the train station and held me like I was a baby, vile blue cigar smoke making me choke, the hair on his arms touching my bare legs, his lips kissing me—he was disgusting. Saying how I looked like my mother and then crying when he saw Pete because Pete had Daddy's face. But I hated his wife the most. Rae Lee. I'd never seen anyone like her. Dark and skinny and very beautiful. She tried to put on like she was nice, but she had slit eyes and when she kissed Mother on the cheek I could tell by the way she bent her head that she didn't want her lips to really touch my mother at all. Her arms were thin and dark and weighted down with silver charm bracelets, clattering and banging together. She put her slit eyes on us, looked us up and down, took us in, disapproving. I could feel her laughing behind her eyes and I hated her. I wanted desperately to go home. I wanted to see Gagee and all my friends, wanted everything to be the way it was. I wanted to die. I didn't speak in the car and Mother said later I was rude, but I didn't care. I knew they were being kind to us, or at least he was, saving his brother's family from poverty and such, Mother said, but I hated them for it. And I hated Daddy more because it was all his doing.

I didn't have to see too much of them; they left us pretty much alone. Mother saw Uncle Ned every day at work, and of course we went there for holidays and all, but I didn't have to pretend I liked Rae Lee much, because we weren't together all that often. She made it clear we weren't "good enough" for her and her friends.

Even then I said a lot of Hail Marys and Our Fathers over bad thoughts about Rae Lee. She told me and Pete right off not to call her Aunt. "You're too grown up for that," she said, "and I'm far too young, aren't I, Ned?" She laughed with her mouth open too wide, tossed her head, and punched at my uncle with her hand. I thought she looked like a horse. Pete thought she was gorgeous. That was his word. From the first. I said she wasn't our kind and he said, "That's how much you know, Nita." He was fifteen years old and he already knew who he was. I just didn't.

The first time I saw any of you was at Harrison. I was sure nobody was gonna speak to me. I had made myself a wreck about it after breakfast. I'd changed clothes three times before Mother had to leave to catch her bus. Uncle Ned had called Mother over and over in Tupelo, trying to convince her to let us go to public school.

"Alice Maude, you're bein' stubborn for no good reason. Good Shepherd is miles away, you'll never get those children there on time, and Harrison is just two blocks from the house. It's a fine school, Alice Maude—why, it's the best damn high school on the Missouri side."

She finally said yes, but it was very hard for her. Gagee and Poppa bought me new clothes as a goodbye present, since I'd only had uniforms my whole life. I was sure that as dear as those clothes were to me, they'd never fit in right at this school. Pete didn't care. He was never afraid people wouldn't like him. I wonder how it would have been if I had turned out like Daddy and Pete like Mother. Then maybe I'd be dead and Pete would be here. Most likely that would please everybody a lot more.

I saw you first, Frances. You were standing outside a classroom, whispering with Ellen and Mike Shapiro, when they walked me up. Your notebook propped against your hip and your hair flipped up all perfect. You looked so confident. I passed by with that lady from the principal's office and you smiled right at me. Then before lunch when I got my locker stuck Anne came to help me and asked me to eat with you all. I met Tee in the cafeteria. She was late and breathless, slamming her books on the table and taking an apple right off Anne's tray, biting into it without even asking. When I said it was nice to meet her, she screeched real loud, "My God, she sounds like she just stepped off fucking Tara!" I was appalled at her language, but you-all didn't seem to notice. You just accepted it as a part of her, so I tried not to judge. I wasn't about to walk away from anybody who was being friendly to me, and Anne took me in right from the start. Maybe because she was shy and I was shy, maybe because we were both older than you-all and a grade ahead. I never stopped to question it, I was too thrilled to have made a friend.

I didn't meet Jessie till two days later. That was the first time Pete ever spoke to me during school. Jessie came back from being sick with flu and at lunch Pete came over to borrow money from me. That's what he said, but I knew it was 'cause he wanted to look Jessie over up close. Look all of you over.

Pete was thrilled with my newfound popularity, that I had been accepted into your little clique. He told Mother at supper, "There's five of them and they're all crazy about her, Mother. You wouldn't believe it. It must be the way we sound, the drawl . . . it gets them every time. After all, what else could it be? She was never popular before . . . were you, Nita?"

"Your sister is lovely, Peter Chickery. I don't appreciate your words one tiny bit."

"Well, you don't have to get yourself in an uproar about it," he said, exasperated. "She knows I didn't mean anythin' bad about her," and he slammed away from the table.

Mother looked at me and touched my hand. It was very rare that she touched me, and I was surprised.

"I'm very glad you're gettin' on so well, Anita. Very glad."

"Thank you, Mother," I said, embarrassed.

Pete was always after me to find out where we were going and what we were doing. Would we be at Winstead's after the movie? Or were we going on to somebody's house? Who was driving? He was overtly interested in the comings and goings-on of all five of you. He was also interested in cheerleader practice, Girls Glee Club rehearsals, the tearoom at Emery Byrd's on Saturday afternoons— wherever females were, my brother knew about it.

My whole life he made sure he told me about his escapades to upset me. Made sure that he got the words out before I could leave a room, slam a door, or put my hands over my ears, all the gory details of what he did in the back seat of Ronnie Green's car with whoever, how he did it, the noises she made. He went out of his way to make me sick with his talk. I knew about the waitress at Winstead's, the one who carhopped, the tough one with the short uniform and her hair all sprayed up into that teased French twist, the one we thought was so old then. When we all were seventeen she must've been at least thirty-two. I doubled with Pete right after Uncle Ned and Rae Lee surprised him with that Ford Fairlane on his birthday; I had a date with Alan Patash and Pete was with Razie Garris, and when that waitress brought the tray over and hooked it on his car window, she said, "I like your new wheels, Pete," and ran her fingernail down my brother's cheek. She was standing real close so he could look down inside the front of her uniform. Alan got hysterical.

"Well, now we know, Chickery, what a stud you really are. . . . Now we know why Miss Tit's always giving you a double with fries and only charging you for a Coke . . . huh, Chickery?" Spitting all over themselves, they thought it was so funny, my brother with that waitress. I was sick to death about it.

When we got home Pete came barging in on me in the bathroom. He said I had better stop being such a prude and a goody-goody or soon nobody was gonna take me out.

"You don't have to put out if you don't want, Nita, but you sure could do a little flirtin'. . . . Stop actin' like you're one of the goddamn nuns at Good Shepherd."

"Don't cuss," I said. "You know I hate it. And get out of my way—I'm goin' to bed." I switched off the light.

"I'm tellin' you somethin' for your own good," he said, blocking my way out of the bathroom. "It wouldn't hurt you any, either, to do a little kissin' . . . might warm you up. You act like a goddamn statue or something!"

"I'll act any way I want," I said, "and I certainly wouldn't take lessons from you on how to behave. You act like scum. . . . You act lower than scum, with your waitresses and barmaids and who knows what."

He grabbed my arm. He was mad. "Let me tell you somethin', Nita. I don't know who the hell you think you are all of a sudden, but I better had remind you. You're the same flesh and blood as me, Nita—you're just exactly like me, not one bit better, you hear?"

I started to cry. "I'm not like you. I'm not a bit like you, not the tiniest part of me."

His eyes were cold and his fingers tight on my arm. "Yeah? Well, let me tell you somethin', darlin': there's only one part of you that's not like me, and I know it's true in my heart—you're mean, Nita . . . you're mean and cold as ice."

Mother was there. I felt her presence. She was standing in the hallway in her robe, staring at us in the bathroom. We'd woke her up with our words. Pete saw me looking at something over his shoulder. He turned and saw her too, dropped my arm, and walked past her down the hall and into his room. She looked at me for a minute and then she just quietly reached forward and pulled the bathroom door shut, leaving me there standing alone in the dark. I cried myself to sleep that night.

When he married Jessie I never trusted he'd be true to her, but I tried to put all those evil thoughts out of my head. I told myself, He's a married man now, he'll mend his ways and be responsible . . . but I didn't believe it, so I prayed for him.

They had been married just a year when James was born. I knew Pete would name him for Daddy. It thrilled Mother, of course, but something about it bothered me. Neil and I were on our honeymoon, burning up in Miami Beach, when the baby was born. We came home and went directly to the hospital to see him. Mother was there with Uncle Ned and Rae Lee. Pushed up against the glass, all of us making fools of ourselves cooing at a baby who couldn't even hear us. Then we went to Jessie's room and drank champagne Billy and Tee had brought. I can't remember there being another time when everyone was quite so happy as standing round that room. Pete sitting next to Jessie, holding her and gazing at her like he loved her so much his heart was gonna break. I glanced at Mother and saw happiness in her eyes. I felt so good. Pete was fine, I thought, he and Jessie were just fine.

Neil and I took the elevator down with Rae Lee and Uncle Ned. Rae Lee was wearing red shoes, cheap red shoes, but I knew she thought they were beautiful, so I complimented her on them, wanting to be nice, feeling the warmth of the evening and not wanting it to end. She reminded me I still had her good soup pot from Easter dinner and would I return it. Said I should be more responsible with other people's things. Talked in that cool, uppity voice she always used with me. My face got hot but I apologized, said how I was so sorry, what with my wedding and all I had forgotten. Said I'd bring it by just as soon as I unpacked and tended to everything.

I pointed out to Neil in the car how she talked to me in that tone. "You see? She just can't be nice no matter what I say or do; she always finds fault with me."

About a week later I was coming home from a ladies' luncheon at Good Shepherd and when I crossed Ward Parkway at Meyer, I suddenly remembered I'd put Rae Lee's old pot in my trunk to return.

I turned right back round and drove to her house. Pulled up the drive, took the pot out of my trunk, and walked up the little path to her back door. I was pleased with myself, glad that I'd remembered, so she wouldn't have anything more to say about me.

I looked in the kitchen window right before I rang the bell. I don't know why, I just did.

The man was up against Rae Lee from behind, ramming himself into her. She was moaning. Bent at the waist, her head hanging down, wild hair flying back and forth across the yellow floor. She cried out each time he pulled in and out, her arms flying, those bracelets clanking against each other. Clanking and clanking. I couldn't get my breath—I thought I was gonna suffocate. Her ribs stuck out in back, poking at her skin like she was a poster child, pasty and dry. He pushed at her breasts and she cried out. He stuck his fingers into her mouth. I could hear her suck his fingers. My ears started to ring. My hands were frozen on that pot, icy fingers clutching at the handles. I couldn't move my feet. She yelled, "Oh, God, baby, oh, God," and my eyes shut. Rae Lee's kitchen was the very same yellow as our kitchen back in Tupelo. I could see the curtains blowing by my mother's head. Little red flowers on yellow cotton. I opened my eyes. She was on her back on the floor, her head thrown to one side, her face wet. Her legs were stretched open wide and he had his head buried in her place. She was moving, jerking her body, arching herself up into his mouth, whimpering, begging. Vomit shot into my throat. Wearing those red shoes she had on at the hospital, high-heeled red shoes on that yellow floor. I was falling into the darkness, and the man yelled, "You come now, Rae Lee, hear me? I wanna see you come, darlin'."

My eyes flew open and he was looking right at me. My brother Pete was looking at me through the open window.

I couldn't bring myself to go home. I drove practically to Latawanna before I realized what I was doing. When I finally got home it was nearly five-thirty, but Neil wasn't there yet. The pot was sitting in the front seat with me. I ran to the basement and hid it behind all the white boxes from the wedding presents and then

I ran upstairs and into the shower. When Neil got home I was drying my hair. Said I had a surprise evening for him, said Gagee had sent us money in a letter to go to supper and a show. "She wants us to go out on her," I said, smiling at him. "Well, that's great, honey," he said. "I'll just change my pants."

I was sick inside. I had lied. I just couldn't think what else to do. I couldn't sit home all evening waiting to see if Pete would call, waiting to see if the phone would ring, what I'd say . . . so I told my trusting new husband a lie. And he was happy.

We went to the Trailhouse to eat, and to the movies, but I didn't see one bit of it. I only saw Rae Lee and Pete. All night I never closed my eyes, and it was all I could do in the morning to not scream until Neil left for work, and then I had to wait until Pete got to work before I could call. I couldn't call him at home. I was afraid Jessie would answer. I couldn't have talked if she'd answered. He said okay, he'd meet me at Joe's at ten o'clock for coffee. He sounded just like he always sounded—fine, just fine, as if nothing at all had happened.

I got there first, Frances. I sat in the last booth on the right, the one near the bathrooms. I didn't want anybody to hear us.

He was right on time. Walked in and looked around, smiled when he saw me, came to the table, kissed me on the cheek, all natural like. Sat down across from me in the booth, touched his fingers to the menu, and the waitress came right over. He ordered coffee and pie, pecan pie. He asked her if it was good. My teeth were clenched so tight they hurt, watching him smile at that little waitress, play with her, flirting. She took his menu, turned, and left, and he looked at me, waiting for me to speak. I was biting on the inside of my mouth, trying to get control, not wanting to cry.

"You're disgustin'," I said quietly.

"What?" he said.

"I saw you. I saw you and Rae Lee."

He looked at me. "What in the name of sweet Jesus are you talkin' about, Nita?" he said.

Something snapped inside me. "Don't you take the Lord's name!" I said. "You know what I'm talkin' about! I'm talkin' about you and Rae Lee on her kitchen floor. I saw you. You looked right at me!"

He leaned forward and stared at me. "I don't know what you're talkin' about, Nita." His eyes searched mine, concerned, as if I had lost my mind, as if I was the one. I sat there shock-still.

"You're crazy," I said.

The waitress put down our coffees and his pie. I put my paper napkin in my water glass and wiped my face, trying to get control of myself.

"Well, thank you, sweetheart," he said to the waitress. "This looks just fine." He picked up the fork and she kind've waited there for him to taste it, as if she had baked it for him herself.

"Perfect." He smiled up at her, chewing. She smiled back, pleased he was happy. Then she walked away. She never glanced my way.

He took another bite and pushed the plate toward me. "Want a taste?" he said.

I started to shake.

"You're sick," I said. "Crazy sick . . . like you don't know what you're doin'. I don't understand how you turned out like this—it's like you're tryin' to be Daddy."

His eyes got angry. "Don't you open your mouth about Daddy."

"Please, Pete, think of Jessie and the baby . . . you've got a brand-new baby. Don't they matter to you?"

"I love Jessie and the baby," he said, real quiet. He put his fork down. Something about the set of his shoulders scared me. I didn't know what it was, but I could feel something happening that I couldn't stop. Something awful. Tears were blurring everything.

I wanted to touch his hand, but I didn't. "I don't understand," I said, "I just don't. How could you do it? How could you?"

He looked at me. Angry eyes, mean, looking inside me. "Do what?" he said real low.

I felt the blood drain out of me. I knew what he wanted. He wanted me to say the words out loud, say what I'd seen him doing to Rae Lee. He wanted to watch me say it, look at me . . . I could tell from his eyes. Pushing at me to be bad like him. Pushing like he always had since we were little. Wanting me to be bad just like him.

"You're trash," I whispered, "nothing but trash. You're not like Daddy at all . . . I was wrong. You're worse than Daddy, you hear me? Worse."

I couldn't see him. I was crying too hard.

"Am I?" he said, looking at me.

I picked up my car keys. They were making a racket, my hand was shaking so.

"I hate you," I said. "You've made me hate you just like I hate Daddy."

I stood up. His eyes stayed right on mine. My knees were trembling. "I'll be polite to you, you hear? Polite for Jessie and for Mother and for the baby, but that's it. That's all I'll be. Because I don't want you in my life. As far as I'm concerned, you're dead to me, Pete, you understand? As far as I'm concerned, you're as dead as Daddy."

His eyes flashed. "Boy, you sure don't bend, do you?" he whispered.

"No," I said. "I'm not Mother. I don't make allowances for little boys." I took hold of the table with my fingers; I thought I was gonna fall.

"You think you're perfect, huh, Nita?"

"I never said I was perfect. Never."

A little smile crossed the corners of his mouth. He put his hand over my fingers that were clutching at the table, patted my fingers with his hand, and then pushed down on them tight.

"No, that's right—you're not quite perfect anymore, now are you, darlin'? You've kinda slipped a little, haven't you?"

I didn't know what he meant. I tried to pull my hand out from under his, but he wouldn't let me. Like when we were kids playing that game where you slide your hand out from under the other person's, only Pete would grab mine, hold on to it until he'd hurt me, until he'd make me yell.

"What do you mean?" I whispered. His fingers were white on mine, he was pushing down so hard.

My lip caught on my tooth; I was trying not to cry out. Sweat stood up on my face. "What do you mean, Pete?" I said.

He was breathing hard, but his eyes never left mine. He looked right at me when he said it: "I mean the watchin', Nita. You certainly haven't forgotten how you watched, now have you?"

He smiled and picked his hand up fast, trying to catch me off balance, hoping to make me fall. He stood up quick and was gone—leaving me standing there with his words all round me.

I never told anybody. I never told a soul, not even Leonard when we married, even though he noticed right from the start how cold I was with Pete. Right off he could tell, asked me what went on between me and my brother. I never told him. I never told one soul until today, and as bad as I feel about there not being any magnolias, I won't cry for Pete. Not now. Not ever.

Frances

So I'M HOME. Kansas City, my mother's house . . . home. And you're not here. I never thought that could happen. Searching for something, that creepy feeling that I forgot something. Looking . . . looking . . . throwing clothes around the room. What was it? What the hell was I . . . ? Panic coming up my chest, into my throat. What am I missing? Can't think . . .

And then I remember.

It's Pete, I say to myself.

It's Pete.

George gets in tonight. Over the Pole. He's not bringing the new wife. And I'm not picking him up. "I'll take a cab, Frances. I don't want you to drive. Okay? Don't drive. Did you hear me?"

"Okay, George. Okay. I hear you."

God knows I hear you. Still directing my every move. I'm not married to you anymore, you bastard.

He actually speaks with an English accent. You'd fall down. Trevor Howard lives in the body of George Massimino. I didn't want to pick him up anyway; I only made the damn gesture because it seemed right somehow. I don't know . . . us together, coming back together.

Frances and George, Best Couple, now divorced, reunite to bury their best friend. Wait . . . their best friend brutally shot and killed in Ellen's upstairs powder-blue bedroom . . . powder burns

in the powder blue . . . God, Pete. I can't do this. Look at me. I'm
making jokes. . . .

George was crying. I didn't expect to get him like that. So fast.
I just dialed and he answered. In an English cottage a million miles
away with his dumpy English wife asleep beside him. All cozy, cozy.
The damn thing's probably rose-covered.

George fuzzy with sleep, half asleep, all asleep.

"Hello? Hello?"

I didn't say anything.

Standing there, staring out the window at the night, at the guy
in the apartment across the way. Staring, hearing the traffic down
below. Standing and shivering. Listen to New York, I said to myself.
New York doesn't care. Shivering, suddenly icy cold, naked except
for my underpants, holding the phone.

George waking up then. Fear in his new English voice, the
accent suddenly disintegrating, disappearing . . . his Kansas slipping
out.

"Hello? Hello? Frances, is that you?"

Now, considering I haven't said one word to the bastard for
four and a half years, isn't it just perfect that he knew it was me?
Could he tell from my breathing? I have such gorgeously identifiable
breathing, don't I? I couldn't say anything. I was crying too hard.

Each of us crying. One by one, little kids playing telephone:
pass the story, see if it changes. One by one. Guess what, George?

Tom was crying when he called me. Not at first. Not when I
first answered.

"What's the matter?" I asked right off.

Knowing it's never Tom who calls; not once in all these years I've
lived in New York has it ever been Tom. It's Ellen who calls, not
Tom. Knowing that, starting to get nervous, feeling something . . .
He called me Frannie. God. Like when we were little. "Sit down,
Frannie." He said that. He actually said that—sit down. You can't
say that, Tom. People don't really say that, do they? You're making
me nervous. Don't call me Frannie, you're scaring me. I laughed
at him. God forgive me, I laughed at sweet Tom.

We don't know how to do this, you see. Don't know what to say
to each other. We're not prepared. Don't know the protocol. He
should have looked it up. Checked it out in his Emily Post, in his
Emily Dickinson . . . surely she would have known. Delivering the

News of a Death, Do's and Don'ts, Chapter Seven, page one hundred forty.

Standing there wet from the shower, my underpants in my hand, the towel falling away to the rug as I let go of it to put them on. Watching my feet step in.

"It's Pete, Frannie," Tom said.

I don't have time for this. I'm supposed to meet Jeremy in exactly twenty-two minutes and I'm never gonna get a cab, and why am I putting these on? I was gonna wear black panty hose with that dress. Looking at my toes stepping through the circles, the phone wedged tight between my shoulder and my ear, water dripping onto the phone from my wet hair.

"What?" I said, brushing water off my nose, looking backward at the clock again, counting backward. . . . What time is it there? Where is everybody? Picturing Tom in Ellen's kitchen at the wall phone by the fridge, seeing everybody . . . seeing you. Your face, that imbecilic grin on your face, laughing to myself, what the hell did you do now, Pete?

That's when Tom started to cry. That was it for me. Oh, God, don't tell me. Please don't tell me. I don't want to know. Call someone else. Tom saying the words as I sat down on the rug—*fell* to the rug—one leg in the panties and one out, tripping and falling against the edge of the bed, the phone slipping off the end table and crashing on top of me as the black lace ripped. My legs spread-eagle, insides out, banging my knee. How unladylike, how unsexy. How you would have laughed.

What semifamous New York actress makes a fool of herself alone in her own bedroom?

Tom sobbing by then. Deep grinding sounds wrenching my insides, like a big truck, his gears slipping. And of course you couldn't make it simple, could you? Couldn't just get hit by a semi on I-435, could you? Had to make it big, heavy-handed, god-awful, didn't you?

Major high drama. Tom's gun, Ellen's house, Jessie's hand . . . everybody gets into the act. Everybody gets to feel horrible. Jesus, Pete. You never ever could be boring, could you, my dearest?

I just realized Milly is listening to the farm reports. Humming to herself, cooking Daddy's supper with the farm reports on in the background. Your favorite thing about my mother.

"You oughta get yourself some crops, Milly"—you in her kitchen, drinking coffee, making her laugh, turning her pink, embarrassed, happy.

She's boiling up green beans from a can. Green beans that were cooked to death by Del Monte before they ever got into the can. Four o'clock and she's already boiling for six-thirty.

I gave Daddy fresh green beans once in New York. "That's what they're supposed to taste like, Pop. What do you think?"

"Well, they're not for me, honey. I like 'em fine just the way your mother fixes 'em. That's good enough for me."

Dead green beans he likes. Well, give the man what he likes, I always say. God forbid we should try to advance our tastes here. God forbid we shouldn't stay just as we are. Only Frances descends into the outside world. Only Frances is willing to change.

Look, it's clear to me, I can't do this. I really can't. I don't know how to behave if you're not gonna be here. Who's gonna understand my jokes? Who's gonna smoke with me behind the garage? Who's gonna commiserate with me about Milly's cooking? Who's gonna love me? Huh, Pete?

You should see this room. The guest room. She's painted it the exact same pink as my bedroom in the old house. The new house is very small, but every stick of their furniture is crammed inside. The giant claw-footed dining-room set? Squeezed into a teeny-tiny room. When Pop pushes his chair back from the table he slams into the wall. Every time. You should see Milly. Not a word, but oh, boy. The only evidence of her irritation: hand jerks up to clutch the pearls, and the lips tighten—just a touch. She's desperate to run for the Comet can, but not in front of anybody. In the dark of night she'll be at the wall—scrubbing, scrubbing in her night-gown. My mother does Lady Macbeth in Kansas with her stockings rolled down around her ankles. I forgot how tiny the two of them are. Milly and Isadore, two tiny people in their cute tiny house. Jeremy and I would kill each other in here. Oh, that's great. Did you hear me? Kill each other. Cute, Frances.

It doesn't matter. He's not coming anyway. He offered to come—but why would I want him here? After all, what are you to him? A man he met once in a hospital room, right? Someone he doesn't know at all.

"Yeah . . . my wife's old friend, her childhood buddy . . . yeah . . . some guy."

Some guy all right.

My room is exactly the same. She may be calling it the guest room, but she's not fooling me. It's definitely my room. Nineteen sixty lives in my mother's house. A permanent time warp. Seventeen forever.

There's a picture of you in that drawer over there. I found it this morning, looking for a robe. The insides of the drawers nearly gave me a small stroke. It's like time stopped. She never cleaned them out. Never put everything into a Hefty bag and marked it and put it in the basement. She moved from house to house with my drawers intact. Copies of *The Wheel* with our names underlined in red wherever mentioned. "It's All in the Game," Tommy Edwards: Frances to George. "The Twelfth of Never," Markny Mathis: Tom to Ellen. Be still my heart. Black-and-white wallets from DeCloud's Studio . . . ponytail over the shoulder, lips wet with spit, slightly open, each of us . . . identical. There's letters tied with ribbons. And the picture of you. The one from Lackland. In uniform—hat and all. Young, spiffy, a regular fly-boy. On the bottom, in your up-and-down script, "For Frances from Pete, with love." Very noncommittal. I dropped it into the pocket of Milly's housecoat and touched it while I talked to Daddy about the funeral. Excuse me—*your* funeral. Your smiling face against my thigh.

He was on the porch. It was only ninety degrees out there already. Me with sleep in the eyes and a big cup of coffee, and Daddy with a sandwich already, up for hours already, as I tried to face it all at ten. The sun beating through the aluminum canopy covering the porch, beating down and cooking everything. I told Tee I'd be at her house before noon.

"What are you doing out here, Pop? It's awful hot out here, don't you think?" His face looks too pink to me. I watch him, listen to his breathing as he talks. The man could have another heart attack from this heat. His stutter comes back when we talk about you. Anything serious and it reappears. I always forget about the stutter.

"I always l-l-liked P-P-Pete, F-Frannie. You kn-kn-know that. A g-g-good b-boy, P-Pete Chickery."

Tears in his eyes, embarrassed by the stutter, by the conversation. A man of few words, my father, his heart breaking. To bury your children, that's the worst, he always said to me. For a parent to bury a child . . . oh, God, spare me this, won't you? Please don't make me watch my father cry. Please.

"Let's go into the house, Daddy. I'll buy you a cold drink."

Milly hides her eyes from me. Doesn't look right at me. "Have you called all the girls, dear? Are they coming over?"

She's sure if we're just all together, it'll be okay again. It'll go away, this horror story.

We'll never be grown up to Milly. She looks at us still the same as when we were seventeen with our lives out there in front of us. Loving us totally, believing in us totally. Not a drop of envy in her heart, my mother. You gotta give her that.

They were waiting for me. The girls. From the second my plane landed, they were waiting. To tell me their secrets. To tell me about you. None of them ever thinking I already knew.

Of course, how could they know that you already told me? How could they know that you always told me everything? They never saw us. Looked at us but never saw us. Not this group. They haven't got a clue. Kind of amazing, isn't it?

I was thinking . . . you know, in all these years of me flying in and out of here, all these years, they've always been waiting for me. Telling me their stories. It's not just now—not just because of you and what's happened. It's always been like this. Telling me their stories, filling me in, waiting to hear what I'd have to say. Banking on my advice. He did this and I did that and she said this and I said that and what do you think, Frances? What should I do, Frances? Help me, Frances.

Why me? I'm the youngest, for god sakes. I'm the one who didn't finish college, remember? The one who didn't take finals her freshman year. Came home with a suntan dark enough to make everyone think I'd gone to Miami, not Missouri. How did everybody forget? I'm the baby. How did I become everybody's official listener? How am I supposed to give and give and give to them while I'm dying inside because you're gone? How come nobody's said to me, "How are you, Frances, how are you going to live your life without Pete Chickery?"

It's because I left, you know. Went to New York. Became an actress, for god sakes. It turned their heads. I come home now a veritable sage. Transformed by my vast experience in the Big City, I return with sound judgment, stunning vision, infinite wisdom. Frances of the East. Worthy of being venerated by my childhood buddies. All because my name is in the papers. My picture once in *Vogue*. God.

I can't stand this. I don't know how to do this. It hurts too much. I thought we'd end up together. You never knew that, did you? Ha! I kept something from you. The only secret I never shared. Couldn't. Thought maybe you'd laugh at me. The picture in my mind was simple, very Norman Rockwell. Me in your lap, you holding me close in to you. Older, wrinkled, gray—I don't know . . . fat maybe. All your kids grown and gone away, all the kids I never had grown and gone away. Just us. I don't know where Jessie and Jeremy are supposed to be in this picture. Dead? Disappeared? I don't know. I never got that far. I never got this far.

I was thinking about the baby. Well, now, come on, Frances . . . it wasn't really a baby, was it? It was a blob. Our little blob, destroyed before it could blossom. So long ago. Hell, the blob would be over thirty years old now. A regular grown-up. Probably with your eyes . . . my nose. Well, we would have had it fixed. You could have taught it how to drawl. You know, I've never thought about it. Never. Not in thirty years. Of course, I never thought of me with a baby in the first place. Not even when we were little. Playing house. Ellen always being the mommy, knowing how to be the mommy. Me always being the daddy. Being the maid. Being the nurse. Never knowing it was okay not to be a mommy. Okay just to be a woman. I was before my time, huh, kid? Maybe it wouldn't hurt so much if the blob were here now. He could pat me on the shoulder, take my arm. She could cry with me. We could tell each other sweet stories about you. Something.

Sometimes when it snows in New York and I'm out in it—you know, a real big thick snow with fat flakes smashing themselves on my cheeks, melting in my eyes—sometimes, just sometimes, I find myself remembering. . . .

You and me in the car, the seat tilted back, cheap bourbon on my lips, laughing—you and me always laughing—and then not laughing anymore. The shock of it all, the hush, the cold. The ridiculous cold. It was supposed to be spring already. A snowstorm

in March. How untimely. Untimely all right; you can say that again.
You had on your topcoat. Me losing my virginity to a boy wearing
a topcoat. What if the papers ever got hold of it? And that ain't
all, fellas—a topcoat, a suit, a tie, shoes, socks . . .

God.

March 2, 1960. The spring before we graduated. The spring
before the summer: the summer you fell for Jess, the summer I
promised it would always be George, the summer of all our summers.

Windows steamed white as the snow, your eyes big, my pulse
pounding in my throat when I swallowed, your lips on my lips,
whiskey breath, icy fingers on my breast inside my sweaters, my
dyed-to-match pink cashmere sweaters.

"Hey! Hey, Chickery, what are you doing?"

"I don't know, Frances. What am I doin'?"

God. My God. Look at that, boys, there's a penis inside me. A
penis in a Chevy in a snowstorm on Seventy-third and Cherry, two
blocks from my mother's house.

Now wait a minute here! That's not George Massimino's penis!
Well, no, sir, he's away at college, sir, he's not here. Well, then,
whose penis is that anyway? It's Pete Chickery's, sir. Pete Chickery's?
What? Don't be silly . . . Frances and Pete are just good friends.
Well, you can say that again, sir. Look what they're doing with that
penis.

I'll tell you the truth. If I had had a daughter, the one thing I
know for sure I'd have taught her, the one single piece of advice
I'd have given, would have been this: the first time you do it,
darling girl—the very first time you feel what it's like—do it with
a friend, someone you can laugh with. That's all I know for sure.

Hours I spent afterward looking at myself in the mirror, sure
that Milly would know when she saw me at breakfast. I kept looking
deep into my eyes, searching . . . laughing out loud in the bathroom,
my hands clenched over my mouth. Inspecting my body, giggling.
Don't wake anybody up, you dope. My heart beating so loud, sure
they could hear it crashing in my chest. I was so excited. God. What
if they know? Oh, God, they're gonna know. They'll see it. They
probably have parent radar. *Frances did it.* Blue neon going on and
off across my vagina. *Frances did it and she's glad.*

Hell, they didn't know. Milly shuffling back and forth to the
table. Scuff, scuff go the slippers.

"Did you have a good time, dear?"

"Uh-huh," says I, my face down into the coffee. Avoid the eyes, avoid the eyes.

They were eating lunch already. Corned beef on rye every Sunday at noon. No matter what. A ritual in our house. Like kishke with the turkey on Thanksgiving. You mean the Pilgrims didn't eat kishke? Well, I'll be. . . .

My brother was making a terrible noise, clanking his knife around against the inside of the mustard jar, hoping it would hurt my head. They always did that. Knew I couldn't take loud noises when I first got up, knew I hated it. Even Daddy. He'd pass a plate and bang it down on the table, his eyes shifting slightly to see if I winced . . . jiggle his ice cubes practically out of the glass, a little twinkle on his face. The two of them chuckling to themselves when they'd get me.

Milly tilting her head at them. "Now, Isadore, don't do that . . . please."

Did you have a good time, dear? Boy, did I.

But you know, Mom, it was just a little uncomfortable, what with it being so cold and all and us having to keep all our clothes on so we wouldn't freeze. So tonight we're gonna go to the Holiday Inn down by the Trafficway and Pete's gonna really show me. You know, all the details, the positions, everything. Don't you think that's a good idea, Mom? Huh, Daddy, don't you think? Well, my brother would have liked hearing that. Hell, he would have loved it.

Good old Holiday Inn. Doing it over and over. Like rehearsing for Broadway. Do it until we get it right. God. I was raw. And happy. So happy.

Who would have thought all that happy would end up in some scuzzy doctor's office in Raytown. You pale and me brazen and Ronnie Green sitting in his car with the motor running—the getaway car—waiting while they butchered away the blob.

And who would have thought that my womb would decide to wash its hands of the whole business? That's it for me, no more of this conceiving stuff for me—not if that's what happens. No, thank you, said my ovaries.

George never got over that. That I couldn't conceive. The idea of no little Massiminos toddling behind him with identical quirks was just too much for old George. It's good we never told him about the blob.

The new wife gets pregnant if he so much as breathes on her. She must truly be a remarkable woman—pudgy but remarkable.

Well, I should have known. I'm the one who's Jewish, after all. I certainly know you're not allowed to have too much fun without paying the price. It's in the rulebook. Hey, not too much fun over there, you kids; think of the stab in the gut that comes after. I should have protected us, should have circled our hands and feet with bright-red kine-ahora ribbons. Shaken a broom in room 311 of the Holiday Inn, shushed away the evil eye with chants and put a mezuzah on the lobby door. You can't be too careful. I should have known.

The saving grace was that we never fell in love. That's what saved us all these years. I do know that.

You were always in love with Jessie.

I was always in love with George.

Since the beginning. Probably even now. But that never mattered with us, did it?

You know, in all these years—the ones when we did it and the ones when we didn't . . . the long stretches of years when we didn't touch each other, didn't even think about it—I'd come home and see you and we'd talk and talk, catch up, listen to each other's heartaches, look into each other's eyes . . .

And the ones when we'd start up again, suddenly unable to stop touching, teasing . . . in all the years, it never mattered to me, either way. It just didn't matter.

It was always you and me that came first. Always the friendship that I needed first. Never the sex.

But they wouldn't believe that, would they? The girls. Bet they wouldn't believe that I never felt disloyal to Jessie or George. Never felt I'd betrayed them, been dishonest, been bad. I didn't, though. Not for a second. Not ever. It just didn't count. It was you and me from another time. It was part of us, part of our friendship. An extension. Well, now, that's a nice way to put it. Cute, Frances. Anyway, to me it didn't count as being bad. Never.

When I came home that Christmas of 1978 after *For All We Know* was such a smash . . . my picture in the paper, photographers actually waiting at the airport, actually interviewing Daddy while he shoveled snow off the front walk, the girls all excited . . . Frances returns a star. Well, a semistar. Finally.

At Jasper's, in the parking lot. You kissed me. We'd said goodbye already at least four times. Had too much lunch and said goodbye and I was about to turn and get into the car. Head back to Milly's, back to New York, back to my regular life, where I might have been recognized as a semistar but, let's face it, people were damn sure I wasn't seventeen anymore . . . especially George.

And you kissed me. And there we were all over again. We hadn't touched each other in all those years we were both married. Hadn't even thought about it—well, I hadn't. Laughing, holding on to each other and laughing . . .

"Well, Frances, darlin', what have we got here?" you said to me. Goodbye thirty-five, hello seventeen.

My knees were shaking from your kiss, actually shaking, like the first time. Like the snowstorm. God. And I changed my flight to the next morning and never told my folks. Actually let them drive me to the airport. Stood there as they drove away, waved, blew kisses, and then ducked into a cab to go back to town. Wearing dark glasses even, so I wouldn't be recognized. Keeping my head lowered as the cab drove through the plaza, slithering into the lobby of the Raphael. Talk about drama. Maybe I'm not totally Jewish—there must be some Episcopalian in here somewhere. And then I wasn't home for six months.

Home. And it was summer—like now. Only I was different. I was dee-vorced. Not officially; just waiting to sign the papers. Not a Massimino anymore, scraping the *M*'s off the towels, the stationery, the heart. Well, not quite . . . but trying.

It was hot here that summer. Like now. Sticky, humid brown heat frying everything, making everything be still, making everything lie down. The corn, the grass, us. Too hot to move. Sitting on the hood of Daddy's Buick in that field way out south. Watching a thunderstorm make its way across the sky. Drinking a six-pack of malt liquor to celebrate my emergence from George-dom.

"You guys just shouldn't've gotten married, Frances. You were never right for each other. I told you a million times. He wasn't your type."

"You know, if you say that again I'm gonna pour this beer right down your pants, Tupelo."

You grinning at me.

"He was always too busy combin' his hair, makin' sure it stayed up there in that wave like that . . ."

Me taking a big swig, letting the cold beer run down my chin onto my chest. God. It was so hot. Smiling at you.

"I thought you guys were such good friends," I said.

"He is my friend," you said, "but he's too uptight. You need somebody looser, somebody who'll let you be."

"Oh, really. Think you're so smart, do you? Think you know what women need?"

"I know some stuff," you said.

You reached over, pulled my T-shirt softly out just a little ways from my body, your head bending, your tongue barely skimming the tops of my breasts. My breath catching. Licking my sweat.

"Yeah?" I said, trying to speak. "What do you know?"

"About what, Frances?" Your mouth encircling my nipple, the blood rushing around my body like the Indianapolis 500, my ass slipping back down across the hot Buick. I pulled your head back, my hand pulling your blond hair, your mouth still open.

"About us, tell me about us."

Your face above mine. "Who? You and me?"

"No, us, the girls."

A smile lit up your face like the lightning flashing around the sky.

"Oh, the girls . . ." you gushed in that sweet drawl. "Well, let's see . . . you want to know what I know about you girls . . ."

You hooked your thumbs inside the waistband of my shorts and my panties and scooched them down about a half-inch. I yanked your hair back hard.

"Tell me what you know, Mr. Smartie."

"All right, all right . . . let's see . . . what do I know . . . you like pickles and mustard on your cheeseburgers and hate ketchup."

I yanked at your hair.

"C'mon, you Southern bullshit artist. Tell me what you know."

"Shit, Frances. All right."

My back was burning against the metal of the car, the beer can freezing my hand.

You bit your bottom lip between your teeth.

"Tell me."

"My sister is sad and stunted and doesn't bend. If she'd give herself a break, then everybody else would. Maybe even me."

"Jesus," I said.

"Exactly, Frances. Jesus messed her up but good."

Your eyes were sad. I held on to your hair but raised my head up and kissed you lightly on the lips.

"Ellen. Tell me about Ellen."

"You all think she's borin' and conventional but I think she's fine. She's direct, you see. You always know where you stand with Ellie." You grinned. "And, she's the best wife of you all."

"You smug son of a bitch. How do you know that?"

"Because she would be, she'd make sure of it. That's the way she is."

"Better than Jessie?"

"Probably, but not for me."

"Well, well . . ."

You bent your mouth to mine and moved your thumbs gently against the skin across my stomach inside my underpants. I tried to get out from under your hands but I couldn't. I yanked your hair back hard.

"Goddamn, Frances. I'm busy here."

"Anne. Tell me about Anne."

"She's generous. And givin'. She's childlike. And she's a dreamer just like me."

"You're a dreamer, Chickery?"

"Sure, Frances, I just got the dream I wanted the most, so I don't dream much anymore."

"You mean Jessie."

"That's right."

"What about Jessie?"

"She's everythin'."

"How?"

"Because of how she makes me feel."

"How does she make you feel?"

You grinned. "Like *I'm* everythin'."

I laughed.

"Okay. Tee. Tell me about Tee."

"Tallulah? She's just adrift, that's all, she needs somethin' to hold on to."

"Oh. You mean you?"

"Hell, no, Frances. Somethin' about herself. So she can remember who she is, that's she's worthwhile and good and not a failure. She'll come round, Tallulah."

"Okay, smartie. Do me."

"I'm tryin' to do you, Frances, but you won't hold still."

Grinning at me.

"Tell me about me, goddamn it!"

"Your language is gettin' atrocious since you became a semi-star, that's what I'll tell you. You sound like a sailor."

"Tell me!"

"You're funny . . ."

"Everybody knows that, that's nothing new."

"You're dramatic . . ."

"Oh, great. Of course I'm dramatic, you jerk, I'm an actress."

"You're delicious . . ." you said, bending your head to mine, since I had loosened my grip on your hair.

"Oh, no, you don't," I said, pushing your chest back up away from mine. "That's easy. Tell me something hard."

You stopped and looked at me.

"Somethin' hard, huh?"

"Yeah."

"You think you can take it?"

"Try me."

"Okay."

Your eyes were very blue when you said it.

"You don't think you're pretty, Frances."

You caught me by surprise. I tried to turn my head away so you couldn't see my eyes, but you held my face with your hands. Your face was very close to mine.

"You don't think you're pretty but you are. You're more than pretty. You're beautiful. That's somethin' I know."

"Oh, really," I said, clearing my throat.

"Yes, ma'am," you said, "you're beautiful, Frances Freeman, you always were."

"Think you're so smart, huh?"

"Yep."

"Think you know about us girls, huh?"

"A little, just a little."

"Well," I said, lowering my eyes, "thank you, Pete."

"You're welcome, Frannie," you said, and as you bent forward to kiss me, I smiled, and poured the whole can of Country Club malt liquor down your back.

"I'll tell you what you know about us, Chickery," I yelled, sliding off the hood of the car and running. "You don't know dick!"

"When I catch you, you're gonna be dead meat, Frances," you yelled behind me.

Chasing each other around that field, splashing each other with malt liquor, stomping on corn, straw husks scratching my legs, losing a sandal. Laughing.

Thunder echoed far across the plains and the wind started to whip up, bending the brown field down, bending us, blowing our sweat dry. The smell of heavy rain intoxicating me before the drops even splashed. A regular Kansas spectacle. Making me cry from its sheer sweetness. Totally out of control. Totally thrilling. We didn't take cover until we were drenched. Exhausted, laughing. Always laughing.

Now look here, Frances, why weren't you ever pissed off about Pete doing it with everybody? Why is that? Aren't you a regular woman? Don't you have feelings? Aren't you jealous?

Nope. Never jealous. Never. Maybe it's the man side of me, the masculine side. Don't laugh. Maybe it's so. All I know is, anything you did with anybody else had nothing to do with us. Ever. Simple as pie for me. I know it's not the same for any of them. Hell, it's probably not the same for anybody at all. Milly always said I was different.

I listened to all their stories, watched their eyes, heard their hearts crack.

You know I love them. It hurts me sometimes now when I come home to see them: new lines in their faces, pain in their eyes, bodies slipping a little, here, there . . . older, frightened. Well, thank God you won't see that happening to me. Thank God I'm still seventeen. It's coming home that keeps me going, you know. When I come home, I remember who I am. The last one on the end, right after Jessie. Hey, I'm Frances . . . the baby.

And it doesn't matter here if I got the part, if I was good in the part, if the reviews singled me out, if the reviews shit on my face. It just doesn't matter. Because here I am totally loved. I'm home.

You know, when I went to Dr. Norman after George and I

finally split and I was so messed up—all that time I went to him he used to get a real kick out of pointing that out to me: "Do you realize, Frances, that you left Kansas City in 1966 and you still call it home? Don't you think you ought to take a look at that, Frances?"

Well, sure, Doctor. Now let's see . . . why would I want to call that silly old place home? Could it be because that's where my pieces come together? Where I feel safe? Where I'm loved? So loved. Could it be that, Doctor? All that abundance of love that makes me call it home? You know, with all Norman's smarts, sometimes he had the sensitivity of a brick.

There's only one story I'm missing now. Jessie's. Except for yours, of course, but the odds on me hearing that one person-to-person appear quite slim, wouldn't you say?

Wait a minute! Maybe you could send me signs. You know, little signals so I'd know you were listening to me, getting all this. Big signals even. Especially if I'm gonna spend the rest of my days talking to you like this. Is that what I'm gonna do? Maybe it will pass . . . but I don't think so. Hopefully my lips won't start moving when I do. God. What if I begin to acquire large and obvious hand gestures, facial tics, talk out loud? Think of the repercussions. Think of my career. And just when Hollywood has finally beckoned. Talk about bad timing. People looking at me funny on the street, pointing, "Look, Mommy, isn't that Frances Freeman?" "No, don't be silly, dear, that's a bag lady." "But she's wearing a mink coat, Mommy." "Don't stare, Marsha, it's impolite."

Hey, Pete. I know how I'll know if you can hear me. All kidding aside. Make me a thunderstorm at the funeral.

Oh, Pete, do it. I know you can do it. Ask the archangel or somebody. A great big fat thunderstorm. Think about it. It would be perfect. All of us standing at the graveside, looking at each other, shuffling our feet, high heels sinking into the sod, trying to guess how to behave . . . and you can save us. Thunder crashing, lightning streaking, and you make it pour. Soak us. Drench us to our souls. So we can run to the cars, so we won't have to watch as they lower you down . . .

Oh, God.

Do it for me, Pete. I never asked you for much, did I? Well, let's see . . . did I?

No, I didn't. Just that one time. To take me to that formal at the Carriage Club because George didn't have the balls. All that crap about Jews not really being wanted there and his father "a little agitated" about it and his mother "a little nervous" about it and why did I feel it was necessary to make such a fuss, to possibly cause embarrassment, why did I always have to make a stand about everything, and gee, we could go to a movie or something instead, couldn't we?

"I mean, really, Frances, you know I love you. Why do you have to do this, huh? C'mon, Frances, for me, huh?" Running his hand through his hair, making sure his wave was just so, his clothes just so, his Corvette just so, his girl just so.

The bastard. How could I have loved such a bastard? And for so long. Talk about taste . . .

You were right. He wasn't my type. Hell, he wasn't even close, was he? I got blinded, that's all. The big brown eyes, the long lashes, that lanky tall stupid body, the letter sweater, the halting speech . . . I thought he was romantic. I always looked the other way when he went into his "Now let's not get involved, Frances" speech. George never wanting to make waves, me always nearly drowning. Well . . . so shoot me, I'm a slow learner. A late bloomer.

Do you know the only person besides you who ever told me not to marry him? It was Jessie. Did you know that?

"He's not strong enough for you, Frannie."

"What do you mean, not strong? I don't need strong. *I'm* strong. I need sweet. I need romantic. I need shy, quiet, refined . . . I need *Gentile*. It's him."

Jessie, holding the baby on her shoulder with one hand, moving the pot roast around the pot with the other.

"It will never last, Frannie."

"What are you, for god sakes, the voice of doom?"

Jessie kissing me gently on the cheek, her black curls brushing up against my face as she laughed softly and handed me a bundle of damp baby, your firstborn, your James.

"Burp him, will you? I've got to put this in the oven."

"That's it? The voice of doom predicts and that's it?" I asked.

Your son was drooling on my blouse, pushing his little knees up against my breast. Just like his father, I thought. A tit man already. Amazing.

Jessie turned back to me from the open oven door, flushed,

beautiful. "I just think you need someone smarter, Frannie. It's just what I think, that's all . . . it's not a big deal."

"Oh, it's not a big deal. Well, if that's the case, then I'm gonna marry him. Okay?" I asked, kissing James on his little forehead.

"Okay," she said quietly.

"So you'll be my matron of honor?" I asked.

"So I'll be your matron of honor," she answered, walking past me and James with a handful of silverware and a stack of paper napkins, making a face at me, crossing her eyes, sticking out her tongue . . . funny Jessie.

You know, none of them has so much as said her name except in passing. Except in stories about you. Like they're afraid to say her name: maybe if they don't say it, this whole thing will go away.

I went over there, to the Prairie Village jail. Iz drove me. He said it wasn't good for me to go alone, that he'd wait in the car and that I didn't have to talk to him about it after if I didn't want to, but he didn't want me driving home alone. Not a good idea, honey, he said to me, my pop. Sweet darling Pop, always taking care.

I didn't even know where the Prairie Village jail was, Pete. I didn't even know it existed. Not in all these years.

But she wouldn't see me. They wouldn't let me in.

She's alone now, Pete. Jessie's totally alone.

And they won't tell us anything, either, won't divulge any information. Won't even tell us if she'll be at the funeral. All we know is that the boys are doing it, making the arrangements, that Jessie sent them word. She won't even talk to Anne. Oh, God, Pete, I'm talking to you about your funeral. . . . How can I do this?

Anyway, none of us are running the show . . . none of our generation. It's hard to believe I can say that, isn't it? Our generation. When did we become the grown-ups? Why don't I feel grown up, Pete? Is it because I'm home?

All these months I've been waiting to come home. You know that—to tell them. Share the secret at last, bare my chest to the girls. I was gonna come last winter. February—that's when I had picked. When everyone was dying for a little breath of sunshine, something to perk up the gray. I was gonna come and change the mood. And then the offer came—play the part in the film that I did on the stage. They almost never do that, you know. They always hire somebody else, never the one who did it in the play. Especially after so much time has passed.

Well, it's gonna be me up there, seventy-eight feet by forty-two feet or however big that screen is. Me. And you won't get to see it. I just realized that. You never even got to see me do it on the stage, did you?

Too far away, too little time . . .

We never know, do we? Jeremy says that. Live each day as if it may be your last. But who does that, really? Nobody does that. Schmucks maybe, they live like that.

Well, excuse me . . . maybe you lived like that. As I look back, it's certainly obvious you didn't spend too much time worrying about how your actions would affect others, now did you? You gotta admit it looks like you pretty much lived your life for *you*, Pete. Did what you wanted every minute. You did, didn't you? I wish I could.

Maybe I should, huh? Especially now. Especially in the light of my drama.

You know, I was really looking forward to telling them. Showing them. After all, this is the best secret I ever kept. The longest secret I ever kept and certainly the best. None of them know. Nobody but you. And I still don't know how you figured it out. I'm a great actress, haven't you heard? Don't you read the papers? How could you say my voice gave me away? I thought I was brilliant on the phone. Thought my performance was award-winning material when I called you back, when Jeremy said you called the day before. You fucker. You could always read me inside out, couldn't you?

Blinking awake from one of those drugged naps with that god-awful taste in my mouth, pain shooting around my body like rockets, my mind beginning to unfuzz, remembering . . . oh, no, don't let this be real, please . . . shutting my eyes to make it go away . . . wanting to reach up and touch myself, not wanting to. . . . Hey . . . who's holding my hand? Who is that? Jeremy?

Opening my eyes . . . and there you were, grinning at me from behind the IV.

"Hello, darlin' girl. How you doin'?"

God, Pete.

You and Jeremy sizing each other up for the first time in a

green room in a New York hospital and me without a breast. Talk about bad timing.

Flying in and out without Jessie knowing, without anybody knowing, keeping my secret, not telling.

"For the life of me, I sure can't understand why you don't want one of them to come here and take care of you . . . or you come home. Why is that, Frances?"

"When I'm ready, Tupelo. In my own time. Then I'll go. Just not yet. Okay? You're not gonna tell, are you?"

I would have known if you had told. Ellen would have given it away. When we talked, she would have slipped. She never could lie. And she would have told the world too. She never could keep a secret. It's a good thing you never slept with her, you know. They would have known all the way across Kansas *and* Missouri. Maybe even into Arkansas . . . Oklahoma . . .

So you didn't tell. You waited.

But you knew I couldn't handle it, didn't you? And you were right, I couldn't. Even with all those sessions of talking it out in the hospital. Even with Jeremy trying to be sweet and dear, talking softly to me through a locked bathroom door while I lay on the cold tile and puked my guts out from the chemo all those months. Telling me he loved me. Hell, what does he know? He hardly knows me, right?

I had tried to do it myself. Tried to convince myself that I was okay. Hell, I even told myself that from my point of view the scar wasn't ugly at all. . . .

Why, really, Frances, from your point of view it looks like an owl winking. Doesn't it?

I was trying. But I wasn't making it. Angry, shocked, repulsed, sickened, petrified. All of the above. Everything in the book. The only thing I knew deep inside of me was that I wouldn't die. This cancer is not going to kill me. I refuse. But that was it. I hated all the rest. I hated the new me. I hated being lopsided.

And there you were. Eight months after the surgery, there you were again. Conniving with my agent, getting her to lie. Only you could pull that off, with your goddamn Southern charm, with your honey-dripping drawl, you fucker.

Leaving the theater—no cabs, of course—making my way uptown, sloshing through the slush, my shoes soaked, the wind whipping through me, pulling my coat tight . . . where the hell are my gloves? It's freezing, goddamn it; why the hell did she say The Plaza? What the hell am I signing anyway? I don't want to do this. I don't want a drink, I want to go home. I want to go to bed.

Going in the Fifty-eighth Street entrance, through the side lobby, raising my eyes only to look at Eloise. I always look at Eloise. I send her up a little prayer, like she's a candle at Saint Pat's.

The maître d' at the Oak Room walked me to the table. I kept my eyes down—didn't want to be recognized so I'd have to smile, not feeling like smiling at anybody—lowered myself into the dark-red leather, hiding . . . and then looked up. And you, you fucker, there you were, sitting across the table from me. Grinning.

I had to grab hold of the chair arms for at least twenty seconds. Did you know that? Good recovery, huh? I told you I was a great actress.

What did you tip the maître d', for god sakes? Ship 'n Shore blouses?

A bottle of Bud in front of you.

A vodka in front of me, making a round puddle on the table. One olive . . .

One room key sticking out of the peanut bowl.

Talk about subtle. Leave it to a Southern gentleman every time.

"I was thinkin' about how I was in need of ravishin' you, Frances, and I thought I'd better just fly in and take care of it. Okay?"

Grinning at me. Making me cry at a table in front of a bunch of stupid strangers having cocktails. Boy, did they get an eyeful. You fucker.

How did you know? How did you know when Jeremy would be away? How did you know how long to wait? How much time to give me? How did you figure that enough was enough? Know that I needed you then? Know that I needed to feel seventeen again? How did you always know everything about me? I never got to ask you. We never had the time, did we?

Kissing the scars. Kissing the radiation burn. Saying you'd never had a high-voltage woman before. Saying I was radiant from the radiation. Silly, dopey jokes but making me laugh. God. I was laughing. I hadn't laughed in so damn long.

When you kissed my spine from my tailbone up to my head

and down again, I thought I was gonna explode from the wanting. I was weeping from the anticipation. Begging you to start, begging you to stop, begging you for everything . . . my darling friend, my Pete.

You kissed the front of me. Turned me over and *looked* at me and kissed *all* of the front of me. Both sides of the front of me. The side with, the side without. The good side, the bad side. The east side, the west side. Oh, you don't know how much that meant . . . you just don't know.

Astounded. Astounded at my need. Like standing in the middle of a song. Coming. And crying. Coming. And laughing. And most of all—God, most of all—knowing. I was free. I could stand naked. *Naked*. No more hiding, not anymore. You'd freed me. Why, you're a regular Southern Lincoln, sweetheart. You emancipated me. You made love to me until I knew for sure.

Oh, Pete, it doesn't matter if I have three breasts or eighteen breasts or no breasts at all. It truly doesn't matter. I know because you showed me. I'm still me. Still Frances, even with the butcher's marks. Still Frances, the last one on the end, right after Jessie. Frances, the baby. I'm still Frances, Pete. You saved me. Thank you for that, my darling friend. Thank you.

But now I'm home and I need you. I need to talk to you. And you're not here. You'll never be here again and I will never get over it. Never. I ache to see your stupid face and hear your stupid voice all dripping with honey. You fucker . . .

Well, you're not gonna believe this. It's Milly. She's calling me to dinner. I have to go into that tiny room with my two tiny parents and eat those damn dead green beans.

Oh, shut up, Pete. Stop laughing.

The Funeral

TEE SIGHED into the phone and there was a short pause as neither of them spoke.

"Wait a minute, Frances. Can't we just go together? I mean, the five of us."

"It's fine with me, Tee."

Frances watched her mother move around the kitchen. Milly wagged a glass jug of orange juice at Frances; Frances shook her head no.

"I don't want to go with Billy. I can't. He'll be breathing on me all the way to Mount Mariah, watching me to see if I crack or something. Can't we just go together? Aren't we allowed?"

"It's fine," Frances said.

Milly plunked an oversize white china cup of coffee down in front of her daughter. Some of the coffee sloshed out onto the table.

"Is that gonna piss anybody off?"

"I don't think so."

"Not that I care . . . I mean, I don't really give a flying fuck, but—"

"It's okay, Tee," Frances interrupted. "We can go together. I'll drive."

Tee sighed again. "God," she said.

Neither of them spoke for a few seconds. Then Tee added quietly, "Could you call them, Frances?"

"Sure."

"You don't mind?"

"No," Frances said into the cup, inhaling hot coffee. The cup was so big you could practically drop your whole face down inside it. It was the cup Frances always used when she came home. On one side was a man reading a newspaper, with a terrible mean look on his face, and the words painted across the bottom of the cup read "Good morning, Grouchy," and on the other side was the same man reading the same newspaper but with a wide smile on his face, and the words on that side of the cup read "Good morning, Darling." Pete had given the cup to Frances's folks years ago for an anniversary present. Frances remembered her mother pulling the cup out of the box of tissue, turning it round and round in her hand, her smile fading into a blank. Iz took the cup from his wife, read it, and laughed. "Always keep 'em guessing, huh, Pete?" he said. Milly didn't throw the cup out or give it away. She just pushed it back in the cabinet behind the juice glasses, and Frances retrieved it every time she came home.

Frances held the cup up in both hands now as Milly swiped at the puddle of coffee with a big orange sponge.

"You do it, then, okay?" Tee said. "If I have to talk to anybody else this morning, I'll spit. My rotten mother called already to see how I was doing—just what I needed—and Ellen called to ask what I was wearing. I mean, Jesus . . ."

Milly stood at the refrigerator door, holding it open with her hip. She had one hand on the eggs and held a loaf of bread with the other. She waved the bread at Frances. "Want your special breakfast, baby?"

Frances tilted the mouthpiece up away from her face. "No, thanks, Mom," she whispered.

"What?" Tee asked.

"Nothing," Frances said.

Milly frowned at Frances and made a small *tsk* sound of disapproval.

"I didn't sleep at all," Tee said. "I was so tired, but I just lay there with my eyes open."

Frances smiled at her mother's small back. Milly had put on stockings but hadn't pulled them up yet to attach them to her girdle. They were rolled down around her ankles like thick beige doughnuts. She refused to wear panty hose. "You look like a fool putting those things on," she said, "and what's more, they don't allow for proper ventilation."

Milly had very specific views on all things female. When Frances got her period, Milly refused to let her wear Tampax like the other girls. "Nothing should ever be inserted into the female parts except what is expected," she said to Frances. "Do you understand, dear?" she asked, her head tilted, her eyes searching Frances's eyes. Milly conducted all "female" discussions with Frances in the aqua bathroom of their old house on Seventy-third Street, Frances sitting on the closed toilet seat, Milly perched on the edge of the bathtub, and the small dark-blue booklet Milly had sent away for from the Modess company lying on top of the clothes hamper. Frances watched and bit the inside of her cheek as Milly traced the diagram of a woman's vagina with one perfect oval Fire and Ice fingernail and lectured in a sweet whisper.

"I thought I'd scream," Tee went on. "I don't know why I just didn't get up instead of lying there like an idiot. Frances? Are you listening to me?"

"Mmm-hmm," Frances said.

Milly wore powder-blue scuff wedgie slippers, a blue print cotton housedress with a zipper up the front and a crumpled white handkerchief tucked in the sleeve, all her makeup, all her jewelry, and three silver clips from the beauty shop, which held her hair securely in place. It was only eight o'clock in the morning, but Milly was ready. The funeral was set for noon. High noon.

"Not one wink. I had another one of those fucking *nuit blanche* nights. You know?" Tee said.

As Milly left the kitchen she touched her daughter's shoulder softly with her hand and bent down to kiss the top of Frances's head. Frances could smell her mother's Zibelene perfume, and her eyes filled with tears.

"What?" she said into the phone.

"I said I had one of those fucking white nights, so if I drive I'll crash us into a goddamn tree or something."

"I'll drive, Tee," Frances said, and took a gulp of hot coffee out of the "grouchy" side of the cup.

"Frances, is she gonna be there?"

"Hmm?"

"Is she gonna be there? Jessie? Do you know?"

"I don't know, Tee. Nobody knows."

It wasn't difficult making the arrangements. Tee told Billy and he said it was fine, she could go with the girls and he'd meet her there. Even if it wasn't fine he wasn't about to fight with her. He was sure she was right on the edge. He'd said as much to his mother-in-law the night before.

"I don't think she'll make it through the funeral, Ma," he'd confessed to Mrs. Shafton. "I think she'll fall apart."

Actually he was grateful to drive out alone. He wasn't all that sure how he was handling everything himself. Just that morning he'd found himself crying. He'd been standing at the bathroom window, staring out at their backyard, and the lather had dried on his face. That's what made him turn around to the mirror; he could feel it pulling at the skin on his cheeks. As he lifted the razor to finish the job, he saw tear tracks down through the hard white lather crusts, and that was the shocker—he hadn't even known he was crying.

Frances called everybody else.

Anne said she was relieved. She said she'd been counting on going with Frances all along. After all, she explained, they'd both come in from out of town and were virtually alone—that meant without husbands—and besides, the kids, Pete and Jessie's, would go in the limo from the funeral parlor and she didn't want to do that. Her only concern was whether the Freemans' car had air-conditioning. "It's so sticky already," she said. "I just hate it." Frances shook her head yes into the phone, but she didn't say anything. Anne had been discussing the humidity since they were old enough to notice it.

Ellen, of course, wasn't sure. Shouldn't she go with Tom? And how did it look? "After all, Frances, we're not girls anymore, we're grown-up married women now, and isn't our place with our husbands or families?" Frances talked her into it. It didn't take long. Tom didn't mind. Everything was always fine with Tom; he hadn't changed one bit.

The only surprise was Anita. There was practically no discussion at all. "Do I have to drive?" she asked. "No, I'm driving," Frances said. "Well, then that's fine, then I'll go with y'all," she said.

And so it had been arranged. They would go together and

stand together at his grave. The five of them. All of them but Jessie.

Of course, George thought it was ludicrous.

"What do you mean? You mean you're *not* going with *me?*" he said on the phone to Frances when he called from his hotel an hour later.

George never stayed with his folks when he came home. He stayed at the Raphael and before that the Hilton or the Alameda and sometimes even downtown. It didn't matter to him where he stayed as long as it wasn't with his folks, and they didn't seem to mind either. That was the part that really threw Frances, that they kind of expected it or accepted it or something Frances could never understand. It was beyond her. She couldn't possibly imagine coming home to Kansas City and not staying with Milly and Iz as long as they were alive.

"We're not going together?" he said, his voice distinctly changing from sleepy to very wide awake. He was on England time and all turned around.

"No, we're not," Frances said, searching the bedroom and then realizing with a shock that she was looking for cigarettes. She hadn't smoked in over ten years. She sat down on the bed.

"But I just got in," he said. "I assumed we were going together. I mean, really, Frances." He used his huffy tone at her. She knew exactly what his face looked like on the other end of the line, the frown deepening on the right side of his forehead, the look in his eyes.

"I'm sorry, George. We'll be together later. All of us. But I'm going with the girls."

"The girls," he said flatly into the phone, and sighed.

"That's right," Frances said right back at him. She stood up next to the foot of the bed and realized she was furious.

"He just acts like he's still married to you 'cause he's home, that's all," Tee said when Frances called her. "He always did push you around."

"No, he didn't."

"Frances Freeman, he did too."

"Well, I don't remember that it was that blatant."

"It was blatant all right—you did whatever he wanted. You were never yourself with George."

They were both quiet on the line.

Tee cleared her throat. "So where's he staying this time?"

"I don't know; I didn't ask. I got so mad I hung up."

"Right," Tee said. "What are you wearing?"

"Oh, heels," Frances said quietly.

"Heels," Tee repeated, and she laughed.

Frances stood naked in front of her mother's bathroom mirror long after the steam from the running shower had obliterated her image. She didn't move; she just stood there clutching both sides of the sink. She was stunned by the thought that it was somehow entirely possible that all her life she had been herself only with the man she was about to bury.

AT ELEVEN, Frances pulled her father's top-of-the-line charcoal-gray Oldsmobile up Ellen's driveway and beeped the horn. She was tempted to try their special honk they used in high school but she thought better of it. She smiled at Anne sitting beside her in the front seat, but Anne didn't smile back. She was too busy adjusting the skirt of her dress underneath her on the seat.

Frances honked again.

The front door opened and Tom came out, wearing a light-gray summer suit, a pale-pink shirt, and a pastel-striped silk tie. His blond-gray hair was wet and looked darker than usual. He walked over to the car and put his hands on the ledge of the open window. They all knew Ellen wasn't ready.

"She'll just be a minute," he said softly, and leaned his head inside the car to kiss Frances on the cheek. Then he reached across the front of Frances to touch Anne. "Hello, Anne pie," he said. Anne looked at him and started to cry. "Oh, no," she said.

Tom walked around to the other side of the car, opened Anne's door, helped her out, and held her while she sobbed. Frances cut the engine.

"It's okay," Tom said gently to Anne, and the front door of the house opened again and Ellen came out. She'd forgotten something. Frances knew it. Ellen took two steps out the door, fumbled in her purse, looked at Frances, shook her head helplessly, turned, and ran back inside the house.

Frances opened the door and got out.

"It's gonna pour," Tom said, looking at her over the roof of the car.

"I know," she said. She took a deep breath of the heavy air and smiled at him.

"Pete's making a storm," Anne said, sniffing into Tom's jacket. "Frances arranged it."

Tom patted Anne's shoulder. "Well, that seems right," he said, and the three of them turned together as Ellen came out of the house again.

"I went back in for my wallet," she said. "Isn't that stupid? Why would I need a wallet at a funeral anyway? Hello, Anne," she said, and held out her arms.

"We gotta go, guys. We gotta get Tee and Anita," Frances said, and she opened the car door and got in.

"I'll see you there," Tom said. He helped Anne and his wife into the back seat and moved away from the car as Frances backed down the driveway, alone in the front seat like a chauffeur. Then he stood there waving at them as if they were going off on a long trip somewhere instead of just to Mount Mariah.

Tee was waiting out in front. She was actually kicking at a little pile of dirt heaped around her rosebushes as Frances came down 108th. She opened the car door and slid into the front seat before they even came to a stop.

"Jesus. I've been standing out here forever," she said to no one in particular. "Could it be more fucking humid? It's gonna pour any minute. Billy left hours ago. Oh, Anne, look at you in all that linen—doesn't it wrinkle?"

She scooted herself around in the front seat so she could face Frances behind the wheel and Anne and Ellen in the back at the same time and continued without taking a breath.

"Well, so . . . oh, shit, look—it's raining."

A few scattered raindrops hit the windshield, but by the time they had crossed back over the state line and into Missouri, which was only some twenty blocks away, the sprinkles had stopped and the sun stood blazing out of a black-and-blue sky.

Leonard stood on the curb with Anita. He had one hand on her arm and the other draped around the curve of her back and clasped at her waist.

"They look as if they're skating," Frances said as she pulled up.

"Anita looks old," Ellen said.

"We all look old today, baby," Tee said.

Leonard nodded to each of them as he helped Anita into the back next to Anne. He didn't say anything. Anne leaned over to kiss Anita on the cheek, but it was just as she turned to kiss Leonard goodbye, so all Anne got was a mouthful of Anita's pale-red hair. Leonard smiled, gave a little wave, turned, and walked back to a silver Mercedes parked in the driveway. Frances took off up Ward Parkway. She glanced at Tee, in the front seat next to her. She looked up into her rearview mirror at Ellen, Anne, and Anita in the back.

They were together.

Each woman rearranged herself on the gray leather upholstery.

"So . . .," Frances began. "Do we want the air?"

"God, no, I hate it," Tee piped up.

"Well, that settles that, then," Ellen said.

Tee turned. "Well, you know how I hate it. It freezes one part of you and not the other. But hell, if you all want it, then don't—"

Ellen interrupted. "No, it's fine. I didn't mean . . . I just thought . . ."

"It's awfully sticky," Anne said, moving her back away from the seat, "but whatever everybody else wants is fine with me."

They were quiet. It appeared that the subject of air-conditioning was closed. They would be hot. Frances moved her hand away from the knobs.

They rode in silence for several blocks, the hot air from the open windows moving their hair, blowing their skirts up softly off the seats.

"Well," Ellen said, "here we are together."

Anne smiled at her.

Ellen went on: "California certainly agrees with you, Anne. You look wonderful."

Anne smoothed at her dress. "You think so? I miss it here."

Tee turned around again. "You do?" She was always shocked when someone missed Kansas City. She kicked off one shoe and tucked that foot under her body.

"Sure," Anne said. "I miss it all the time. I think about you guys and I wonder why I'm there."

"Would you move back?" Ellen asked.

Anne sighed. "Oh, well . . . I don't know; it seems like I just got settled."

"What about you, Frances?" Ellen asked.

Frances watched Anita in the rearview mirror. Her eyes were staring straight ahead and fixed on something. . . . Frances couldn't figure out on what.

"Frances?" Ellen asked again. "Would you move back?"

"What? Oh . . . move back? God, I don't know. I'm always counting backward in my head to see what time it is here, imagining what you're all doing, but . . ."

"But you wouldn't move back, would you?" Tee said.

Frances looked at her. "No, I guess not, not now, not with my work and all."

"Maybe you'll move to Hollywood," Ellen said.

"Oh, yes, come to L.A., Frances," Anne said. "Be with me."

"And be a big star," Ellen added.

Frances laughed. "It's a little late, guys. I'd be the oldest ingenue in town."

Tee whipped her head around to Frances. "Hey, nobody can tell how old you are. You look fucking great. Oh, shit. I ripped my stocking. Goddamn it!"

"Tee, please, couldn't you just not—" Anita said.

"Sorry," Tee said quickly, cutting her off.

"Where are you stayin', Anne?" Anita said. Her drawl was quite pronounced.

"I'm at Mother's."

"You mean you didn't sell the house? After all this time?"

"No. We've had three different agents since Daddy died. Nine months. And nobody wants Mother's house."

"Everybody wants to be further south is all it is," Ellen said.

"Just think, Anne," Tee said, "when you sell that house, you and Jessie will be rich."

"Tee, really," Ellen said.

"What?" Tee said, turning around. "It's true, isn't it, Anne?"

"Well, when it's settled, the house and all of Daddy's other property, when it's sold, all of his estate, then I guess we'll be taken care of."

"Taken care of? You'll never have to work another day of your life."

"Oh, I wouldn't quit working."

"You wouldn't?"

"No, Tee. I like to work."

"And the children too?" Ellen said. "James and Luke and Amy, they'll be taken care of too?"

"There's some kind of trust fund, I don't really understand it all."

"Well, that's a blessing, then, isn't it?" Ellen said.

"Hell, it's more than a blessing," Tee said. "When my rat bastard father died all we got were twelve moth-eaten editions of the Reader's Digest Condensed Books from 1963 and 1964 and a box of black-and-white snapshots of him prancing around Europe during the Second World War, him and all his army buddies leaning against their jeeps smiling in undershirts and boots."

Frances glanced at Tee.

"Of course the books were hardcovers, not paperbacks. I guess I shouldn't put that down, huh?"

Frances smiled at Tee. Tee turned her head away.

"I probably ought to throw that shit out. It's in a box in my basement. I wonder what I'm keeping it for?" she said.

They were quiet.

Ellen opened her purse and took out a pack of Doublemint. She took a stick for herself and offered the pack to Anne. Anne shook her head and so did Anita. "Frances, gum? Tee?" Ellen said, leaning forward.

"Okay," Tee said.

"Frances?"

"No; no, thank you."

Ellen gave Tee a piece, unwrapped her own piece, folded it into her mouth, put the pack back in her purse, and clicked the purse shut.

"Well," she said, sitting back against the cushioned seat, "we haven't been together in a long time. You haven't been here, Anne, and neither have you, Frances. When were you home last?"

"Uh, I don't know . . . two summers ago, wasn't I?"

"No, you weren't," Tee said, looking at Frances.

"Anne, you weren't either," Ellen said to Anne. "Was she, Anita?"

Anita didn't answer.

"Of course, I guess that's the way it is now. Even the four of us who still live here—we're hardly ever all together anymore. Unless one of you comes home. Or for a special occasion . . . you know, a wedding or a funeral—" She heard herself and stopped.

No one spoke for a few minutes. Frances moved the Oldsmobile up the Wornall Road on-ramp to I-435 and got in the second lane.

"Oh," Anne said, "guess who I saw? In L.A., I mean. About two weeks ago."

"Who?" Ellen said.

"I was sitting at McDonald's and there he was, as big as you please, eating a Quarter-Pounder right across the room from me. I was so surprised. I said, My goodness, have you moved here? But he said no, he was just visiting. He looked absolutely the same."

"Who, Anne?" Frances said.

"I haven't seen him in a million years, maybe since I moved. How many years ago is that?"

"Well, let's see," Ellen said. "You left the summer after Adam was born, and Frances and George had gone the January before . . . so it must have been June of—"

"Wait a minute, Ellen," Tee interrupted. "Who was it, Anne?"

"Oh, you know . . . ," Anne said. "Sweet little beady eyes, sandy hair, a wonderful sense of humor . . . you know . . ."

"You mean you *just* forgot his name?" Tee said.

"Give her a second," Frances said. "Who, honey?"

"Oh, you know . . . he went to Pemday." She turned to Ellen. "Ellen, help me."

"With beady eyes?" Ellen asked, frowning.

"Yes, yes . . ." In her mind's eye, Anne could see him sitting there plain as day, chewing on a hamburger, smiling. It was so exasperating. "He was a year ahead of me. . . . His mother was rich and his father died when he was a baby; I think he had a heart attack."

"Great," Tee mumbled. "That'll help me remember."

"Shhh," Frances said to Tee.

"He dated Mulligan my junior year and he had a powder-blue Thunderbird and he crashed all our dances; he was a good dancer but he had sweaty palms—"

"David," Frances said. "David Paul."

"Praise the Lord," Tee said. "Sweaty-palmed Paul."

Ellen looked at Anne. "But David Paul doesn't have beady eyes, Anne."

Anne frowned. "He doesn't? Well, I think they're beady. They're squinched into his face like raisins pushed in pie dough."

Tee turned around. "I'll tell you what he's got besides sweaty palms: he's got one big cock. Sally Thurmond told me."

Frances laughed.

"Tee!" Anne said, laughing.

"Tee, you're making that up," Ellen said.

"I am not!"

"But Sally Thurmond was a virgin when she married Witzer; how could she know about David Paul's . . ."

"Cock." Tee laughed. "You can say it, Ellen, you're old enough."

Anne laughed and so did Frances.

"How can you be talkin' about this now?" Anita's voice cut through the laughter.

Everyone stopped.

"Shit, here we go," Tee mumbled to Frances.

"I heard you, Tee," Anita said.

"Hey, I was just trying to keep it light, keep our minds off where we were going."

"Well, I know exactly where we are goin'. We are goin' to bury my brother. I couldn't forget it no matter what smut you talked about!"

"Anita, Tee didn't mean anything," Frances said.

"I'm so sorry," Anne said. "Please forgive us, Anita."

"It wasn't your fault, Anne."

"Oh, no, it was my fault. Right?" Tee said, her voice raised. "Everything is always my fault."

She turned her body around in the seat and faced front.

"I don't know why I wanted us to go together—I must have lost my mind. We're not together, we haven't been together . . . hell, we probably never should have been together. We were just too young to know we didn't get along."

"Come on, Tee, don't say that," Frances said.

"Why not? It's the truth."

"No, it isn't," Ellen said. "We're still friends; we'll always be friends."

"How can you say that? Why don't you open your eyes?"

"I assume you're referrin' to me," Anita said.

"No, she isn't."

"I'm not referring to you; I'm referring to the whole damn thing. It's a memory is all it is. This friendship is just a fucking faded memory."

No one spoke.

Hot air blew Frances's hair across her face. She caught it with her hand and brushed it out of her eyes. She glanced at Tee. Tee's eyes were shut, her bottom lip caught between her teeth. In the rearview mirror, Ellen was looking to the left, out the window, Anne was staring into her lap, and Anita's hand was across her face.

Anita leaned forward a little in her seat.

"I tried to see Jessie," she said. "I went there, to that . . . jail, but they wouldn't let me in. She refused to see me."

"It wasn't just you, Anita. She wouldn't see me either. She wouldn't see any of us," Anne said.

"Who any of us?" Ellen said. "I didn't try to see her; I didn't go back there. I mean, after they took me to question me, I didn't go back." She looked around. "Did you go, Frances?"

"Yes."

"I went," Tee said quietly, her eyes still closed, her head back against the seat.

Frances turned. "You didn't tell me you went."

"Well, why didn't somebody tell *me*?" Ellen said. "I didn't know *anybody* went."

"That's 'cause everything's a secret," Tee said. "That's how close we still are."

"Jessie hasn't seen anybody," Anne said. "She's been totally alone."

"Maybe she wanted it that way," Tee said.

"Oh, Tee," Ellen said, "nobody wants to be alone."

"Maybe she didn't have a choice," Frances said.

Anne leaned forward. "Why do you say that?"

"Because I think we did it. The five of us. I think we walked out of her life."

"Oh, and whose fault was that?" Tee said, opening her eyes and turning toward them. "You can't blame that one on me—not all of it. Huh? Whose fault could it be?"

"Oh, Lord," Ellen said, and Frances swung the Oldsmobile through the Mount Mariah gates.

JAMES STOOD ALONE, looking at his father's casket. Luke had told him it wasn't fancy. "I picked plain," Luke said. "Plain. Okay, Jimmy?"

Okay, James thought. It looks okay.

He had planned to be with Luke, of course, but he and Callie got hung up changing planes in St. Louis, with a four-hour layover. Hell, I could drive there faster, he told the guy at TWA. Goddamn airlines, they could make a person crazy.

He looked at the casket again. Hell, I don't know . . . we don't know what we're doing here anyway; what difference does it make?

James frowned.

We don't know how to make a goddamn funeral.

What did she say to me? That stupid wiseass cop. It doesn't matter that she was a woman—she was still a stupid wiseass cop. Your mother says you boys should make the arrangements, your mother doesn't wish to see you, I think it's best to leave your mother out of this.

Leave my mother out of this . . . Boy, that's a good one. Hell, I begged my mother to be out of this.

Every goddamn time. Even when I was little, from the time that I could see. All the goddamn times.

Please leave him, Mommy. Please, he'll never change.

Standing there in her nightgown, holding it together where he'd ripped it off her. Standing in the hallway, where I'd stopped her, whispering so Luke and Amy couldn't hear.

Please, Mommy. I'll help you.

You don't understand: he doesn't mean to be this way.

Shivering in the moonlight, tiny and white, not like a mommy at all.

But he always says he promises, and he always lies.

No, it's gonna be different now, baby. Daddy loves me. You'll see, it's all gonna change this time.

All the goddamn times. All the promises that it would change.

James frowned.

Well, it sure as hell changed this time, didn't it, Dad?

A bead of sweat slid down James's neck and melted into his collar. What difference? The whole shirt was damp already anyway. Goddamn humidity. He brought a white-on-white monogrammed handkerchief out of the inside pocket of his jacket, unfolded it, and blotted his forehead and throat. He looked up at the moving sky. Goddamn clouds building up in the west . . . gonna be a storm. . . . Hell, that's just what we need here, a storm. Great, Dad.

He grimaced as he exhaled, and then he looked at the casket once more. It's perfect, he thought. Polished pine with straight brass handles. Plain and perfect. I guess he would have liked it.

What am I saying? How would I know what the bastard would have liked? We probably exchanged less than ten thousand words my entire life. Besides, who gives a damn? We could bury him in a cardboard box, for all I care. James had a sudden vision of a tan cardboard casket being lowered into the ground. Big red block letters warned: FRAGILE. THIS END UP. HANDLE WITH CARE. Then the side of the box snapped open and his father's feet began to slide slowly out one end: Pete's cordovan loafers gleaming in the sun, white ribbed socks, frayed cuffs on the blue jeans— James blinked. Okay. Let's just slow down here, boy. Watch what you're doing.

He folded the soft white piece of cotton into a perfect square and stuffed it back inside his jacket pocket. Then he focused quickly on the toes of his shoes on the grass; they looked too long somehow, too pointy. James squinted at them, lowering his eyelids into tiny slits and then opening them slowly, watching the light change, trying to make his feet appear smaller.

He's not wearing jeans anyway; he's wearing a suit. A navy-blue suit with a thin pinstripe and a button-down shirt, a light-blue Sea Island cotton button-down shirt. I ought to know—I picked it out. Luke couldn't do a thing after the casket. He fell apart like a little kid.

James shook his head. A closet full of light-blue shirts to match your goddamn eyes, huh, Dad? He frowned, yanked his tie, and bent his head to the right, trying to catch another drop of sweat as it made a path down the side of his face and into his collar.

He watched his sister, Amy. She stood by Luke. Luke was telling her something and Amy's head was bent forward, her eyes down, her black hair falling straight across her face. Poor Amy, James thought, poor kid. She's just a kid. What is she now anyway?

Sixteen? Seventeen? A baby. A small grumble sound came out of him; he coughed and cleared his throat to cover it. He felt his wife's eyes on his face, but he didn't look up.

Okay. Where was I?

I say hello or something . . . goddamn, what am I supposed to say? Welcome to my father's funeral . . . that would be good. Okay, wait a minute here . . . I say something simple like hello and then I go right into the Twenty-third Psalm and then I say, Okay, whoever wants to stand up and say something about Dad, stand up and say it . . . and then they do, and then . . . What the hell were we gonna do next? Shit. Wait a minute here . . . I know, I know . . . the Lord's Prayer. That's right . . . attaboy. I got it.

Okay. Let's see . . . Hell, I know the damn thing since I'm five years old, what the hell's the problem here? The Lord is my shepherd. I shall not want. He maketh me to lie down in green pastures. James looked at the emerald grass beneath his loafers. Green pastures, all right. He leadeth me in straight paths for his name's sake. What the hell does that mean? Goddamn. Luke should be doing this, not me. No, Luke's a wreck. All that talk about me being the firstborn. What the hell difference does it make who says it? Firstborn to see their shit is all I was anyway. Firstborn to hear him beat her up with his mouth. Beat her up with all he had. Firstborn, my ass . . . Where was I?

Uh . . . He restoreth my soul. Yeah. No. Wait a minute. Where's the part about the still waters? Wait a minute. Back up, boy. Back up. Where are you anyway? Uh . . . oh, yeah . . . He *leadeth* me beside the still waters, then He *guideth* me in straight paths for his name's sake. Right. You leadeth and then you guideth—everybody knows that. Now you're cooking', boy. Thou preparest a table before me in the presence of mine enemies. My cup runneth over.

Well, then, looketh out, Dad, James thought, looketh out.

His wife touched his arm. She had come up to him without James even realizing it.

"Are you all right?" she asked.

James stared at her. "What?"

She lowered her head a little, and one yellow wisp of a curl brushed against his chin. James was overwhelmed by her smell.

"I said, Are you all right?"

It seemed to James that her words came out after her breath had struck his face. Instant replay, he thought. Slow motion . . .

Let's see that one more time, folks, once for the guys in the back of the . . . James swallowed and looked at her harder. Her mouth is moving, that's for sure. What's the matter with me? Concentrate, boy. Is she speaking in code?

He kept his eyes focused on Callie's soft pink lips as they moved up and down. A sudden and powerful desire to knock her right off her feet rushed through James. It was so strong he had to hold on to himself.

He coughed. "I'm fine. I'm just hot."

"You could take your jacket off, sweetie," she said softly.

In his image he pushed her at her shoulders and she fell backward across the perfect cemetery sod, one leg up and the other broken in an odd position under her body, her mouth frozen open in a pink strawberry O and the stupid piece of white lacy stuff she'd stuck to the top of her hairdo undone now and lying cockeyed across her face.

James closed his eyes. Erase it, boy, he thought. He felt his fingers curl into fists.

"Jimmy?"

"I'll be fine."

"But you're sweating."

He looked at her closely. She was white and pink and yellow and far too soft to touch. Bubble gum, James thought, sweet bubble gum. I'm choking on a Double Bubble wife. Somebody help me. It was suddenly clear to James that he couldn't remember why he'd married her.

"I'm fine, Callie. Really."

"Okay," she said. "I was just trying to help."

She was hurt. The whine of crushed feelings was just on the end of her words. She was waiting for him to say something; she was waiting for him to say he was sorry.

I have to bury my goddamn father here, James thought. Don't you get that? He watched Callie closely. She moved slightly to the left, but her eyes didn't leave his.

Well, you can wait until hell freezes over, girl.

Her eyelashes fluttered softly, curled and coated with black sticky paint.

Trapped moths, James thought. We're nothing but a bunch of poor trapped moths stuck in the tar, Dad.

When her husband didn't say anything for at least two long

minutes, Callie March Chickery turned and walked away from his side. James watched the play of apple-green shiny fabric stretched across his wife's ass. Then he reached once more for the white monogrammed handkerchief and mopped the sides of his face.

Where the hell is everybody anyway? Just where the hell is everybody so we can get this goddamn show on the road?

GRADY WAITED PATIENTLY. She was afraid to get any closer to the people who were standing together near the rows of chairs set up by the grave. After all, she was the only person there who wasn't white. She pulled at the rim of her straw topper.

I'm getting a headache from this hat, she thought. Or maybe I shoulda had a bigger breakfast. Maybe that's what it is and not this hat at all.

She missed eating eggs and bacon for breakfast, but Dr. Ben had said bacon was a big fat no-no. He laughed at her when he said fat no-no, like it was a huge joke.

Ha! He wouldn't even discuss eggs. A fine how do you do. I wonder what the man would do if he knew I still ate fried potatoes, Grady thought. She had to cover her mouth with her hand to keep from laughing out loud just thinking about the look on Dr. Ben's face.

She hoped it wasn't wrong to wear a red hat. You never did know with them. She looked around. Well, it was too late now. She adjusted her hip up against the fender of her husband's Cadillac. Actually it was her Cadillac, but she always thought of it as Maurice's. It was too big for her, too wide, too hard to park. She should have sold it years ago and gotten herself one of them cute little things to drive around in, but she just didn't have the heart. After all, it was Mrs. Connell's, and when she died, Mr. Connell had given it to her.

Wouldn't take a penny for it, that man. Not one penny. Poor soul, he was beside himself when she died. Cold as she was, cold and mean. And for no good reason. Why, the woman had everything, didn't she? A good man, two beautiful girls, all that money—what more could a woman want? And her so mean and hateful and he loved her anyway. Well, there's just no accounting for love, Grady thought. Thank the good Lord they're not here to see this, neither one of them. And not his poor sainted mother either. Lord have mercy on their souls; they're better off up there with Him than down here watching this.

Grady looked up at the dark sky. Big black thunderclouds were making their way across the blue. Well, look at that—it's gonna pour right down in the middle of this. She moved her backside a little to the right and put her weight on the other foot. Then she reached up and patted at some sweat collecting on her upper lip. She squinted at the horizon. Sweet Jesus, what's gonna happen to my baby now? Tell me that, dear Lord. Grady shook her head and frowned.

She never shoulda married that boy anyway. He wasn't right for Jessie. I told Maurice. I told him once if I told him fifty times. He's too wild and good-lookin'. There's gonna be nothin' but trouble over him, I said. Nothin' but heartache. She coulda had her pick of all of 'em, but oh, no, she wanted that wild Indian.

Grady shook her head again. And then, remembering, she smiled. She sure did shake up the missus, though. That's for sure. Comin' home from that college all skinny and sick and scarin' everybody half to death, and then she up and announces she's gonna marry Pete Chickery. Well. The missus runnin' around the house all hysterical, lookin' for some way to stop that baby, a magic potion . . . draggin' her off to all them psychiatrist doctors. Why, she coulda given me the money, all the good it did. That baby had her mind made up. "I love him, Grady." Well, that's all it takes. There's no talkin' to a child in love. A waste of a grown person's breath, that's all.

But I knew what was comin'. I knew, Maurice knew. . . . You could see it in that boy's eyes—those were the devil's blue eyes starin' out at you, Lord knows. Too much for my Jessie to handle.

Grady smiled.

Of course, you hadda like him. You jes couldn't help yourself. He had a way about him, a particular way. Even right from the start I liked him; it was never any different with me. Not for all these years.

But the missus hated him. That's what made her sick, if you ask me, all that hate, that's what made her head go bad. That and Jessie marryin' him. She couldn't take that. Oh, no. Couldn't take Jessie defyin' her right in the face.

Grady took a big sigh and raised her eyes to the moving clouds.

Well, she had it comin'. Lord forgive me, but that's the way I see it. Never layin' a hand on them children, pushin' at that man, lips all clenched up in a line . . . it was unnatural.

Grady pulled a bit more on the brim of her hat.

Unnatural, that's what it was. She was an unnatural woman. Why, I raised those babies. And that's the God's honest truth. Everybody knows it. Everybody.

She moved her backside again on the Cadillac and shifted to her other leg.

She never did understand about my rheumatoids anyways, expectin' me to stand up when she came into a room no matter what I was doin', like she was a queen or somethin'. The idea.

And then her actin' like I was her best friend all of a sudden when the trouble started, askin' me to go over there and mix in. "Oh, Grady dear, she'll listen to you. Tell her to leave him. Tell her to come home." Come home? As if Jessie would come home to her anyway. And you couldn't fool me with that Grady *dear* business. Talkin' to me like that, like butter would melt in her mouth, and after the way she done me all those years. Why, I never.

I told Maurice. I told him but good. I said, "I ain't gettin' in the way of those children. I ain't messin' in Jessie's marriage. Not a word, do you hear?" And Maurice says, "Hey, I didn't say nothin'. Did I say somethin'? I ain't the one," he says to me.

And then she makes poor Mr. Connell to come and ask me. The man so embarrassed he like to died, sittin' me down in his dining room, no less, lookin' at the floor, tryin' to discuss his personals with me. It just wasn't right and she knew it and I knew it and she pushed him to do it. Pushed him and pushed them girls. Pushin' at everybody her whole life is what she did. Right up to their limits.

Grady sighed and licked her top lip. My Lord in heaven, am I gonna bury them all? Is that your plan for me, sweet Jesus?

Her brassiere strap inched down her shoulder a little ways and she pushed it right back up where it belonged. Too hot for this slip, she thought. Nobody wears slips anymore but me. I told Maurice I didn't need a slip in this heat. I told him.

Lightning flashed off in the west and a crack of thunder

followed. Grady looked up. Well, that's all there is to it, it's gonna pour right down on us but good, soak everybody through to their quick.

An unfamiliar car went by and Grady thought she saw a hand flapping at her from one of the open windows. She didn't know anybody who drove a charcoal-gray Oldsmobile, so she kept her eye on it. The car slowed at an empty space, turned in, parked, and the driver's door swung open. Frances got out, raised her hand, and gave Grady a little wave. Tee got out of the passenger side and Ellen stepped out of the back, with Anita and Anne behind her.

Well, now we're gonna do this, now that my babies are here. Clutching her Bible under one arm and her pocketbook and umbrella in the other, Grady moved her Sunday-best black dress off the fender of Maurice's Cadillac, gave her bottom a little brush, and adjusted her hat. Lord, I'm gonna miss me that boy, she thought, but she smiled bravely as she walked toward the girls.

GEORGE MASSIMINO SWERVED away from a cluster of people ahead of him and stopped under the shade of a big oak. He wasn't ready to say a bunch of hellos yet; he was waiting for Frances.

Where is she anyway? Using that tone with me—I know that tone. "I'm going with the girls, George. We'll be together later." You bet we will, Frances.

His cock got stiff in his pants.

What the . . . ? Boy, nothing changes, does it? I'm fifty years old here. Look at this.

George reached down and adjusted himself. Then he leaned back against the tree and studied the people.

God, there's Patash; he looks the same. . . . Who's he holding on to? Is that Tanner? What happened to her hair? Why would Leonard be here? Is that Leonard on the end? Who is that anyway?

Mike Shapiro moved toward George with an outstretched hand and a small smile.

Well, look at this. Shapiro must have lost forty, fifty pounds at least. Hell, you can see the bones in his face. I wonder when this happened.

"How you doin', Mass?" Shapiro asked, shaking George's hand and patting him on the shoulder.

"I'm fine, Shapi. Just fine. Except for this, of course." George gestured at their surroundings.

"Oh, right," Shapiro said. He shuffled his feet a little on the turf, moved a few steps closer to George. "So when did you get in? Middle of the night?"

"Yeah. I had to change planes in New York."

"Right," Shapiro said, "I get the picture. That time change sure is a bitch, huh?"

"Yeah," George said.

What the hell is going on here? What are we talking about?

Shapiro looked around. "So, buddy . . . where's Frances?"

Here we go. "She's coming with the girls, Shapi."

"Oh, right," Shapiro said, shaking his head with understanding. "Anne got in all right?"

"Yeah."

"Where's she live now?"

"L.A."

"Oh. Right. So . . . uh, any of 'em seen Jessie?"

"I don't know, Shapi, I just got in."

Shapiro frowned and then smiled. "Oh, yeah, forgot for a minute. Sorry." He rubbed his hand across his face.

This is ridiculous. I know this guy my whole life and we're standing here talking about . . .

"So it's not this humid in England, huh, Mass?"

"No, it sure isn't."

The weather. We're having a totally moronic conversation here about the weather . . . me and Shapiro, who know each other since the third grade.

Shapiro put his hand back on George's shoulder.

"So, Mass . . . uh, what's gonna happen here, huh?"

"What do you mean?"

"I mean, you know, with Jessie and all . . . I mean, you're a lawyer, you know about this stuff. Hell, I don't know anything about murder."

"Murder?"

"Well, hell, Mass, she blew his head off, didn't she?"

"I don't know, Shapi. I don't know what went on."

"Well, then let me tell you, buddy, it was bound to happen sooner or later—nobody's surprised. After all, old Pete never could learn to keep his pants on. Just a shame it had to be Jess who did it, that's what I say, a cryin' shame . . . one big cryin' . . ." He looked off into the distance for a second and then put his hand back on George's shoulder. "Hey, look at that, Mass—isn't that Bridgie Block walking up with Packer? What a set of jugs, huh?"

GRADY HELD ANNE'S ARM.

"When they bringin' Jessie?" she whispered into Anne's ear.

"I don't know. They wouldn't tell me anything," Anne said, wiping at her nose with a little piece of wet Kleenex. "I don't even know if she's coming. None of us do."

"Here, child," Grady said, and handed her a freshly ironed white handkerchief from out of her pocketbook.

Tee held on to Billy. Tom was on the other side of him. Billy had been all right until he saw the casket, perfectly fine, and then he fell apart. Tee had never seen him cry like this. Not even when she had the awful miscarriage right after they got married. Not even when his mother died.

"I'm sorry, Tee. I . . . I . . ." He tried to speak.

"It's okay, Billy," Tee said. "It's okay." She put her arm around him. She was filled with a tremendous wave of closeness to him, and it stunned her.

Frances held George's hand. She had to admit she felt better as soon as she saw him standing there. Something about his hand in hers just made her feel safe. She didn't know why. Probably the comfort of old times, the familiarity of his fingers twined in hers. Good old George. Jesus, I can't believe we're doing this.

Anita saw them all. Ronnie Green and Larry Yord, Tip Rutten, Fiskin, Lax and Kazanjian, Mike Shapiro, Patash, Bill Vallely—they were all there. All the boys who ran with her brother. All those awful boys who made her so miserable in high school. She held on to Leonard's arm and kept her head down. She didn't want to see any of them; she didn't want to look into their eyes and remember.

And then James came over. He kissed the women he had known since childhood and shook hands with the men. "I'd really appreciate it if you could sit with us in the chairs, Aunt Anne. And you too, Aunt Anita." He nodded at the stranger who had married Anita. "And you too . . . uh, Leonard," he added softly.

Grady kind of pushed Anne over to the chairs. Anne was suddenly very white and her feet didn't seem to be working properly. Anita sat down at the end of the empty second row, with Lenley at her side. Grady fixed Anne into a chair next to them and stood behind her.

The children sat in the front row: James with Callie, Luke and then Amy. All the seats in that row were taken except for the first chair, closest to the casket. It was empty.

People moved forward as if someone had given them a cue. They didn't sit down in the other rows of chairs; they remained standing. A hush moved through the group until there was only silence. They were ready.

James leaned across his wife's body to confer with his brother. Callie turned around and scanned the area. Luke leaned in closer and said something. James shook his head. Callie's yellow hair fell over one eye as she bent to join them. She poked it back up into place.

Then James stood, walked to the casket and the banks of flowers, and looked out at the people who had come to bury his father. He blinked and cleared his throat.

"Uh, hello. Uh, we decided we'd do this ourselves. I mean, there's only us here." He smiled at the people. "You all know that Dad wouldn't have wanted a priest or anything like that."

There was a low rumble of acknowledgment.

Anita took a breath and clenched her hands tighter in her lap. Her head was bent forward and her shoes lay flat on the grass in front of her. Her knees pressed white and hard up against one another, and her back was straight and held away from the chair. Only Leonard could see she was shaking.

Ellen had a sudden vision of Pete winking at her through the peephole in her front door. She closed her eyes and held tightly to Tom's arm. He looked at her and then back at James.

"So, uh, I'm gonna start and then, if any of you want to say something about Dad, well, we'd be most obliged."

A sob came out of Billy. There was a small scuffling as Tom practically pushed him into one of the chairs. He was sure that if he didn't, Billy would fall on his face. Tee sat next to her husband.

"Sit down, Ellen," Tom whispered to his wife, gesturing with his hand at the next seat.

"But . . . we're not family," she said.

"I said sit down," Tom said firmly. Ellen folded gently into the chair next to Tee, and Tom sat beside her. He looked at James.

James cleared his throat. "If anyone else wants to sit, just go right ahead."

He held on to the lectern in front of him and looked at the assembled group. His voice was firm.

"The Lord is my shepherd. I shall not want. He maketh me to lie down in green pastures."

Ellen reached over and took Tee's hand in hers.

"He leadeth me beside the still waters. He restoreth my soul. He guideth me in straight paths for his name's sake." James looked at his brother. He continued. "Yea, though I walk through the valley of the shadow of death . . ."

Frances's body swayed a little. George moved her into one of the chairs. He sat down beside her and put his arm around her shoulders.

"I will fear no evil, for Thou art with me. Thy rod and thy staff, they comfort me. Thou preparest a table before me in the presence of mine enemies . . ."

Frances buried her face in George's neck. He realized with a start that her nose was cold against his skin. Her nose was cold and so was her forehead.

"Thou has anointed my head with oil, my cup runneth over. My cup . . . runneth over . . . and . . ." James heard his voice creak. He held tightly to the lectern and tried to gain control.

Callie stood up and walked to her husband. She put her hand on his chest and looked into his face.

James took a breath. "Surely goodness and mercy shall follow me all the days of my life," he continued. "And I shall dwell in the house of the Lord forever. Amen," James said to the others.

"Amen," they echoed back.

"Amen." A woman's voice was heard alone.

James's eyes searched for the voice that came from behind the crowd. He didn't move. Callie followed her husband's gaze.

Everyone turned. There was no bustle of movement and hardly any mumble of words; there was virtually no sound at all.

Across the grass and under a wide, leafy maple, Jessie stood alone, silhouetted against the sky.

"Mom!" Amy yelled. She jumped to her feet, turned, and ran, long hair flying out behind her in a thick black wedge.

"Mom . . . Mom . . . Mom!"

The lightweight folding chair she'd been sitting on fell backward, smashing into the front of Ellen's legs, ripping both stockings and breaking the skin on Ellen's left shinbone.

Amy raced to the rear—around the side of Tom's chair, around Frances and George, in between all the people who separated her from her mother. She threw her body into the front of Jessie, her face pushed into Jessie's hair, her thin tanned arms wrapped around Jessie's small waist. And then, as if locked, the two bodies, mother and daughter, swayed slowly in front of the maple tree.

"Oh, Lord," Ellen said. Tom put his arm around her shoulders.

"Billy . . . it's Jessie," Tee said, getting up.

"Okay, hon," he said, pushing back his chair.

Frances held George's arm and they stood up together.

Anita didn't stand. She didn't even turn around in her chair. Leonard rose to see what was happening, and when he realized his wife was still seated, he quickly sat back down.

"Oh, Jessie," Anne said. She took a few steps toward her sister, but Grady held on to her by the shoulder. "Wait a minute now, baby," Grady said. "Jes wait a little minute now."

James stood frozen in his spot by the casket, Callie beside him, one hand on her husband's shoulder and the other open wide across her chest, fuchsia-pink nail lacquer catching the light.

Amy moved forward with Jessie. The crowd parted to let them through, as if they'd been rehearsed. Luke stayed at his chair, his eyes glued on Jessie, his face rigid.

By the time they reached the first chair in the first row, everyone was standing. James kissed his mother and settled her into the chair. Luke stood motionless; he made no move to touch her. James squatted down on his haunches in front of Jessie, one hand resting on her knees, the other dropped down between his legs, holding the ground for support. He leaned his head in close to her and said something. She moved to the side. He said something else. She turned her head away. James looked up at Luke, said something, and Luke squatted down beside him.

The people waited. They watched the back of Jessie's head, the set of her shoulders as she bent to her boys, her pale arm around her daughter's thin back, her tiny hand pulling Amy in close. They watched and they were quiet. Some of them sat back down.

She wore blue. Pale ice blue. The blue of her husband's eyes. None of her friends had ever seen her wear blue before; none of them had ever seen this dress. It was a simple short-sleeved sheath and it was clearly expensive; you could tell by the way the fabric moved and the way the dress was cut. She wore no jewelry except her wedding band. She wore no makeup. She carried no purse and no handkerchief and she was bare-legged. Her shoes looked new; pale beige heels with a closed toe and a sling back. She had on large square sunglasses with tortoise frames and dark smoked lenses.

Ellen knew the glasses. She'd gone with Jessie to buy them when Rusty chewed up Jessie's old ones. He'd lifted them out of her purse in Ellen's front hall and by the time they'd all chased him out from under the dining-room table and through the whole downstairs, the frames were ruined forever. Ellen even knew how much these glasses cost, because she'd insisted on paying for them; after all, she'd argued, Rusty was her dog. Jessie thought the frames were too big for her face, but Ellen disagreed.

"You look mysterious . . . you look daring . . . you look like you're . . . like you're somebody else. Oh, come on, Jessie, you need something dramatic in your life."

Ellen could remember saying those words, those exact words, in that little optical shop at Ward Parkway. She couldn't remember the name of the shop, but she remembered what she'd said.

We bought the glasses and had lunch. Chicken salad, Ellen thought. Chicken salad stuffed in a tomato and iced tea.

She sat back in her chair.

And a week later she threw that drink at me.

Ellen leaned over and touched Tee's arm. "Those are Jessie's glasses," she whispered in Tee's ear.

Tee turned and frowned. "What?"

"Those are Jessie's sunglasses. Who went to the house to get them for her?"

"Hell, I don't know," Tee whispered back. "Why?"

"I don't know. I mean . . . that's not her dress, is it?"

Tee squinted at Jessie's back. "I don't know."

"Well, have you ever seen it before?"

"No."

"Well . . ."

"Well what?" Tee said. Her voice was raised.

Ellen blinked. "Well . . . I don't know. I just . . . I mean, where did she get those clothes and who did they call to get her sunglasses? If they didn't call me and they didn't call you, then—"

"For crissakes, Ellen, who gives a fuck what she's wearing? What the hell's the matter with you?"

"What's going on?" Tom said, leaning across his wife and looking at Tee.

"Nothing," Ellen said.

"What's the matter?" Billy asked.

"Nothing," Tee said.

Both men sat back.

Tee looked at Ellen. Ellen dabbed her eyes and patted her nose with a white lace handkerchief. She didn't blow her nose—she just patted it around the nostrils. Her leg was stuck out in front of her, but the piece of Kleenex she had stuck to the cut had fallen off. The bruise was lavender now, lavender and red and about the size of half a kumquat, rising up through the torn stocking.

Tee put her hand on Ellen's knee. "I'm sorry, Ellen," she said softly. "Really, I didn't mean to be such a bitch."

Ellen shook her head up and down. "It's okay," she said. "You're right, I'm a moron. A stupid, simpleminded moron."

"Oh, God, Ellen, please, you're not a moron. Okay?"

Frances watched Tee and Ellen in front of her, their heads bent toward one another. She closed her eyes and bent her own head over to the side, resting it on George's upper arm.

"Are you all right?" he asked.

"I'm fine."

"I mean it, Frances. Are you all right?"

"I'm fine. I just . . ." She looked up at him and smiled weakly. "Did you know they'd let Jessie come?"

"No."

"Can you see what's happening? Can you see her?"

"They're talking, that's all I can see. The boys are talking to her. They're probably figuring out how to proceed."

"You sound like a lawyer."

"I am a lawyer."

She interrupted. "It was a joke, George . . . a joke." She moved her cheek against the nubby material of his jacket. "I can't believe any of this is happening. I can't believe we're here."

He looked at her. "Sit tight, baby," he said, and stood up. He moved around Tom, walked behind the first row of chairs down to where Jessie sat, and stepped in front of her.

James was saying something, but when George appeared he stopped.

Jessie looked up. She moved her hands from her sons and daughter, took off her sunglasses, put them in her lap, and raised her arms to George. He took her tiny hands in both of his big ones and squatted down in front of her, next to James. Jessie's eyes never left his. She said nothing.

The boys turned and looked at George.

"Can I help?" George asked quietly. His question was directed to all of them, but his head stayed face-front, his eyes fixed on Jessie.

"We were deciding what to do," James whispered. "We wanted to see if Mom here wanted to change anything. Not that we had a real plan. We were just gonna talk a little, each of us say a little something, and then whoever else . . . you know, like I said before." He gestured with his hand toward the casket, where he'd been standing when Jessie appeared. "But we're having a little trouble here with Mom: she won't talk to us."

"George," Jessie said.

"Well, I'll be damned." James shook his head. "That's just about the first word she's said."

"Hello, Jessie," George said softly.

"Mom?" Amy asked.

Jessie's eyes stayed locked on George.

"Mother," Luke said, "there are lots of people waiting. Decide what you want to do."

"Leave her alone, Luke," Amy said.

Luke frowned. "Hey, Amy, just let the grown-ups handle this. Okay?" He turned back to Jessie. "Mother, what do you want to do? Huh?"

"Give her a minute, brother," James said.

Amy put her face up close to Jessie's. "Mommy?" she said.

Jessie stared at George. She gripped his fingers with her tiny cold ones. Her grasp was very strong; her short oval nails cut into George's flesh.

"Jess?" George asked, looking into her eyes. "Are you all right?"

"Mommy, please say something," Amy said, and started to cry.

"Oh, God, here we go." James sighed. "Amy, honey, please."

Callie touched Jessie's shoulder. "Mother, please, tell us what you want us to do."

"This is ridiculous," Luke snapped, his voice raised. "She wasn't supposed to be here anyway. Let's just do what we want."

"Hey. Watch your mouth," James said. "And keep it down, would you? We don't need everybody listening to this."

Callie put her hand on Luke's arm. "Give her a minute, Luke," she said gently.

Luke shrugged Callie's hand away. "Get your hands off me!" he said.

James turned. "What's going on, Luke?"

"Jessie?" George asked again, bending forward, searching Jessie's eyes. George looked at James. "Is she drugged?"

"Hell, I don't know. Nobody tells me anything. The goddamn cops wouldn't even tell me if she was coming."

Callie leaned in. "Jimmy, please, people are gonna hear you."

Luke whipped his head around to his sister-in-law. "Stay out of this, Callie. It's none of your business."

"I said watch your mouth, boy!" James snarled.

Luke looked at James, his face red. His fists were clenched. "Fuck you," he growled, and swung fast to the left on his haunches, crashing his knees into his brother's knees. James fell over in a heap on the sod.

"Jimmy!" Callie squealed.

"Don't you tell me what to do!" Luke said. "Don't you ever tell me what to do!"

"Jesus H. Christ!" James sputtered. "Have you lost your goddamn mind? Look where we are!" He put his hands behind his back to push himself up, but Luke shoved him hard in the chest. The shove was unexpected, and James fell backward again on the grass.

"I'm so sick of you with your big mouth and your big ideas and your big fucking attitude," Luke said.

Callie made a grab for Luke's arm to stop the punch that was about to connect with James's face.

"Get away from me," Luke said as he shook off Callie's hold. Callie teetered on her high heels and toppled softly next to James on the grass. James's mouth gaped. He reached for his wife. "What's the matter with you, Luke? What in God's name is the matter with you?"

"In God's name? Don't tell me about God's name! What's Mom doing here? What the hell's she doing here? *She blew him all to kingdom come!*"

Amy threw herself off the chair, slapping at Luke with both hands, knocking him over, her little body sprawled across his.

"Jesus! Amy!" James yelled.

White lightning flashed across the charcoal sky. Three claps of thunder echoed across the cemetery green, and it started to drizzle.

Everyone looked up.

Jessie tugged gently on the lapel of George's jacket. He turned to her.

"Oh, George," she said, punching him softly in the chest with her hand. "Oh, George . . . look what I did. I . . . I . . ." The trembling started in her rib cage but soon overtook her body. "I . . . I . . . I forgot to put on stockings!" She collapsed onto George's shoulder in a fit of hysterical giggles. He held her, her thin lovely body shaking with laughter.

"My God," George whispered. "My God, Jessie."

He spun around to her grown children, sprawled across the lawn. "Get up! Do you hear me? Get up now and finish this thing! It's enough!"

James struggled to his feet and helped Callie up. He brushed the back of his pants; there were grass stains that would never come out across the seat of his seersucker suit. Callie reached up to fix her husband's hair, but he pulled his head to the side, avoiding her touch. She straightened her skirt and the bit of white lace on her head. James lifted Amy off the ground and set her back in her chair. He looked at Luke, crumpled in the grass, and bent down, helping him to his feet. Luke slumped into a chair, sobbing. James gave Callie a look and she quickly sat down.

George grasped Jessie by her upper arms and gently pushed her back off his chest and into the chair. Her laughter had subsided. She heaved a deep sigh and grinned at George. He wiped her face softly. And then Jessie winked, a big exaggerated wink as if they shared a joke.

George stood.

Amy looked up at him, her eyes wide with fear. "It'll be okay, honey," George said, touching her hair. "It's all gonna be okay."

He squared his shoulders and moved to James. "All right, James?"

"Yes, sir."

"All right, then. Finish it before it pours."

George gave Jessie one last look and walked back to his seat. He kept his head down; he didn't want to connect eyes with anyone.

James moved to his place in front of Pete's casket. He mopped his face with the white handkerchief as he walked. He folded it slowly and was going to put it back inside his jacket pocket, but he forgot. The handkerchief stayed in his hand.

He raised his eyes and looked at the people. He had no idea how much they had seen or how much they had heard. He knew his face was flushed, he could feel that. He knew his tie was pulled too far to the left. He reached up and centered it with his left hand. He blinked a few times.

What a tribute, he thought.

Should I say something? Should I acknowledge what just happened?

He smiled at the assemblage.

Should I say I want to puke?

He shook his head a little.

We had a real one down here, Dad. Just like you would like. A humdinger.

James frowned.

Oh, wait a minute . . . they were gonna talk. I was gonna ask them all to talk . . . talk about Dad, wonderful Dad . . . or have we had enough? Was that display of family tradition just about enough?

Shit, James thought, they're waiting. C'mon, boy . . . think of what you want to do here.

He cleared his throat and spoke.

"Uh, Mom . . . Mom wants us to go on," he said. "Uh, she *wants* us to go on but, well, now it's raining." He looked up at the sky. "It's only drizzling but . . . so we're . . . we're just gonna. . . ." He rubbed his face with the folded handkerchief. The people waited. "Well, we'll just . . ." He looked at Callie; she lowered her eyes.

I'm in this thing alone, James thought.

His gaze drifted across Amy and Luke.

That's right. Don't anybody help me. After all, I'm the firstborn, right?

His eyes stopped on Jessie. She was watching him. Her chin was raised and her head was tilted slightly to the right. It was the same way she'd watched him the night he had his first date, the same way she'd watched him when he learned to ride his two-wheeler, the same way she'd watched him when he was five years old and played the second Wise Man in the Country Club Christian Church's Christmas pageant.

"We'll say the Lord's Prayer," James said.

Jessie smiled at her firstborn son.

It's enough, James thought. Let's finish it.

"That's right," James said out loud, taking a breath, setting his shoulders straight. "We'll say the Lord's Prayer, and then . . . then we'll all go home."

He bowed his head. "Our Father," James began.

"Who art in Heaven," the others followed.

"Hallowed be Thy name," they all said together. "Thy kingdom come."

The tears rolled openly down James's face. He made no attempt to wipe them with his handkerchief; he just let them fall.

Thy kingdom come, Dad, James thought, thy fucking kingdom come.

The sky moved, the sun came blasting out from behind a bank of black, and the rain abruptly stopped.

ANNE STOOD ALONE in the Mount Mariah parking lot. She gave a small wave at the back of Ellen's Chrysler wagon as it pulled out through the gates and onto the road. She couldn't tell if Ellen waved back; there was a glare across the rear window.

She'd convinced them all to go. "I'll wait for Jessie," she said. "I'll wait and go with her."

She had no idea where Jessie was going or why the car was waiting for her. She assumed it was going back to the Prairie Village police station. Where else could it be going?

It really doesn't matter. Jessie is my sister; it's my place to be with her. It's my place, Anne thought.

She stood a little ways across from the Mercury. She had been standing right next to it, but she leaned back a couple of times and her dress brushed up against the fender, so she moved. The car was filthy.

It was a four-door tan sedan and it was very plain. It wasn't that it was stripped of its chrome or anything like that; it just seemed plainer than other cars. Anne had no idea what year it was, but she knew it had definitely been driven a lot; it looked lived in. There was no writing on the doors and no light on top; there was nothing to suggest that it was a police car even if you were standing right next to it. Billy had said it was an unmarked car. He knew about things like that.

The woman behind the wheel smiled at Anne and took a sip of something out of a Styrofoam cup.

This morning's coffee, Anne thought. She's drinking this morning's cold leftover coffee. She's probably used to that; she probably never has the time to sit and finish it while it's hot.

The car was parked sideways on the asphalt, not flush inside the painted lines.

Because they were late, Anne thought. Of course, *they* can park any way they want; they don't have to park in the lines, do they?

She looked at the wheels of the car, at the deep grooves in the thick black tires.

Treads, they're called treads. Pete gave Jessie tires once for a present. Was it her birthday? Big fat snow tires wrapped in pink paper and tied with Christmas ribbons. Christmas, it was Christmas. Oh, God, why do I remember that?

Anne looked quickly away from the tires and back inside the car. The woman was sitting sideways behind the wheel, with the car door swung open and one leg out, her foot flat on the asphalt.

She needs new shoes, Anne thought. New summer shoes. She probably can't afford them on what she makes. The woman wore low-heeled white pumps that were clearly scuffed on the heels and toes and a simple yellow print shirtwaist dress with a self-belt. Anne discreetly looked her up and down.

Her stockings are too dark for that outfit. They're probably the ones you buy in the grocery, the ones that come in those plastic egg-shaped containers that they advertise all the time. Legs. That's what they're called. Only they spell it wrong, with two g's or two l's . . . something like that. They're cheap. They're for people who have to go through a lot of stockings. She probably runs stockings all the time, chasing people or whatever she has to do.

Anne studied the woman's face. She looks vaguely familiar. But that's impossible, I couldn't possibly know her; I've never met any policemen. How could I know her? Besides, she's younger than we are. Definitely. She's in her mid-thirties is all. I wonder if she has children. She looks like she does. She must. Little boys. She looks like she has two little boys. With dusty-blond hair and dirty faces. Snails and sails and puppy-dog tails . . . how does that go? . . . Puppy-dog tails, that's what little boys are made of.

Where do they go after school when she's out in this car being a policeman, her little boys? Maybe to their grandmother's. That's right. They go to their grandmother's, and when the mother comes to pick them up, the grandmother has the lights on and the dinner all ready, and they sit down together and eat and laugh and it's lovely.

Anne's eyes filled with tears.

I was married to Joe when I was in my thirties. Oh, Joe, where are you? Why aren't you here to pick me up and hold me?

She took a quick step forward as if it would shake off her thoughts of Joe and automatically brushed the back of her dress with one hand. She could feel the wrinkles already set in the navy linen, and her mother's disapproving face popped into her mind. She closed her eyes and tried to think of something else.

Frances's mother makes her that special breakfast whenever she comes home, doesn't she? Poached eggs on white bread toast with chocolate milk. Isn't that funny? Frances living in New York and being a famous actress now and all, and she still loves that silly breakfast, like a little girl.

I'm hungry. Oh, how can I be hungry at a time like this?

The woman turned and smiled at Anne.

She looks tired. She probably doesn't sleep well at night. She probably wakes up thinking about criminals or something. Oh, dear God, won't you please send Jessie down here now? I can't wait anymore. Please. I can't. I'm going to scream.

The woman leaned over and offered Anne a folded newspaper. "Would you like the paper?" she asked. "It's this morning's."

"No, thank you," Anne said.

The woman shook her head in agreement, as if she had just realized why Anne wouldn't want to read the paper.

Anne smiled at her. "I didn't mean to be staring at you; you just look a little familiar to me."

"I do?"

"Yes, isn't that funny? I mean, I'm sure I've never met you; I haven't lived here in years."

"It's my sister; you must have known my sister."

"Your sister?"

"Uh-huh. She's just a few years older than you are, I think. My sister graduated in fifty-seven."

"From Harrison?"

"Uh-huh. Sherry Glazer. I mean, Bumpas. It was Bumpas then and then it was Worrel and now it's Glazer."

"Sherry Bumpas? My goodness! Of course I remember your sister. I mean, I didn't know her personally. She was head cheer-leader; she was very popular."

The woman smiled at Anne. "Uh-huh. Now she's fat."

"Fat? Sherry Bumpas? I can't imagine. She was so petite; she was the tiniest little thing."

"Not anymore. Now she's enormous, a size twenty-four for sure."

"She couldn't be."

"Well, let's put it this way—she couldn't do a cheer now if her life depended on it," the woman said, laughing. "She has trouble getting out of a chair."

"Oh, dear," Anne said.

They looked at each other. The woman smiled at Anne. "Things change, don't they?"

"Well, yes," Anne said. "I guess so. Yes, they do."

"She's married to Nat Glazer now. Wasn't he in your class?"

"Nat? Nat Glazer? Why, he was in Jessie's. He and Pete and Tom were all dear friends, Billy, everybody. They used to spend practically every summer down at the lake on Nat's boat; he had a boat at Latawanna and we were always down there . . . well, I wasn't as much as they were, but—"

"Yeah, I know," the woman interrupted. "He told me. You know, when all this came up and I was put on the case, he told me, you know, that he knew your sister and how there were a bunch of you and all."

"A bunch of us . . . yes," Anne said. "I guess there were."

The woman smiled.

"Well, isn't this something," Anne said, looking at her. "So you're Sherry Bumpas's sister."

"Yes, ma'am, I am," she said, extending her hand to Anne. Anne shook it.

"Detective Barbie Lucas," the woman said, smiling. "Barbie Bumpas Lucas," she said, "but I'm divorced."

"Anne Bombara," Anne said, "Anne Connell Bombara. I'm divorced too."

"Small world, huh?" Detective Lucas said.

"Yes," Anne said. "Isn't it?"

They smiled at each other.

"And you became a policeman. Now isn't that interesting? What made you think of that?"

"Well, my pop was a policeman, a detective—he's retired now—and my uncle Leonard and my uncle Lawrence too."

"Well, it runs in your family, then, doesn't it?"

Detective Lucas laughed. "Yes, I guess it does." .

"But Sherry isn't a policeman, is she?"

"Just a mom, that's all she is."

"Just a mom," Anne said softly.

"You know," Detective Lucas said, "you could sit down here if you like." She patted the beige vinyl beside her.

"Oh. That's very kind of you. I would, but I think I'll just stand right here and wait. I mean, if that's okay with you."

"Of course," Detective Lucas said.

"Jessie's right up there. You see her, don't you?"

Anne pointed up the graded lawn and the woman's eyes followed in that direction. "Yes, I see her."

"Do you need me to go get her?"

"No, it's fine. Whenever she comes."

"She's just . . . you know. . . ."

"It's really fine," Detective Lucas said.

"Okay. Maybe I'll just walk around a little. Is that all right? Until she comes, I mean."

"Of course. Whatever," she said, and smiled at Anne again.

Anne turned and looked up the hill to where Jessie stood alone at Pete's grave. She had to squint to keep her eyes in focus; heat waves shimmered across her view. She lifted her hand to shield her eyes and watched her sister.

Jessie didn't move. Her back was perfectly straight in the pale-blue dress, her arms at her sides, her head bent.

I should go to her. No, she wouldn't want that. James said she wanted us all to go. Everybody. Even me. She's gonna be mad when she comes down and sees that I'm still here. But how could I go? Oh, God, is Frances right? Is that what we did? Left her all alone?

Anne raised her other hand, both hands now cupped over her eyebrows like the curved beak of a baseball cap.

I have to eat. If I don't eat something, I'm going to fall.

She let both hands drop down to cover her eyes.

I should go to her. For the life of me, I know I should go to her, but I can't. I'm afraid.

Anne lowered her hands and smiled sweetly at Detective Lucas.

"I'll just take a little walk until she's ready, just right around here."

"Fine," Detective Lucas said.

"You won't have to look for me or anything. I'll be right in this area."

"Okay," Detective Lucas said. "I'm just giving her a ride."

"What?" Anne asked. "What do you mean?"

Detective Lucas looked at Anne. She tilted her head a little to the right.

"I mean I'm giving her a ride to wherever she wants to go." She smiled at Anne. "And you too, of course."

"But . . . doesn't she have to go with you? Back to where she was . . . ?"

"No."

Anne frowned at the woman. "You mean she's been let go—what do you call it?—released . . . you mean she's been released?"

"Yes."

"You mean she's free?"

"Well." Detective Lucas exhaled softly and smiled again at Anne. "I'm sure she'll explain it all to you."

Anne looked at her. She turned and looked at Jessie up on the hill. Then she turned back.

"Please, Miss Lucas, when was she released?"

"Barbie. It's Barbie."

"Barbie, please tell me, how long has Jessie been released?"

"Well . . ."

"Are you not allowed to tell me?"

"No, I just think . . ."

"Is it because you're on duty?"

"No; I'm not on duty."

"I'm her sister, you know, her older sister . . ."

"Yes, I know; I just . . ."

"I love her," Anne said softly.

Detective Lucas took a little breath, caught her top lip between her teeth. She looked at Anne. "She's been released for a day . . . well, actually it's a day and a night and a day now."

Anne's mouth opened slightly. "But where has she been?"

"Well, she's been with me, at my apartment."

Anne stared at Detective Lucas. "With you?"

"She asked if she could stay until this morning, until the funeral. And I said fine."

"My God," Anne whispered.

"Well, she wanted to be by herself—she was adamant about not wanting to talk to anyone—and she was going to check into a hotel and I said she should stay with me. I felt that it would be better that she wasn't alone in some hotel."

"She didn't want you to call me?"

"No; she said she didn't want to talk to anyone until after the funeral."

Anne turned and looked at Jessie; she stared at her up on the hill. "My God," she said again. She kept her eyes on her sister as she spoke. "But how was she released?"

"Well, we presented the case to the DA, and he agreed with us and declined to prosecute."

Anne turned her head back to Barbie. "I don't understand."

"Well, it was clear from the evidence. We figured it would either be 'death by the hands of another by accident' or 'self-defense.' Like my pop said to me, this one won't take you long, honey—after all, it's a slam dunk, not a whodunit."

"A slam dunk," Anne repeated quietly.

"Well, we already knew who done it," Barbie said. "I'm sorry, I didn't mean to be crass. It was just cop talk, you know, between me and my pop."

"Of course, but I still don't . . ." Anne frowned at Barbie.

"The statement of Mrs. Ellen Scott. That, along with the nitrate residue on Mrs. Chickery's hands, the flash burns on Mr. Chickery's right hand plus his prints on the barrel of the weapon—we felt it was apparent."

Anne took a little breath and changed her weight to her left leg. She exhaled. "Uh-huh," she said.

Detective Lucas looked at her. "We feel it was self-defense."

"I don't understand," Anne said. "You mean you think Pete was trying to hurt Jessie?"

"It's clear that she was running from him, isn't it? Distraught, barefoot, naked except for a bathrobe? Running like that to Mrs. Scott's house?"

Anne stared at Detective Lucas. "But Pete wouldn't hurt Jessie; he loved her."

"His demeanor at the door changed from charming to angry, so angry he forced entry when Mrs. Scott refused to let him in. He broke through the kitchen door."

Anne squinted, the frown lines deepening between her eyes. "But Pete didn't have anything to hurt her with when he got to Ellen's house. . . . He didn't have a weapon, did he?"

Detective Lucas tilted her chin up a bit and looked Anne right in the eyes. "Male presence can be a weapon, Anne. Take it from me, I know."

JESSIE SAT DOWN on the pile of dirt heaped to the side of Pete's grave. She didn't sit directly on the dirt; the dirt was covered with thin mats of a bright-green material that looked like AstroTurf, and that's what she sat on.

The three men stood behind Jessie and watched. Deeter looked at his uncle Matt. He'd never heard of anybody sitting on the ground at a cemetery before, but he really didn't know anything about this stuff, he'd only been doing it for three days. Matt was watching the lady too. He had a small frown going on between his eyes, but he hadn't moved off of leaning on his shovel, so Deeter stayed put.

Deeter ran the back of his hand across his forehead.

Boy, if my friends knew I was digging graves . . . boy oh boy, would they go nuts. Well, I need the money for the truck and it's only for July and Matt made a whole big deal about what was the big deal anyway, after all, it was only shoveling dirt, wasn't it? And then askin' me if I was a sissy or what . . . hell.

Deeter stared at Matt again but Matt wouldn't catch his eye; he was watching the lady. Deeter turned back and watched her too.

She's good-lookin', that's for sure. Old. Older than Mom even, but still good-lookin'. Nice little body. Compact, Deeter thought. And pretty legs. Solid ones like I like.

And then he remembered what Ashley had done to him last night in his truck and he smiled and closed his eyes so he could remember better.

Jessie slipped off her shoes. She held one in each hand and moved her hands behind her on either side of her waist. She dropped the shoes, letting them fall one at a time down the little slope of dirt behind her.

The three men looked at each other. Deeter's uncle Matt pursed his lips together and shook his head back and forth. He shot Deeter a look and then shot the old black guy a look. Deeter watched. The old black guy'd been leaning up against a big oak, picking at his teeth, but when the lady dropped her shoes he stopped picking and chuckled. Deeter glued his eyes to the lady's back. Something about the whole thing was making him edgy.

I never shoulda said I'd do this, I shoulda gotten a job at Wendy's cookin' french fries or something. This shit's too spooky.

Jessie could feel the men watching. She knew they were waiting for her. Waiting for her word. That's what the tall one had said when she'd asked him if she could have a couple of minutes alone. "Sure thing, lady. Just let us know when you're ready, just give us the word."

Jessie ran the palms of her hands slowly across the shiny green needles of the AstroTurf. She stared down at the deep hole in front of her.

I wonder which word, Jessie thought.

* * *

THE BLACK STRETCH LIMOUSINE MOVED slowly into the right lane and up the on-ramp to I-435.

"Stop jiggling, sweetie," Callie said softly to Amy.

"Oh, sorry," Amy said.

It was the third time Callie had asked her. Amy was jiggling her foot against the seat and it made the whole seat shake. It was giving Callie a queasy feeling in her stomach.

"Thank you, sweetie," she said, and gave Amy a smile.

She opened her purse and took out her compact, looked at her face in the mirror and frowned. She adjusted the white lace on top of her head. She'd lost two bobby pins when Luke pushed her, and now she couldn't get it to stay on straight. She sighed, took out the remaining pin, lifted the lace off her head, folded it neatly, and slipped it into her purse. She fiddled with the wave of blond hair that fell over her right eyebrow.

Nobody can tell I'm older than Jimmy, can they? Nobody can tell I'm over thirty.

She squinted into the mirror.

This color is perfect. Armando was right; it's better more to the gold than to the ash.

She turned her head a little to the side, scrutinized her face in the glass.

It's amazing I didn't get hit. Goodness, the way these people behave. That whole thing on the grass was pathetic. And embarrassing. So embarrassing. Can you imagine a thing like that happening at a funeral in my family? My mother would up and die.

She glanced at James, in the seat beside her. He was folding his handkerchief into thirds.

Poor Jimmy. What a mess.

And then that business with Luke about where he was gonna sit.

Callie shifted her eyes from the mirror to the front seat of the limousine. Behind the glass partition were the backs of the driver and of her brother-in-law, Luke.

Sitting up there with the driver. What a thing! There was absolutely no reason for him to sit up there, with only three of us back here, but no, he had to make a fuss.

"Well, then, just sit there if you want!" James had yelled at his

brother. "Goddamn bullheaded cuss," he'd said to Callie as he
followed her into the back seat of the limo and slammed the door
himself, not waiting for the driver to shut it.

"We have lots of room back here," she said quietly to
James.

"There's no talking to him; there never was. That's why he only
talks to computers all day, he doesn't know how to talk to human
beings!"

"It's embarrassing for him to be up there with the driver instead of back here with us," she whispered. "What will people
think?"

"I said let it be, didn't I? Didn't you hear what I said?" His
voice was loud in the padded, upholstered car.

"I heard you, Jimmy. There's no need to address me in that
tone."

"I'll address you in any goddamn tone I want."

Callie settled herself back against the black leather. She took a
breath to compose herself.

"That's misdirected anger, Jimmy."

"Don't shrink me, Callie! *Goddamn it!*"

Callie pushed the wave back off her brow.

She would have gone on with it, but Amy was watching
them.

"Are you all right, sweetie?" she said now, patting Amy on the
arm.

"Sure. I'm fine," Amy said softly. "Thank you."

My goodness, Callie thought, what a mess this whole thing is.

"What a goddamn mess that was," James said, loud enough for
Luke to hear through the partition. "A goddamn stinking mess we
made of Dad's funeral, Luke!"

Callie looked at her husband.

"I better call the store as soon as we get to my mother's and
make sure those jerks aren't giving away more muffins than they're
selling," he muttered, "goddamn it."

"All right, sweetie, we'll call as soon as we get there."

She wiped at the raspberry lipstick in the corners of her mouth
with her finger, closed the compact, and put it back in her purse.
She gave Amy another little smile and put her hand on Jimmy's
arm.

Goodness, wait till my mother hears about this. She thought *our* family was bad.

BILLY CHECKED HIS REARVIEW MIRROR. Tom was right behind him. He shifted into third and changed lanes.

"Well, talk about drama," Tee went on. "All we needed was the fucking Philharmonic playing Mahler's Second. That's all that was missing."

"Tee," Billy said.

"Well, hell, they had a fistfight."

"It wasn't a fistfight."

"Okay. It wasn't a fistfight. What was it?"

"It was a scuffle. I don't know. A disagreement."

"A disagreement? Billy, they were shoving each other around all over the place."

"Honey," Billy said.

She sighed and looked out the window. "It was a circus," she said. Hot wet air whipped her hair across her face and into her mouth. She tugged it back and caught it behind her ears.

Billy looked at her. "Honey?"

"It should have started raining right then, you know? Right when Jessie appeared at the tree. That would have really been dramatic. Rain pouring down, thunder and lightning behind Jessie's back, and all the violins could have come in then. Men with violins in chairs strewn across the lawn—"

"Tee."

"—playing Mahler's Second."

"Tee!"

"Did you know that the chairs we just sat in are the exact same chairs you sit in at a garden party? Did you know that? The same identical white fold-out chairs. It's amazing. Think what a boon they've been for mankind. So practical. So useful. You can bury people in them, marry people in them—"

"Tee, let it be," he said firmly.

She leaned her head back against the red vinyl and blew her nose into his big checkered handkerchief. "Well, shit," she said. She sighed and looked out the window again. "Why doesn't it just pour already? What the hell's it waiting for?" She wadded the handkerchief into a ball and held it in her lap.

"Relax, Tee. Really, honey. Take it easy."

"Jessie looked nuts. You know that? Nuts. And I know from what nuts looks like. Don't I, Billy?"

"Tee, please."

"Well, I know from nuts." She sat quietly for a second and then turned to him. "So what's gonna happen now? Huh?"

"I don't know, baby. I know the same as you. We'll find out when we get there. Okay? We got plenty of time to find out everything. Now take it easy. I don't want to have to worry about you."

She glared at him. "What the hell does that mean?"

"Just what I said. I don't want to worry about you. Come on now, will ya?" He took his hand off the gearshift lever and patted her right leg above the knee. He kept his eyes on the road. "I love you. Okay?"

Tee didn't answer. She closed her eyes. She saw Jessie up against the tree. Jessie's black hair blending with the black of the sky, her face white and distinct against the darkness.

The orchestra could have been in a semicircle around her, Tee thought, around Jessie and the maple tree. In white jackets, of course, because it's summer. White dinner jackets and white chairs and Jessie's white face.

Billy looked at her. Her eyes were closed. "I kind of lost it when I saw the casket, didn't I?" he asked.

She didn't answer.

"Tee?"

Tee didn't move. She was listening to the orchestra in her head, watching Jessie and listening.

"Tee," Billy said again.

Summer. Summer and Jessie's white face. White roses in her black hair. White tulle, white lace . . . I hid behind the white stall door. "Hey, Frances, you stuck a pin in my head." "She didn't"—Anne, laughing. "Where?" "Hold still." "C'mon, ya'll"—Anita, from the door—"they're waitin' for us." "I can't go, there's a pin in my head." "Shut up"—Frances, laughing. "I got it, I got it." "Tuck the veil in there. . . ." Then Ellen's voice, in awe: "Oh, Jessie, look how beautiful you are—you look like the cover of a magazine." "Yeah, *Field and Stream*." "Oh, Jessie, I meant *Bride*." "She knows, silly; she was kidding." "Come on, Tee, we're going." "If ya'll don't hurry, Pete's gonna run out of this place." Frances, yelling: "C'mon, Tee, get the hell out of that toilet—we're walking down the aisle." "Let's go, you guys." "Come on, Tee"—Jessie, calling—"I won't get married without you." "Tee . . . come on, Tee . . . Tee . . ."

"*Tee! Hey, Tee!*" Billy yelled.

She turned, frowning. "*What?*"

"What the hell are you doing? I'm talking to you."

"I was thinking. Okay? Am I allowed to think?"

They stared at each other.

"C'mon, honey," Billy said, "that's enough. You know what Knelman said."

"Oh, fuck Knelman."

"It's not good for you, you know that."

"Well, that's great, Billy. That's just great. I won't think, then. No thinking and no remembering. I won't do anything, okay? I'll just sit here like a *goddamn stump! Okay?*"

"You stop this shit right now. I'm telling you, Tee. You just stop it."

"Why?"

"Because I said so, goddamn it!"

"Oh, great. Terrific, that's just terrific."

She glared at him. Her nose was pink. "Fuck you," she said.

"Tee, you're scaring me," Billy said softly.

Tee looked at his face and then slumped back against the seat.

Billy took a right up the on-ramp to I-435, and the hair behind Tee's left ear came loose when he picked up speed. It blew across her face and into her eyes but she made no move to fix it. Billy reached over, caught a handful of hair, and tucked it behind her left ear. Then he put his hand gently back down on her leg. "I love you, Tee," he said. "Okay?"

Tee looked at her husband. She looked into his eyes and then at his hand on her leg. "I ripped my stocking," she said. "I ripped my goddamn stocking."

Billy moved his hand gently across the torn nylon, tracing the rip with his finger. "It's okay, hon," he said. "Everything'll be okay."

After riding in silence like that for several minutes, she tentatively took her hand and placed it down on top of Billy's hand on her leg.

"So are Ellen and Tom still behind us?" she asked.

Billy checked the mirror. "Yep."

She smiled.

"Well, Pete would have loved this. First a circus and now a parade."

SITTING THERE on the pile of dirt, Jessie took off her sun-glasses, turned, and let them fall out of her hand and roll down the little hill behind her, after the shoes. She watched as they landed right side up next to the upside-down high heels. Then she raised her face and looked directly at the three men. The young one caught her eyes, but the other two looked away.

Jessie turned back, propped her elbows on her knees, dropped her chin into her hands, and looked down at the coffin in the hole.

There wasn't any dirt on top of it and there weren't any flowers. She didn't want flowers—that was the only request she had sent to James. No flower-dropping. She didn't care what else they did, but no flower-dropping. She remembered with dread how her father had insisted that each person at her mother's funeral throw a long-stemmed yellow rose down on the coffin. Every single person filed by and threw a rose as her father stood watching, and then when he threw his rose he nearly collapsed into the hole after it.

He would have pitched himself in if Anne and I hadn't had ahold of his arms, Jessie thought. I know it. Grady and Maurice had to practically carry him back to the car, he was so hysterical. Poor Daddy. Poor demented Daddy, how he loved that witch.

Jessie sighed and stared down at the coffin.

She remembered when it was her turn to throw a rose. She had looked down at the pile of yellow flowers heaped high on her mother's coffin and she had fought hard her urge to spit. A big fat glob of spit, Jessie thought, that's what I wanted to throw, not a rose. It was all I could do to stop myself, all I could do. If Pete hadn't squeezed my arm, reminding me that Daddy was there . . . hell, if Daddy hadn't been there I could have danced on her grave.

Jessie smiled down at the coffin top. Couldn't I have, Pete?

In Jessie's head, Pete smiled back.

She raised her head to the sun. The storm had moved. The bank of black clouds was hovering now in the north, and the day was very hot. Hot and thick and yellow. Bright butter yellow. Like the roses, Jessie thought. The fucking yellow roses.

She squeezed her eyes shut until the yellow turned to black. There. That's better.

ELLEN LEANED HER BODY FORWARD from the back seat and put her hand on Tom's shoulder as he drove. They were in Ellen's Chrysler station wagon.

"But what if there's nothing there? If I don't know anything about this and neither does Tee or Frances, then who's bringing the food?"

"I don't know, Ellen," Tom said.

"Well, I don't understand this," she said. "Everybody's starving. You can't have people without food."

She sat back in the seat and reached down to touch the bruise on her leg. It was throbbing. She patted it with her handkerchief. She thought about taking off her ruined panty hose but knew she couldn't possibly stick her bare feet into brand-new shoes.

"Can I put the radio on?" Stevie asked. He was up front with his father.

"No," Tom said.

"Why not?"

Tom looked at him.

Stevie shrugged his shoulders. "Sorry," he said.

"Nobody's had a thing since breakfast," Ellen said. She was looking through her purse for an aspirin. She'd dumped most of the contents onto her lap. She thought she had one of those little tin purse containers of Bayer, but she couldn't find it. Her hair was curling despite all the spray; she reached up and tried to smooth it. "Lord, it's hot," she said.

"Am I going with you guys?" Stevie asked his father.

"Yes."

"*I am?* How come?"

"To pay your respects," Tom said quietly.

"Oh," Stevie said.

"Don't you want to see Amy?"

"Yeah, sure I want to see her. But it's not like I haven't seen her. We've been together practically every day, you know, Mom, since this happened."

"I know."

"Well, I think you should go," Tom said.

"Okay. I was just asking. No big deal."

Tom looked at his son on the seat next to him; he didn't say anything.

"Goddamn, that was weird, wasn't it? The way Amy's mom just appeared out of nowhere like that? Wasn't it weird?"

"Don't say 'goddamn' like that," Tom said firmly.

"Sorry."

"What?" Ellen asked from the back.

"Nothing," Tom said.

"So what's gonna happen now?"

"What do you mean?" Tom looked at his son.

"Well, she's gonna have to go to trial, Dad. I mean, goddamn, she blew him away."

Tom's eyes flashed. "Jesus fucking Christ!" he yelled, and hit the steering wheel with his hand.

"What happened?" Ellen said, quickly sitting up and leaning forward. All the things on her lap fell to the floor. She saw her brand-new Sunset Coral lipstick roll under the front seat.

Stevie's face was pale.

"Watch your mouth, Steven. Do you hear me?"

"Yes, sir," Stevie said. "I'm sorry, Dad."

"What did he say?" Ellen asked.

"You're seventeen years old!"

"Yes, sir."

"You're going away to college in the fall!"

"Yes, sir."

"Then act like it, damn it!"

"What did you say?" Ellen asked Stevie.

"Is that the way you and your friends talk about this thing?"

"No, sir."

"That was one of my best friends. You know that, don't you? Since I'm seventeen years old; since I'm sixteen years old! Do you understand that?"

"Yes, sir."

"Your mother and I were sixteen years old once upon a time too, you know? We were young too, all of us."

Ellen touched Tom's shoulder. "Tom, please, what did he say?" she asked again. Her eyes were wide in her face as Tom looked at her in the rearview mirror. Her face . . . he could see her face the day they were married, his hands shaking as he lifted the veil, tears in her eyes. . . .

"When I married your mother, who do you think was standing next to me?"

"I know, Dad."

"Who do you think was *standing there right next to me, Steven?*"

Shaking so hard, my knees banging, wanting to bolt and run up the aisle, loving her but wanting to run, Pete right there in his white jacket, handing me the ring, looking at me, knowing, putting it in my hand, whispering, "Piece of cake, Tommy," smiling. "Piece of cake," he said. . . .

"*Who do you think, Steven?*"

"I'm sorry, Dad. I didn't mean anything, Dad. I just said it the wrong way."

"Tom," Ellen said.

"And when you were born? Huh? When you were born and when I bought the store and when—"

"Tom, please, what are you—" Ellen interrupted.

"*Who was there, Steven? Who?*"

"Uncle Pete, Dad. Please, Dad."

"*My whole damn fucking life, who do you . . .*"

"*Tom!*" Ellen said.

He pulled the car to the side of the road and stopped. His shoulders slumped and his forehead leaned against the steering wheel. The car idled. Ellen's fingers clutched the seat. Nobody moved for a long time.

"You think your life's there ahead of you. You think your whole life will always be there . . ." Tom mumbled into the steering wheel.

"Please, Dad, I'm sorry," Stevie said. "Goddamn—oh, shit— sorry . . . I'm sorry, sir, I'm sorry."

"Tom?" Ellen asked softly. "Honey?"

Tom picked his head up off the wheel. He rubbed his hand across his face. He sat there. Then he looked at his son. Slowly he reached out and touched Stevie's hair. He didn't ruffle it; he just touched it.

"Tom?" Ellen said again.

He didn't turn to look at her.

"I love you, son," he said softly to Stevie.

"Yes, sir. I know."

Tom sighed. "Good," he said. He shook his head. "That's good that you know."

He put his hands back on the wheel, shook his head again, and pulled the car out onto the interstate.

A sigh came out of Stevie.

"It's okay now," Tom said. "All right? It's okay."

"Okay," Stevie said.

Ellen took a deep breath and sat back in her seat. Then she reached down to retrieve the fallen items from the floor.

"Well, it's probably because everybody's starving," she said. "That's what it is. We all have low blood sugar. Nobody's had a thing since breakfast."

She was having a hard time getting the lipstick. Her fingers were on it but it was wedged in the seat-moving apparatus. By the time she did get it out, she had cut her finger. The lipstick was covered with dust and hair from the car floor, and her blouse had pulled out from her bending over so far. She tried to tuck the blouse back in and got a little blood from her finger on the waistband of her new outfit. She sucked on the finger, wrapped it with a hankie, pushed the blouse back in, and wiped the lipstick tube off as best she could with her last Kleenex. She was shaking and could feel sweat collecting under her breasts. She dropped the lipstick and everything else back in her purse, clicked it shut, took a deep breath, and looked out the window. She tried to put the nagging concern about food aside but she couldn't. She visualized all the people from the funeral milling around the kitchen with empty plates and glasses. She bit her lip and watched the back of Tom's head as he drove. She looked at the new gray hairs mixed in with the blond, a tiny scrape where the barber had clipped him too close, the suntan on the back of his neck. She loved him so much. She sighed and moved forward in her seat. She reached out her hand and placed her fingers ever so gently on her husband's shoulder.

"Tom? I really think we ought to stop, honey. We could go to that little place in Waldo where they make those hero sandwiches and—"

"Ellen, let's just go to the house, okay? If they need stuff, I'll go get it."

"But it's right on the way. I don't know why you're being so stubborn. I'll just pop out and—"

"*Ellen! Would you just let up with the goddamn food?*"

She connected eyes with him in the rearview mirror. There were little circles of pink high up on his cheekbones. She could not remember a time when he had spoken to her like this.

They stared at each other. Ellen could feel her son's eyes on her, waiting, listening for her answer, watching. . . .

"Ellen?" Tom said.

She didn't move. She could feel her teeth touching, the muscles of her jaws pulled up tight to her ears.

I have feelings too. Do they think I'm cold? Is that what they think? Is that what everyone thinks of me? That I'm some cold, distant woman who doesn't feel?

She slid back in the seat and held her body, her arms crossed under her breasts, her fingers spread against the ribs at her sides.

Nobody remembers it was me.

Taking Jessie out my front door, those two policemen putting her hands into those plastic bags, the handcuffs, her face all splattered with blood, her robe, her hair. I'm the one who had to see that. Doesn't anybody remember it was me?

Ellen bit at her bottom lip.

Taking me away in a squad car like a criminal.

Ellen closed her eyes.

"Ellen?" Tom said, watching.

Blood in my closet, Pete's blood all over my clothes.

I'm the one who saw that. It was me.

She shook her head slowly from side to side.

I want it to be right, that's all. I just want it to be right.

She released her bottom lip from between her teeth. She took a breath.

We can't bury Pete without food. Not Pete. He wouldn't have wanted that. I know.

Ellen smiled.

"You make the best fried chicken in the world now, Ellie. Even Grady can't make it this good. Why, we could put you in a competition."

Standing at my stove, a three-pronged fork in his hand.

"But you taught me how."

"I don't care who taught you what. You have far surpassed me, darlin'. You are now the fried-chicken champeen of the world. You hear me?"

Smiling as we slipped the pieces into the hot fat together, flour splattered across his nose, down the front of his shirt.

"You really are somethin', Ellie."

Kissing the tip of my nose.

Teaching me how to make his aunt Eula's rum balls at Christmas. Letting my babies roll them in the powdered sugar with their pudgy fingers, putting waxed paper down on the floor so they could do it on their knees, feeding them cookie dough, making them laugh.

"Now look here, Ellie, you can't put dark meat in this chicken à la king, that's the problem." Winking at me, the spoon at his lips. "Only the white meat, darlin', only the sweet young breasts."

"Cut that out, Pete, don't you start with me."

Pie dough and biscuits and mashed potatoes and tomato sandwiches . . . how to cut the bread the exact same round of the tomato . . . Pete taught me. And johnnycakes and beer muffins . . . and mint juleps. I can make a mint julep that's perfection. Me—Ellen. The best julep this side of the Mississippi, he said.

She felt the warmth of her skin under her breasts, her thumbs tucked up into the folds. . . .

A julep that's really somethin' . . .

Ellen shook her head softly and started to cry.

I just want it to be right. Don't they understand that?

Tom watched his wife in the rearview mirror.

He turned to Stevie. "Turn on the radio."

"But, Dad, you just said . . ."

"I know what I said! Turn it on!"

Ellen looked down at the purse in her lap. She put her fingers on the black patent leather, picked them up and put them down, watching the iridescent sweat marks come and go. She made a circle pattern of six fingerprints on the patent leather and watched them disappear. Then she placed her finger down once more and made a last mark in the center of the circle.

Oh, Pete, she thought, nobody knows I'm something. Nobody knows but you.

When the last print faded, Ellen lifted her head.

"There won't be a thing there to eat," she said softly, wiping the tears off her cheek with her hand. "Not a thing, you mark my words."

JESSIE SAT MOTIONLESS by the side of the grave and listened to the quiet. There had been a high whine of an electric power mower for a while, but it had stopped, and now there was nothing but the rustle of leaves as hot air blew in from the west and moved across the grass.

She closed her eyes and concentrated on the sun searing the skin on her arms and legs, scorching the hair on the top of her head. Bake me, she thought. Bake me brown.

She moved a little under the sun's rays and adjusted herself, extending her arms out to the sides of her body like a teenager determined to get an even tan.

Brown. Flat and brown and crispy on a silver tray. A cut-out cookie in a Jessie shape. Raisins for eyes, sugar on top. Grady can carry me out with the lemonade. Carry me out and away.

No. Wait. She can hide me. Oh, that's better. She can hide me in the cookie jar and they won't know where I am.

Jessie smiled at the thought of herself being broken into bits as Grady slammed shut the lid of her mother's porcelain cookie jar. She saw Grady stand guard in front of the cookie jar, fold her arms across her big breasts, and stare down at Jessie's five best friends as they raced into the kitchen. "Well, I ain't seen her," Grady said. "She ain't in here! She went thataway!"—pointing her fat brown finger in the direction of the garden.

That's right. You tell 'em, Grady.

In Jessie's daydream she saw the backs of the five little girls run out of the kitchen into the backyard, the screen door banging loud behind them. Grady moved to the cookie jar, raised the lid, and winked at Jessie inside.

Good, Grady. We fooled 'em.

Jessie sat very still, baking in the sun. She didn't flinch and she didn't move. She was motionless.

Anyway, even if they found me I'd be crumbs. That would fix them. They couldn't talk to a pile of crumbs. Right? Of course not. Imagine.

In her mind, her five best friends circled a pile of chopped brown cookie crumbs, only this time they weren't little girls anymore, they were grown-up women.

"Oh, tell us, Jessie," Ellen pleaded. "Tell us what he did."

"What'd the bastard do now?" Tee demanded.

Frances searched her face. "What happened, sweetheart?"

"He was never any good. I told you that," Anita said. "I told you."

"Tell us what happened," Anne asked quietly. "Tell us, Jessie."

Tell us, tell us . . . Well, I don't have to tell you anything. You're not my friends anymore.

She squeezed her closed eyes tighter, the sun painting the insides of her eyelids red-orange.

I saw all of you today, don't think I didn't see you, the five of you with your stupid sad hawk eyes staring at me, wanting to know, waiting.

She didn't move, but the slightest frown line appeared in the space between her eyes.

Best friends . . . not anymore . . .

Her body moved. It was ever so slight, but if you were standing close to her you would have seen that her body had moved, her concentration had been broken. Her arms lowered a bit from their position. Her shoulders sagged.

She moved her hand to her hair and fiddled with it.

I'll think about something else.

She wrapped a curl around one finger.

Okay, okay, okay.

She bit the inside of her cheek.

Think about something else. Something pleasant. Something lovely, something absolutely lovely.

She moved her bottom a little on the AstroTurf.

Her face relaxed and she smiled.

The babies! I'll think about my babies . . . when they were little. Little and sweet, smelling like heaven, soft and warm . . . James's little pudgy legs so dear, and Luke, my darling Luke, looking just like Pete . . . from the moment he came out, scowling just like Pete . . . his face just like Pete's.

She frowned and shook her head fast.

No, don't think about that! Something else, find something . . .

No! I don't smell Shalimar! There's no Shalimar here; I'm

outside. There's only trees, trees and flowers and grass. Come on, smell the grass, smell the nice fresh grass. . . .

Tears started to run down her face. Soft, glistening tears, one at a time, ran slowly down her cheeks.

Oh, Jesus, please help me.

Her fingertips covered her eyes, her face fell softly into her hands, and sobs shook her shoulders.

No! It hurts my head! Please, no. Don't make me hear the sound. Don't make me see the blood. Oh, Jesus . . . oh, God . . . please help me.

Oh, Pete . . . Pete, look at your face . . .

"No," Jessie said out loud. "Pete! What's happened to your face?"

"*No!*" she yelled, her voice ringing loud with fear, ringing out across the green of Mount Mariah. "*Pete!*"

THE DARK-BLUE RENTED PONTIAC PASSED Ellen's Chrysler wagon, parked on the shoulder, but George didn't notice; his focus was on Frances. She was laughing as she spoke.

"Can you believe I forgot? I forgot the whole thing until you started, and now it's all coming back . . . isn't that crazy? Where were we anyhow?"

"I don't know. I don't think I could ever find it again."

"I remember the car sinking, I do remember that. And the mud and the guy with the tractor—I think I remember him. Didn't he say not to come back or—"

"No, no; he said, 'Hell of a place to park with your girlfriend, kid. I don't think you'll be doin' this again.' "

"Oh, George"—Frances laughed—"I do remember. He had on coveralls and a farmer's hat . . ."

George laughed. "Yeah, straw . . ."

"God," Frances said.

George looked at her. "It was spring," he said, "or maybe it was fall, but we were having an Indian summer kind of day . . . fifty-eight or fifty-nine . . . it was a Sunday; I picked you up right after church."

"Oh, George . . . church," Frances said.

"That's right . . . it must have been twelve-thirty, one o'clock, I would guess. It had rained for a day or two but that day it hadn't rained, it was beautiful, and we ended up driving way out south and into this wooded area that suddenly opened onto a track with a grandstand and a railing. What it probably was was a quarter horse racetrack. And there was no one around; it was completely empty . . . deserted."

Frances sat motionless, watching George's face as he recounted the story, the look in his eyes.

"The grandstand was green, the railings were white, and the sun was coming through the trees . . . dappled sunlight. It was incredible, I remember . . . like a sylvan glade. Suddenly it just opened up and there it was right out of nowhere. I must have gotten out of the car to open the gate to the track and I must have said let's see how fast we can go around or something. We got in and I started driving as fast as I could . . . but it was so muddy that as we drove we sunk up to the floorboards of the car, the wheels were encased in mud, and—" He began to laugh.

"You had to go out the window. I remember."

"That's right. I had to climb out the window to find help and when I stepped into the mud I lost my shoe, it just got sucked up off my foot by the mud."

"Weejuns, you had on Weejuns. . . ."

"Sure," George said, laughing. "*Of course . . . Weejuns.*"

"And you found the guy with the tractor," Frances said.

"Yeah . . . with the overalls, the coveralls . . . God, Frances—"

"Why were we there in the first place?" she interrupted.

He looked at her and smiled.

"I don't know . . . just screwing around together on a Sunday afternoon, looking for a place to make out. Seems like yesterday, doesn't it?"

"Yesterday," Frances repeated softly, and smiled.

Then she wrapped her arms around herself and moved ever so slightly on the seat. George immediately turned the air conditioner down a notch and moved one of the jets so it didn't blow directly on her. "Too much air?" he asked.

"Just a bit."

Frances sat up straighter and flipped the visor down to look at herself in the mirror.

He can still read me, she thought. All these years and he can still tell what makes me move. Jesus God . . .

"Still cold?" George asked, breaking her train of thought.

She flipped the visor back up and looked at him.

"No. I'm fine. Thanks."

"You're welcome," he said. "I'm glad you came with me, Frances. I'm glad you let your folks take home the other car."

Frances smiled at him. "I'm glad too. George?" she said.

"Yeah?"

"It's a beautiful memory."

"Yeah, it is nice, isn't it?"

They looked at each other. They didn't say anything for a minute or two. Then Frances said softly, "Why won't you tell me what happened back there? Was there something wrong with Jessie?"

"I think they gave her something, but I don't know." He looked at Frances. "I don't know, baby. Really. It was just a little nuts, everybody was just a little off their . . . hell, I don't know. We'll find out soon enough, right?" He gave her a little smile. "Right?"

She sighed. "Okay," she said. "You don't know anything else, do you?"

"What do you mean?"

"I mean about what's gonna happen to Jessie. You don't know anything, do you?"

"No."

"You'd tell me if you did, wouldn't you?"

"Of course I would, Frances." He looked at her. "Okay?" he asked.

"Okay." She peered out the window, watched the land flying past. "Look at all that corn."

"Yeah. Looks great, doesn't it?"

"It doesn't taste the same in New York, you know . . . corn, I mean. Not tomatoes either. At least not to me."

George smiled. "Your mom grow 'em behind the new house?"

Frances smiled back. "Sure. You can pick one when we go . . . when you take me home."

"Great. Just like the old days."

"Right," Frances said. "Just like the old days."

She took a deep breath. "George, when did you talk to Pete last?"

He frowned before he spoke. "Oh, not for a while. Maybe two, three months . . . No, wait . . . he called me on my birthday. That's right. I forgot."

"He did?"

George laughed. "Yeah. The bastard woke me up in the middle of the night to remind me I was older than him."

Frances laughed. "That sounds like Pete."

"Yeah. So how about you?"

"What?"

"When did you talk to him last?"

"Oh. About a week before. Not quite a week . . ."

"And how did he sound?"

"The same. You know. Like always, like Pete. I don't know." She shrugged her shoulders. "Happy, joking . . ."

"Right."

They rode a little ways.

"I'm glad it's over," Frances said. George looked at her. "The funeral, I mean."

"Oh, yeah," he said. He shook his head slightly and ran his hand through his hair.

She knew he wasn't going to tell her what had happened with Jessie and the boys. She had asked him repeatedly since they left the cemetery, and it was clear he wasn't going to discuss it, so she didn't ask again.

George loosened his tie and unbuttoned the top button of his shirt. It was beautiful; soft cream linen. He had hung the suit jacket on a hanger from a hook in the back seat. Only George would have thought to put a hanger in the back seat of a rental car so he could hang up his coat. It was so . . . so *George*. She smiled and watched his profile as he drove. How close he had shaved without making a nick, the soft brown hairs at the top of his chest where he'd opened his shirt, his long lashes, his hands on the wheel . . . Frances realized with a start that she knew what those hands felt like on her body.

George turned and looked at her. She felt as if he'd caught her stealing. She laughed.

"What?" he said.

"You look the same."

"Oh, sure."

"No, really, George, you do. I mean it."

"Thanks, Frances." He smiled at her. "*You* don't look the same."

"Oh, really? Well, thanks a lot."

"You're more beautiful."

She unconsciously touched her neck with her hand.

George laughed softly. "Have I embarrassed you with the truth?"

"No, of course not; don't be silly."

"You're blushing."

"I am not."

"Yes you are."

Frances laughed. "Oh, stop it, George."

"I can't help it if you're beautiful."

"I'm not beautiful. I never was."

"Okay. What are you?"

"Attractive. I'm an attractive woman."

"You're beautiful, Frances. But different somehow; it must be the work or something. I can't put my finger on it, but you look more complete somehow, more full . . ."

She jabbed him gently on his upper arm with her fist. "Hey! Are you saying I look chubby?"

"I'm saying you look better than you ever looked, baby. I don't know what it is . . . somehow you've come into your own."

"Oh, George," she said, smiling, "what am I going to do with you?"

"I don't know. I'm certainly open to any and all suggestions."

Frances turned her head away and watched the fields race past her window. Well, I'm certainly not complete, she thought. There's a piece of me missing.

She closed her eyes for a second and took a breath.

Why can't I just tell him? This is ridiculous. We were married for years.

George, I have something to tell you.

George, I've had a mastectomy.

George, I've lost my breast.

Pete's face flashed into Frances's head. He grinned at her. "It was here a minute ago," Pete said in Frances's head. Frances laughed out loud.

"What?" George said.

"Nothing," she said quickly.

They rode in silence.

Tell him, Frances thought. Just tell him.

"So," he said, "uh, how's Jeremy?"

"What?"

"Jeremy. How is he?"

"Fine. And Livvy?"

"Fine."

"That's good," Frances said. She smiled at him. George smiled back and then they both started to laugh.

"God, this is strange," Frances said.

"It sure as hell is."

"I feel so . . . I don't know, it must be 'cause we're home, riding in the car, being together. I feel like we're still . . . like nothing's changed, like we don't have other lives, like . . ."

George reached over and touched her face with his hand.

"Like we're still together," he said.

Frances closed her eyes and shook her head. "Yes," she said. "Were you reading my mind?"

"I used to," he said. He moved his fingers down her cheek and cupped her chin in his hand. Frances took a breath but didn't move. He traced the outline of her lips with his thumb.

"I remember," she said softly.

George put his hand back on the wheel. "What do you say we stop and have a drink?"

"Now?"

"Yeah."

"But we're supposed to be—"

"C'mon, Frances, I could use a drink." He looked at her.

She made a feeble gesture at the cars in front of and behind them. "But Tee and—"

"C'mon, baby," he interrupted. "Pete wouldn't mind. Let's go have a drink together."

He reached out and touched her hair softly, pushing a curl back off her forehead. His fingers trailed softly against her throat as he moved his hand back to the wheel.

"Okay?" he asked.

Frances was suddenly aware of the skin all over her body. She looked at George. "Okay," she whispered.

She flipped the visor down again and checked her face in the mirror.

Why am I making such a big deal out of this? I'll have a drink and then I'll tell him. And that will be that.

She turned and looked at George. He smiled at her and hit his turn signal. The Pontiac moved into the right lane and took the State Line off-ramp from I-435.

"GET UP, PETE!" Jessie yelled, and the three men raised their heads. "I said *get up!*"

Deeter's uncle Matt let his shovel fall and held his hand out at his nephew like a traffic cop. "Stay put, boy," he said to Deeter, and took off in long strides across the lawn toward the lady. "Jedediah," he said, and the big black man was instantly a step behind him.

Jessie scrambled to her feet on the AstroTurf. She looked down. "I said get up! What's the matter with you?"

Deeter stood with his mouth wide open. The lady had put her hands on her hips and was yelling down into the open grave.

"Don't try to fool with me. I know you're faking. I know what a liar you are! Get up, goddamn it!"

Deeter's uncle Matt reached the mound of dirt and hesitated for just a second. Jedediah stopped beside him and put his hand on the white man's arm. "Jes watch yourself here, Matt," he said. "We done got ourselves a lulu."

"Hey, lady," Matt called out.

"*Get up out of there, I said.* Get out of all that blood. I know you're lying. Take off that stupid mask—I know that's not your face!"

Matt and Jedediah took one step together up the pile of dirt. Matt held his hand out to the lady. "Hey, lady," he said gently, "come on down here with us."

"You just won't stop, will you?" Jessie yelled into the grave. "You just won't ever stop! Why won't you let me be!"

She stomped her bare feet on the AstroTurf like a two-year-old in the middle of a tantrum. The thin green mat moved, and a small avalanche of dirt gave way under her and rolled down the little hill into the grave. It thudded loudly as it bounced around on the lid of Pete's coffin.

The two men reached Jessie just as she lost her balance and began to fall with the earth.

"He just wouldn't let me be," she sobbed into the chest of the old black man as he scooped her up in his big arms. "He just wouldn't," Jessie sobbed, looking up into his handsome face.

"No, ma'am," Jedediah said gently back to Jessie, "I surely knows he wouldn't."

"I WONDER WHERE they're going?" Leonard said, watching George's Pontiac exit the highway at State Line. He accelerated the Mercedes and it passed the eighteen-wheeler in more than enough time.

What a spectacular piece of machinery, he thought. He turned and looked at his wife. She mumbled something and moved the beads around in her hands.

"Honey? Are you all right?"

She looked at him. "What?"

"I asked if you were all right."

Anita poured the beads from one hand to the other, as if they were sand. She shook her head. "I was thinkin' about Daddy."

"Oh."

"Pete looked like him but for the hair. Have I told you about that? About Daddy's fire-orange hair?"

Leonard smiled at her. "Just like Mary's, right?"

"I've told you."

"Just a few times," he said gently.

She frowned and looked back at the beads in her hand.

"Do you want to do this?" he asked.

"What?"

"Go there. I mean, we don't have to, you know. We can go home and you can lie down. I'll call if you want and say we'll be over later. You can rest. What do you say?"

"No. I want to go." She twisted the beads around her fingers, looping them over and under like a child making a cat's cradle.

"What a sham it all was, wasn't it, Leonard?"

"No it wasn't, Anita."

"Yes it was. A horrible sham. There was somethin' goin' on up there with the children, wasn't there?"

"I couldn't tell."

"There was. I know there was. You can tell me."

"Anita, I couldn't see what was going on. You know that. I was right next to you."

"Okay, you don't have to go on at me."

"Well, you said I—"

"Okay, Leonard. Okay!"

Her lips were pinched and white with anger.

She held the beads in the palms of her hands on her lap and looked out the window.

"You think I'm a bad mother, don't you, Leonard?"

"What in the world are you talking about, Anita?"

"I'm talkin' about tellin' my girls not to come home for this funeral. You think that was bad, don't you?"

"No. I don't think it was bad. It was what you thought was right, and after all, the girls are certainly old enough to decide for themselves. I mean, if they had really wanted to come, they—"

"But you think it was wrong, don't you?"

"I didn't say that, honey."

"But you do." She looked at him. "I didn't want them here. Do you understand? I didn't want them all mixed up in this dirty affair. I didn't want them to see all this . . . this horror."

"It's okay, Anita."

She wrapped the beads around one wrist, pulling them tight with her other hand. Her wrist was white where the beads were tightening. "He didn't care about them anyway. He didn't care about my girls. He didn't care about anybody but himself. Never."

"Please, honey. It's okay."

She unwrapped the beads from her wrist and let them fall into her lap. "It should have been in a church."

"It was fine."

"No. It wasn't fine. You don't know. It wasn't fine at all. It was outside and without a priest. It should have been in a church, the right way, not like that, not with nothin'. Even though that's all he deserved, it should have been right."

"But he wouldn't have wanted a—"

"I know what my brother wouldn't have wanted, Leonard. I know very well."

"All right, honey," he said.

She put the rosary beads back in their satin envelope and slipped them into her purse. She closed the purse and placed it on the seat beside her, then folded her hands in her lap.

"I remember everythin'," she said.

"Okay," he said.

"Every single thing, every single word. It's all burned into my brain. All of it."

"I know, Anita," Leonard said. "I know, honey."

She looked at her hands.

"What's goin' to happen to Jessie?"

"I don't know, Anita."

Anita turned and looked at Leonard. "She loved him, you know. She always loved him. Always."

"I know. You told me."

She stretched her fingers out in front of her. "I'm glad my mother's not alive," she said. "Lord forgive me."

Leonard passed Billy's blue Ford pickup, his fingers sliding easily around the polished wheel, the big Mercedes gliding in silence past the little Ford truck. Billy gave him a wave as they passed.

Leonard looked at Anita. "There's your friends, honey," he said. Anita didn't answer. She was staring at her fingers.

"He killed her, you know. With his dirty words and his dirty deeds. He killed my mother. He broke her heart."

"Anita, are you sure you want to do this?"

She clasped her hands together and dropped them back down into her lap. She looked straight ahead without answering him.

Leonard looked out at the moving sky and then back at his wife. "Boy, I sure wish it would rain already. Maybe if it poured, it would cool things off. You think?"

Anita turned. Her eyes flashed green out of a white face. "I should have shot him myself years ago," she said. "I could have saved Jessie all the trouble."

"EXCUSE ME, MA'AM," a voice said from behind Anne.

She was standing in front of the baby part of the cemetery. She'd been standing there for quite some time, standing perfectly still after she'd wandered upon it, stunned that she had forgotten it was there, stunned that she had blocked that it was there, so she wouldn't have to remember. She hadn't gone in after finding it, but she hadn't gone away either. She'd just stood there, her fingers perched gently on the rough white wood of the little fence, her mind running back and forth until she could see Pete and herself in among those small headstones, remembering that day and everything about it and trying to assimilate that with everything Barbie Lucas had said.

She frowned and shook her head.

I can't believe that Pete would hurt Jessie, he wouldn't, he wasn't that kind of man. . . .

And he loved her, he adored her.

She squinted at the headstones in front of her.

He was dear . . . and kind . . .

Anne took one hand off the fence and dabbed at the moisture on her upper lip.

They're only policemen. They could be wrong, couldn't they? How do they know?

"Excuse me, miss?"

But she wouldn't have hurt him either. Not on purpose. No matter what.

She cocked her head to the right.

They're wrong. I don't care if they're policemen. It was an accident. What did she say? Death from another person's hands by accident? Is that what she said? That's what it was. A tragic, horrible accident.

"*Hey! Lady!*"

Anne turned. A boy stood a few feet back from her. A teenage boy. Sixteen, seventeen . . . with scruffy beige hair curling up around his ears, dirty blue jeans with slashes and cuts across the legs, a white round-neck T-shirt stained under the arms, and big brown work boots with thick laces and ugly crepe soles.

Anne looked at him. She looked to either side of her to see whom he was talking to.

He held his ground.

"I'm sorry. Me?" she asked. "Were you speaking to me?"

"Yes, ma'am." He frowned and looked at the ground. "I'm supposed to come get you 'cause they brought the lady down."

"Down?" Anne said. "What do you mean, down?"

He looked at her and frowned again, lowering his eyes.

"Well, she . . . you know . . . she got a little nuts. I guess . . ." He sucked his lower lip up under his top teeth on one side, blinked a few times, and then released the lip. "I guess it kinda got to her."

Anne's eyes widened as she took a step toward him. Her hands flew to her chest. "What? What do you mean?"

"Hey, don't have a fit or nothing. She's okay now. My uncle Matt's got her, and he knows all about this stuff."

Anne couldn't imagine who this boy was, or what possibly could have happened; the only thing she did know was that she didn't think she could bear it.

"Thank you," she said politely to the boy, and, lifting the stiff linen skirt of her dress, broke into a ladylike run.

The Wake

IT WAS NEARLY THREE O'CLOCK. The whistle on the kettle had been screaming for several minutes, but Jessie made no attempt to get up. She sat on the ottoman of her father's club chair, tracing a crack in the caramel leather with her finger. The shutters were tilted to stop the sun's glare, the windows shut tight against the heat. White muslin sheeting covered all the furniture except where she sat.

High heels clicked on a hardwood floor, and the kettle whistle screeched to a stop.

Jessie slid her body off the ottoman and onto the chair. She burrowed her back deep against the cushions and laid her arms down along the cold leather. Then she turned her head and pushed her face into the back pillow, smashed her nose against it, and breathed in and out, long deep breaths, inhaling the chair.

"What are you doing?" Anne said.

Jessie looked up. Anne stood in front of her. Two little up-and-down frown lines pinched above Anne's nose. She had a flowered cup and saucer in each hand and she held one out to Jessie.

Jessie stared at the lines above her sister's nose.

"Jess? What are you doing?"

"I was smelling Daddy."

"Oh." Anne raised her chin slightly. "I see."

"Don't say 'I see' to me."

"Okay."

"Don't patronize me, goddamn it." Jessie blew air out of her mouth. "Goddamn it," she said again, and slapped the chair arms with her hands.

Anne bit her lip. "I'm sorry. Are you all right?"

Jessie sighed.

"Are you speaking to me now?" Anne asked, and held the cup out farther.

Jessie shook her head back and forth.

"You're not speaking to me or you don't want tea?"

Jessie rubbed her hands along the arms of the chair. She didn't look up. "What difference does it make?"

"Which?"

"I don't know. Shit. Any of it."

Anne put one of the cups down on a side table next to the chair, lifted the muslin off the couch, and sat down across from Jessie, the den windows behind her head. She took a tentative sip from the cup she still held. The sip was loud; it was the only sound in the room except for the air-conditioning hum. She turned and looked out the windows, stared for a minute at the real estate sign on their parents' front lawn, then lowered the cup back into the saucer and set it on the table in front of her.

Anne sighed. She waited. Jessie didn't move. Anne looked out the window again, stared at the FOR SALE sign.

"Do you think we'll sell the house? With these people, I mean . . . do you think they'll be better? Pete said—"

Jessie looked up quickly. Her eyes flashed.

Anne stopped midsentence, closed her mouth. Jessie turned her head away. Anne looked at the teacup on the table. Then she looked at the bookcases in the corner, the rows of their father's books, the embossed leather bindings.

"I love this room. The books, the ivy-leaf fabric, all the green . . . I don't know, it's old-fashioned but I love it."

Jessie exhaled.

"Hmm?" Anne asked, leaning forward in anticipation of Jessie's reply, but Jessie said nothing.

Anne sat back. "It would break my heart to change it. I mean, re-cover the furniture or anything. I couldn't stand to see that.

Maybe we ought to just sell all the furniture with the house. Except what you want, of course, or what Grady wants; I don't care." She looked around the room. "What do you think?"

Jessie didn't move.

"We could do that, couldn't we? I mean, I'd rather just see it all go at once rather than change any of it—in my head, I mean. Do you think that's silly? Jess?"

Anne patted a pillow, ran her finger along the soft green fringe at the edge. She moved the pillow into her lap, pushed her finger back and forth on the fringe. "Remember moving your finger back and forth on Mother's mink coat? Making the fur move, the nap of the fur with your finger? When you had to sit next to her at church. Hmm? Jess? Remember?"

Jessie reached up and brushed at some hair at the back of her neck. She didn't look at Anne.

Anne put the pillow back carefully in the corner of the couch, punched it so it stood straight up against the arm of the couch, like a picture in a magazine—perfect, like everything in their mother's house. She looked at the pillow, sat back, folded her hands in her lap, and looked at her sister. "Mother's fur coat was the only thing soft about Mother, wasn't it? I mean, that's really the truth, isn't it? No matter how I wish it weren't, that really is the truth. How she smelled soft . . . but she wasn't. It was all a lie."

Jessie looked at Anne and then turned her head away.

"God. What a stupid thing for me to be talking about," Anne said. She leaned forward and reached out her hand, nearly touching Jessie's knee. "I don't know what to say to you. That's what it is, that's why I'm talking about Mother. I'm just sitting here babbling because I don't know what to say. Aren't you going to talk to me? Aren't you going to tell me anything?"

Jessie didn't look at Anne.

"Please, Jess. You have to talk to me. I know you've been released. She told me—the policeman, Barbie—she told me."

Jessie turned her body away from Anne.

"Why are we at Mother's? Don't you want to go home and see your children? Jessie, please. I don't know what to do, I don't know what's happening. Jess?" She touched Jessie's knee with her fingers.

Jessie turned and looked Anne right in the eyes. "I hate tea. Do you understand? I hate tea and I hate this house and everything in it. All the furniture, including that stupid couch you're sitting on and those pillows and everything. It all reeks of Mother and her awful face, do you understand? I only want this chair. Daddy's chair and his ottoman. I want it for James. That's all I want. Okay?"

Anne blinked, her mouth open, her lips apart.

"Okay?" Jessie asked again.

"Okay," Anne said quietly.

"Good." Jessie nodded her head, turned away from Anne, and looked out the windows.

Anne took a breath. "I didn't know you hated tea."

"Well, now you know."

"I didn't remember."

"It's okay."

"I just didn't remember. I'm sorry."

"You don't have to be sorry."

"But I am."

"Anne, stop it."

Anne moved forward, her arms extended to take Jessie around the waist, her head forward to lean against Jessie's. "I'm sorry, Jessie, I'm so terribly, terribly sorry."

Jessie stood up fast, leaving Anne on her knees in front of the club chair, in front of her standing sister.

"I don't want to talk about it."

She turned abruptly and walked out of the den.

"But, Jess," Anne called, "we should go to your house. No one knows where we are."

"Good," Jessie said, as she ran up the stairs. "Why don't you go there with them? I don't need anybody here with me."

PETE AND JESSIE'S HOUSE WAS PACKED with people. They were everywhere. Moving in and out the front door, sitting on the steps out front, standing in the driveway, under the weeping willow, even on Steve Lonza's new zoysia grass next door.

Tom drove past the house, down to the corner, and made a right to go around again; he'd already circled three times. He looked at Ellen in his rearview mirror. She had her eyes averted to somewhere in her lap. She hadn't looked at him or said a word since the scene in the car.

"Why don't we just go home and walk back?" Stevie said.

"What?"

Stevie gave his father one of those looks that kids give their parents when their parents are being morons. "You know, Dad, park at our house and walk back . . . you know? It's only like fifteen blocks." Tom glared hard into the rearview mirror, but Ellen wouldn't look at him.

"Ellen?" he said.

She didn't answer.

"You want to do that?"

"What?" she said, her eyes still down.

"Park at our house and walk back."

"Don't be ridiculous."

"But, Mom, we can't find a place for miles; our house is closer than all this driving up and down—"

"I'm not walking. I'm going in this car."

"Honey, I've been around three times," Tom said softly.

"Well, go around again."

Stevie shrugged. Now they were both morons.

"Why don't I drop you off?" Tom said.

"What?"

"I'll drop you and Stevie off, go home, put the car in the garage, and walk back."

"I'm not going in without you."

"Ellen, you know everybody in that house; what's the difference?"

She raised her eyes to meet his in the mirror. "I said I'm not going in without you, and I'm not."

Tom sighed, turned the corner, and looked over at his son. Stevie rolled his eyes at his father. We're okay, Dad, but Mom's a moron, his eyes said.

Tom shook his head, but a trace of smile crossed his face. He made another right and drove the Chrysler wagon around the block again.

ANNE SAT ON THE RUG, looking off in the direction where Jessie had stood, looking at the empty staircase.

Then she leaned her head down on the seat of their father's club chair and shut her eyes.

I don't smell Daddy, she thought. I don't smell Daddy at all; I only smell Mother in this house.

She frowned.

I can't wear the pearls. Five separate strands of perfect pearls in different lengths, and when I open the boxes my head swims. I know I'll be sick if I wear them, they smell so like her.

Anne raised her head up off the seat cushion. She moved her fingers gently across the leather of her father's chair.

"They're yours now, Anne pie," he said so gently, handing me the velvet boxes. "She wanted you to have them." But then his eyes fell. Poor Daddy. I knew he was lying. I knew she would rather have been buried wearing them than give them to me.

Anne smiled. And Jessie wouldn't take them. "I wouldn't wear them on a bet," she said when I tried to give them to her.

Well, don't worry, Daddy. I'll give them to Amy when she's old enough, when she realizes how important they are.

She laid her head back down on the chair and closed her eyes again.

Oh, Daddy, why can't I smell you?

And then in her mind her mother appeared in the doorway; as if by magic, she stood in the doorway from the foyer to the living room. Poised and perfect and still, her dark hair pulled away from her face, caught in a tight chignon at the nape of her neck. She was wearing dark-brown suede pumps and a brown-and-beige tailored tweed skirt and a chocolate cashmere sweater. The ivory pearls lay glistening in rows against the cashmere across her breasts. Her face was as pale as the pearls, and her lips were very red.

Anne closed her eyes tighter, the little up-and-down frown lines deepening between her brows.

"You're mangling that Bach, Anne."

Anne's ten-year-old fingers leaped off the keys as if they were hot. "I'm sorry, Mother. I was just trying—"

"I heard what you were trying. Why don't you go do your homework?"

"I finished it."

They looked at each other.

Mrs. Connell took a little breath. "Maybe you should forget about the piano, Anne," she said.

"But I love it, Mother. I'll work harder. You'll see. I'll practice all the time."

Mrs. Connell brushed at the side of her skirt with her hand.

"One needs talent to play the piano, Anne. It doesn't matter how much you practice if you don't have that."

Anne watched her mother in the doorway. Her little heart was slamming around inside her chest under her cotton blouse.

"But Mrs. Falk says that if I practice I'll be—"

"Maybe it would be easier in the long run if you would just admit to yourself that you don't have the talent for the piano. Maybe it would be easier if you did that now rather than going on with it. I think that would be a very brave thing to do." She tilted her chin up a little and looked her older daughter in the eyes. "What do you think?" Mrs. Connell said.

"But I love the piano, Mommy, you know I love it. I want to play like you do. I want to—"

Mrs. Connell interrupted. "All right, Anne, then do what you want." She reached up with her right hand, stroked a single hair back into her chignon, looked at her daughter, turned, and vanished from the doorway.

Anne sat at the piano for at least ten minutes before she moved. She didn't cry; she just sat there. Then she closed her little red *Anna Magdalena Bach* book, slid silently off the piano bench, and left the living room.

She cried now. She sobbed into the seat of her father's club chair until the tears were gone and she had nearly drifted off to sleep. But then she realized that something was poking into her, something extremely uncomfortable. She reached behind her and pulled one of Jessie's high-heeled shoes out from under her backside. She didn't look at it, she just held it in her hand. Then she stood it upright under the side table. She never raised her head from the seat cushion.

"I'd better call them to come over," she whispered, but still she didn't get up.

LEONARD LED ANITA through the crowd in Pete and Jessie's house. He bypassed the living room, off the foyer, and veered left into the dining room. Anita had said to go that way, right into the kitchen; that's where they would be. Around the long pine table, the chairs with the tied-on blue-checked cushions, past the Irish hutch with the curlicued curves and the blue-and-white plates, he pulled Anita by the hand behind him. Someone stopped her every two feet to say their piece about her brother, but Leonard pushed through despite the interference. He figured he didn't know most of them anyway, so what was the difference; they could be mad at him.

He pushed open the swinging door to the kitchen, pulled Anita through, and let the door shut.

"Well," Tee said. She was sitting up on the tile countertop next to the sink.

"I knew you'd be in here," Anita said.

"Why?"

"I don't know . . . I just knew it."

"She knew it," Leonard said to no one in particular.

"Jesus," Billy said as he and Leonard shook hands. "It's a mob scene, huh?"

"Where are the children?" Anita asked.

"Luke's in the backyard, Amy's upstairs, and James and Callie are somewhere, probably having another brawl," Tee said.

"Tee," Billy said.

"What?"

Anita sat down on a kitchen chair.

"Anita," Billy said, and gave her a peck on the cheek.

She closed her eyes. "You want some water, honey?" Leonard asked.

"Yes, please."

"You look like you could use a stiff one," Tee said.

"I'll have water, Leonard," Anita said, opening her purse. She took out a brown plastic prescription bottle, turned the white top to the arrows, uncapped it, and poured two long red capsules into her hand.

Tee looked at Billy.

Leonard took a glass from a cabinet, filled it with tap water, and handed it to his wife.

The kitchen door swung open and Grady walked in. Her eyes moved around the room and settled on Anita, who was downing the pills.

"What's that?" Grady said. "Tylenol?"

"Hi, Grady," Tee said.

"Hello, baby." Grady put her Bible and pocketbook down on

the kitchen sink by the telephone and leaned her umbrella up against the wall next to the back door. She looked at Anita. "I said what's that you're takin', girl?"

"She has a headache," Leonard said.

"Mmm-hmm," Grady said.

Billy smiled at Grady. "That's some hat you got there, Grady."

"Yeah, well, you jes like it 'cause it's red. I know how you firemen are partial to red."

Billy laughed, and the door to the kitchen opened.

"We had to park in Steve Lonzo's driveway. Tom had to ask him; there's not a spot for miles," Ellen said as Tom walked in behind her.

Tee jumped down from the counter. "Well, now all that's missing are the rings and the ponies. Where's the booze around here, Grady? It's time we had a drink."

LUKE LEANED AGAINST THE OAK TREE in the backyard, took a pack of Marlboros out of his shirt pocket, and lit a cigarette. He took off his suit jacket and threw it across a redwood chair next to the barbecue. He yanked at his tie, pulling the knot loose until it hung down in front of his chest, left the cigarette between his lips, and rolled up both shirtsleeves.

He frowned and ran his hand through his thick blond hair.

Well, that takes care of that. Now I can get away from this house and these people.

We buried you, Dad. In our own inimitable style. A real Chickery shebang.

Luke dropped the cigarette on the flagstone and stomped it out with the toe of his black loafer. He walked back and forth in front of the redwood table and chairs.

Am I supposed to forgive her now? Is that it? Forgive her for what she did? Take all my feelings and bury them with you? Is that what I'm supposed to do, Dad?

"Shit," he said out loud.

He took the pack of Marlboros out of his pocket again, shook out another cigarette, and lit it. He took a deep drag.

Why didn't you leave her, Dad? Why didn't you leave her long ago? I would have gone with you. You and me without her and

James. I mean before Amy was born. When you still had a chance to go. When me and James were already big.

Luke stood in front of the rosebushes. He took the cigarette and held the burning tip to the petal of a pale blush rose and watched it burn.

You could have gone if it wasn't for Amy.

He touched the tip to another petal.

Why did Mom have to have another baby? Why didn't you tell her no? Not that I don't love Amy; she's my sister, I love her. But we didn't need her. Hell, there's a dozen years between me and Amy. Well, eleven anyway. That's why Mom needed another baby. To keep you from going, that's why.

Luke dropped the cigarette in the dirt by the roses and stomped it out with his shoe.

Nobody'll ever hold on to me like that, that's for damn sure.

Luke turned and walked across the lawn to the old swing set. He ran his hand along one of the metal poles.

Look at the rust, Dad. Boy, oh boy.

He sat down on one of the swings, squeezing his rear onto the board, feeling the chain links tight against his thighs. He backed up and gave a little push-hop, swinging forward in the air.

He swung back and forth. When he swung forward, the swing set rose from the ground, one of the back poles lifting up, and when he swung back, the pole sank back into the ground with a clunk.

Luke smiled. I'm too heavy for this now, Dad. Remember when you got it for me? My seventh birthday.

He moved his fingers on the links. No rust then. Fire-engine red. And you let me help you put it together—just me and not James, 'cause it was my birthday.

Luke let the links push into the crooks of his elbows and clasped his hands in front of his chest. His tie flapped against his neck as he swung back and forth. He looked up at the chairs on the flagstone patio.

Mom sat up there, drinking a soda and trying to amuse James. He was so mad. And you and I put the swing set together until it got dark. And then we went to Gates for barbecue 'cause that's what I picked for my birthday supper.

Luke swung and closed his eyes.

And it started.

James said there was nothing for him to eat at Gates 'cause he hated barbecue, and she said we'd stop on the way home and get him something else, and you said no we wouldn't. You said it was my birthday and if I picked barbecue then that's what it was. You said there was no stopping for anything else. You said that was the deal on birthdays and we all knew that and James could just make do.

She ordered him coleslaw. And beans. And garlic toast, his favorite. But he wouldn't touch it, none of it. He just sat there, sulking, sitting on his hands. I knew he was hungry, I knew how much he loved garlic toast.

Luke ran one hand through his hair.

He was always such a pain in the ass. Such a baby.

She said why couldn't we just stop and get him something on the way home, what could it hurt? And you said that wasn't the way we did it; it was my birthday and I picked barbecue and that was what it would be.

You smiled at me and I ate my ribs. "I bet you can eat a whole slab all by yourself now. You're so big, Lukey boy," you said, and you winked at me.

Luke swung a little higher.

And James started to cry. He said he was starving.

Luke squinted into the sun.

Such a fat pain in the ass.

Nobody said anything for a long time. You and I ate and James cried and she watched him. It seemed to go on like that forever, and then Mom stood up. She said she'd take him to the car, they'd wait for us out there. James stumbled to his feet beside her, he kept his head down, he wouldn't look at you or me.

"This is Luke's birthday supper, Jessie."

"I know, Pete, but James—"

You didn't let her finish. "You'd best sit back down there, Jessie, and put that crybaby back in his chair."

"It's okay with me, Daddy. I don't care. I don't want him here anyway."

You didn't look at me. Your eyes never left hers.

"I said sit down, Jessie. Did you hear me?"

She stood still, like she was frozen. She had her hand on the back of James's hair; he was crying into the front of her by then, into her front under her breasts.

People at the other tables were watching.

"Please, Pete," she said, "don't do this."

"It's okay by me, Daddy. I want that crybaby to go."

"Mind your manners, Lukey, I'm talkin' to your mama here. . . . Do I have to get up, Jessie? Are you gonna make me get up?"

"I'll just take him to the car."

"You will not."

"It's okay, Daddy," I said. "We can get him something else to eat on the way home. I don't care, really I don't."

"Sit down, Jessie." She stood there, staring at you.

I was holding tight to my ear of corn; the kernels were squishing under my fingers.

You put your bread carefully at the edge of your baked beans, you wiped the sides of your mouth with your napkin and then your hands. You folded the napkin precisely and laid it on the table by the side of your plate. You pushed your chair back slowly; it scraped against the wood floor in the restaurant. And you stood up.

You were very tall.

"Sit down, Jessie," you said to her.

"Please, Pete, don't do this."

James sobbed and hiccuped, but other than that I don't remember any sound. I didn't know I was biting my lip until I tasted the blood. Blood and barbecue sauce in my mouth.

"I said sit down in that chair, Jessie, before I sit you down."

No one else could hear you except James and me and her.

I watched her chest go up and down, her eyes on yours.

She sat down.

And so did you.

And so did James.

All the noise in the restaurant jammed into my ears like somebody had turned the volume up real fast—silverware clanking and plates banging and kids screaming. I jumped, it was so loud. And everybody was moving all of a sudden—waitresses walking back and forth carrying platters of ribs and stuff and saying do you want more iced tea or coleslaw. And I couldn't let go of the corncob; it was stuck to my hand. . . .

Luke swung his feet forward and up together to get more leverage. The swing went higher. The back pole clunked up and down. Two black loafers gleamed in the sun in the blue in front of his face.

"It's okay, son," you said to me, smiling. "We're gonna finish our supper now. You want another root beer?" Like everything was fine.

Luke ran his fingers across his upper lip and forehead and wiped the sweat on the side of his pants.

They didn't talk all the way home. You and I sang "Way Down Upon the Swanee River" and you let me do the whistle part by myself. And when we got home, she took James with her into your bedroom and locked the door.

You taught me casino and said I could stay up late. And then you brought out my birthday cake, chocolate with chocolate icing, the one you'd baked for me.

Luke smiled as he swung higher.

Nobody else's dad could bake, nobody else's dad baked them their birthday cakes.

And when it was time to blow out the candles, you called her. You called her and called her and knocked on the door. But she wouldn't answer and she didn't come out. You put me to bed after the cake and you hugged me, you said you loved me very much.

Luke squinted up toward the patio as if he could see into the house.

She tried to make it up to me the next day. She said when you were so angry it was better for her to stay away from you, and that was why she didn't come out. She said she'd make it up to me real special and what did I want, but I didn't care by then. All I knew was my seventh birthday was over and she didn't see me blow out my candles and she didn't see me make my wish.

Luke ran his hand across his eyes.

I woke up when you were yelling. I never told, but I could hear. "*What kind of a mother are you?*" you were yelling. The night-light wasn't on in our room, but I could see James anyway, down there in the bottom bunk, holding the pillow over his face. "*You didn't kiss him good night on his birthday!*" you were yelling. "*What kind of a mother are you?*"

Luke began to sob as the swing slowed down.

"What kind of a mother are you?" he whispered to the empty backyard.

I don't think I can forgive her, Daddy. I'll never see you again, and it's all her fault.

"AW, COME ON, FRANCES," George said. "Just one." He reached across the table and touched her hand.

"Okay, okay," she said reluctantly, and looked up at the waitress. "I'll have a Bloody Mary."

"Spicy," George said. "She likes them spicy."

"Spicy," the waitress said, smiling sweetly at Frances. Then she turned and walked away.

"This is crazy, George," Frances said.

"Okay, it's crazy. I need a little crazy in my life right now."

"You do? What's the matter with your life?"

"Nothing. It's fine. I just—"

"What?"

"I just wanted to have a drink with you, Frances. I wanted to be alone with you and have a drink, that's all."

"Okay."

"Okay then."

Frances pushed the little paper cocktail napkin back and forth in front of her on the table.

"So now is the wake, huh?"

"Well, not really," George said.

"What?"

"Well, the wake is supposed to be beforehand. Actually, the wake or watch is supposed to take place over the body *before* the body is buried. Literally, that is. That's the wake."

"Oh," Frances said, nodding her head slowly.

The waitress returned to the table and put a Bloody Mary down in front of Frances on the napkin. "Spicy," she said, still smiling. "And a martini for you, sir. Beefeater. Anything else?"

"Not now, thank you," George said. The waitress flashed another smile and left.

Frances pushed the cubes around in her drink with the plastic swizzle stick, took the stick out of the glass, and put it in her mouth.

George mixed his drink and laid his swizzle stick in the glass ashtray at the center of the table. He smiled at Frances.

"So . . ."

Frances looked at him. "Jews don't have wakes."

"I know that."

"They just sit around afterward and tell wonderful stories about the person and laugh and cry and remember . . . you know, but it's not called a wake."

"I know that, baby. I didn't forget."

"I knew what it was. I just—"

"Frances, let it go. I wasn't trying to upset you, I was just explaining the actual meaning of the word 'wake.' "

"Right."

"You know how I am. I remember stuff like that."

"Okay."

"Wake: a watch over the body of a deceased person before burial, sometimes accompanied by festivity. Wake: the visible track of turbulence left by something moving through the water. As in the wake of a ship. Wake: a—"

"Okay, George," Frances interrupted.

"I didn't mean to upset you. I just got carried away."

"I know."

"I was being too literal." He looked at her. "I was being . . . my old asshole self."

"Right," Frances said, and she smiled. "I forgot."

"I'm sorry," George said.

"It's okay."

"You sure?"

"Sure."

He looked at her.

"The visible track of turbulence left by something passing through . . . is that what you said?"

"Yeah, but that's for a ship."

"Well, Pete wasn't a ship."

"No."

Frances looked down at her drink, ran her finger around the top edge of the glass. "If anything, he was more like a buoy than a ship."

"What?"

"You know. A buoy. Those things in the water that help you mark your place."

"Oh, a buoy. I didn't hear you at first."

"Help you when you're lost," she said, and then she smiled, but she wasn't smiling at George, she was smiling out into the air somewhere. "That keep you afloat, keep you lifted up," she said softly. "You know . . . a buoy, George."

"I know what a buoy is, Frances."

She shifted her gaze to him. He was frowning.

"Right," she said, "of course you do."

They looked at each other a moment.

"Uh . . . ," George said, looking nonplussed and raising his glass. "So, uh . . . to Pete?"

"Of course," Frances said, smiling as she lifted her glass to his. "To Pete."

JESSIE STOOD at her old bedroom window, looking out at the backyard: the banks of honeysuckle along the fence, the perfectly clipped hedge, red rosebushes in a line, green-and-white-striped canvas lawn furniture arranged on the flagstone as if on painted markers—everything in order, everything in place, as if her mother were still there.

Jessie cocked her hand over her right eyebrow and saluted the garden. "Ten-hut!" she whispered at the window.

She turned, walked back to her desk, flipped off the muslin sheeting, ran a hand along the polished cherrywood, and then methodically pulled out each one of the drawers from the desk and placed them side by side on the pale-blue carpet.

She sat down on her knees in front of the drawers, closed her eyes, and pointed her finger out in front of her. "Eeny, meeny, miney, mo'," she said, pointing the finger from drawer to drawer, "catch a tiger by the toe. If he hollers make him pay, fifty dollars every day. My mother told me to pick this very best one. Icka, bicka, soda cracker, icka bicka boo, icka bicka soda cracker, out goes *you*." She picked up the drawer she was pointing at and dumped the contents onto her lap.

A small gray stuffed elephant, once plush and now worn, rolled out and fell facedown on the rug. Jessie pushed all the envelopes, papers, and photos off her lap and picked up the little elephant. "Oh, José, look—your trunk is torn." She ran her finger along the soft felt. "And here, on your little foot. Well, we'll have to fix that, won't we?"

She held the tiny toy elephant to her breast with one hand, leaned forward on her knees, and rummaged in the other drawers until she came up with a plastic hotel sewing kit.

Jessie moved to the bed with the sewing kit and the elephant and stretched out on top of the pale-blue bedspread, with her back up against the padded silk headboard and her legs out in front of her.

"I'm sitting *on my spread*, Mother," Jessie said out loud as she threaded the needle. "Ha ha ha!"

"AMY?" STEVIE SAID.

He knocked tentatively on the closed bathroom door off the master bedroom of the Chickery house. He put his ear to the door but he couldn't hear anything. Of course, it was hard to hear anything with the madhouse going on downstairs. He jiggled the doorknob.

"Amy?" he said again, his mouth close to the door.

He knocked again. Louder this time.

"Come on, I know you're in there. I already looked in your room."

He listened some more and knocked again.

"Come on, Amy, before some asshole comes up here to use this john."

He sighed and listened at the door again. Nothing.

"Amy?"

He tapped the door again softly with his knuckles. Then he started beating out a little drum riff with his knuckles and his fingers. Not loud, just barely tapping the door, a soft beat.

"Chhh, ch, ch, chhhhh, ch-chichicka, ch, chhh, ch, ch, ch," he said softly as he tapped. He was really getting into it when the lock clicked and the door swung open.

Amy was on her knees on the tile floor, with her hand on the doorknob. "What the hell are you doing?"

"Jesus," Stevie said, waving his hands in the air. "You're smoking up a storm in there."

"You sound like your mother," Amy said, taking another drag from the joint in her hand.

"Fuck you," Stevie said. He smiled. "Hey, now I sound like your father. Oh, shit. Sorry."

"You in or out?" she said.

"In, in."

She backed up on her knees. He took two steps into the bathroom, closed the door behind him, locked it, turned, and looked at her.

"Why are we in here? What's the matter with your room?"

"Everybody keeps looking for me in my room."

"Ahh . . ."

Amy sat down on the floor again, her back up against the cabinets. She handed him the joint, he took it and sat down across from her on the floor, supported by the bathtub.

"Where'd you get this shit?" he asked, taking a deep drag. He immediately began to choke.

"You."

"What?" he said, coughing.

She leaned forward, patted his chest, and took the joint out of his hand. "You—I got it from you."

"Me?" He coughed some more.

Amy stood up, took the porcelain cup next to the toothbrush holder, filled it with water from the tap, and handed it to him.

"Here, you ninny."

"Shut up," he said. He took the cup and downed the water. His face was red.

She put the cup back on the sink and sat down next to him, her back against the tub.

"It's the shit you stole from your brother when he came home from Syracuse," she said.

"Last *Christmas*? You've been saving this stuff since last Christmas? No wonder I'm dying here."

"Well, then don't have any more."

"Fuck you," he said, and held out his hand. She passed him the joint; he took a couple more hits and sat there holding it in his hand.

"The stuff from Adam, huh?" He laughed. "I love it."

She didn't say anything. He took another drag and looked at her.

"So how you doin'?"

"Oh, I'm great, Stevie. I can't tell you when I've had such a great day."

"Come on, Aims, stop fucking around. How are you? I want to know."

She looked at him. "I don't know. I guess I'm numb."

"I think that's best," he said. "Numb is good, numb is better than falling apart."

She frowned and held out her hand. He passed her the joint and she took a hit.

"So'd you see the main bout?"

"What? Oh, yeah, part of it. What the hell was going on up there? I was standing in the back with Jennifer; I couldn't see it all."

"Oh, was Jenn there?"

"Sure, everybody was there. Everybody from East and even some guys from South. You know, the ones you're close to and all."

"The event of the season, huh? Did we have a bigger turnout than the prom?"

"Come on, Amy, you can let up with the tough shit. It's me."

She smiled a weak smile at him and passed back the joint.

"I'm sorry, I forgot it was you."

He smiled at her. "Your other brother."

"My only brother, as far as I'm concerned—blood or no blood. You should have seen those two bozos; it was positively ludicrous."

"Hey, *ludicrous*. Definitely college material. Look out, Mizzou."

"Oh, shut up, Stevie."

"Pardon me." He took another hit and passed it back to her.

She took a drag.

"You still think I'll go?"

"To Missouri? Sure. Why not?"

She gave him a look.

"Oh. No, sure you'll go. You know, you'll hang out all summer, sit around, get your head together about all of this, take care of your mom, whatever. And then September . . . sure you'll go. Hey, what's gonna happen with your mom anyway?"

"I don't know." She handed him the joint. "I wish you were going to Missouri with me."

"Hey, not me, babe; it's Emory for me. I'm gonna wallow in Southern babes."

"You're gonna come back with an accent."

"Yeah, I'll sound like your dad." He looked at her. "Shit. Sorry."

"It's okay." She smiled and bit her lip. "I wouldn't mind if you sounded like my dad."

They looked at each other. He put his arm around her shoulders.

"Okay, it's a deal," he said. "I'll drawl by Thanksgiving."

They sat there.

"I loved my dad, Stevie."

"I know."

"And I love my mom."

"I know."

She sighed. "Jesus," she said quietly.

"Yeah," he said.

He took the joint from her and tried to take a drag; it was getting tiny and hard to hold.

"Shit. You want any more of this? It's burning my lip."

"No. Here."

She got up on her knees and opened a door under the sink. Taking out a cosmetic bag, she unzipped it, threw some lipsticks, blushers, and brushes on the sink, and unfolded a Kleenex. She handed him a fresh joint. "Here's the other one."

"I gave you two?"

"Yes, you gave me two. Whatja think? I stole them?"

"No, I just don't remember. I must have been stoned at the time." He laughed, threw the tiny roach in the john, and lit the fresh one. They sat back down together on the floor.

"Here," he said, putting the joint in her mouth. "So what was the fight? What was goin' on?"

"Oh, I don't know. They're so grown up, my two big brothers, that they ended up lying all over the grass. And I'm the one who's supposed to be the baby."

"What happened?"

"They were pushing at each other, angry, pissed off the way they always are, until they knocked each other over—even the blond bimbo, with her legs up in the air. . . ."

"You're kidding. Jimmy's nymphette wife? With her legs up in the air? I missed this?" Stevie began to laugh.

"Oh, yeah. And me too. I jumped off my chair like I was a Flying Wallenda and threw myself at Luke. . . ."

Stevie laughed harder. "A what—a flying what?"

"A Flying Wallenda . . ." Amy started laughing. "You never heard of the Flying Wallendas?"

Stevie doubled over, laughing.

"Wait, Stevie, wait. . . ."

"What the fuck is a Flying Wallenda?"

"It's a group—I mean, a troupe—"

"A troupe, a poop . . ." Stevie laughed some more and then snorted through his nose.

"Oh, no, don't do that," said Amy, convulsed with laughter. "I can't take it when you do that. . . . Oh, Jesus, wait"—she laughed—"wait, I'm trying to tell you." She tried to control herself and then slumped against Stevie when he snorted again. The two of them laughed so hard they rolled over onto the floor and the green throw rug.

"Wait a minute—stop it."

"Poop, shmoop," he said, seized with more laughter. "Is it shit—a Flying Wallenda?"

"Cut it out." She snorted, holding her sides. "Cut it out, you shit."

"Shit is right," he said, howling. "Hell, this is great shit. I'll have to thank Adam."

"Oh, right," she said, laughing hysterically, "and when he finds out you stole it from him, he'll shoot you— Oh, Jesus . . ." She laughed some more and then began to sob.

"Oh, Jesus, Amy," Stevie said. "Oh, Amy, please don't cry."

She rolled over on the floor, sobbing, her face in the green throw rug.

Stevie flicked the joint into the toilet and took her in his arms.

"Oh, Amy . . . God, Amy . . . oh, Amy, I love you, please don't cry."

"Stevie, what's gonna happen to me?" she said through the sobs.

"It'll be all right. It'll be all right," he said, kissing her hair and holding her close. "It'll be all right. I promise."

"I miss my daddy," she sobbed.

"Oh, God."

"I'll never see him again." She clung to Stevie and he held her. "Do you think my mom will come home? What if I don't have my mom?"

"Oh, God, Amy, you'll have your mom." The tears began to

roll down Stevie's cheeks. "You'll have your mom, Aims, I promise."

"What if I don't?" she sobbed. "What if I don't have her? Then I won't have either of them."

"Oh, God," Stevie moaned. "Come on, Amy, please."

He rocked her in his arms, the two of them crying. Stevie gently stroked the top of her head. And when her sobs subsided, he still held her. She moved her face against his chest and they lay down together on the tile floor on their backs, exhausted. His arm was under her neck, her head was turned into the hollow between his shoulder and his chest.

She sniffed and shuddered. She wiped her nose with her hand.

They lay there together for a long time, staring up at the ceiling, neither of them speaking, just breathing in sync. Occasionally she trembled, a sob escaped her lips. Occasionally he patted her shoulder or kissed her gently on the hair.

"Anyway," he finally said softly, "I missed the whole thing."

"That'll teach you to stand in the back." She sniffed.

He smiled, leaned to the right, and kissed the top of her head and part of her left eye.

"Yeah." He took a breath and exhaled. "So hey, you want to hear what happened with my folks? Maybe it'll perk you up."

"What?"

"He went ballistic on the way over here. I thought he was gonna leave us on I-435."

"You're kidding."

"No. He practically ejected himself out of the car, he was so mad."

"What'd they fight about?"

"Who knows? Who can understand them? I think it started with me, but then it got so out of hand . . . I don't think I could explain it to you."

She sniffed and rubbed her face against his chest.

"Are you wiping your nose on my shirt?"

"No, I am not, Steven."

"Okay, okay."

They lay quietly.

He patted her shoulder. "I was only kidding."

"Do they fight a lot?" Amy said.

"Who? My folks? Nah, not really."

"Oh." She sighed. "Mine fought in spurts, you know? Sometimes they'd be fine forever and then all of a sudden, I don't know, it would be all bad again."

"Yeah."

She sighed another sigh and moved her face against his shirt. Then she raised her head and looked at him. "But they loved each other. I know they did, Stevie. Didn't you think they loved each other?"

"Yeah, sure. I guess. I mean, when I saw them and all. You know."

She leaned her head back down and rested it on his chest. "Well, they did. I know they did."

He ran his fingers gently over the top of her hair.

"I guess they're all crazy," she said softly.

"Parents?"

"Yeah."

"It's a true story," he said.

Amy smiled. "Now you sound just like your dad."

"Right." He laughed gently. "Another true story."

"They should have gotten a divorce."

"Who? My folks?"

"No, mine," she whispered.

"Well, it would have been a lot easier than this."

She giggled. "Oh, Stevie."

"Shit. Sorry. I was just trying to change your mood."

"What'll I do without you?"

"At Missouri? You'll pine for me. You'll miss me. By Thanksgiving you'll be a wreck to see me. You'll forget that I'm three months younger than you and that you've known me all your life. You won't be able to keep your hands off me."

"Yeah?"

"Yeah. That's my plan."

She smiled into his shirt.

"So? What do you think?"

"What? About your plan?"

"Yeah."

She raised herself up on one elbow and looked him in the eyes.

"Well, Stevie," she said, sounding exactly like Pete, "it works for me."

She leaned over and kissed him full on his mouth for a very long time.

"Jesus, Aims," Stevie whispered when their lips broke apart. "Jesus."

He looked at her. Her eyes never left his. And then he reached up, bent her head down to his, and with everything he had, he kissed her back.

GRADY STOOD AT THE KITCHEN WINDOW, watching Luke in the backyard. He'd gotten off the swing. Now he was sitting in a redwood chair on the patio, smoking a cigarette.

She made a little *tsk* sound, shook her head, and moved to the stove. She crossed her arms over her breasts and watched a pot of coffee percolate.

"Where's George and Frances already?" Tee asked, stirring vodka and ice in a glass with her finger.

"Why don't you put some juice in that, babe?" Billy said, opening the refrigerator door and squatting down. "There must be orange juice . . . somewhere."

"There's nothing," Ellen said. "I looked."

Tee sat down at the table across from Anita. "I don't want juice. So where are they? Huh? Anybody know?"

"They turned off the highway at State Line," Leonard said.

"They did?" Billy said, pulling a carton of orange juice out of the fridge and sniffing it. "Here, Tee, I found some."

"Yeah," Leonard said. "He was in front of me and they turned off."

"I don't want any, Billy," Tee said. "Where's George staying? Did you talk to him?"

"Who? Me?" Leonard asked.

"Hell, I don't care . . . anybody."

Billy walked to the table with the carton of orange juice, extending it to Tee. Tee shook her head no, put her hand out flat, covering the top of her glass. "No, thank you," she said in a singsong voice to her husband.

"He's at the Marriott. I talked to him," Tom said.

Tee raised the drink in front of her face. "Well, he's probably gonna try a fast one with Frances at the Marriott."

"Tee, really," Ellen said. "That's awful."

"Why is it awful? You know George. Do you think he's changed? He already pushed her around plenty this morning."

"He did?" Ellen asked.

"Come on, Tee, this is hardly the time," Tom said.

"Oh? Is there a time? I didn't get the schedule when I came in. Cheers." She lifted the glass and took a big swig of vodka.

"Tee," Billy said.

"What?"

Grady put a white china cup and saucer down in front of Anita at the table. She gave Tee a look and poured coffee into Anita's cup. "You want sugar, baby?"

"No, thank you, Grady. This'll do fine." Anita raised the cup to her lips and took a sip.

Tee watched her. "I'm sorry, Anita," she said. "I'll watch my mouth."

"It's just 'cause she's hungry," Ellen said. "That's all it is. We're all hungry. Maybe we should get some food."

"I didn't say anything, Tee," Anita said.

Tee took another swallow of her drink. "I know you didn't." She turned. "They sent out for food, Ellen."

"Who sent out?"

"The kids, before you got here. I don't know, James's wife or somebody, they called and ordered and somebody went to pick it up. Or maybe it's gonna be delivered, I don't know—I lost track."

"What? What did they order?"

"Pizza."

"Pizza?" Ellen stood staring at Tee with her mouth open. "They ordered pizza? You must be kidding."

"No, I'm not."

"Pizza? You can't have pizza at a funeral. We can't have pizza at Pete's funeral."

"It's all right, Ellen," Tom said.

"No, it isn't! It isn't all right. He wouldn't have wanted pizza. It isn't right at all!" Her voice caught. She turned. "Oh, Grady, they ordered pizza."

"It's all right, child," Grady said. "It sure don't matter now."

The phone rang. Tom reached over and picked up the receiver.

"Hello? . . . Hi. Where are you? . . . Why'd you go there? . . . Yeah . . . No, she's not here yet. . . . I don't know, honey. . . ."

"Who is it?" Ellen asked. "Is it Frances?"

"What do you mean?" Tom said into the phone. "Yeah . . ."

"Who is it, Tom?" Ellen asked again.

He held out his hand at Ellen to wait a minute. "Yeah . . . What does that mean? Yeah . . . But I don't understand . . . Where is she now?"

"It's Anne," Ellen said.

"She what? . . . Well, can't you . . . Okay, okay. Wait a minute." He turned to Tee. "She wants to talk to you."

"Great," Tee said, getting up with the drink in her hand. "Send in the clowns." She took the receiver from Tom. "What's the matter, Anne?" she said into the phone.

"You want coffee, Mr. Kintner?" Grady said to Leonard.

"It's Leonard, Grady. You can call me Leonard."

"Yes, sir," Grady said. "You want coffee?"

ANNE WALKED SLOWLY UP THE STAIRCASE and down the thick rose carpet in the upstairs hallway of her parents' house. After the door to her parents' bedroom and before the doors to her room and Jessie's, there were several framed photographs lining both sides of the wall. All were in identical frames, plain-edged sterling-silver classic Tiffany frames.

Anne's eyes moved along the photographs without seeing them; she knew each one by heart. Her parents' wedding, Jessie's wedding to Pete, her wedding to Joe. Jessie and Pete's children—two photographs of each: one taken on their first birthday and one taken for high school graduation. The silver frame for Amy's graduation was already there, hanging empty in its place, waiting.

James, Luke, Amy . . . babies in a row. All the photographs alike, all taken by Strauss-Peyton on the plaza as per Mrs. Connell's instructions, three perfect babies, one little chubby leg tucked under the other little chubby leg, all of them smiling except for Luke.

Anne walked by the photographs, touching each one with her fingertips, her hand gliding across the wall until she reached the door to Jessie's room. She stood in front of it.

"Jessie?"

She waited.

"Jessie, I called them. I had to."

There was no sound at all. "Jessie? They're coming over."

Anne bowed her head forward until her forehead rested against the wooden door.

"Please don't be mad," she said softly. "Jessie? Hello?"

"WHAT'S HE DOIN' NOW?" James asked Callie.

"I told you," she said from the window. "He's just sitting there, smoking a cigarette. The same thing he was doing the last time you asked me." She turned. "Can I leave here now? I feel like a spy."

"Yeah, yeah."

"It's strange being in here anyway."

"Why? It's just my parents' bedroom."

"I don't know, I feel funny; I feel like she's gonna walk in and wonder what we're doing in here."

"I wish she *would* walk in. Why the hell doesn't my aunt Anne call and tell us where the hell they are?" James exhaled through his teeth. "I should have stayed with her at the cemetery—what the hell was I thinking?"

"She asked you, Jimmy, she asked you to go. You did what she asked."

"Yeah. What a good boy am I."

Callie turned and walked to her husband. He was sitting on a chaise longue in the corner of the room. He wasn't leaning back, reclining; he was perched on the edge. Callie ran her hand along the polished cotton upholstery, tiny white and blush-peach roses with soft green leaves on a pale-beige background. At the foot of the chaise lay a tan throw. Callie picked it up and held it.

"Goodness, this is cashmere," she said.

"Goddamn jerk."

"Hmm?"

He looked up and frowned. "My goddamn brother."

"Oh."

"Well, he can just stew in his own juice for all I care."

She rubbed her face against the cashmere.

"I could never talk to him anyway."

"Siblings don't get along, especially when they're so close in age."

"Where didja read that?"

"It's a common fact, Jimmy."

"You don't have any siblings; don't believe everything you read."

She raised her eyebrows and tilted her chin at him. "Well, it seems to be true, doesn't it?"

He didn't answer. He sighed and ran his hand through his hair.

She refolded the throw with perfect precision and laid it back where it had been.

"Luke was always on his side, always looked the other way when it came to Dad, perfect Dad to Luke."

"I've never seen a chaise lounge before. I mean, in somebody's house. You usually only see them in the movies, you know, in old movies that are black and white."

She ran her hand along the fabric again.

"How come your mother has a chaise lounge, sweetie? Does she lie on it a lot?"

"Huh? What?"

"On the chaise lounge."

"What chaise lounge?"

"The one you're sitting on, Jimmy!"

He looked down at where he was sitting. "I don't know. Goddamn it, what are you talking about?"

"You don't have to get angry. I just said it was romantic. I didn't *say* it—I was just thinking how romantic it is."

"What's romantic?"

She sighed. "Having a chaise lounge."

He looked at her. "What the hell are you talking about, Callie? Are you saying my parents were romantic? Is that what you're saying?"

"No, I . . . Oh, what's the difference, Jimmy, you turned it all around. I was just . . . Don't you think we should go downstairs? All those people are waiting. Don't you think *you* should go and talk to them, since Luke certainly isn't?"

"They were about as romantic as Punch and Judy, my parents, for crissakes, carrying on the way they did."

"Okay, Jimmy."

"You don't know the half of it, the stuff I got in the middle of."

"I know."

"No, you don't know. Nobody knows."

Callie didn't say anything.

"Even my goddamn brother doesn't know. And certainly not Amy; she doesn't know a goddamn thing. She probably thinks they were romantic as hell. She probably thinks everything was hunky-dory with the two of them!"

"She couldn't think that, Jimmy. She had to have heard them fight."

"Yeah, well, if Mom would have had the guts to leave him none of us would have had to listen to them fight. That's all I heard my whole goddamn life!"

Callie exhaled softly. "The fighting was part of who they were, it was part of the dance they did."

He looked at her. "You know, you read too goddamn much." He shrugged. "Some dance. It was more like a bullfight."

"Jimmy, you know she never would have left him. She loved him. And he loved her. You know that."

"Yeah, thank you, I remember. It looks like I'll never forget." He rubbed his face with his hands. "I just wish they'd done their goddamn dance in front of somebody else."

Callie put her hand gently on James's shoulder. "We pick our parents before we're born."

"What the hell is that? Some goddamn new mystical crap?"

"It's a theory; you don't have to put it down."

"Okay, okay, I'm not putting it down. I just wish I'd known about it sooner. I could have asked to be the son of somebody else."

"Who?"

"Hell, I don't know . . . somebody who was boring"—he looked up at his wife—"somebody who wasn't romantic and didn't have a chaise lounge."

Callie smiled.

James rubbed his face. "I guess we better go downstairs," he said. He held out his hands and she took them and pulled him up. "For the life of me, Cal, I never understood why they were together. It never made any sense."

"People never understand why people are together, sweetie. It's been like that since the beginning of time."

He smiled at her. "Oh, yeah?"

"Sure. Look at all the couples that people didn't understand."

"Who? Name three."

"Well . . ." She tilted her head. "Alice and Ralph Cramden . . ."

"Uh-huh."

"Uh . . . and Beauty and the Beast, and, uh . . ." She frowned and then she smiled. "You and me, Jimmy; people never understand about you and me."

James grinned and burst out laughing. He put his arms around his wife. "Goddamn, you know, you're good, Callie. Sometimes when I'm sinking, you just pick me right up again."

"Well, there you have it," she said, snuggling into him. "That just proves my point."

"WELL, ARE WE GOING?" Tee said, draining her drink and handing Grady the empty glass.

"Well, which of us?" Ellen asked.

"What do you mean, which of us? *All* of us."

"Well, who'll wait for Frances and George?" Ellen asked.

"I'll wait here for Frances," Grady said.

"Do you think we should take the children?"

"Which children?"

"Jessie's children," Ellen said. "Should we tell them and see if they want to go?"

"Jesus, haven't they seen enough?" Tee said.

"Maybe we should handle this," Tom said. "I think Tee's right."

"At last," Tee said, "somebody thinks I'm right."

"Look, it won't be a big deal. We'll get Jessie out of the bedroom and bring her and Anne back here," Billy said.

"I'll keep an eye on the children. You all go on," Grady said.

"Do you think there's really a need for all of us to go traipsing over there?" Leonard said.

Tee looked at him.

Anita turned in her chair and faced Tee. "What did Anne say again?"

"She said that Jessie's been released. That the DA isn't going to prosecute."

"But what does that mean?"

"I don't know; I never finished law school, remember? We'll have to ask George."

"Does that mean she's free?" Ellen said.

"We have to find out, honey," Tom said.

Anita looked at Tee. "And what else did she say?"

"She said she wants us to come over there and get Jessie out of the fucking bedroom."

"That's what she said exactly?"

"For crissakes, Anita, she said that Jessie's locked herself in her old room, she won't answer when Anne calls, and Anne's afraid."

"There's no reason for her to jump to any conclusions," Leonard said.

Tee looked at him again.

"I wonder what set her off?" Ellen asked.

"What is that—a joke?" Tee asked. "Are you kidding?"

"All right, Tee," Billy said. "Take it easy."

Ellen looked at Tom. She went on. "I meant what upset her specifically, Tee, not the whole thing, not the situation; just what . . . what specifically, you know."

Tom moved to his wife's side, put his arm around her shoulders. "I know, honey," he said to Ellen.

"To even go there . . . She won't go there, you know. She won't go to that house. She hasn't gone there since her daddy died. Has she, Grady?"

"No, she ain't, child."

"Well, then, why would she go there now?" Ellen said to Tom.

"Do you want to do that, Anita?" Leonard asked.

Anita turned to him.

"What do you mean?" Tee said. "You mean Anita isn't going?"

"I mean," Leonard said directly to his wife, "do you think it's good for you to go over there, *Anita*—is that what you want to do?"

"What do you mean, is that what she wants to do?" Tee asked.

"Stay out of it, Tee," Billy said.

"Well, what does he mean?"

Leonard didn't answer. He just stood there, looking at Anita in the chair.

"What do you think, that she's some goddamn wilting Southern belle all of a sudden, that she can't take it?"

"Tee," Billy said.

"Well, what's the matter with him?" Tee said, her voice rising. She turned and took a step toward Leonard. "What's the matter with you? We just put your wife's brother in the ground and Jessie's probably lost her mind and you're gonna stand here and discuss with us whether you want to go or not. . . . What have you got, a previous engagement?"

"Wait now, baby," Grady said, putting her hands on Tee's shoulders.

"No! I won't wait. The hell with you, Leonard."

Leonard opened his mouth, looked at his wife, and closed his mouth. Anita's head was lowered, her eyes were closed, and her face was very pale. She sat perfectly still in the kitchen chair.

"Tee," Ellen said, "maybe it would be better if we just—"

"Just what?" Tee said. "I'm telling you Jessie's nuts. You hear me? Nuts. Did you look at her? Did you look in her eyes?" She spun on her heel, her back to them. "Let's go, Billy."

"Wait a minute, Tee," Tom started. "We're all gonna go." Tee stopped at the back door and whirled around at Anita.

"What's the matter with you? Too much for your whitewashed soul to go see dirty Jessie? Is that it? You too much of a saint, Anita? Sittin' here poppin' Seconal like a goddamn princess—"

"Those weren't Seconal," Leonard interrupted.

"Don't you tell me; I know what Seconal look like."

Anita stood up and faced Tee. "Don't you talk to me about what I do, Tee. You look to yourself, don't you look at me."

Tee took a step forward. "What the fuck does that mean?"

"Oh, please don't do this," Ellen said, and turned to Tom. "Don't let them do this now."

"Does the Catholic Church approve of drugs nowadays, Anita? Huh? Do they?"

Billy moved across the room to block Tee. "Take it easy, Tee."

"Those were not Seconal," Leonard repeated firmly.

"Be quiet, Leonard," Anita said sharply.

"Then what the fuck were they?" Tee said, her voice raised.

The kitchen door banged open and Shapiro stood there with Larry Yord, Alan Patash, and Tip Rutten behind him.

"Yeah, what the fuck were who?" Shapiro asked, smiling.

*   *   *

JESSIE LAY ON HER STOMACH across the blue carpeting. The little stuffed elephant was at her side. Tiny stitches of red thread stuck in and out of the side of his trunk and along the bottom of his left foot, where Jessie had mended him.

She was raised up on her elbows, looking down at the dark-green leather diary in front of her. She ran her finger across the gold Girl Scout insignia on the front cover, picked up the tiny gold key, inserted it in the tiny gold lock, and turned it until it clicked. Then she laid the diary carefully on top of an open box of unsharpened pencils. Her name was engraved on each pencil in the box—"Jessie Connell," stenciled in red script across each blue pencil and in blue script across each red pencil.

She ripped the lined pages from inside the diary and spread them out, mixing them up on the rug in front of her, shuffling them so they weren't in sequence anymore.

She pulled a page out of the pile and read it. "Oh, look at my handwriting, José, look how little I was. 'Dear Diary, Grady made oatmeal cookies today and she let Anne and me eat the dough.' " Jessie laughed. "Look how I spelled 'dough': d-o-e."

Jessie picked up another page and read aloud. " 'Dear Diary, Mother took me for shoes on the plaza today. She wouldn't take Anne. She said Anne didn't need shoes but I did. She said it in her tone like I wore my shoes out on purpose just to make her mad. I got brown and white saddles. She wanted me to get black and white, that's why I got brown.' "

Jessie smiled. She dropped the page, scooped up a handful, and turned over onto her back. She held the pages up in the air above her head and went on reading.

" 'Dear Diary, Oh, no, Ellen has the chicken pox. Now we'll all get it. They're all over her, in her ears and on her eyeballs. I don't think that's possible but that's what Tee said. Ellen's mother told Tee's mother and Tee told me at school. Ellen's mother says Ellen has the most horrible case of chicken pox ever reported in the state of Missouri. I don't know how she knows that but that's what she said. She even has them inside her you-know-what. How pucky . . .' " Jessie brought the page in closer to her face. "Pucky?" She squinted at the paper in her hands. "Oh. Pukey. 'How pukey,' it says."

Jessie laughed. " 'How pukey,' José. Let's see . . ."

She pulled up another page.

" 'Dear Diary, Mother made us go to Garavelli's last night for dinner. I'm never going there again. I don't care what she does to me, I'm not going. She says now that Anne's twelve she's big enough to get over her unfounded ridiculous childhood anxieties—that's what mother called it—but I can't watch my sister go through that again, her face gets all white and sweaty and she looks like she's gonna fall off the chair. I said in the car on the way home that Garavelli's food stinks and I wasn't going there anymore but she told me to watch my language. Daddy didn't say anything but he made sure Anne's window was open in the car and he patted her hand a lot at the table. You can see Anne's eyes lifting up to that balcony while we're eating, Diary. That's where mother told her the man was gonna come from, that if little girls didn't finish their dinner, the man would come out of the door at the end of the balcony and down the steps and take the little girls away and they'd never see their mommies or daddies again. . . .' "

Jessie stopped reading.

She lay there for at least a minute, the paper in her hands above her head, her chest moving slowly up and down.

Then she crumpled the paper into a tiny ball and threw it across the room. "Come on, José," she said as she sat up. "We've got work to do."

FRANCES PUT HER DRINK DOWN. "I did not nearly drown."

"Oh, come on, Frances, we were pumping water out of you."

"You know, Tee said the same thing. . . ." She shrugged. "Well, I don't remember it as being so dramatic."

"Sure you don't remember. It's 'cause you nearly drowned."

"Well, I know I never swam after that, that's for damn sure."

George laughed. "Hey, sweetheart, you didn't swim *then*."

Frances took a sip of her drink. "I do remember flipping out of that Pontiac in the Cornerville parade, I sure as hell remember that, landing upside down in my bathing suit in the middle of the street. Wasn't that the same summer?"

"It wasn't a Pontiac, Frances. It was a Chevy."

"Turquoise and white and long."

"Right."

"With big fins and that thing on the back . . ." She looked at George. "I know," she said, "a Continental kit."

George laughed. "And Pete creamed the shit out of it." He laughed some more. "On both ends."

Frances frowned. "Who did we hit? I can't remember. Who was in front of us?"

"Rowlands."

"With McGraw."

"Right. And Rowlands hit Polotsky."

"God. And Pete had to call up Mr. Blackman and tell him what he'd done to Mrs. Blackman's beautiful convertible."

"Yeah," George said, and laughed again.

Frances looked at him. "Well, you're sure getting a kick out of this."

"Well, it was his own damn fault, Frances. He couldn't keep his eyes where they were supposed to be—on the road."

"What do you mean? I thought Rowlands stopped too fast."

"You don't remember any of this, do you, Frances? Rowlands didn't stop fast. Pete just had his eyes on the rearview mirror and didn't know Rowlands had stopped at all, that's why he crashed into him. He was watching me behind him."

"Why?"

"Because Jessie was in my car. She was sitting right next to me."

"So?"

"So he wanted to make sure I didn't try anything."

"George, what are you talking about? He wasn't even going out with Jessie then."

"That didn't matter. He had his eye on her."

"He did not."

"Sure he did, Frances; you just don't remember."

Frances drained the last of her Bloody Mary. Her eyes flashed. "I guess I don't," she said. "I guess I don't remember anything at all. It must be all that water on my brain."

"What?"

"From when I nearly drowned, George."

"Can I get you folks another?" the waitress asked from behind George's shoulder.

"No," Frances said quickly. "We have to go."

"Aw, come on, Frances."

"George, we have to go; everybody's there by now. I want to know what's going on."

George put his hand gently on Frances's arm. "How 'bout we call and tell 'em we'll be there in thirty minutes. . . ." He looked at her. "Twenty minutes . . . ten minutes; we'll drink fast." He waited for her smile. "Come on, Frances, they'll be there all day—all night, for that matter. We all will. This is the only chance we have to be alone." He looked at her.

The waitress cocked her head to one side and smiled at Frances.

"Well . . . ," Frances said.

"Great," George said. "Two more, thanks."

The waitress laughed. "Yes, sir."

Frances sighed. "You're awful."

"No I'm not."

"Yes you are. You always get what you want from me."

"I do not."

"You do too. Everything. I married you, didn't I?"

"Yeah. But you divorced me."

Frances laughed. "I nearly forgot."

George looked at her. He put his hand over hers on the table, gently rubbed the top of her hand with his fingers. "Was it really so bad with me, Frances?"

"No. But I let you push me around. I always did. I still do. Look at me. I'm here, see? I could never stand up to you; you could always make me . . . Oh, what's the difference?"

She shook his hand off hers and reached for her purse.

"What?"

"Nothing." She took out a lipstick and compact.

"What? Tell me."

She opened the compact and took the cap off the lipstick, turned the tube until the red-wine color was exposed, held it to her lips. George stopped her hand, held her wrist between his fingers. "Tell me, Frances. Please."

"Weak in the knees," Frances said, looking directly at him. "You could always make me weak in the knees." Then she shook his hand off hers again and moved the red around her mouth. "One more, George, and then we're going. Understand?"

He smiled at her. "Yes, ma'am," he said. "I promise."

TOM TOOK A LEFT onto Ward Parkway and drove north. Ellen sat next to him in front, Tee and Billy were in the back. Leonard and Anita weren't with them; Leonard had insisted on taking his own car even though Tom had pointed out that they had plenty of room in the wagon.

Billy was laughing. "So we're at JuCo, and you're all away at your fancy schools, and we go up to Topeka, me and Pete and Shapi—Shapi had a girl up there. We go up for some dance or something, and we're staying at this Holiday Inn and we're shitfaced, I mean, really shitfaced, and somebody wants more ice, I don't know who, probably the girl. . . ." Billy laughed again. "And the goddamn phone in the room won't work, so Pete goes out the door into the hall, he presses for the elevator and the elevator comes and he stands inside it, with his foot holding the door so it won't close, and the next thing you know, he's trying to order ice from room service . . . *on the elevator phone.* The door is slamming back and forth on his foot, trying to shut, and Pete's yelling into the phone—it has this little-bitty short cord, you know, like elevator phones have—and he's yelling, 'We need some ice up here, god-damn it, this is an emergency.' Oh, Jesus . . ." Billy laughed some more and wiped his eyes. "Jesus, it was funny. God, he could make me laugh."

Ellen smiled at Tee.

Billy shook his head. "Jesus, what a guy," he said.

They rode a few blocks in silence. Then Ellen turned and looked at Tee. "Tee, what was the name of those stories that Pete used to tell? You know, to the kids when they were babies and he did all the voices. Remember? I can't think what he called them. . . ."

Tee smiled. "My God, I forgot about those. . . . The adventures of Gwendolyn and Johnny."

"That's right. And he did Gwendolyn's voice real high—"

"And Johnny's voice real low," Tee interrupted. " 'Let's go to the park today, Gwendolyn,' " Tee said in a deep, gravelly voice.

" 'Okay, Johnny,' " Tom answered in a high-pitched, squeaky little-girl's voice.

The four of them laughed.

"I remember those," Billy said. "He told 'em to Jenn when she was little."

"He told them to all the kids," Ellen said. "Ben loved them. Remember, Tom? How he'd crawl in Pete's lap when they were over at the house, make sure Pete would tell him one before he went to bed."

"Sure," Tom said. He picked up speed and made the light at Eighty-third.

"Well, his dad did stuff like that. Pete took after his dad," Billy said.

"You didn't know his dad, Billy," Tee said.

"No, but I know what he told me. He was crazy about his dad. He said as far as he was concerned the wrong one died, that it should have been his mother who died first instead of his dad."

"What a terrible thing to say," Ellen said. "I thought Mrs. Chickery was very nice."

"Well, he couldn't get close to her. It was because she was so Catholic, I think. I mean, she was really, really Catholic. Pete was too funny to be Catholic."

"Pete was funny?" Tee asked.

Billy looked at Tee. "Of course Pete was funny. He was the funniest guy I ever knew."

Tee shook her head. "Well, I give up."

"How did he die?" Ellen asked. "Pete's dad."

"He drove into a tree."

"Oh, my goodness," Ellen said, "I never knew that."

"Was he drunk?" Tee asked.

"They never told them," Billy said. "Maybe Mrs. Chickery knew the details, but she never told Pete or Anita. Pete told me how he imagined it, though. He said he could see his daddy's truck—it was a Ford, a green Ford truck—and Pete said he could see it plowed head-on into a tree by the side of the road. A black sky, lots of stars . . . nothin' around for miles . . . crickets and cicadas making a racket . . . a quiet Southern country night. He said he could see his daddy's door was thrown open and one of his legs was sticking out . . . and he said the car radio was on . . . some lady singing some country song, some slow, sad song spreading across the night. That's how he saw it, his daddy dead in the truck, just sitting there with the music still playing until they found him. . . . That's how Pete imagined it in his head."

"But he never knew any of that," Ellen said.

"Hell, no. He just made it up. All he knew was that his dad had plowed into a tree."

Nobody said anything.

"Well . . . ," Ellen said.

They stopped for the light at Seventy-fifth.

Tom ran his hand through his hair, turned, and looked at Billy in the back. "Did you know that when I got the store, the first store down on Troost, it was Pete who set it up?"

"What do you mean?"

"The loan. I had a chance to get the store, but I couldn't get a loan." He shook his head. "Hell, I didn't have anything except a pharmaceutical degree"—he turned to Ellen and smiled—"and a wife and a baby and another baby on the way. . . ."

The light changed and they took off.

"Who was gonna give me a loan? I'd been working for old man Boyer five years when he had the stroke. It was over for him. And they had nobody, the Boyers—no kids, nobody to take over. They wanted me to have it, they were making me a great deal, but I couldn't get a damn loan. I went everywhere. I was about ready to put Ellen and the baby up for collateral . . . or my soul. Anyway, I told Pete. And that was that. He told Jessie's father, and the next thing you know, Pete takes me over to talk to Mr. Connell—told him how responsible I was, gave me a great buildup—he takes me over to the Connells' and I talk and talk. And you know how connected Mr. Connell was . . . so before I could even call Ellen, Mr. Connell takes me in his big car over to United Missouri and cosigns the loan with me. Just like that. We just sat there in all that walnut paneling and they gave me the money. Nobody batted an eye. Except me; I practically collapsed."

"I'll be damned," Billy said.

"Well, it's a true story," Tom said. "I wouldn't have had any of the drugstores without Pete. Not a one."

"He was a hell of a guy," Billy said, "one hell of a guy."

"I'll tell ya, Billy," Tom said, "there were certain things in life that I couldn't talk about to anybody, not the way I could talk to Pete."

"You mean personal things?" Tee said.

"No. I mean ideas. Things about the physical world."

"What do you mean?"

"Oh, about the way the world works, technical things."

"Like what? I don't understand."

"Like why it rains over here and not over there. Things like that."

"You talked to Pete about things like that?" Tee said. "Pete Chickery?"

Billy turned his head. "What's the matter with you, Tee? You act like you didn't know Pete at all. What do you think, he wasn't smart enough to talk to Tom about things like that 'cause he didn't finish school?"

"I never said that, Billy. I never said Pete wasn't smart."

Tom braked for the light at Gregory.

"Oh, they had a language all their own when they got going," Ellen said. "It was like the two of them were speaking Bulgarian— at least it was to me." She sighed. "Of course, I was never good at things like that. It's just like those thought problems we had in math. If a boy gets on a train going twelve miles per hour and the train goes twenty-three miles and then it stops to let people off and then goes thirteen more hours at only seventeen miles per hour, then how many . . . Oh, I hated those things. I always started thinking about where the boy was going and who would be there to pick him up and if he would be all right. . . ." She smiled weakly at the three of them.

The light changed and the cars in the other two lanes moved ahead, but they sat there stopped, the motor of the Chrysler wagon idling quietly. The man behind them honked his horn.

"Tom, the light's green," Billy said.

"Well, *he* won't be all right," Tom said softly from behind the wheel. "*He* won't be all right anymore." His head lowered as if he couldn't hold it up. "God, why did it have to be my gun?"

"Oh, honey, please," Ellen said.

"Now come on, Tom," Billy said, "we've been all through this. There was no way for you to know, no possible way." He leaned forward and extended his hand, touching Tom lightly on the shoulder. "Come on, buddy, before this guy plows into us."

"My goddamn fucking gun," Tom said.

The man behind them honked again. Louder. Three times.

"Hey, Tom," Billy said gently, "you want me to drive?"

Tom slammed his foot hard on the accelerator. The Chrysler wagon jerked and screeched as it laid a stretch of rubber down Ward Parkway at the intersection of Gregory.

"A loaded gun in the closet," Tom said. "Where was my goddamn fucking mind?"

LEONARD LOOKED AT ANITA. "Are you okay, honey?"

"You're goin' awfully fast," Anita said.

"No I'm not." He made a left onto Ward Parkway off Eighty-third. "I hate the way she talks to you."

"It's okay; it's the way she is."

"What? Rude?"

"No. She's just"—Anita shook her head—"she's passionate. She gets excited about things. Tee's always been like that."

"Well, she better watch her mouth with me."

"You're gonna get a ticket."

"No I'm not, Anita."

"All right, Leonard, all right."

"God, I'm hungry," he said.

She looked out the window. She watched the big houses go by.

They rode in silence for several blocks, and then Anita smiled and began to laugh.

"What?" Leonard said.

She turned to him. "Hmm? Oh, I was just thinkin' about how Pete was afraid of Jell-O."

"Jell-O?"

"When he was a little baby. Mother had him at Aunt Eula's for a picnic and someone had made a Jell-O mold, you know, with different colors and fruit inside, and she scooped some onto a saucer to feed to him and when she moved the spoon up to his mouth, oh, he screamed and cried." Anita laughed. "And nobody knew what was the matter. She'd take the spoon away and he'd stop, and she'd bring the spoon back and he'd carry on." Anita looked at Leonard. "They couldn't figure out what it was." She laughed again. "You see, he'd never seen Jell-O before, and the way it was movin', he thought it was alive, you know, jigglin' on the spoon as she'd lift it to his mouth."

Leonard smiled at her.

"He was just a little baby," Anita said softly.

"Were you there, honey?"

"Oh, I guess so. I don't remember it happenin', though. I was just a year and a little more older than him. It's just that they talked about it so much that sometimes I think I remember."

"Uh-huh."

"I don't know what made me think of that."

"Maybe you're hungry too," Leonard said.

"Such a silly thing, Pete bein' afraid of Jell-O."

Leonard braked for the light at Seventy-fifth.

"He was afraid of loud noises too."

"What is it—Sixty-eighth?"

"Hmm?"

"Is it Sixty-eighth Street?"

"Mmm-hmm. Halfway up before State Line." She turned and looked out the window. "Motorcycles or a big truck, anythin' loud, he'd hold his little hands over his ears. 'No helicopter,' he'd say." She looked at Leonard. "He didn't like helicopters the most, so that's what he'd say for any loud noise. 'No helicopter.' " She smiled. "Of course, that was when he was little, not after he got big."

"Uh-huh."

"Then he wasn't afraid of anythin'." She sighed. "Of course, sometimes I think I remember things and then I realize it was just the movies."

"The movies?"

"Daddy had a movie camera, Leonard. One of those old home movie cameras they had back then. It didn't have any sound on it or anythin'."

"An eight-millimeter."

"I don't know, I guess so. Somebody owed him on a bet—that's how he got it, we wouldn't have had it otherwise. He didn't have any money for a thing like that. We didn't have any money for anythin', much less a movie camera."

Leonard looked at her. She was staring into space.

"All those little yellow boxes. She had them all stacked on their sides in shoe boxes, my mother, with the labels facin' up so you could see what you wanted to watch. Anita's sixth birthday, or Christmas at Gagee's with the dates—you know, so you could pick. We would sit and watch for hours; we didn't have a television then."

"Uh-huh."

Anita opened her purse and closed it. She turned it over in her lap.

"Daddy was always takin' movies. It didn't matter what we were doin'—sprinklin' each other with the hose, just walkin' back and forth or runnin' around in the yard—it didn't matter . . . anythin'. There he'd be, capturin' it for posterity to put inside another little yellow box."

She opened her purse again. And closed it.

"That's what he'd say to my mother: 'I'm capturin' this for posterity, Alice Maude, so you can look at it when I'm dead and gone.' And he'd laugh. Sometimes he'd make us get all dressed up like we were goin' somewhere and act like we were leavin' just so he could make a movie of it." She frowned. "Of course, he was hardly ever in them. He wouldn't let anybody hold the camera except sometimes Poppa, but if Poppa tried to get Daddy in the movie, Daddy would frown and wave him away."

She turned and looked at Leonard. "You know, Leonard, I have no idea what she did with that camera. I never saw it again afterward."

"Afterward what?"

"After my daddy died."

"Oh," Leonard said. "What happened to the movies?"

"All the little yellow boxes? When we moved away from Tupelo, she didn't bring them. I guess she didn't want to see them anymore."

Anita opened her purse again and took out a white lace handkerchief. She unfolded it and held it in her hand.

"Everythin' was on there, though."

Leonard reached over and patted her arm. "Are you okay, honey?"

"Everythin' "—she sighed—"captured for posterity." She turned to Leonard. "Did I ever tell you we had a dog?"

"No."

"Well, we did. Gagee got him for us. Oh, he was the cutest little thing. We named him Butchie, I don't remember why. He was a fox terrier, I think, and oh, he could jump so high. He used to chase Pete and me around the back and jump and jump. . . ." She sighed again. "He was on those movies, Butchie."

He looked at her. "Anita?"

Her eyes had filled with tears but she was staring straight ahead. "Poor Butchie."

"Honey?"

"They gave him away. Just like that. I woke up one mornin' and went to feed him his breakfast and he was gone. And his bowl and his bed and everythin'. Just gone. They got rid of him because he was too wild, but they didn't tell us that. They said he left to get married. That's what they said. And I believed them, Leonard. Pete said it was a lie, but I believed them with all my heart."

She looked at Leonard. The tears rolled down her face; she didn't wipe them with the handkerchief.

"Until I was big and Mother told me. Wasn't that a terrible thing to do to children, Leonard? To tell them a lie? I never lied to Mary and Charlotte. I didn't. Not ever. I always hated lies after that. I always hated that Pete lied."

ANNE STOOD AT THE WALL PHONE in her mother's kitchen. She dialed the area code and the number again, but this time hung up before it rang twice. She kept her hand on the receiver and took a breath.

Oh, God. What am I doing?

He wouldn't be at home now anyway. It's too early. His wife would answer in that high voice, and what would I say? Is Brennan there, please? I need to talk to him. My sister's locked herself in the bedroom and I don't know what to do. Is he home, please? This is . . . who? Who would I say I was? I could pretend to be Spanish. Oh, no, I couldn't. The last time I called there I hung up when she answered.

Anne looked at her watch. She frowned. He's at lunch.

She counted backward two hours to L.A. time again. She sighed.

He's at lunch; he's on late shift this week, he told me. He's sitting with his crew in the commissary, at that table on the left.

Anne smiled.

With sawdust in his hair and on his face, wood shavings on his T-shirt. Crinkles around his eyes. Muscles in his arms.

What did Pete say when I told him? When he was teasing me? What was that thing he said? Anne frowned and then she smiled.

"Carpenters are number two, darlin'. Of the six sexiest occupations, carpenters are number two. You better watch yourself."

"What's number one?" I said.

"I'm gonna hang up on you, SF. How could you ask me that? You know what's number one—travelin' salesmen are number one!"

"Well, he's just my friend. I don't have to watch myself. And he's married. I don't have relationships with married men. I told you that."

"Okay, SF."

Friends. We're pretending to be friends. But it's not the truth. I know it's not. I know how he looks at me. How I look at him. How he makes me feel. I know.

Anne sat down on one of the stools at the tile counter. She perched her elbows on the counter and put her face in her hands.

What did Pete tell me? Don't make it into a drama; men don't like drama.

Okay, okay.

But it is a drama, isn't it? I've fallen in love with him. I know I have. I've fallen in love with a married man. Me. Anne. Of all people.

A wife, two boys, a dog—no, two dogs. Wasn't it two dogs?

"What do you know about this guy?"

"What I told you . . . that he's married, he has two boys—"

"No, not that, Anne. What do you *know*?"

"Oh . . . that he's funny, that he's kind, that he cares about me. When I get there and he's waiting, he looks at me and I . . . I . . ."

"Okay, okay, then just take your time, just wait and see what happens."

"But it's wrong, Pete. He's married."

"Well, you haven't done anything but talk to him. You are allowed to talk, aren't you?"

"But I . . ."

"Don't get yourself in a commotion, darlin'; there's no way to plan."

Anne took her hands off her face. She sat up straighter.

But that's what I'm in. Isn't it?

A commotion.

She got up off the stool.

I'd just feel better if I could talk to him. Tell him about Jessie. See what he thinks I should do. He sees things so simply. I can't explain it. I have something on my mind and I tell him and he just sees it this other way, clearer, cleaner. . . . I don't know how he does that.

Maybe he'll call me. Even though I already talked to him this morning. Maybe he'll call me after he finishes lunch.

Anne walked to the refrigerator and opened the door. The shelves inside were empty. The air was cold against the front of her legs; cold, musty air. She closed the door.

She turned and looked around the kitchen, at the spotless white appliances, the round breakfast nook with the pale sea-green cushions and the windows looking out onto the lawn, the happy wallpaper with the apples and cherries and green leaves on a white background.

I lived here.

Jessie and I lived here.

We ate breakfast right here. Grady at the sink, Mother upstairs, Daddy already gone to work. Pancakes and orange juice . . .

God, was I happy? Have I ever been happy?

Joe made me happy. Didn't he?

Yes. But not comfortable. I always felt on edge; I couldn't tell him everything I felt. Not every part of what I felt. He wouldn't want to hear it, or he'd get angry or be bored. . . . Maybe he wouldn't, but I thought he would.

Maybe you can't tell anybody what you feel.

Maybe I've never felt comfortable.

Oh, but Brennan makes me comfortable. I can tell Brennan.

And you, Pete, I could always tell you.

Ice cubes clunked into the ice-machine part of the refrigerator, and Anne turned.

Oh, dear. Where are they? What's taking them so long?

What's Jessie doing up there?

Anne ran her hands through her hair, straightened her skirt.

She looked out the windows.

I nearly told Frances yesterday. Yesterday when we were talking. I nearly told her about Brennan. But I couldn't.

Besides, they wouldn't believe it. Or they'd laugh. Well, Frances wouldn't laugh, but Tee probably would. I can hear Tee: "Oh, that's great, Anne. The lady and the carpenter."

Oh, God, Pete, I can't tell anybody but you.

Anne looked at the telephone.

I told him all about you. Everything. When he drove me to the airport. I told him everything. He was so sweet. So dear. He held me while I cried. Right there in the America West parking lot with the sun going down and people all around, going to their cars, carrying their luggage. He held me and I cried. He didn't care that people could see us while he held me. They probably thought I was crying because I had to leave him. They didn't know I was crying about you, Pete. I told him everything. All about you, about you and Jessie, about all of us at school, about you and me at the cemetery . . . everything. How you've been my friend nearly all my life, how I—

The telephone rang. The sound was very shrill in the quiet kitchen. Anne was standing right next to it and she stumbled backward when it rang.

"Oh," she said out loud. "Oh, please . . . please, Brennan."

She grabbed the receiver before it could ring again.

"Hello?"

She closed her eyes.

"No. No, I'm sorry; no, we don't need a subscription for the *Kansas City Star*. No one lives here anymore."

JESSIE SAT ON THE FLOOR in the middle of the room. All the drawers in the desk were empty now; photographs and papers surrounded her. Old copies of *The Wheel*, four *Sachem* yearbooks—1957, 1958, 1959, 1960—swizzle sticks, bits of ribbon, cocktail napkins, matchbooks, and dried broken flower petals from dead corsages lay strewn around her on the pale-blue carpet. The little stuffed elephant sat upright on her lap.

If she heard the cars pull up, she gave no sign of it. She didn't rise, didn't go to the windows, didn't look up.

Wearing white underpants and a T-shirt of her father's—her dress tossed on a chair arm—she sat barefoot and cross-legged, Indian-style, on the rug, her head bent over some pages she held in her hands.

Slowly and methodically, Jessie ripped the pages into tiny pieces. Scraps of thin sky-blue paper sent from Lackland Air Force Base, August 1963, fell into the overflowing wastebasket in front of her. Pete's black slanted writing blurred in front of Jessie's eyes.

The doorbell chimed, but Jessie didn't look up.

"IS SHE STILL UPSTAIRS?" Tee asked Anne at the front door.

"What?" Billy asked, walking up behind her.

Anne nodded yes.

"She's still upstairs," Tee said to Billy. "Has she said anything?"

"No."

"Nothing? All the way here?"

"No. She just sat in the car and the policewoman drove."

"Did the policewoman say anything?"

"Just what she told me at the cemetery, what I told Tom on the phone."

"Who was on the phone?" Ellen asked, walking in with Tom.

"Wait a minute, Ellen," Billy said.

Anne touched Ellen's arm. "Ellen, you'll never guess who the policewoman was. Barbie Lucas. I mean Barbie Bumpas Lucas. She was a Bumpas before she married. Now she's divorced."

"A what?" Tee said. "What the hell is a Bumpas?"

"A Bumpas; she's Sherry Bumpas's little sister."

"I don't know Sherry Bumpas," Ellen said.

"She was two years before Anne and me," Tom said. "She was a cheerleader, a little blond."

"Not anymore," Anne said. "Her sister says she's huge now."

"Jesus, wait a minute," Billy said. "Who cares? What did she say about Jessie?"

"That she's been released, that it's over."

"They're not gonna prosecute?"

"No. The police think it was self-defense."

"What the hell does that mean?"

Anne frowned and looked as if she might cry. "I don't know, Billy. I'm just telling you what she told me. She didn't say anything else."

"But what did Jessie say?"

"She wouldn't talk about it; she would hardly talk to me at all."

"What were you talking about when she went and locked herself into the bedroom?"

"I don't know," Anne said. "It was nothing. We were just talking—well, I was talking, she wasn't saying much—about the house and all. I don't know . . . nothing specific, not about what happened, really, not about anything, and then . . . I don't know . . ."

Tom sat down hard on a side chair by the door. He rubbed his face with his hands. "Okay, we'll find out, we'll talk to her. Why don't we all calm down."

"Are you all right, honey?" Ellen said to him.

He didn't answer.

Tee moved to the piano, pulled up the muslin sheeting, and let her fingers touch the keys. She turned and looked at Anne. "It feels like your mother's still here."

"Does anybody have an aspirin?" Ellen asked, looking at Tom.

"Where's Frances?" Anne asked.

"Somewhere with George," Tom mumbled through his hands.

"Having a quickie," Tee said, and sat down at the piano.

"Tee, please," Billy said.

"Please what? I wish everybody would get the hell off my back."

"I thought you were in such a hurry to get to Jessie," Leonard said, coming into the doorway with Anita right behind him.

"Oh, go fuck yourself, Leonard," Tee said.

Nobody said anything or moved for at least a minute. Leonard stopped short in the foyer, Anita bumping up against him. Tee stayed where she was at the piano bench, her back to everyone.

Anne searched their eyes. "What's happened? What's the matter with you-all?"

Tee turned around. "We're not adjusting well to grief. No, I take that back. *I'm* not adjusting well. Everyone else is fine."

"Aren't we going upstairs to Jessie?" Ellen asked softly. She stood by the piano, one hand touching her chest and the other out in front of her, the palm extended up as if she were stopping something.

"We're not fine, Tee. Nobody's fine," Anita said.

"Oh, right. Good. I'll remember that."

Leonard took a step in front of Anita. "Why don't you just shut up, Tee."

"What?" Billy said. "What did you say?"

"I said I'm getting a little tired of your wife's mouth."

"Oh? Really?"

"Oh, dear," Ellen said.

"Wait a minute here," Tom said, getting up. "I think we ought to go upstairs and see to Jessie; I don't think we ought to start anything here."

"You know," Leonard said, "I don't need you to protect me, Tom. I can take care of myself."

"Oh, great," Billy said. "This is great."

"Tom," Ellen said.

"Hold on, Billy," Tom said, moving across the room.

"Hey! I don't need him telling my wife to shut up."

Leonard took a step toward Billy. "Oh? But it's all right for your wife to tell me to go fuck myself? Is that it?"

"You know, I'm really getting sick of you. Why don't you go on home?"

"Stop it, Billy. That's my family you're talkin' to," Anita said.

"Your family, Anita? What about the rest of your family? What about Pete?"

"Back off," Leonard said, putting himself in Billy's face, making distance between Billy and Anita.

"Get out of my way, asshole," Billy said, pushing Leonard back. "When's the last time you saw Pete, Anita? Huh? How many years has it been?"

"Leave her alone!"

"I said get out of my way!" Billy yelled.

"Oh, my God," Ellen cried. "What are you doing?"

"OH, MY GOD," Frances said, looking up into George's eyes. "What are we doing?"

"I thought you knew," George said, and he kissed her again, pushing her back against a cement pole at the entrance to the parking garage, pressing his body into hers, his legs against hers, his cock hard inside his pants against her groin. He moved his mouth off her mouth onto her ear and down her throat, inside the collar of her blouse.

"George . . . wait a minute . . . I was trying to tell you something."

"What . . . ?" he whispered. "Tell me."

"It's hot."

"It certainly is."

"No, I mean the cement . . ."

He pulled her to him from the pole, holding her fast to his chest with his left arm. "Sorry, baby."

"George, I was trying to—"

"What, what?" His right hand moved between them, skimming against the silk of her blouse, across her right breast. He felt the nipple harden under the silk, her legs bend as he held her, even though she flinched. "I got ya, baby."

"Don't do that!" she said, trying to dislodge herself.

"Where you going, baby?" he said, his lips at her cheek, his fingers moving gently against the silk, brushing the nipple softly as he kissed her again.

"Stop it, George!" Frances said, struggling.

"You're right. Let's go upstairs," George murmured, his lips covering hers.

"What?"

"I said, let's go upstairs."

She managed to pull her head back. "What?" she said, her eyes wide, red lipstick smeared around her mouth.

"Upstairs. To my room, Frances."

She looked at him. "You're staying here?"

He smiled.

Frances pushed his hands off her. "You're actually *staying* here? At the Marriott? You never stay at the Marriott!" She ran her fingers across her mouth. "You fuck!"

"What?"

"You planned this. You son of a bitch!" She pushed George hard in the chest. "How could you?" she said, her voice raised, mocking him. " 'Let's get a drink, Frances. I need a drink, Frances.' You fucking son of a bitch!"

A man and a woman with two little girls in party dresses walked to the car next to them and proceeded to unlock the doors. The little girls were smiling. They were holding pink balloons attached to long gold ribbons.

"Hey, Frances . . . ," George said, in an attempt to keep her quiet.

"I should have known. 'Let's get a drink, Frances.' 'Let's go to my room, Frances.' *What am I? Crazy?*"

"Frannie, please," George said, smiling sheepishly at the man and woman at their car, at the two little girls who stood there wide-eyed, gaping.

"Don't call me that! Don't you fucking call me that!" She yanked at her suit, pulled hard on the blouse, trying to tuck it in. "I came here to talk to you, and I'm necking with you in a goddamn parking lot! My God, how could I? I must have lost my mind!"

"Get in the car, Margaret Anne, get the kids inside the car," the man yelled at his wife.

George reached out to touch Frances on the shoulder.

"Don't touch me, goddamn it! *Don't you fucking touch me!*"

"Mommy!" said one of the little girls.

"Get your butt inside that car!" the man yelled.

"Alan!" the woman said.

"I'm so sorry," George said to the man and woman. "You see, our good friend died and she's very upset."

"What?" Frances screamed. *"What?"*

She hurled herself at George, tears running down her face, her dark hair flying, her hands batting at him.

"Frances, please," George said, trying to catch her arms. "Get ahold of yourself."

Frances's right arm swung back and she slapped George hard across the face as one pink balloon took off across the Marriott garage.

JESSIE PUSHED AT THE PAPERS in the wastebasket with the swizzle stick she took from her mouth. It was a black swizzle stick that said "Milton's Lounge" in white letters down the side. The letters were tilted as if written by a drunk, and at the end of the swizzle stick was a listing martini glass.

Jessie popped the stick back in her mouth, stood up, carried the wastebasket into the bathroom, and held it upside down, watching the debris float into the already overflowing sink. Everything that had been in the drawers now lay broken or ripped in the sink. Jessie took the stick out of her mouth, cracked it into pieces, and threw them on top of the pile.

Clasping the wastebasket to her chest, she carried it back to the bedroom and set it at the foot of the bed. Then she slammed each empty drawer back into the desk, brushed at some broken dried rose petals scattered on the spread, snatched up a piece of a black-and-white photograph caught on the dust ruffle, picked up whatever bits and pieces she had missed on the blue carpet, and threw them into the wastebasket.

Jessie surveyed the room. She moved to the moiré club chair in the corner and picked up her blue dress. Under it lay a shopping bag from Swanson's department store. Jessie left the dress on the chair and took the shopping bag with her.

She sat down on the rug, put the stuffed elephant back in her lap, and dumped the contents of the shopping bag out in front of her. Two sealed plastic bags slid to the rug.

"Look at this, José. Just like she promised."

Jessie picked up the bag closest to her knee. Inside was the terry-cloth robe she was wearing when Pete died. It was clear, through the plastic, that the robe was stained with blood, but Jessie didn't notice; she tossed that bag into the wastebasket without a glance.

"Detective Barbie Lucas, true to her word."

Jessie pulled the other bag over and held it in her hand.

"Took me to her house, bought my dress and shoes . . . and now this, José."

She ran her fingernail down the seal, opened the bag, and took out Pete's wallet and his pocketknife, the one he had carried since her father gave it to him the day they were married, the one with the mother-of-pearl handle, his initials on one side.

"You see, sweetheart, everything we need."

Jessie put the pocketknife on top of the elephant in her lap. She held Pete's wallet in both her hands and opened it. As she removed each item, she studied it thoughtfully and then tossed it into the wastebasket after crumpling it in her hands: their wedding photo, smiling at each other in a tuxedo and a gown, several small, square school snapshots of their kids, a formal family photo of the five of them around a Christmas tree, all dressed in red and green, an old cracked black-and-white Polaroid of Billy, Tom, and Pete with crew cuts, their arms slung casually over each other's slender shoulders, horsing around in front of Nat Glazer's motorboat down at the lake, a clipping from *TV Guide* with Frances's name circled in red, an old baby picture of Jessie and Anne wrapped in their father's arms, a dime-store photo-machine strip taken some years back of Pete and Grady—he's tickling her as she tries to leave the booth—a MasterCard, a Visa, a green American Express card, four gas credit cards, a driver's license and a Triple A card, a thick stack of cheap white business cards with "Pete Chickery, Sales Representative, *Ship 'n Shore*" embossed on them in black raised ink, a four-leaf clover pressed in cellophane tape, and a tiny scrap of pale-pink paper, folded and worn.

Jessie opened the paper. The writing was faded, but you could still read the words across the folds. "I love you, Pete," was written in Jessie's hand.

She crumpled the paper into a tiny ball and tossed it in with all the rest. She closed the empty wallet, ran her finger across the tiny tear on the edge of the fold, and threw it in the basket.

Jessie picked up the pocketknife and held it in her right hand. She opened it and stood up.

"You wait right there, José," she said to the little elephant. "We're almost nearly done."

She picked up the wastebasket with her left hand and took it with her to the closet. Putting it down by her foot, she opened the closet door.

It was virtually empty inside—a few discarded shoes, three round hatboxes on a shelf, bare metal hangers, a pink chenille bathrobe with an obvious wide rip in the right sleeve, a child's yellow rain slicker, and—pushed way over to the side of the closet—a wide gray plastic floor-length garment bag, zipped to the top.

Jessie slid the garment bag along the clothes rod until it hung directly in front of her. She closed her eyes and then opened them. She reached in, pulled down the zipper, leaned her shoulder against the closet doorjamb to steady herself, and touched her wedding gown.

THE FRONT DOOR OF THE CONNELL HOUSE slammed open and Leonard stormed out. He ran down the porch steps to the circle drive, with Anita pulling on his arm, trying to hold him back.

"Please, Leonard, don't go. I need you here."

"Calm down, Anita," Tom said, following them. "He's not going. We're all friends here."

"He's not my friend," Billy shouted from the doorway. "I don't even know him."

Leonard crossed the driveway to his car, with Anita in tow.

"I don't need this, Anita."

"You sure as hell don't," Billy said, starting down the steps. "Why don't you just go home?"

"Hold on, Billy," Tom said, "for god sakes."

"I'm not staying!" Leonard yelled back, "so you don't have to worry about it!"

"I can't believe this is happening," Anne said to Tee and Ellen as they all watched from the porch.

"I can," Tee said. "Billy, wait," and she went after him.

"You're not goin'," Anita said to Leonard. He had opened the door of the Mercedes and was starting to get in.

"Oh, yes I am. Now let go of my arm, Anita."

"Leonard, please."

"They don't want me here. I'm not staying where I'm not wanted."

"Leonard, please. I've got to talk to Jessie."

"Well, you don't need me to talk to her. Now let go of my arm. I've had enough of this!"

"Len, wait a minute here," Tom said, grabbing hold of Leonard's other arm.

"My name's not Len," Leonard growled, trying to shrug Tom off. "You people don't even know my name."

"Well, wait a minute, man. I was just trying to—"

"Let go of me, goddamn it," Leonard yelled at Tom, flapping his arm to loosen Tom's grip.

"Okay, okay, don't get nuts," Tom said, letting go. "I just thought we could work this out."

"*We?* I'm not a part of this. I never was!"

"Well, that's fine with us," Billy said.

"For crissakes, Billy," Tom said. "Let's just—"

"I don't need any of you, you hear me? And I didn't need Pete Chickery either—phony bastard that he was!"

Tom's face drained. "Hey, wait a minute here."

"Watch your mouth," Billy said.

"Watch my mouth? I'm sick of watching my mouth! That's the goddamn trouble. I've been watching my mouth too many years, watching my step. The hell with it—that's what I say!"

Leonard stuck his face right in front of Billy's. "Pete Chickery was a phony rotten bastard who fucked around his whole life, and if she hadn't shot him, someone else would've!" He turned and yanked his right arm hard. "Now let go of me, Anita!"

"Leonard," Anita cried.

She lost her hold on his arm and stumbled backward. Tom caught her before she fell.

George Massimino's dark-blue rented Pontiac raced up the driveway and screeched to a stop in front of the house, wedging Leonard's car in behind Ellen's Chrysler wagon.

"*Shit!*" Leonard yelled, smacking the roof of his Mercedes. "Move your goddamn fucking car!"

The Pontiac door flew open and George jumped out. "Where the hell is Frances?" he asked no one in particular.

GRADY MOVED THE BIG CADILLAC down Eighty-third and took a wide turn onto Ward Parkway. She adjusted her foot on the gas pedal and held the car steady at thirty-one on the speedometer. She took one hand briefly off the wheel, pushed at the brim of her straw topper, turned her head slightly, and looked at Frances in the passenger seat.

Frances felt Grady's eyes. She turned toward her.

"I stay under the speed limit," Grady said, her eyes back on the road.

"It's okay, Grady."

"They can jes go round me if they want. All of 'em. I make it a rule." She settled her body back against the seat cushions and shook her head positively. A little *humpft* sound escaped from her. Frances smiled. "Rushin' to nowhere is what I say, goin' round Meyer Circle like demons. Think they're Andy Granatelli."

"Mmm-hmm," Frances said.

"And not stayin' in the lines, slippin' over into the next person's lane like they do—it's not right."

They rode a few blocks. Frances looked out the window at the big houses lining Ward Parkway, brick and stone houses surrounded by large expanses of green, well-manicured lawns, neatly clipped hedges, tall oak trees.

"Stay in the lines, that's what Mr. Connell taught me. 'It don't matter the car, Grady, jes stay in the lines. Like colorin',' he says to me." She looked at Frances. "That's the trick, you know."

Cars passed the big Cadillac on both sides, but Grady held her ground, doing thirty-one in the center lane of the wide street. "So," she said.

"So," Frances repeated.

Grady smiled. "So one a my babies is a big movie star now, ain't she?"

Frances laughed. "Well, hardly, Grady."

"You are to me, child. That's one a mine, I say to everybody— do you believe that? Not that I raised you like I raised Anne and Jessie, I know that, but you're one a mine all the same." She cocked her head toward Frances. "Ain't you, child?"

"Yes, I am," Frances said, smiling.

"That's right. All a you mine since you're little girls. Six little girls."

"In two straight lines," Frances said.

"Hmm?"

"Nothing. Just something I remember." She smiled. "So, Grady . . . you went to see the movie?"

"Oh, I seen everything, baby, right from the start. All the TV, you know, even when you'd just walk by and say a little somethin' and be gone real fast. Tee'd call me up or Ellen, sometimes even your mama, so I'd know when to put it on. They all know I don't put the TV on as a general rule."

"Well, I'm glad they called you."

"Every time. I seen everything. Of course, I couldn't see that play—that was the only thing. I tried to get Maurice to go, but he wouldn't hear of it. 'Not up for discussion,' he says to me. 'I ain't got no business in New York. I ain't never been to New York and I ain't goin' now.'" Grady shook her head. "Never wants to go anyplace except his lodge. That's it. Otherwise he don't move. He don't even like to go out and eat."

"So did you like watching me, Grady?"

"Well, not all the time. I got to tell you that, Frances. Some a them things they put on the TV make me mad. Like that low-life picture where you was trash walkin' around in your underthings with all that shootin' and carryin' on. I like to died watchin' that. 'Get away from the set if you gonna take it to heart, woman,' Maurice says to me. 'It ain't real, you know, ain't nothin' bad happenin' to Frances in her real life.' What does that man take me for—a fool? I know it ain't real. I just don't like those shows. The devil's tools is what they are."

"Well . . ."

"No. You should talk to them people, Frances, make them think twice about the folks sittin' home stuck watchin' that trash. Put on some a them nice shows like they used to have—people singin' and dancin' . . . Why, whatever happened to that nice Italian fella who sang wearin' all them sweaters?"

"Sweaters?" Frances looked at Grady. "Oh, my God, Grady, you mean Perry Como?"

"That's the one. What happened to him?"

"Well, they don't have much call for him anymore, Grady. People don't want to watch shows like that."

"Well, people'd be a lot better off watchin' Perry Como than all that fightin' and killin', I can tell you that."

"I'm sure you're right, Grady."

"A course I'm right. People go crazy from watching too much crazy, and that's the God's honest truth."

A bright-red Porsche flew around the Cadillac on their left side. The driver was doing at least sixty and blasted his horn at them as he passed.

"See? Look at him. Where's he goin' in such a hurry? He don't even know, I can tell you that. None of 'em knows. Racin' to die is what Maurice calls it."

"Racing to die?" Frances asked softly.

"That's right."

Frances sighed and looked out the window. She had a sudden vision of Pete standing in the doorway of Ellen's bedroom closet with his arms stretched out in front of him, the palms spread, his fingers opened wide. "Don't shoot me, Jessie, I don't want to die," he said in Frances's daydream. The muzzle of the gun popped out from behind some dresses. It moved to the right and to the left, tracking like a radar scanner, until it pointed directly at Pete's chest.

"Well," Grady said, "we'll jes go on over there and see if they got her out."

She pursed her lips and frowned. "She's hidin', you know, that's what she's doin'. Used to do it when she was little. Whenever things got bad, Jessie'd go and hide." Grady shook her head. "She's hidin' 'cause she don't know how to live without him. Ain't no secret to me."

She looked over at Frances.

"Frances?"

Frances stared off into space, her eyes frozen on the daydream, a frown across her forehead.

"Frances?"

"Mmm?"

"Did you hear what I said, child?"

Frances didn't answer.

Grady took her right hand off the wheel and touched Frances on the shoulder.

"Whatchu thinkin' about, baby? How you smacked that boy?"

"George," Frances said.

"George. I know. George Massimino. You think I don't know? Don't be too hard on yourself—there's a reason you hit that boy. And besides, there's no accountin' for grief. When my daddy died, me and my stepmother, Lurene, we done had ourselves a knock-down screamin' match right there in front of his casket. It was terrible, let me tell you, a terrible, terrible thing. That's right, chile. When you breakin' apart inside, you just don't know whatchu gonna do, what evil gonna fly outta you when you least expect it." Grady sighed a big sigh, shook her head from side to side.

"Grady," Frances interrupted, "when did you see him last?"

"Who? Pete? Why, I seen Pete all the time. Once a week, 'cept when he was on the road with the blouses—that could change it. Used to see him lots more when I was still over to the Connells', but when Mr. Connell passed—may the good man rest in peace—I jes—"

"Once a week?"

Grady looked at Frances. Frances was staring at her.

"What?"

"You saw Pete once a week?"

"A course, baby. He's been comin' to my house for breakfast Monday mornin's, seven a.m., since I don't know when. I used to

go there too, to his house, couple times a week until my rheumatoids
got too bad. Used to help Jessie with the babies, iron Pete's
shirts—he always liked the way I did the collars—but then when
my knees couldn't do it no more, then we was down to once a
week. Monday mornin's, seven a.m."

Frances stared at Grady.

"That's right, that's what we did. And if he was on the road
sellin', then he'd call from where he was." Grady chuckled. "A
telephone breakfast, that's what he called it. Like on the radio. See,
he bought me this special talkin' phone so I can move around the
room, make my coffee, do whatever I want; I don't have to hold
on to no phone while I talk. You ever seen one a them?"

"A speakerphone? Pete bought you a speakerphone?"

"That's it, a speakerphone. I can't ever remember that name.
See, I'm not supposed to sit in one place; my knees freeze up bad,
so I'm supposed to keep movin'. . . . This way Pete says he can
check up on me, hear me movin' on that phone. 'I don't hear you
movin', lady, you better be movin',' he'd say to me on that phone."
Grady laughed and her eyes filled up with tears. "Lord, I'm gonna
miss that boy."

Frances sat there, half turned in her seat, shaking her head.

"What?" Grady asked.

"I don't know. He just never stops amazing me."

"Well, he was that kind of a boy. Had a way about him, a
particular way. I always said that."

"A speakerphone."

"That's right."

"Breakfast every Monday."

"Uh-huh, and I made him the same exact thing all these years,
eggs basted and biscuits with a splash of gravy. And then, all of a
sudden, last December he up and changes his mind, says he wants
somethin' called eggs benedick. I said, 'I can't make that, Pete. I
don't know nobody who can make that.' So he got me the recipe
from a place in New York where he liked it. See, the sauce is the
trick—you got to get it just right or it curdles up on you."

"The Plaza!"

"What?"

"The Plaza Hotel. In New York. He got the recipe from The
Plaza Hotel. He asked me to get it for him."

"Oh, that's right; he ate it there when he went in to see you."

Frances turned and looked at Grady, her eyes wide.

"Oh, Lord," Grady said softly, "now what have I gone and done?"

"You knew he came to see me?"

"Well, now, Frances, I did, but I never told a soul."

"He told you?"

"Pete told me everythin'. Always. I never told one soul, not even Maurice."

"You know about me?"

"Whatchu mean, Frances?"

"I mean why he came to see me last winter—last December, to be exact. Why he came to see me then?"

"I do."

"Oh, Grady." Frances put her hand up against her face, her fingers flat across her mouth.

"Now, Frances, I never told one soul. Nobody knows about your troubles. I couldn't even say nothin' to you, on account a how I never breathe a word of what Pete tells me in our personals. That's why I couldn't call you up or write you a letter, but I been prayin' for you, I been prayin' for you every day since I know. He told me that very day, the day he came home from New York that first time; he came right to my house from the airport. Sittin' at my kitchen table, cryin' like a baby, and he says, 'Now, Grady, this is a big one, you gotta watch yourself on this,' and he told me the whole thing. About your trouble and what they done to you in the surgery and how he knew before he even went, felt it in his bones, knew somethin' was wrong and had to see for himself, just fly in there on the spur of the moment and see if you was okay. Surprisin' you like that—so sweet, that boy."

"Oh, Grady."

"But he said you was fine in December, Frances. He assured me. Said you was a little under the weather in the spirits department, but he said he fixed you right up. The cancer is gone, he said to me. 'It's gone, Grady, and it ain't comin' back.' I tole him only the good Lord knows about things like that, but he said no, he looked in your eyes and he knew it was true. You know Pete, how he could tell a story, made me feel like I'd been right there with the two of you."

Frances laughed, remembering how they had been in the bed at The Plaza Hotel.

"He knew I'd be fine, huh?"

"That's right."

"He knew I'd be fine," Frances said again, and then she covered her face with her hands and she was sobbing, shoulders hunched forward and horrible sounds coming from deep inside her.

"Oh, now, child, don't cry like that . . . sure you gonna be fine."

Grady watched Frances out of the corner of her eye while she drove.

"Now, Frances, you don't want to do that, baby, that's not good for you . . . Frances . . . child . . . oh, Lord, look what we got here."

Grady flipped on her turn signal, changed lanes, and took a left on Sixty-eighth Terrace. She pulled the Cadillac up to a nice shady spot in front of the second house from the corner, parked evenly against the curb, cut the engine, and moved over.

She took Frances in her arms. "Shh, now, baby. Grady's gotchu."

Frances folded up into Grady's big chest and Grady rocked her as one might a small child. She sobbed until Grady's neck and shoulder and the front of her Sunday-best black dress were soaking wet with tears.

"He said I was down in the spirits department?" Frances asked. "Is that what you said?"

"That's right. Said how you was feelin' poorly about yourself, 'bout how you looked and all—you know, what with . . ."

Frances attempted a smile. "What with my breast missing?"

"Now, Frances . . ."

"And he was crying? Did you say he was crying?"

"Well, a course he was cryin', child. He loved you very much."

"He loved me very much," Frances whispered, and she lowered her head again.

"Now, Frances," Grady said. She put her fingers under Frances's chin and raised her head. "You know Pete Chickery loved you."

"Yes, I know."

"That's right."

She smoothed back a piece of hair that had stuck on Frances's wet cheek, pulled a white handkerchief out from the sleeve of her dress, and wiped the tears from Frances's face.

"He loved you and you loved him."

Grady looked hard into Frances's eyes.

"And you shoulda married him."

"What?" Frances sniffed.

"You shoulda married Pete, not that George Massimino."

"What are you saying?"

"I know what I'm talkin' about. I tole Maurice once, I tole him a thousand times, 'They all marryin' the wrong ones; it's gonna blow up in their face.' "

"Grady."

"Don't Grady me, child. I knew it from the time you was startin' out. I knew it even then."

"What?"

"That it wasn't right."

"What wasn't right?"

Frances took the handkerchief from Grady and wiped around her eyes.

"That Jessie needed Pete too much. And you needed George Massimino too much. That's why you're always actin' funny whenever he's around."

"What do you mean?"

Frances blew her nose into Grady's handkerchief.

"You know what I mean. Not smart like you are, but like half your brain's missin', your eyes flyin' around in your head, tongue-tied and silly . . . You're still doin' it today."

"I am not."

"You are too, Frances. That's why you smacked him in the head."

"Grady, this is absurd. You can't mean this."

"Oh, I mean it, all right. Jessie couldn't look at Pete—she needed him too much. And he couldn't live with that—that's what made him run around. Made him crazy and it made her crazy too."

"But, Grady . . ."

"No. I'm tellin' you. That's why she's hidin'. She couldn't live with him and she sure can't live without."

JESSIE STOOD ANKLE-DEEP in shreds of thick cream satin. She bent, scooped up another armful, and threw those into the wastebasket. Scraps of satin kept sliding out of her arms. The bodice of her wedding gown was all that remained on the padded hanger. She grabbed hold of it and slashed it with the pocketknife until it was barely recognizable. Then she threw it and the hanger at the wastebasket and shut the closet door.

Wisps of satin and ivory lace clung to the old T-shirt of her father's that she was wearing and to the curls of her hair. She crunched across the tiny seed pearls scattered under her bare feet. Picking up the stuffed elephant, the overflowing wastebasket, and the pocketknife, she carried them into the bathroom. Then she put the wastebasket down under the window, laid the pocketknife and the elephant on the edge of the bathtub, and turned on the faucets. She felt the water and adjusted the temperature, adding more hot, then pulled her T-shirt off over her head and let it fall to the floor, stepped out of her white underpants, bent down, picked up both items, and threw them into the hamper.

Jessie stood naked at the bathroom window. She tugged gently on the cord to the oak venetian blind until the slats were perfectly horizontal. She looked out across the grass to the big pine where her parents' front lawn touched up against the Glazers'.

She stared at the street, at the cars parked up and down, at the two big weeping willows in the yard across the way. She saw a little girl pedal a bike with training wheels down the sidewalk. A large Irish setter lumbered along beside her.

She glanced back at the FOR SALE sign stuck in her parents' grass by the hedge and then looked at her friends standing in the driveway.

Her mother's old black Cadillac moved slowly down the street and turned into the drive. George ran to the passenger side and opened the door. Frances got out. Tom opened the driver's door and held out his hand. Grady got out. Tee had her hands on Billy's chest. Ellen moved toward Tom. George said something to Frances, but she turned and walked away. Anne stood by the hedge, her arms wrapped around her waist as if she were cold. Anita stood alone at the curb. Jessie watched.

In her mind, snow fell and covered the grass, thin icicles formed and hung down from the gutters, the pine tree branches bent with white. Jessie's body swayed slightly at the window. She took a breath, leaned forward, and let her forehead touch the wooden blind. She looked out at the snow.

"A sandwich or what?" she asked him again. He was behind her, still lying in her bed.

"I don't know. Is it still snowin'?"

"A little. It's beautiful."

"It is, huh?"

Jessie raised the venetian blind, put her face up to the glass, laid her cheek against the windowpane. "Cold," she said. "So what do you want—a sandwich?"

"How much time we got?"

Jessie's eyes moved to the clock on her dresser. "Forty-eight minutes."

"No sandwich. Come back here."

"Come look at this."

"Come back here, Jessie."

"Pete, come look at this—it's beautiful."

"You're beautiful. Come back here."

"Nope," she said, smiling into the glass.

A pillow hit her in the small of the back. She didn't turn around.

"Jessie . . ."

"Pete, come look at the snow."

Another pillow hit her on the left shoulder.

"If I have to come get you, you'll have to pay the penalty."

"Oh, yeah?" she said, grinning at the window.

"You don't want that," he said.

"I don't?"

"No, you don't," he said. Another pillow hit her in the back.

"I'm tough. I can handle it."

"I don't think so," he said. "The penalties are very hard this afternoon."

She laughed. "It's nearly dark . . . the light is changing . . . it's my favorite time of the day."

"Jessie."

"What?" Her heart was beating fast in her chest. She put her fingers next to her nose on the cold glass. She breathed a little cloud of frost onto the window.

"Don't change the subject."

"What's the subject?"

And he was behind her. He put his hand on the back of her

neck and gently lifted up her hair. He breathed softly on her neck, kissed her skin from the nape of her neck to behind her right earlobe. "I had to come get you," he said. "Big penalty"—grazing her ear with his breath, his face next to hers at the glass—"for disobeyin'."

"Oh, yeah? What?"

His chest up against her back. His hands around her body, crossed at her waist, cupping her breasts.

"What?" she asked again, leaning back against him, her breath catching in her throat.

"Big, very big," he whispered in her ear.

His thumb brushing her nipple, so soft . . . and then not so soft.

"Tell me," she whispered, her knees shaking.

His other hand on her other breast, his lips against her ear.

"Of course, maybe we don't have time." His penis hard up against her back.

"We have time," she whispered, her hands pushing against the glass.

"What time will they be home?"

"Five; not till five."

"I don't know," he said, turning her around, his head bending, his mouth circling her nipple, sucking her breast.

"Oh, Pete," Jessie said. She was wet.

He raised his head. "What?"

"Tell me the penalty," she said softly.

"Rug burns," he said, grinning at her, pulling her down beside him on the pale-blue carpet.

Jessie laughed.

She laughed out loud at the window and opened her eyes. Sunshine. The snow was gone, the grass was green, the weeping willows bent and dipped in the thick June air.

Grady stood in the driveway, looking up at Jessie's face. Jessie felt Grady's eyes. She pulled the cord fast to shut the venetian blind, dropped it as if it were hot, and stumbled back. She grabbed the sink and saw her face in the mirror. She ran her fingers up the sides of her cheeks and into her hair. She pulled the dark curls taut away from her face and stared at her eyes.

Pete stepped up behind her. He smiled at her in the mirror. Jessie closed her eyes and shook her head.

"Don't do this," she whispered. "Don't do this to me." She opened her eyes, and Pete was gone.

She released her hair, moved to the bath, checked the water in the tub, and turned off the taps. She looked down at the little elephant.

"Okay, José," Jessie said. "That should be just about enough."

"WELL, WE'RE A DISMAL PARADE," Tee said as they filed back inside the house. "We need pom-poms."

Grady closed the big front door.

"Wait a minute, Grady; you forgot Frances and George," Ellen said.

"They gonna have a little talk. They'll be in directly." She moved toward the kitchen. "I'm takin' off my hat."

"You going up with me, Grady?" Anne asked.

"Yes, baby. I'm jes gonna collect myself. I'll be right back."

Anne watched Grady move down the hall. She stood at the bottom of the steps, her hand on the wooden banister.

Anita sat down on the edge of a sofa.

"You all right, Nita?" Tom asked.

"What?"

"I said are you all right?"

"I'm fine, Tom, thank you."

"Hey, I'm sorry about what happened, about us and Leonard." He leaned forward to say something else, but Anita stood up.

"I know, I know you are."

"Anita," Billy said, "it's none of my business about you and Pete. I shouldn't have opened my mouth."

"It's okay, Billy." She looked at everyone in the living room. "Why don't we just let it go? After all, it doesn't make any difference. Pete and I never would have made our peace. Never. Now all I want is to make my peace with Jessie, that's all I want to do." She turned. "I'm gettin' a glass of water."

"I'll get one with you," Billy said. "You want one, Tee?"

"No."

"Ellen?"

"I'll come with you. I need an aspirin."

"Bring me water," Tom said, "with lots of ice." He sat down on the sofa. "And two aspirin."

"Jesus, what a day," Billy said as he left the living room.

Anne walked back and forth at the bottom of the steps.

"You want a drink of water, Anne?"

"No," she said softly.

Billy patted her on the shoulder as he moved off down the hall.

"It'll be okay," Billy said.

"Mmm-hmm," Anne said, looking up the staircase.

"DON'T TELL ME you didn't, I don't believe you. It was deliberate," Frances said. She moved the palm of her hand across the top of the hedge. "How could you do that, George? How could you do that to me?"

"What did I do that's so terrible? Want to make love to you?"

"Jesus, George, is this the day you picked? Today of all days?"

"Why is this day different from all other days? Huh, Frances? I remember, you know."

"What do you remember—what it was like to be married to a Jew? Don't spout my prayerbook at me, George."

"What it was like to be married to you, Frannie, that's what I remember."

"I told you not to call me that."

"Okay, okay, I won't call you that. Jesus, don't you understand that I miss you?"

"You miss me? This is the way you show me that you miss me? What did you think was gonna happen? I was gonna go upstairs with you and fuck our brains out in between Pete's funeral and his wake? Or whatever the hell it's called! Is that what you thought? Don't you know me at all?"

"Frances, please."

"Please what? Is that what you thought? Is that what you think of me?"

"Are you telling me you didn't like what was happening? You didn't participate? You didn't kiss me back?"

"Of course I kissed you back. I'm not a fucking stone. I know I kissed you back."

He looked at her across the hedge. "You always kissed me back."

"Don't do this, George."

"Jesus, Frances. I think about you all the time."

"I don't care."

"I wonder why we aren't together."

She glared at him. "Oh, that's a good one. Experiencing short-term memory loss now, are we?"

He got up from where he sat on the concrete steps and walked to Frances at the hedge.

"If Pete were here, he'd tell you."

Frances's mouth dropped. "You're gonna use Pete? You'd stoop to using Pete?"

"I told him."

"You're amazing."

"I told him when we talked, the last time that we talked."

She stepped back away from him. "You make me sick, George; you really make me sick."

She turned to move away, but he grabbed her by the arms.

"I told him I was going to go to New York and tell you how I felt."

"I don't want to hear this. Let go of me."

"He agreed with me, Frances. Pete said he thought I should."

"Don't talk about Pete—don't even say his name!"

She struggled to get out of his grip, but he held her fast. "I still love you, Frannie, and I think you love me too."

Frances stopped struggling and looked up at George. She shook her head and smiled.

"You really are a bastard, aren't you? Why the hell do I keep forgetting that?"

BILLY AND GRADY CAME OUT of the kitchen together and moved down the hall.

"You want me to go up with you?" Billy asked Anne at the bottom of the stairs.

"Let Grady try first."

"Call me if you need me. I'll be in the living room."

Grady and Anne went up the steps. Grady held tightly to the banister, pulling herself up, stopping after each step. Anne stayed by her side.

"No good, these knees a mine," Grady said, shaking her head.

"Take your time, Grady; it's fine."

"When I think a how many times I went up and down these steps, polishin' this railin', dustin' down these walls." She made a little *tsk* sound with her teeth. "Up and down . . ." She stopped to catch her breath. "Carryin' the laundry and all my cleanin' stuff . . ." She pulled herself up another step. "That vacuum like to killed me."

Anne moved up another step. Grady followed.

"All the things I carried, no wonder 'bout my knees."

"Oh, Grady," Anne said, and took Grady's hand.

"Up and down . . . up and down . . ."

Anne squeezed Grady's hand. "You carried us when we were little. I remember that."

"Both my baby girls . . . up and down these steps."

They moved up the last step together. Grady dabbed at her upper lip with her fingertips.

"Well, a lot a years has passed," she said. "I sure couldn't carry you now."

Anne smiled. Grady patted her on the shoulder.

"Come on, child, let's go get your sister out."

They moved down the hall to Jessie's room. Grady straightened two of the pictures as she passed.

Anne stood to one side of the door as Grady knocked.

"Jessie? Come here and talk to me." Grady stood still, her head cocked to one side, listening. "Jessie, it's Grady." She looked at Anne. "She's hidin' in there, you know."

Anne sighed.

Grady knocked again. "Jessie, stop your hidin'. All your friends is here."

She looked at Anne again. "Stub-bor-on," she whispered. "Just like your mama." She shook her head from side to side and turned back to the door.

"You worryin' me to death, Jessie Connell—whatchu doin' in there?" Then, a little louder: "You better mind me now."

She waited and then looked at Anne.

"I saw her in the window," she whispered.

"You did?"

"Mmm-hmm. She was lookin' out at them trees." Grady stood there. Then she called out, big and loud, "You want me to have these boys to come and break down this door, Jessie Connell, is that what you want?"

JESSIE SAT NAKED on the closed toilet seat. She ripped the last page out of the 1960 *Sachem* yearbook that lay in her lap, crumpled it into a tight ball, and tossed it in the sink with all the rest.

"And so, ladies and gentlemen," Mr. Shannon bellowed into the microphone. Feedback screeched around the auditorium. He grimaced and stepped back. A couple of kids behind Jessie laughed. Tee turned around from three rows up and made a face.

Mr. Shannon adjusted his glasses and stepped up to the mike again. "Ahem . . . uh, testing . . . excuse, uh, me . . ." He tapped the mike twice with his finger.

"Jesus Christ," Ronnie Green hissed next to Jessie. "What a jerk."

Jessie took a breath and touched her hand to her chest. The fabric of the blue-gray rented graduation robe was scratchy and smelled faintly of cleaning fluid. She moved her body inside the robe; it felt strange to be wearing only underwear underneath. Underwear and stockings and a slip. God, is this thing wool? Jesus, wool in June. Ronnie Green's arm touched her shoulder; she looked up at him. His dimples were very deep when he smiled.

Someone Jessie had never seen before ran out from the wings, did something to the microphone, whispered at Mr. Shannon, and ran off the stage.

"Ah, well . . ." Mr. Shannon positioned his body back about a foot from the mike. "Ahem . . . well, there . . . uh . . . It is with great pleasure . . . Ladies and gentlemen, may I present to you, uh, *now*"—there was some gentle laughter from the crowd—"the, uh, Harrison High School graduating class of nineteen hundred and sixty."

Shoes shuffled on a hardwood floor. Auditorium seats banged back.

Four hundred sixty-eight of us standing up, Jessie thought, there's four hundred sixty-eight of us standing up, sweating in these robes.

Jessie stood up in the bathroom. The broken *Sachem* binder fell from her lap and clattered on the tile floor.

"Jessie, whatchu doin' in there?" Grady yelled from the hall.

Jessie looked back over her shoulder. Where were Anne and her parents? Somewhere in the crowd. And Tom and George and Anita—all home from college to watch them graduate.

Billy gave her a wave; he was three rows back, standing next to Pete Chickery. Pete grinned at her. God, his eyes were blue. She gave them both a little wave and turned around front again.

She studied the back of McGraw's head, her blond pageboy bouncing above her shoulders.

Mr. Bishop raised the baton. He smiled out at them. A wide, strong smile, assuring them that it was true, they could sing.

The piano began.

Oh, my God, we're graduating. . . .

Jessie crossed her arms in front of her chest, clasped hands with Ronnie Green and the girl on her other side. What is her name? I know her. She's a friend of Frances'; she was in my chemistry class last year . . . Jesus, what's her name? She's wearing Chantilly perfume . . . Mr. Lund taught chemistry with moss on his teeth . . . Oh, my God . . .

"*For all we know, we may never meet again . . .*"

Ronnie Green is breaking my hand.

"*Before you go . . .*"

He has a good voice; why wasn't he in choir?

"*. . . make this moment sweet again. We won't say goodbye until the last minute . . .*"

I'm going to Northwestern, I'm getting out of here . . . oh, listen to us sing . . . honeysuckle, I smell honeysuckle . . . it must be coming in the open windows . . . honeysuckle and grass . . .

"*I'll hold out my hand and my heart will be in it . . .*"

Ellen's soprano is behind me. . . . What number was she? Two hundred and thirty-what? I can't remember. I'm seventy-two, good old seventy-two, and Tee is six 'cause she's so damn smart, and Frances is after me . . . and poor Lizzie Jones is last, last-ranked in class and first to go all the way. . . . Oh, God . . . what am I thinking . . . ?

Jessie sang louder as she moved to the sink.

"Jessie!" Grady yelled, rattling the doorknob hard.

"*This may only be a dream . . .*"

We sound like the Mormon Tabernacle Choir. . . . My God, Ronnie is crying.

"We come and go . . ."

Honeysuckle and sweat, gym shoes, Chantilly . . . Suze, that's her name, Suze Rainier, just like the prince . . . look how cute Ronnie is; his dimples are so dear . . .

Jessie grinned at the mess in the sink. She stuck her hand into it and pulled out a shiny white matchbook, took out one match, lit it, closed the cover, and used that match to light the whole matchbook.

"So love me tonight . . . ," Jessie sang as she touched the burning matchbook to the pile in the sink. Scraps of glossy pages from the yearbook caught fire and flamed.

"Tomorrow was made for some . . . ," she sang as she moved away from the sink.

She dropped the burning matchbook into the wastebasket when it scorched her fingertips.

"Tomorrow may never come . . . ," she sang as she stepped into the tub and inched herself slowly down into the hot water. She took the little elephant off the bathtub ledge and clasped him to her breasts in the water.

"For all we know . . . ," Jessie sang.

She did not look at the fire in the sink.

She did not see the other fire burning in the wastebasket.

The matchbook blackened and curled, the silver-gilt letters on the cover that said "Jessie and Pete—June 23, 1961" melted and burned, and everything in the wastebasket under the window began to flame, but Jessie didn't see.

She picked up Pete's pocketknife in her right hand and opened it.

"For all we know . . . ," Jessie sang in a whisper to José, *"we may never meet again . . ."*

"I'M TELLING YOU, I smell smoke," Billy said.

Tee laughed. "It's an occupational hazard—he's got smoke on the brain," she said to everyone as they followed him up the stairs.

"I don't smell anything," Ellen said.

"Jesus! She's burning something up there," Billy said, taking the stairs three at a time.

Tom ran after him.

Billy banged hard on the door with his fist.

"Jessie, open the door!" He put his palms flat against the door, feeling the wood up top and down low. "Shit, we got a fire! Tee, call 911."

Tee ran down the hall.

"Oh, my God," Anne said, leaning into Grady.

"Billy knows what to do, child, he knows what to do."

"Tom, please," Ellen said, trying to pull him back by the arm.

"Jessie," Anita said softly.

Billy backed up, crouched, sprang, and ran at the door, kicking it hard at the knob. The polished oak didn't budge, but little puffs of smoke started seeping out from the edges of the doorframe.

"Oh, Grady," Anne cried, and Grady held on to her.

"Get out, everybody, get out of the house!" Billy yelled. "Tom, get over here—you gotta help me bust this door!"

Tom ran to Billy's side, and Ellen burst into tears.

JESSIE CUT ONE DEEP HORIZONTAL GASH across her left wrist, which sent a gush of blood rising high into the air, splattering across her chest and face.

"Pete," she whispered.

She tried to cut again, but she couldn't keep her hand steady on her wrist and she was having trouble holding on to the knife. The smoke hung low and thick in the bathroom. Her eyes stung. José floated by in the red water. She saw him in a blur.

"Sweet baby elephant," Jessie whispered up at Pete. He handed her the little stuffed toy and took her in his arms.

"Thank you, Mr. Chickery," she said into his chest.

"I love you, Jess," he said, kissing her nose and eyes.

"I'm too big to love."

She tried to manipulate her protruding pregnant belly into his hug. "That's why you bought an elephant." She laughed. "I see the hidden meaning here. You should have bought a truck."

"They don't make stuffed trucks. I wanted somethin' soft."

"I still can't believe I'm pregnant again after all these years."

He kissed her mouth and held her close to his chest.

She smelled his skin, rubbed her face up against him.

"So what do you think it's gonna be—a baby, an elephant, or a truck?" Jessie said into Pete's neck.

"An elephant," he said, lifting her face to his again. "I'm absolutely sure."

The wicker hamper crackled and blew up. Jessie saw the bolt of orange and blue. She shut her eyes.

"Don't close your eyes, Jess," Pete said. "That keeps in the pain. Breathe, baby."

"I'm trying to breathe," she said. "It hurts. And don't get tough with me; in the olden days they wouldn't even let you in here. I did it all myself. Ow."

"I would have been in here if they would have let me. Now look at the elephant, darlin', come on, look at José and breathe." He wiggled the little stuffed toy in front of Jessie's eyes.

"José?" She laughed through panting breaths. "Did you say José?"

"Breathe, Jess."

"I'm breathing, Pete. José?"

The towels burst into flame.

"What's the matter with José? The baby's coming out! I can see the top of his head, Jess, I see the top of his head!"

"I'm not naming him José," Jessie said, grimacing while she pushed. "He's gonna be a girl."

"Come on, baby, you're doin' it!"

"This time a girl."

Fire raced along the wall, lifting the wallpaper as it moved.

"We're gonna name her Amy," Jessie said.

"Fine, we'll name him Amy. Here he comes, Jess, here's his head. Holy Mother, here's his head!" Pete yelled.

"It's not a boy," Jessie whispered, her body sliding deeper into the water as she fought for consciousness. "He's gonna be a girl."

"I love you, baby. Breathe!" Pete said.

The heat in the bathroom was intense. Heat singed the curls around Jessie's face. It burned the ivory skin on her face, her ears, her neck, her chest, her breasts, her shoulders, her upper arms, the tops of her thighs and her knees; it burned every part of Jessie that rose out of the water. She choked on the smoke, her eyes clenched tight against the pain.

"Breathe, Jessie!" Pete yelled.

"I can't," she whispered. "I'm trying, but I can't."

THEY HURLED THEMSELVES at the door, kicking it hard in perfect unison, Billy yelling as they crashed. Thick billows of gray smoke poured out into the hall.

"Get down!" Billy shouted as he dropped to his knees. "Get down flat, Tom!"

Tom fell to the floor.

"Stay here. I'm going in!"

"Jesus Christ," Tom said, spread-eagled on the rug.

On his hands and knees, Billy crawled forward into Jessie's bedroom.

"Jessie!" he screamed as he searched for her.

Fresh oxygen from the hallway fed the flames. Fire chased around the walls, consuming things as it went. The smoke was heavy; Billy stayed low. He crawled from the bedroom to the bath.

"Jessie!"

He found her in the tub.

"Jessie," he whispered at the naked body submerged in the bloody water. "Jesus God, Jessie," Billy said, sweat running down his face.

He raised up on his knees, leaned into the tub, grabbed her tight under her armpits, and pulled her out.

"C'mon, baby, c'mon, baby, c'mon, baby . . . ," Billy chanted. He flipped her over as she passed across the bathtub ledge, her thin white body over and down onto the tile floor.

"C'mon, baby . . . ," Billy said as the heat burned the skin on the backs of his ears and the back of his neck, singed the hairs on his hands and his arms as he pulled her out and onto him.

"C'mon, baby," Billy whispered, coughing into the smoke.

The fire roared with renewed strength. The flames that had started in the wastebasket and then lit the venetian blind leaped greedily across the ceiling and joined the flames burning in the sink.

"Let's go!" Billy yelled under the din.

He grabbed hold of her by the waist and, stumbling backward in a half-run, half-slide, pulled her wet, slippery body out of the burning bathroom.

The window exploded.

"What the fuck was that?" George said, looking up. Jagged glass shards rained on him and Frances, standing on the front-yard grass. Smoke billowed into the sky.

"Jessie!" Frances screamed, and ran for the house.

Jessie coughed and choked. Her eyelids fluttered and opened.

"Let go of it," she mumbled into Billy's chest as he ran with her in his arms.

"What? What'd she say?"

"Jesus, Billy, look at all the blood," Tom said.

A dark red trail followed them down the carpet. Blood ran from Jessie's wrist, over her hand, and down her fingers.

"Shit!" Billy said. He dropped Jessie on the rug at the top of the stairs, fell on his knees beside her, and ripped at his shirt, tore it from his body, the buttons flying as he pulled.

"Grab ahold of her arm," Billy said to Tom.

"Let go," Jessie said, but the words didn't quite come out.

Her eyes flickered. She saw Pete through the smoke.

Pete reached forward and touched the banana in her hair. There were tears on his face.

"Don't you know I love you? Please don't do this, Jess," Pete said. The clothes swung on the hangers behind his head.

She pulled away from his touch.

"Shit, Tom!" Billy yelled. "Hold on to her, I said!"

Tom grabbed Jessie's arm again. He held it tight as Billy twisted the shredded shirt around her wrist.

"Jesus," Tom said, as blood soaked the cloth.

"We're out of here!" Billy yelled. "Go, Tom! Get out!"

Billy threw Jessie's bleeding arm around his neck, his hand clamped to the wound to stop the blood, grabbed her by the waist, yanked her back up into his arms, and ran after Tom down the stairs.

"I got you, baby," Billy said. "You're okay now."

"Let go of it, Pete," Jessie whispered into Billy's shoulder. "Let go of the gun."

Jessie

"I'M GONNA MARRY YOU, Jessie Connell. I've made up my mind."

That's what he said to me, and I laughed.

Pete's blond hair blowing back, his hands steady on the wheel, freckles across his fingers, looking at me.

Marry him? Pete Chickery? I laughed at him.

It was two weeks after graduation from high school. Tom and Ellen were taking Pete out to thank him for escorting Ellen to the prom—Tom had been stuck at M.U., taking finals, and couldn't make it home.

"We'll have more fun if there's four of us," Ellen said. "Come on, Jessie, we're going to the Bali Hai Room; we'll have all those fancy drinks. Please . . . it's just one night."

One night.

I was leaving in September. It was June. Three months of summer and I'd be out of Kansas City, out of my mother's grasp. Escaping. That's all that was on my mind. They pushed me. They liked him. I went.

I didn't like Pete Chickery. He was arrogant and obnoxious. He was handsome. He was a flirt. He was dangerous. He was trouble. He was everything I didn't like. And then, somehow, he was all there was.

Laughing, I was laughing, drunk on rum, and reeking with

vomit. Poor Grady tried to pull me up the steps, shooshed me, tried to save me, shield me from my mother's wrath. Holding her robe tight around her body, tight and white like ice, her eyes making pinpricks in my face, my mother stood fast at the top of the stairs.

"You will never see that boy again. Never. I don't care if he's Anita's brother. You will not see him. Do you hear me, Jessie? Did you hear what I said?"

She thought I cared. I didn't care. I had thrown up all over his uncle Ned's new pink Thunderbird. All those Chinese hors d'oeuvres, all that rum, that dreadful rum with orchids floating in it. I was so sick; I'd never had rum before. Speeding down the Trafficway, the top down, the wind blowing us around. I was up on my knees facing backward, keeping my balance in the wind. My arms stretched wide, laughing. How he looked at me!

"How could you behave in such a manner? Have you forgotten who you are?" the dragon hissed from the top of the stairs.

I don't know. Who was I?

I was alive. Alive for the first time.

She hated him. I loved it. That first date was the only date I ever told her we had. From then on, it was lies.

We were at Winstead's, Mother, Frances drove. Tee drove. Ellen drove.

Standing there in the front hall, her thin tanned arm touching the wood banister—coming out of nowhere to catch me as I ran.

"Where are you going, Jessie?" Cold eyes searching. She was everywhere, my mother.

Where are you going, Jessie? When did you get home, Jessie? Where were you, Jessie?

Oh, we were at Tee's house, Mother. We were at Ellen's. We were shopping. Frances got the cutest blouse at Harzfeld's.

I could do it. Once I got the hang of it, I could do it with the best of them. I was great at it because I loved it, I loved to lie to her.

For every cold and distant move she had ever made to me or Anne, even the ones she'd made to Daddy, I paid her back. The way she'd wash Anne's mouth out with soap—the only motherly gesture she ever made, as I think back. With glee, she would lather up her Lux bar—the famous soap of the movie stars—and stuff the bubbles down my sister's throat until Anne would choke and gag. For that I paid her back. For every good-night kiss she never gave us, every tucking-into-bed she wasn't there for, every story she never read, every hug or talk or look of love she had no time for, I paid her back in lies.

We were here, we were there, we were everywhere. It didn't matter how elaborate, I could do it. I was at Roy's and Ray's, eating onion rings. I was at Katz's, drinking sodas. I was at Bennett Schneider's, looking at the paperbacks. I was at Barnard's, listening to records. I was everywhere—except with Pete.

I was unrecognizable. Transformed. A butterfly. A big fat orange-and-black butterfly, a monarch. Unstoppable, untouchable, totally different than before.

I did everything. He taught me. I ate barbecue and let the sauce roll down my chin, I drove barefoot, I drank Scotch and Country Club malt liquor, I went places with him where I knew I shouldn't go, bars off the Trafficway where hoodlums played pool, I read *Lady Chatterley's Lover*, I bleached my hair, I lied, I touched my body, parts I had never touched before. I was daring and exciting. And somehow I felt safe. Safe for the first time. How could that be, when he was so dangerous? How could he make me feel so safe?

"You will never see that boy again. Never."

June and July, I was giddy with Pete.

Grady knew.

"You're gonna get caught, baby. She's gonna find out and she's gonna get you; she hates that boy."

But she didn't tell on me. Grady refused to be one of my excuses, but she wouldn't tell. She liked him. She couldn't help herself. He wooed her. He'd hang in her kitchen when Mother wasn't home and talk to her, ask her questions about herself. Personal things from Grady. No one in our family had ever asked Grady anything personal except how are you, and no one even listened for the answer. Not until Pete. Pete wanted to know.

He wooed Anne. He made her happy. He bought her presents. He looked at her, he paid attention. She was hardly ever happy. Until Pete.

Daddy knew. He didn't know what, but he knew something. He never looked directly at me when I said where I was going that whole summer, he never caught my eye. He didn't want to know, but he knew.

And if Mother hesitated before she gave permission, if she'd even stop to think, he'd push her gently to let me go.

"Come on, Jean, they're having fun. It's their last summer before they go away to school and have to grow up. You remember how special that is . . . you remember. Come on, let her go."

Daddy knew.

I was innocent. I had always been protected. I had next to no experience. And now suddenly I was alive with nerve endings. I was in love for the very first time and I practically flew out of my skin.

He was everything to me. I was intoxicated.

I had only been kissed before. A couple of kisses from a couple of boys, fumbling baby kisses at the door, kisses that made me feel nothing. They were laughable.

I was fresh, brand-new, aching to know it all. Ready. Scared but ready.

June and July. And then it was August.

August. We were parked behind the Jewish Community Center. We'd been parking there all summer. I was supposed to be at the lake, that's what I'd told them. At the lake with everybody. "We're all going, Mother . . . all of us . . . before we leave . . . all of us."

All of us except Pete. He wasn't going anywhere. He was staying in Kansas City and going to JuCo. He and Billy had enrolled.

I was to be home by twelve-thirty. It was twelve. The sun had gone down hours before, but it was still hot. The end of August. One week left before I was supposed to leave. One week. I tried to put it out of my mind. How could I go? How could I leave him?

My skin was sticking to the car seat. I was dizzy with the smell of him. We'd been necking for hours—necking, petting, reaching a point and then pulling back, wanting to go further, afraid of losing control. I had already gone beyond the limits I had set for myself. They were lost when I kissed him. Lost when he held me. Lost when I touched him. I was a good girl. Good girls waited. Those were the rules.

I stopped his hands.

He'd always been gentle with me, never pushed, always understood when I balked. Said it didn't matter, said he loved me, said it would be okay. . . .

My bra was on the seat. Somehow my blouse was still on—a white cotton sleeveless summer blouse, unbuttoned but still on my shoulders—but my bra was on the seat. And my slacks were on the floor. His hands were in my panties. His fingers were doing things to me and I couldn't breathe right. His mouth was on my breast and then he kissed me, kissed me hard and said "Jessie," and my heart melted the way he said "Jessie." Kisses on my skin, his lips moving down my stomach, down to where I knew I couldn't let him go. Soft baby kisses . . . He pulled my panties off. I didn't stop him. I knew I had to stop him but I didn't. I was dizzy with desire, giddy from the ache of wanting him to kiss me there, afraid that he would and afraid that he wouldn't . . . wanting him to do it. Wanting him to do everything there was to do to me, wanting to scream . . . I forgot that we were in the car in the parking lot behind the Jewish Community Center. I forgot everything.

His mouth was on me. On me there. His lips were on me there and my breath stopped. We didn't move. Neither of us. We lay there for a second, not moving. My head was spinning. What was I doing? I couldn't do this.

His tongue touched me. Sweetly, ever so sweetly and slowly, ever so slowly, ever so gently, ever so quietly, he stroked me . . . like a leaf, a velvet leaf. A sound came out of me. A sound I'd never heard before. I moaned.

I had to go home. It felt so good and I was gonna get caught but I couldn't stop. I just couldn't let him stop. I was caught up in the power of his mouth, I felt my body moving up to him, I couldn't stop my body.

And then suddenly everything changed.

He was turned around. Long and lean and turned around, his face in front of mine, his eyes searching mine. "Jessie, oh, Jessie," he said, and he kissed me.

His jeans were gone. Somehow his jeans were gone and his legs were touching mine. Hot skin on his legs rubbing mine. His penis hard against me, his penis was pushing up against my wetness. I felt myself opening, his fingers opening me. I couldn't stop. I had to feel him inside me. My heart was slamming in my ears. I wanted him to do it. I needed him to do it, to fill me up, needed to feel him inside me. The tip of him was inside me. I could feel it.

I could feel it.

I couldn't breathe.

I thought I was going to die.

My hands flew down—and pushed him. I pushed him away. I was so afraid, so young and afraid, and I pushed him away. Closed my wet legs and rolled back against the sticky leather seat away from him. Panting, sweating.

"Please, Pete . . . please . . ." I said, trembling.

Please what? Please do it? Please don't?

"Please, Pete, please," I said to him, expecting him to know everything, expecting him to understand.

He sat up. He was shaking. He pulled on his jeans. I put my hand on his back and it was wet with sweat.

He opened the car door and got out without saying a word. His shirt was off and I watched his chest moving up and down, saw him breathing hard as he got out of the car. Without saying a word.

"Pete?"

He didn't answer. I was buttoning my blouse—my fingers wouldn't work—pulling on my slacks.

There were trees in the grass right where the pavement of the parking lot ended. A field. Grass and trees, big leafy oaks with still, silent leaves. Nothing was moving. There was no breeze that night. The heat had trapped the air into not moving. He walked slowly to the first tree and stood in front of it. I got out of the car. The pavement was hot under my bare feet. I watched his back.

"Pete?"

I was crying.

He was so young and thin in the moonlight.

He smashed his fist hard into the trunk of the oak tree and shattered every knuckle on his right hand. I heard them break. I remember the sound.

I cried as I drove him to Baptist Memorial emergency. He held his bloody broken hand and apologized softly while I cried. We were stunned, shaken by the intensity of what had happened.

I left for Northwestern a week later. My father drove and tried to make conversation. My mother stared straight ahead all the way to Chicago, and I looked out the back. I don't remember seeing one thing along the way.

Pete arrived at the dorm two hours after my parents left. I was sitting on the bed, surrounded by my luggage, and the buzzer rang from downstairs. I didn't even know what it was—a buzz and then a girl's voice with a thick New York accent came right out of the wall. "There's a boy down here for Jessie Connell."

A boy, the angel said right out of the wall. I flew to the lobby. He was kissing me and holding me and people were staring and laughing. I didn't care. I left the dorm with him and went to a motel.

And we made love.

And I was finished.

From then on there was no more Jessie, from then on there was only Pete.

He stayed two days and then went back to Kansas City. He had to get back to start school.

But there was no school for me. There was nothing except Pete. I had to get home. I knew that no matter what I told her or how I told her, she'd never let me leave, she would never let me be with him. So I stopped eating. And when I weighed below ninety and I didn't get out of bed, Northwestern called my parents to come and take me home.

A discussion, a talk with coffee, like grown-ups, in the living room. Mother would explain to him that this *would not* happen, he *could not* have me.

I was hers to push around.

"I'll take her away, then, I'll steal her."

"I beg your pardon?"

"No matter where you send her, I'll find her. She's mine."

"Are you crazy?"

"Maybe."

Eyes on eyes. Grady in the doorway, behind my mother, so my mother couldn't see her, not moving, not breathing, a silver coffee-pot in her hands.

"I forbid it."

"That doesn't matter."

"Watch your mouth with me, young man."

My father moved his chair, cleared his throat softly. He wouldn't cross her; he knew his place.

"No disrespect, ma'am, but I love Jessie. I'm gonna marry her. You can't stop us."

I knew my sister was in the hall. I couldn't see her, but I knew. In my head, she was smiling.

"I will not allow it."

"I don't care what you allow."

She blinked. It thrilled me that she blinked. "Charles?" she said. I'm sure even my father couldn't believe she had turned to him.

"They love each other, Jean. I think you'll just have to let it be."

Her eyes blazing. "No." She stood up. "I will not let Jessie marry him. I won't!"

As if I weren't there, I didn't count.

She ran out of the room, into the hall, and up the stairs. I'd never seen her run before, except on a tennis court. Her high heels made no sound at all as they hit the flowered Oriental carpet. It was as if she had been suddenly and magically silenced. He had extinguished her. No sound.

And then Pete. "Does that mean it's off for the coffee?" he drawled, grinning at my father and Grady and me.

I laughed till I fell off the chair.

And I married him.

With all the trimmings. My daddy made sure.

A sit-down dinner, an orchestra, white roses on the cake, taffeta and candles, a lace garter on my leg, Grady buttoning my buttons, Anne teetering down the aisle in rose-satin shoes, lift the veil, kiss the bride, Daddy making a toast, the glass shaking in his hand, Billy giving a speech, Frances laughing, Anita crying, Tom and Ellen dancing, Tee frowning, George and Neil drinking until they turned pea green, Pete's shoulder in a tuxedo jacket under my hand, flashbulbs, an airplane, a hotel, a honeymoon.

A marriage.

I open my eyes to his eyes on the pillow next to me.

I close my eyes with his arm slung across my waist, his knees turned into the backs of mine.

I sit on the toilet seat and watch him shave.

I try to iron his shirts.

He leaves me in the morning and comes home to me at night.

A marriage. A history.

Pictures in the album.

Ellen and Tom's wedding. Tee and Billy's wedding. Tears and laughter and rice.

I was still laughing then.

"You're late. Where were you?"

"I was workin'. Why?"

"Nothing. I just didn't know where you were."

"I'm right here, baby. I'm right here with you."

Anita's wedding to Neil. I'm pregnant, hugely pregnant. Laughing in Pete's arms.

A hospital, a corridor, his face as the elevator doors slam shut. Pain. Fear. Blackness.

A baby boy. James. A baby boy with blue eyes and yellow hair, named for Pete's father. Little fingers, little toes, Pete's eyes, Pete's face. Pete is filled with love for me and our darling James.

"I'm right here, baby; I'm right here with you."

A cottage, a tiny apartment behind the hospital off Rockhill Road, a baby and a husband, hot dogs and bologna sandwiches on the lawn, put the pictures in the album. Anita's missing—she's not in the pictures—where did she go? Pete's inside me in the bed, on the floor. "That's my girl, Jessie."

I was still laughing then.

He threw the car keys in the ivy.

"Why did you do that? I want to go—let me go." My hand still out there, extended in the cold air; I'd been holding the keys when he took them and threw them away.

He turned and went back inside the apartment. The baby in my arms in a snowsuit, powder blue like his daddy's eyes.

"I love you. You're not leavin'. Shut the door."

"It's too hot for him in here in a snowsuit."

"Then take it off of him. You're not goin' anywhere."

James's big blue eyes, watching us.

"Let me go. You have someone else."

"I don't have anyone else, Jessie. I only have you."

"You're not telling me the truth."

"I love you, Jessie. *That's* the truth."

The TV was too loud. He was standing in front of the TV and it was too loud. I could hear it. I didn't want to hear it. They were leaving the cathedral. They stood on the steps right behind Pete on the television set. She had the children at her sides. Little blue coats, little red shoes, and the bells were ringing and the drums were drumming and the little boy saluted.

James made patty-cake with his tiny mittened hands, smiling and laughing at his daddy.

"There's nothing more to say. I want to go home. Please, Pete."

"This is your home, Jess. Now go and wash your face."

James put out his little arms to Pete. Pete reached to take him, and I backed up.

"You belong to me, I love you, you're not goin' anywhere."

He loved me. How could he have someone else? Wasn't I enough?

White horses pulled the coffin, the flag draped across the top. And behind that, the riderless horse. Spooked, skittish, throwing his head, wanting to run.

I wanted to run. Do you promise to take this woman? Do you promise? What happened to the promise?

James started to cry. He was hot in his snowsuit. I pulled off the little blue mittens and unsnapped the little blue hat. He smiled at me through his tears.

Walter Cronkite had been crying, crying on the television where everybody could see. "The President is dead," he'd said, crying.

"I'm tellin' you, Jess—on my eyes, I'm tellin' you . . . I don't care what you heard, I don't care what someone told you. I love you. I don't love anybody but you."

James was crying. I tried to shush him.

Pete reached for him; he tried to take him from my arms.

"Hey! Don't do that."

The cortege moved down Connecticut Avenue. Cortege. I'd never heard that word before. Cortege and grassy knoll, book depository—what's a book depository? Is it like a library? Cortege . . . your husband kisses someone else. Grassy knoll . . . sleeps with someone else. Book depository . . . puts his cock in someone else.

Pulling, he was pulling James out of my arms as if we were playing tug-of-war. I let go. I couldn't yank at my son.

James was hysterical.

"Unzip him. It's too hot, Pete. Unzip his snowsuit."

He stared at me as if he couldn't hear what I was saying.

"You can't take my son and leave me. I won't let you, Jess."

She was walking down the avenue, so beautiful, the black veil fluttering across her face, flanked by his brothers, walking behind the body of her dead husband.

"I won't let you leave me," he said.

"What?"

I was twenty-one years old, with a baby boy.

"Promise me you'll never leave me, Jessie."

"What? What did you say?"

Guns and jet planes tore across the sky.

"Promise!"

Promise? No, no more promises.

"You broke the promise," I said.

"Jessie, please," he said, staring. His eyes locked into mine.

Nothing. I said nothing.

He lifted James and turned him upside down, held him by the ankles above my head.

"Promise," he said softly.

James was screaming.

"I'll never leave you!" I cried, my hands up in the air, clutching for my boy.

"I said promise. *Say the words!*"

"*I promise, I promise, I promise I'll never leave you!*"

He handed James to me. He kissed me. He kissed James. He said, "I love you."

They sang "Eternal Father Strong to Save" and she buried her husband and lit the torch and clutched the American flag to her breasts. I clutched a whimpering baby and watched the light change in the room.

Did it happen?

It didn't happen. It couldn't have happened.

See how much I love you? How can I show you? Should I smash my hand into another tree?

Tinsel and ribbons and the smell of pine, lights on the front of the cottage, cookies with colored icing, dancing close on New Year's Eve. Holding hands, hiding together in the doorway of the tiny bedroom, watching James mumbling to himself as he tried to climb out of his crib.

" 'Goodnight clocks and goodnight socks . . .' "

"Where the little mouse, Daddy?"

"Wait a minute, fella, we gotta get to that part. 'Goodnight kittens . . .' "

"Where the little mouse, Daddy?"

" '. . . and goodnight mittens . . .' "

"There he is! There he is! I found him."

"Where?"

"On the cereal bowl—look, Daddy, there he is, on the cereal bowl."

"Well, now, would you look at that! Whoever heard of a mouse who likes cereal?"

Delightful shrieking from James. "Daddy, Daddy, you're tick-ellllling me!"

Laughter. Giggles.

I walk through the room. James's little arms around Pete's neck. Pete smiles at me.

"Hey, Mommy, want to see this mouse?"

Did it happen?

I must have made the whole thing up.

I love you, Jessie.

He loves me. Look at how he looks at me.

I must have made it up.

Another honeymoon.

Pregnant, I'm round and pregnant, high in front like before.

Lending naked together in front of the mirror. He's behind me, his head above mine in the glass.

"Look how beautiful you are, Jessie." His hands on my round-ness, his fingers touching my breasts as he turns me into him.

I was still laughing then.

Luke. Another baby boy with Pete's face and Pete's eyes. My darling Luke, another boy of blue and gold.

And a tiny house to rent off Holmes and Eighty-third.

Frances and George get married, we take pictures in the front of the hall—two and two and two and two—and Anne stands alone.

One car; Pete had two jobs, then three jobs. I type envelopes for money in between the diapers. Kissing in the market, necking at the drive-in, the boy babies sleeping in the back seat of Pete's old Ford Fairlane. Barbecues and ball games, Country Club Dairy, hot fudge sundaes in the night.

"Cut the carrots."

"I'm doin' the onion."

"Do you want celery?"

"Of course, Jess, I want it all. This is miraculous—look at this," he says, grinning, a big hunk of raw beef in his hand.

"It's just a pot roast."

"Jessie Connell Chickery, this is not *just* a pot roast. It is a *stolen* pot roast, lifted out of your very own mother's freezer and given to us by the wonderful Grady. A *hot* pot roast."

"She didn't steal it."

"Okay, she borrowed it."

"She said she thought I needed some meat on my bones."

His smile fades, his shoulders fall, he stands there. "I'll get somethin' good soon, Jess, I promise. A decent-payin' job. I will."

"Hey, I'm happy. Look at me—don't you see that? I love you. Okay?"

"Okay," he says, but he's not smiling.

"I love it when you say my name."

"Yeah?"

"Mmm-hmm." My arms coming around him, my breasts pushing into his back. "All of my names."

"I thought you were doin' the celery."

"I'm busy," I say, rubbing up against him. "You do the celery."

"Maybe we should give this back to her."

"Come on, Pete—what's a little pot roast among friends, huh?"

I wiggle around to the front of him, in between him and the sink and the pot roast, on tiptoe, my mouth searching for his.

"You do the celery," I say, kissing him, "and the carrots . . . and the onions . . . but do me first."

"Jessie."

"No, say the whole thing."

"Jessie Connell Chickery."

"Oh, that's good," I say, my mouth on his. "Say it again."

"Jessie, wait a minute."

"Say it, Pete," pulling at my buttons; I'm pulling open the front of my shirt, kissing the side of his face.

He puts down the wooden spoon and turns off the gas.

"Jessie Connell Chickery," he says. He picks me up in his arms and turns.

"No, do me here," I say, yanking at the zipper on his pants, whispering into his neck. "Here, on the sink."

"On the sink," he says, smiling.

"Yeah, Chickery, what's a little meat among friends?"

And at last he's laughing, he's even blushing. "It works for me," he says, grinning, his face pink.

I was still laughing then.

Frances and George move to New York. Cartons and tissue paper, kisses goodbye. Anne marries Joe and moves to Texas, wave bye-bye to Auntie Anne, baby, she may be happy at last, send pictures, send postcards. Come over Sunday, we'll eat fried chicken and play poker. "Oh, I'm busy," says Anita again and again. That's okay, I still have Ellen and Tee.

Nursery school. I type four hours a day for the Heart of America Tobacco and Candy Company on Troost, for big burly guys in stained T-shirts who love me and give me Clark bars to take home. Pick up the kids and bathtime and stories and "Mommy, I fell." "Here, let me kiss it." Blouses. Pete gets a good job selling blouses on the road. He drives off in the dark on Monday, his arm out the window, blowing kisses back to me. He drives home on Fridays, sometimes Thursdays, in the middle of the night. A honeymoon every weekend. Who could ask for anything more?

"Where were you?"

"In Sedalia."

"I thought I saw your car on Brookside."

"What were you doin' on Brookside?"

"I was getting my sunglasses fixed; Luke broke off the earpiece when he ran over them with his truck. Pete?"

"Huh?"

"I thought I saw your car. Was it your car?"

"How could it be my car? I just got off the road."

He just got off the road.

I knew every inch of him, every part of him, the rough parts, the smooth, the way the skin grew over the cuticle on the index finger of his left hand, the sound he made when the hot water in the shower hit his back, his voice laughing from a phone booth by the side of a highway in the rain, "I'm just slavin' away here, baby, sellin' blouses left and right," his face pensive as he sat with the boys on the floor of the kitchen, building towers with their blocks. His hand on the steering wheel, his hand on my breast, his lips, the piece of hair across his forehead, his stance, his walk, his laugh, his grin, his kiss, above me, below me, inside me . . . I knew.

But that couldn't be him; he just got off the road.

Luke wanders in when we're making love, his blanket and bear in his arms; Pete rocks him back to sleep. James walks in and sees us fight, sees Pete push me hard against the wall; I rock him back to sleep.

"Was Daddy hurting you?"

"No, sweetheart, of course not." Little blue eyes stare up at me, damp pudgy fingers on my leg.

"Are you sure?" He watches me carefully.

"Of course I'm sure." I bend to him, smiling. "Daddy loves me, sweetheart."

Staring at my coffee cup. They see too much, they hear too much, I will save them, capture them in my arms and run away. But when I go to find them, they're playing catch with Pete in the yard. They're laughing; they love him. What was I saving them from?

"Okay, you guys, who wants to learn how to make fudge?"

"Me, Daddy! *Me!*"

"Come on, we'll teach Mommy."

"No nuts!" shrieks Luke.

"Of course no nuts," Pete drawls, scooping the little one up against his chest. "What do you think—I don't know about you and nuts, Lukey boy?" Blowing bubbles with his lips on Luke's stomach, Luke squealing with delight.

James pulls me by the hand. "Come on, Mommy, Daddy's gonna teach us how to make fudge. Daddy is one *champeen* fudge-maker," drawling just like Pete.

"Come on, Mommy," Pete says, putting Luke down, slinging his arm around my shoulders. "I love you, Mommy," he whispers, his lips in my neck as he pulls me to him and the screen door slams.

Car pool, first grade, second grade, third. PTA and Cub Scouts, Pete teaching the boys how to tie knots. Shopping on the plaza, Tee teasing Ellen mercilessly about Ellen's quest for the perfect shoes. Grady and Pete make peach pies, James and Luke gobble up the raw dough as the scissors cut around the pan edges and it falls into their little hands.

"When did you get in?"

"About an hour ago."

"I would have been here. I thought you'd be home last night."

"Couldn't do it, sweetheart. Had to make a stop in Bonner Springs."

"But Bonner Springs isn't far; you could have still come home."

"Here I am, I'm home now. See? I'm home."

"I see that, Pete."

Kissing me, holding me, touching me. Sweetheart? Did he call me sweetheart? Is that who I was?

Years in a jumble. A marriage. A history.

A house. A house from Daddy. On the Kansas side and out south. With a front yard and a backyard and a garage, not a carport where you had to scrape the snow off the windshield as the sleet ran down your neck. And a fireplace and an upstairs and a downstairs and three bathrooms. Three whole bathrooms—be still, my heart.

"That's enough now, kids, I insist. It's an investment for me and I've done it, so there's nothing more to say."

Daddy standing by the sofa as the boys throw a football in the street. My mother sitting there, her hands folded in her lap, her face grim, perched high up on the chair. She says nothing. She hardly lets her bottom touch the chair.

"It's yours, son; enjoy it." Daddy shaking Pete's hand.

A house. A forever house.

"What are those, Pete?"

"Rosebushes. I got 'em for you."

Work boots, his shirt off, just blue jeans, digging holes for bare roots. I watch the muscles move in his arms. The boys chase each other around the yard, making fire engine sounds. Puffy white clouds, a cool breeze. I cross the lawn and count.

Ten rosebushes.

"What colors?"

"They're all the same, Jess, a perfect blush white, the color of your face."

"Oh, Pete." My heart surges. I put my hand on his back, feel the sun on his bare skin.

He smiles, turns his head, and kisses my hand. "I love you, Jess, you're my girl."

His girl. That's who I was.

Pictures in the album. Somewhere I turn the pages and there's no more George—Frances divorces him. Letters and phone calls, and Joe leaves Anne. But she won't come home; I beg her to, but no, she moves farther away, my big sister, or was that later on? But the order doesn't matter; it's the getting to the now.

"I know."

"You don't know anythin'."

Whispering at each other in the kitchen, the boys asleep in their cozy beds.

"There's someone, I know it."

"There's no one, there's only you."

He's mixing Hershey syrup into a big glass of milk, stirring it with a tablespoon, the spoon clinking softly against the inside of the glass.

"Please, Pete, you have someone. I know it."

"Why do you do this to yourself, Jessie? Come on, it's late. I gotta get up at the crack of dawn."

"Just tell me; we'll deal with it."

"There's nothin' to tell you. Now stop it." He takes a big swig of chocolate milk.

"We can deal with it; we've dealt with it before."

He bangs the glass on the countertop. It's still half full. It makes a sharp clunk but it doesn't break. He wipes at the milk on the sides of his mouth with the top of his hand. He looks at me.

"I'm goin' to bed. You comin'?" He holds out his hand to me. I don't take it.

"Please, Pete, tell me."

"I love you, Jessie, that's all there is to tell." He turns to leave the kitchen.

"Then I'll leave you," I say quietly.

"No you won't," he says, his back to me.

"I'll leave you and I'll take the boys."

He turns and stares at me. His eyes are very blue.

I'm suddenly cold there in my nightgown, my bare feet icy on the kitchen floor. I wrap my arms around my chest.

"I will. I'll wake them up, I won't even dress them, I'll take them to Ellen's in their pajamas."

"No you won't."

"Yes I will. Unless you tell me. I won't stay here in this house with you."

He stands still. I hear the faucet drip. I sweat but I'm freezing cold.

I turn and walk to the telephone; it's about six steps. The beautiful brand-new white telephone hanging on the wall. I lift the receiver and start to dial.

"What are you doin'?" he says to me.

I say nothing; I keep dialing.

He walks over behind me. I can feel his breath on my hair. "Put the phone down," he says.

It starts to ring in Ellen's house. One ring.

"Jessie, put the phone down."

Two rings, three.

"Hello?" Tom says.

He shoves me hard with his left hand and pulls the phone out of the wall with his right—maybe with both hands, I don't see, I'm busy falling against the stove. Plaster is flying, chunks and pieces, bits of wire sticking out of the wall. He crashes the phone to the floor in a crumpled heap, plastic shattering and a little bell distinctly tinkling as it hits by my head.

"Round two," I whisper, crying, lying on the cold kitchen floor next to the dead telephone. "Look sharp," I whisper, laughing and crying as Pete's bare feet walk by my face.

I went to Frances.

I waited until he drove away after a night of I'm sorrys and I'll never do it again. By the time the dawn broke, it was as if he'd never done anything at all.

I cleaned up the remains of the telephone and taped a calendar from Burt's Plumbing over the hole in the wall. I made peanut butter and jelly for the lunch boxes and cut off Luke's crusts. I drove them to school like a good mommy and said I had to go someplace important and Grady would pick them up and look after them till Daddy got home from the road. Goody; Grady'd make fried chicken and let them stay up late and was she bringing her dog? They were delighted. I went home and packed my bag.

I made Grady swear she wouldn't tell him where I'd gone.

"I'll do it, child, I'll do it. He won't get nothin' outta me. I'll be a regular double-oh-seven."

The bruises on my shoulder and upper arm where I'd hit the stove were covered with a blouse and a jacket and I told her no details. I never told anyone the details.

"Go to Frances, child; don't worry your head."

I took a cab to the airport and caught the next plane to New York. I used every penny I was saving for Christmas, every penny I had stashed. Flying somewhere over Ohio, surrounded by strangers, I realized that I'd never been anywhere alone.

Frances asked no questions. It was an argument and I was hiding, that was enough for her. My only mistake was forgetting how close Pete was to Grady and what a good wangler he was.

New York. I'd never seen New York. The end of fall, the first of winter, gray; crisp leftover leaves strewn across Central Park; Fifth Avenue, Park Avenue, Bloomingdale's, traffic, the theater, noise, horns, the Empire State Building, checker cabs, coffee shops, nightclubs. I forgot I was upset. Four o'clock on the afternoon of the third day, a brisk wind wrapping crumpled newspapers and torn coffee cups around our ankles as Frances and I walk fast across Fifty-first in our high heels. Thunder, lightning. Our arms linked, laughing, as we race to beat the storm.

"Oh, no," shrieking as the first fat drops pelt us hard.

"Shit," says Frances. "Don't look now, but Rhett Butler's on the corner."

A tall man with blond hair falling into blue eyes, in a gray suit with a blue shirt and a maroon tie and no raincoat, his hands clasped behind his back, his legs spread steady against the wind, smiling, on the corner of Fifty-first and Lexington.

I hold tight to her arm. The rain is hitting us sideways.

"Steady, Scarlett."

"Shut up, Frances," but I laugh. I can't help it.

"Do you want me to take a left?" Her hair already plastered to her forehead and her cheeks.

"Do you want me to never speak to you again?" I sputter, rain in my mouth and eyes.

"Got it," she says, gasping.

Twenty more feet and we're soaked through. We stop short, breathless, right in front of him. Wet stockings, wet faces, wet everything.

Handsome, tall and handsome, his suit jacket glued fast to his shoulders, the cheap maroon tie leaking color now, purple spreading on the wet blue cotton stuck to his chest.

"Well," he says, drawling, extending his arms wide in the beating rain. He grins at me. "I couldn't find you at Ellen's, so I thought maybe I'd try New York."

Rain drips from his eyelashes as he takes me hard in his arms. Wet and shaking, I cling to him as the three of us stand on the corner and laugh and cry.

He couldn't have, he wouldn't have, he didn't.

Did he?

How could I have ever thought? Look how much he loves me. I look.

It will all be different now. You'll see.

Okay, I'm ready. Show me. After all, this is Missouri, the Show Me State.

I could still laugh then.

Pregnant again—after a dozen years. He insisted. I was weak from all his love.

Pregnant, and Pete is everywhere, as if we'd never had a baby before. At the doctor's, at the classes, breathing with me, rubbing my back. Blending me protein drinks, making me take naps, reading baby books, discussing car seats, taking pictures of me as I grow.

A pregnant honeymoon.

Everything is different since Luke was born.

Pete's with me in the labor room. He wipes my forehead, he counts with me, he rubs tennis balls on my back. He squeezes my hand hard as the contractions hit and rise and fall. He coaches me, he tells me to get in there, cut right—I'm a running back for the Chiefs. He's in the delivery room. He cuts the cord. He holds the baby under the lights and weeps with joy while they clean me up.

A baby. A baby girl.

Amy, my Amy.

My white skin, my black hair, my brown eyes; she looks like a Connell, not a Chickery. She looks like me and my daddy. Amy, less than six pounds, loud and perfect and strong. Amy, my little love.

The years blur.

She's one and then she's three. She's against Pete's chest as he runs up and down the street with her in his arms like a tiny football, and then she's standing in the doorway next to him, her hand in his.

"We're going on a venture, Mommy. Bye-bye."

"You're going on a what?"

"A venture. Daddy's taking me."

I look at them from the sink. Her hair is pulled back far too tight with little yellow plastic clips. One sock is yellow but the other is white. Her pants are flowered and her shirt is checked. Her grin is as big as his. One hand is in her daddy's and the other is clutching her stuffed rabbit, who goes everywhere with her.

"Well," I say, my heart melting, "will you be home in time for supper?"

She gazes up at him. "Will we, Daddy?"

He bends and lifts her up into his arms, whispers something in her ear.

"Only if you have noodles," she says with great seriousness.

"Oh, so it's blackmail."

"No, noodles! Not black nails! Noodles!"

"Okay. Noodles," I say, looking at Pete and laughing as they kiss me goodbye.

And Easter floats into Christmas.

"Where the hell is that other piece?"

"Shh. What other piece?"

"The piece that goes on top of the sink, the piece with the window."

"Pete, shh, you're gonna wake them up." I crawl around. "I don't see it."

"Listen, you little elf, what kind of assistant are you?"

The tree lights flicker on and off, red and green shadows across his face, tinsel behind his head.

"How'd you talk me into this?"

"Oh, Pete, she's gonna be so excited."

The pieces of the Sears "you put it together" kitchen are everywhere on the rug. "Here." I retrieve the missing piece from under the couch.

"These damn directions are written in Greek," he mutters, his hair falling in his eyes, his lip caught between his teeth, as he squints at the paper on the rug.

I hold the little plastic dishes in my hands and watch him put together Amy's big Christmas present, the one she wants the most, the one she's sure Santa won't bring.

"Ta dah," Pete says, turning the part of it he's been working on toward me, the little red sink in the little cardboard wall, the little window above the sink with the curtains and the backyard painted on.

"Oh, Pete, it's perfect."

"It's not bad, is it?" He grins at me.

"It's gorgeous, Santa." I kiss him.

"Ho ho ho," he says, lying back and pulling me on top of him. "Come here, my little elf. Santa needs a break."

And Christmas slides into the Fourth of July and another Fourth of July, and then Amy is six.

"Hey, you guys, take me with you—hey, you guys, wait for me. Oh, phooey, damn it!"

"Hey, there, young lady!"

"Sorry, Daddy. Rotten boys," she mutters, as she pedals after James and Luke, black hair flying behind her bike, little red tennis shoes going round and round.

Pete flips the hamburgers and smiles at me across the lawn. I laugh out loud.

I could still laugh then.

Put the pictures in the album. Another Thanksgiving, another birthday, but then where's Tee? Is she with Anita? No, that couldn't be. Where's Tee? I turn the pages back and forth, searching.

A matchbook from the Muehlbach and one from the Red Roof Inn. A cocktail napkin from a bar called Frey's on Sixty-fourth Street, with a number written in blue ink. I dial the number for three days while he's on the road. No one ever answers. I rip the napkin and put the shreds in the garbage under the potato peels.

"I thought you were gonna call me."

"I was. There wasn't a phone for miles."

"What do you mean? They've gotten rid of all the phones in Texas?"

"That's right, Jessie; it's a phenomenon."

"I'm gonna give you a phenomenon," I say, laughing, as I hold the phone against my ear with my shoulder and chop lettuce into a salad bowl.

He's gone and then it's Friday, his keys jingling as he fills the doorframe, says "Hi there," and grins at me.

A marriage. A history.

James is a Cub Scout and then he's standing handsome in a cap and gown. Luke is catching pop flies and then he's reading college entrance requirements, his lip caught between his teeth like Pete. What happened to Amy's braces? When did she say to me, "Mom, there's this boy."

I was going to save them—when did they grow up?

Frances and Anne send letters, but they stay far away. It's okay. I still have Ellen.

Another spring. Well, not quite. It's just March, but you can smell it coming.

"Well, it's certainly none of my business," says Ellen, holding a tall, dripping cocktail away from her chest so it won't make spots on her green silk, "but I can't believe I'm the first one to have told you. I mean, it's been going on for years and everybody knows. I just don't see why you want to put up with it for another minute. I mean, I was looking at you in Marlene's living room and I thought, Why, look at her, she's still the prettiest; why, she could find someone else."

Twilight, the light is changing, my favorite time of the day. I'm the prettiest, that's who I am. People are laughing inside the Thornes' house and there's a record on, but I can't make out the song.

"We're not getting any younger, you know. Your Amy will go away to school soon, the boys are already gone. . . . You should try while you still have a chance."

I rub the palm of my hand hard against the cold stone of Marlene and Jack Thorne's garden wall. I take another sip of my drink and watch Ellen's mouth as her lips say the words.

"I'm sure there are some lovely men out there for you to date, just lovely ones, I'm sure. Look at you, Jessie—you could get someone else."

I watch the sky change as things lose their shape in the missing light.

"Someone who loves you," Ellen says, with a space between each word.

The lights blink on automatically in the Thornes' garden, splashing the maple leaves with gold and white. Someone who loves me. Oh. I thought that was Pete.

"After all, Jessie, he's never going to change. He's probably slept with every woman in town. Except me, of course, but I'm probably the only one."

Is she going to tell me all their names?

"Thank you very much, Ellen," I say, finding breath somewhere to speak. "It's good to know he didn't get you too. Very reassuring."

I have a hard time with the word "reassuring." My tongue gets caught on the *s* part and it comes out a little slushy, but Ellen doesn't notice. She's on a mission; she goes right on.

"There's no reason for you to be hateful to me, Jessie. I'm only doing this for your own good. I mean, it makes me sick to have to say these things, but if I don't say them, who will?" She frowns and then tilts her head slightly; her face softens and tears fill her eyes. "I mean, I love you, Jessie; haven't we been friends for years?"

"That's right," I say, taking two steps forward, my heels a little shaky on the grass. "Well, here's to friendship." I raise my glass and she raises hers. I throw my whole drink in her face, drowning her so she won't have to say these sickening words anymore. After all, what are friends for?

I could still laugh—even then.

More I love you. Spring, summer, and fall.

I know everything. I say nothing. I wait.

I focus on my children, feeding them lots of fat worms so they can fly strong from my nest.

The truth that I've always known inside me has now been said out loud. Like a tiny cancer, it metastasizes from my heart to my brain. It gets harder to laugh, it gets easier to be scared. What am I scared of? I don't know.

Colorado. Another honeymoon. The cancer has spread now, from my heart and my brain into my mouth. There's no stopping it, it's rampant.

"Who is it this time? Someone I know?"

I smile at him in his dark-blue down parka as he prepares to leave our love cabin to go up to the lodge. "Is that why you've brought me here? Guilt?"

"What?"

I lean seductively against the doorjamb from the bedroom, in my white lace bra and panties. "Have they all been women I know?"

"Don't start, Jessie. I'm not in the mood."

"Oh, I see. So sorry. Fuck you," says I.

He blinks—just the way my mother did in my parents' living room a million years ago.

He crosses the kitchen and the hallway in three long strides before I can lock the bedroom door. He carries me like a baby in his arms, out the cabin door into the snow. He doesn't look at me. He deposits me on the front porch, barefoot, in lace underwear, surrounded by eight-foot drifts.

He locks the cabin door.

"Maybe you'll stop this talk now, Jessie," he says to me.

He turns and moves away through the dusk. His size-twelve moon boots make loud crunch sounds in the snow. I listen to the crunches diminish as he gets farther away from me and the porch.

Other than that, there is no sound. Quiet. Cold quiet. Just my teeth slamming.

He doesn't leave me very long. Long enough for it to get dark and for the stars to come out. Long enough for me to get frostbite in two toes and the little finger of my right hand. Not very long.

There is nothing to wrap around me, there is nowhere to go. The next cabin is too far away to run to in my underwear. I stay put on the porch. There is nothing but snow. Everywhere.

I didn't cry in Colorado when Pete came back and held me. I didn't cry. He did. He sobbed. He loved me more than his own breath. He loved me more than his own life. He loved me. He adored me.

And winter turned to spring.

The cold receiver against my ear, his voice in the pale of dawn.

"I just thought I'd tell you I love you before you hear anythin' else, before the light comes into the room."

"What time is it?"

"Six, nearly six."

I hear trucks roar beside the phone booth.

"Where are you?"

"Outside of Columbia. I'll be home tonight."

"Okay." I turn over in the middle of the big bed; I smell him on the pillow next to me.

"I love you, Jessie," he whispers in my ear.

He's everywhere; he hardly leaves my side except to go on the road. He's so good, he's perfect. He's so determined to make it up that I can scarcely breathe.

"Where do you want to eat?"

"Hmm?"

"Where do you want to eat? I'll take you out."

"I have pork chops."

"I want to take you out."

"I have pork chops, Pete; they'll go bad."

He lifts me from the chair, waltzes me past the sink and the stove; even though I try to get away, he holds me fast.

Amy comes in from the dining room.

"Oh, how nice," she says. "Fred Astaire and Ginger Rogers. You guys are crazy," but she's smiling. It's clear she likes this, her parents dancing around the kitchen floor.

"I want to take your mother out on a date, but she won't go."

"Why not, Mom?"

"I have pork chops. Cut it out, Pete. Let me go."

"Screw the pork chops," Amy says.

"Amy!"

"Sorry. I meant, forget the pork chops." She grins at me. My hair, my eyes, my face, Pete's grin. "Go out with him, Mom. Look how cute he is."

"Yeah, look how cute I am," he says, dipping me in front of the refrigerator door.

Amy laughs.

"And I'm a very good dancer," he says as he spins me past her.

"Cut it out," I say, laughing too.

"Not till you say you'll go."

"Go ahead, Mom."

"All right, all right, I'll go. I can't fight the two of you at once."

I was still laughing. Even then.

He holds my hand in the restaurant, he holds my hand as we walk to the car. He holds my hand in the movies, on the couch as we watch TV.

He goes downstairs and brings me up ice cream, potato chips, a drink, whatever I want. He rubs my feet, my neck, my fingers, whatever I want. He covers my shoulders softly with the blanket when he leaves me in the bed. He curls into me when we sleep. He leans against me when we sit side by side, his arm against my breast. He loves me.

He looks at me and he loves me. It's like a sign across his face. You can't miss it. He loves me spring right into summer. A week away from Amy in a cap and gown.

It was morning. A Tuesday morning. We had just made love.

I was naked, standing in the bathroom after a shower, combing my wet hair. It was quiet. I could hear the house hum.

Pete was downstairs.

I could still feel him inside me. I smiled at my face in the mirror.

Cotton bath-mat loops under my bare toes and my heels. Drops of water hitting my shoulders. A gentle breeze against my kneecaps as the air-conditioning clicked on. Soap smells and shampoo. Sun shimmering through the window, making leaf shadows on the tile wall.

I looked at my face in the mirror. The same face. The same eyes. I smiled and I looked at myself. I still had the comb in my hand. I was nearly laughing. Nearly. And then I blinked. Because I couldn't laugh. Because I knew.

I knew the way I'd known every time before. No rhyme or reason, I just knew.

Pete had someone else. Again.

Pete

I FOUND HER under the table, the dinin'-room table. She was flat on her back, one arm at her side and the other thrown up over her face. She was wearin' a white terry-cloth bathrobe, the one she'd had on the night before. There was a stain on the sleeve that looked like coffee.

"Jessie?"

She didn't move.

I wanted to get on the road; it was nearly nine o'clock. I'd been lookin' all over the house for her, to kiss her goodbye.

I walked closer to the table.

"What's the matter, babe?"

I wasn't shocked to find her under there. Jess always wound up in strange places when she had somethin' on her mind. When we were first married it was the bathtub. Not that the bathtub is a strange place, but she could stay in there for hours. I'd come home and look all around before I'd find her, and then I'd sit in the bathroom and talk to her until she'd get out. It wasn't like she did it often; just every now and then. She needed a place to think, she said, a place where it was calm.

"Jess?"

No answer.

Later it was the car, after the boys were born. After I sold the Fairlane and I was on the road, makin' some money, I got her a convertible, a dark-green Mustang that Jessie loved, and I'd find her sittin' in that car, sittin' in the back seat in the middle of the driveway, the top down, sittin' there just starin' at the sky. I'd get home and James or Luke would run at me. "Mommy's in the car." I'd go out by the Mustang and the kids would watch from the kitchen door.

The cigarette trick always worked. Not right away but if I did it long enough. It wasn't really a trick, just this thing I did tossin' a cigarette up in the air and catchin' it in my mouth like people do with peanuts, but I did it with a cigarette. My dad used to do it; he taught me when I was a kid. I could always get to Jessie if I did it long enough. I'd make a big production out of it, act suave and debonair like Fred Astaire doin' a dance, or use an accent like Maurice Chevalier, anythin', until I'd get to her. Eventually she'd look to see if I'd caught it, and once I got her eye, the mood would be broken, she'd forget what she was upset about, she'd laugh and get out of the car. The kids thought it was great, but I only did it for Jessie.

. I don't know if the cigarette trick would have worked to get her out from under the table, but I did think about it as I walked over to where she was. I bent down.

"Jess?"

No answer.

She'd had a shower or a bath—her hair was still damp, makin' little curls around her ears.

I sat down by the table leg, with the mail in my lap. That's what had caught my eye when I was movin' through the house, the mail on the floor where it had fallen through the slot. I turned over a postcard with big fat oranges on the front, spellin' out "Saint Petersburg."

"Hey, look at this, Jess. Milvain wants us to come down. 'We're racin' the boat on the Fourth, why don't you and Jessie come down and crew so I can watch you puke, Chickery?' "

I laughed.

"That fuckin' Milvain," I said, holdin' the postcard out to her.

"Look here, Jess. Julia's written you a note down on the bottom here. . . ."

She didn't move.

I dropped the postcard on the rug and touched her foot. She was barefoot and her toes were icy in my hand.

"Hey, kid, your toes are cold."

She didn't say anythin' while I rubbed her foot, but what she did do was take a very deep breath like she hadn't had any air for quite a while. The terry-cloth robe rose up and down and I could hear her breathe through the sleeve over her face.

I put down her foot and stretched out on the rug next to her. I propped my head up in my hand and watched her lyin' there. Her skin was still the color of cream, cream at the top of a bottle of milk like when I was a little boy. She never got in the sun unless she was covered up. I reached out and touched her hand, the one that was on the rug, little thin fingers like a child's hand.

"Hey, you want to talk to me?"

Nothin', not a move.

"Did you eat breakfast? Is that coffee on your robe?"

She turned ever so slightly, her whole body away from me, just the tiniest of movements.

"You want somethin' to eat?"

I traced her earlobe with my finger and then put my hand into her curls.

"Hey, what's the matter, kid? I'll just be gone three days. I'll be back on Friday. Is that what's on your mind?"

I was goin' to Oklahoma, to call on a couple of stores where I hadn't stopped last week.

"Is that what it is? Come on, talk to me, Jess. . . ."

She didn't move.

"What's goin' on?" I waited. "I'm waitin' for you to talk. . . . You want me just to go? I gotta get out of here; it must be nine o'clock."

The mornin' was shot already. I had two stops in Tulsa, and if I didn't get out of the house soon, I wouldn't be there till dark. I lay there watchin' her chest move up and down, listenin' to her breathe.

"Do you want me just to leave? I can do that, you know."

"You just went to Oklahoma," she mumbled.

"What?" I'd heard what she said; I just wanted to get her to talk. "What did you say?"

"You just went to Oklahoma."

"No I didn't, honey, I went to Texas."

"You went to Oklahoma."

"Jessie, I went to Texas."

"You went to Oklahoma."

"This is ridiculous," I said. I looked at my watch: ten after nine. "Jessie, I went to Texas."

"You had to go through Oklahoma to get to Texas; I know your route."

"But I didn't stop, I didn't call on Penney's or anybody else, 'cause Joe was in New York; that's why I didn't stop. I told you that, I told you Friday when I got home."

I was havin' a conversation with my wife while she lay under our dinin'-room table with her arm across her face.

"You went to Oklahoma."

"Jessie, I went *through* Oklahoma; I didn't go *to* Oklahoma."

"You went to Oklahoma," she said softly.

"Goddamn it," I said. I was losin' my sense of humor.

She took her arm up off her face. The terry cloth had left a pink stripe across her forehead and one cheek. She must have had her arm on her face for quite a while. She must have been under the table for quite a while. I'd been in my office since eight, doin' paperwork and talkin' to the factory back East. It's really not an office, just the den off the kitchen, but I make all my calls from there.

"Goddamn it to you!" she said.

She was beautiful. Even with a pink stripe across her face. She didn't look at me, didn't turn her head, kept starin' at the underside of our pine dinin'-room table. At least her arm wasn't over her face.

"What's this all about?"

"You went to Oklahoma," she said, starin' up at the wood.

"Okay." I sighed. "I went to Oklahoma."

"Right," she said.

"Okay. And so?"

"So," she said. "So."

"What have you got against Oklahoma all of a sudden?"

She took another breath. She closed her eyes.

"I don't think I can do this," she said quietly.

"What? Hey, are you gonna talk to me? What's the matter with Oklahoma?"

She didn't move.

"Okay, listen, I'm tryin' to talk to you. You want to talk about Oklahoma or not?"

Nothin'. She didn't make a sound.

"Okay, I confess . . . I went to Oklahoma! Arrest me!" I raised my hand like you do when you swear on a Bible in court, but she didn't see me. "Is that what you wanted to hear?"

Nothin'.

"I thought you liked Oklahoma, honey; I thought you liked all that red dirt."

I touched her cheek with my fingers. And then I started to sing. I know all the words to "Oklahoma"; Anita did it in high school and she played the record so much I know the words without tryin', they're ingrained in my head.

"*O----k-lahoma, where the wind comes sweepin' down the plain, and the wavin' wheat can sure smell sweet . . .*"

She flung my hand off her cheek and laid her arm back across her face.

"Jesus Christ, Jessie!" I looked at her. Nothin'. "Okay, I've had enough of this. You hear? I'm gonna get a cup of coffee and then I'm gettin' on the road."

I sat up.

"You want to talk to me about Oklahoma?"

Nothin'.

"I'm goin', then." I watched her, but she didn't move her arm, didn't look at me. I stood up. "I'll be in the kitchen," I said. I took two steps backward. "I'll be in the kitchen, Jess."

You cannot do the cigarette trick for someone who has their eyes closed and their arm across their face, that's for damn sure. Even if I still smoked, and I didn't; I hadn't smoked in thirteen years.

I turned away, went into the kitchen, walked to the percolator on the stove, and put the gas on under it. I stood in front of the already made coffee, waitin' for it to boil up again.

You just never knew with Jessie. Usually I could get to her, but you never knew. She was hard to predict. Even from the start, I never knew which way she'd go.

I never even thought she'd go out with me, and then there she was in my uncle Ned's pink T-bird, up on her knees, facin' backward on the front seat next to me, her arms stretched out wide in the wind. First she was all dressed up and proper, and then she was laughin' in the wind, her hair blowin' across her face, so beautiful, and I knew she was the one for me. There was never any doubt, she was always the one.

I never stopped to think that she was unattainable, a Connell, out of my league. I never stopped to think about anythin' except how much I wanted her. I knew from that moment, and it had never changed for me.

I realized I was starvin'. The cornflakes box was on the counter; Amy must have had cornflakes before she went to school. I got a bowl out of the cabinet, a banana from the basket, and put them and the cornflakes on the kitchen table. Then I went back and stood in front of the pot.

I'll tell you, you have to hand it to women. I had no idea why she was under that table or when she was comin' out. No idea at all. Not a clue.

The coffee started to boil. I turned the heat off, refilled the mug I'd left on the sink earlier, and took it with me to the table. I didn't do anythin'. I didn't eat the cornflakes and I didn't drink the coffee. I just sat there.

Any man who tells you he understands women is either a liar or a fool. It doesn't matter how many women a man knows in his life—we don't think the way women do; there's no way for us to understand.

I took a sip of coffee and peeled the banana. I got up to get a knife to cut it into my cereal—that's when she came into the room.

She stood in front of me at the sink. Neither of us moved. I had the banana in my hand; she still had the pink stripe across her face.

"Who's in Oklahoma, Pete?" she said.

"Hell, is that what this is about?" I moved to the right to go past her, but she stood in front of me. I took a step to walk around her, but she moved to block my way. The whole thing was pretty silly considerin' Jessie's five one and I'm six two, but I stopped anyway.

"Who's in Oklahoma?"

"Jessie, don't start this crap."

She was blockin' me like a miniature basketball guard. I stepped to the right, she stepped to her left in front of me. I stepped to the left, she stepped to her right in front of me. I might have laughed if I hadn't been so pissed.

"Answer me," she said.

"No one's in Oklahoma."

"Why am I never enough for you?"

"You're everythin' to me. You know that."

"No. You always need someone else."

"There's no one else. I told you."

She looked at me and frowned, then she backed up a couple of steps.

"I just don't get it. Why am I never enough for you?"

She took another step back, yanked at her bathrobe belt, pulled the knot loose, and held the terry cloth open at her sides. She was naked under the robe.

"Is it my body? Is that it? Is it my body that's not enough for you?"

"Jess, stop it. I love your body. Please . . ."

She dropped the edges of the robe. "Is it my face, then? Is that what it is? Am I not pretty enough for you?"

I moved toward her, but she kept backin' up.

"My eyes? My cheeks? Is it my hair, Pete? I thought you loved my hair."

She backed into a kitchen chair and knocked it over.

"Jessie, stop this. I love you. I love your hair."

"No, I'm not enough. I never have been. Even from the start."

She stumbled around the fallen chair and the kitchen table. I moved toward her.

"I love you. Please, baby, this is crazy. . . ." I picked up the chair. "Stop it—"

"No. You want someone else."

"Jessie, please . . ."

I reached out to get her.

"Don't lie to me!" she screamed, and she grabbed the banana out of my hand. "Here. I'll fix it. Now you won't have to look at me. You can pretend I'm someone else!"

She was mashin' the banana on her face. It happened right in front of me, but it was so fast I couldn't believe it—on her cheeks and across her lips, on her forehead and in her hair, she was smashin' the banana.

"*Stop it!*" I shouted.

"*There. Is that better, Pete?*" she yelled. "*Now do I look like someone else?*"

"*What the hell are you doin', Jessie?*"

I grabbed for her wrists; she was strugglin' to get away, yankin' hard with both arms. It was hard to hold on to her—there was banana everywhere.

"*There's no one in Oklahoma!*" I yelled.

We were movin' in a circle around the kitchen table; we knocked over two more chairs. I had ahold of her wrists, but she was thrashin' to get free.

"*Jessie, stop this! There's no one in Oklahoma. I'm tellin' you the truth!*"

I backed her up against the sink. I pinned her with my body so she couldn't get away.

"*Listen to me. I promise.*"

We were both pantin', trying to catch our breath.

"Please stop this. I love you. Don't you know I love you?"

Her mouth was open, her eyes on mine.

"Please, Jess. I mean it. There's no one but you."

She stared at me.

"Come on, baby, please."

She didn't say anythin', she just kept lookin' at me.

"Jessie? Come on, baby, let's get the banana off your face."

I held on to her wrists with one hand and reached for the sponge with the other. I wet the tip of it and wiped some of the banana off her cheek and forehead.

"Jesus Christ, Jessie. I love you. Look what you did to yourself."

"You can let go of my hands," she whispered.

I looked her right in the eyes and told her again. "There's no one in Oklahoma. Okay?"

I let go of her wrists. She fell against me. I put my arms around her.

"C'mon," I said, movin' her to a chair. "You'll be okay now, it'll all be fine."

She looked up at me. She was whiter than her robe.

"Come on, we'll sit you down and clean you off and put this whole thing where it belongs."

I let go of her with one arm and reached for a chair. I still had the other arm around her, but I wasn't holdin' on to her tight—that's how she got away from me.

"You just don't get it, do you?" she said quietly. "Look at me, Pete. Don't you see me? I can't do this anymore."

She turned slowly and padded out of our kitchen in her bare feet, out of our kitchen and out our back door. I didn't move at first. I just stood there holdin' on to that chair.

There *was* no one in Oklahoma. I was tellin' the truth this time.

When I got outside, she wasn't in our yard; she wasn't in the yards adjoining ours. Sarah Branz waved at me; she was waterin' down her tomatoes by the fence.

"Hey, Sarah, have you seen Jessie?"

"No. But I just came out." She smiled. "What's the matter, honey, did you lose her?"

I smiled back at her and walked around to the front. She wasn't in the front yard. She wasn't in the garage, the basement. I thought maybe she'd gone inside while I was out back, but she wasn't anywhere. Her smell was upstairs. Perfume, shampoo—Jessie's smell.

I went back downstairs and into the kitchen. I picked up the phone and stood there. I realized I didn't know who to call. I didn't know who she talked to. I didn't know who was in her life anymore. She hadn't mentioned Tee. . . . I knew she didn't see Anita because the whole thing with my sister was a stick in my craw. . . . Anne was in L.A. . . . Frances was in New York. . . . I dialed Ellen's house. I stood there thinkin' about what I didn't know.

I could hear Frances laughin' at me. "You don't know dick about women, Chickery, no matter what you think."

I put the receiver down. It must have rung thirty times. Ellen wasn't home. I walked through the house and out the front door.

There was no one around. A quiet Tuesday mornin' . . . quiet and hot. Next week, school would be out, there'd be kids every-where, bikes in the street, toys on people's lawns . . . another summer.

I sat down on the front steps. I didn't know where to go; I tried to think.

I couldn't believe it. Jessie standin' in front of me, puttin' banana all over her face.

I loved her. Didn't she know that? How could she not know that? I'd been tellin' her all her life.

I watched the cars go back and forth on Mission. She didn't have any money, she couldn't take a bus or a cab. And anyway, where was she goin'? Runnin' away naked in a bathrobe . . . Jesus fuckin' Christ.

She was everythin' to me. She always had been. I thought it was obvious. Hell, we'd had three babies together, raised them, been through thick and thin. Wasn't that what you were supposed to do? Wasn't that what this was all about? I was a husband, I was a father—what the hell more did she want?

I stood up and walked back and forth.

I would never leave her. Not for anythin' or anybody. I thought that was clear.

Hell, I couldn't live without her. Didn't she know that? I loved her. What more was there? What more did she need?

Sarah Branz came round the side of her house. She unwound the hose and pulled it with her to the rosebushes linin' her front walk. She put her hand up to shield her eyes.

"Did you find her, Pete?"

"No."

She put the hose down and left it runnin' in a trickle on the roots. She walked over to where I was. She was wearin' a big straw hat.

"What's the matter, honey, did you all have a fight?"

"Yeah, I guess so."

She laughed. "You guess? You're not sure?" North Carolina in her voice.

"Okay, we had a fight." Crinkle lines around her eyes, blue eyes like mine. "She's run away in her robe."

"Oh, Pete, you musta been *very* bad."

"I can't figure where she is."

"Oh, she'd go to a friend's, honey, that's where she is."

"But the closest friend is past Nall, and besides, no one answers there; I tried."

"Nall isn't that far."

"Well," I said, "it is if you're barefoot."

"Barefoot and in a robe . . . well, well, well." She tilted her head and grinned at me.

"Okay, I was bad."

"Honey, I coulda walked to Oklahoma when Ed made me mad, with or without my shoes."

"Oklahoma?"

"What?"

"Oklahoma, you said Oklahoma . . ."

"Oh, you know, honey—I mean I coulda walked a million miles when he got me really mad. I'd go there if I were you; they're probably not answerin' the phone."

It had never occurred to me that Ellen could be there and not answer the phone. That's another thing women do that men can't understand. A man would answer a ringin' phone.

I took off down Ninety-first, crossed Mission, and ran west and south. It was really too hot to run; it must have been nearly ninety already and it wasn't even noon. I looked at my watch: twenty after ten. Why hadn't I taken the car?

I waited for the light at Ninety-fifth, crossed, and then cut through some yards. The clouds were high up in the sky, maples dippin' in the breeze, the smell of fresh-cut grass. I jumped over a hedge and cut behind a house.

The woman was lyin' on a blanket in the middle of her yard. She sat up fast when she heard me, and the top of her bathin' suit stayed behind.

"Jesus," she said, gropin' for her top on the blanket. "What the hell are you doing?"

"I'm sorry . . . I'm really sorry . . . I was just cuttin' through, I didn't realize you were here." I stopped and stood there huffin' and puffin', tryin' to catch my breath. "I'm sorry, really . . . I live a few blocks up." I pointed north. "I'm just . . ."

Her mouth was open. "You've got a hell of a nerve," she said, her arms across her breasts, tryin' to cover herself.

"I was just cuttin' through to . . ." What the hell could I say to her? To get my wife, who's run away from home? "I'm sorry . . . really . . . I'll be goin'. . . ." I moved across her grass and into her neighbor's yard.

"Well, I never . . . ," she said, but I didn't hear the rest.

Jesus. What the hell was I doin'? I should have taken the car. The look on her face. Jesus fuckin' Christ. I'd scared the hell out of that woman. Jesus. Sittin' up without her top on. A stranger in her yard. Her suntan line clearly etched above and below her breasts . . .

I could remember Mrs. Dee's breasts . . . Tupelo long ago . . . runnin' to her house. I was fourteen years old . . . fourteen and playin' ball.

Me and a bunch of guys throwin' the ball around at Hargrove's lot. Me and Mark Dee, Clayton Dale, his brother Joel; just some guys tryin' to keep it goin' before it got too dark. And then I had to pee. I would have done it right there, but old lady Magers and her sister were sittin' on chairs out in their yard and I figured gettin' caught with my dick out was not such a good idea. It had been a hard summer for me, the first one since my daddy died, and I'd been in trouble most of the time. Dee's house was the closest, so that's where I ran.

Everybody and their brother was on the street, fightin' to get some air. Nothin' was movin'; it was just too hot. The light was changin', things were losin' shape, not quite nine o'clock yet. I knew the game was over, knew they'd have to chuck it 'cause they wouldn't be able to see the ball.

Up Dee's steps and into his house; nobody latched their doors back then, at least not in Tupelo. It was pitch-black inside. They hadn't turned the lamps on yet, tryin' to keep the house cool.

I knew somebody'd had a bath, but it didn't register with me. A fourteen-year-old kid, his mind is on the game, not on somebody havin' a bath, but there was still some water in the tub, a sweet smell in the air, bubbles smudged on the porcelain edge. . . .

The thing you have to understand is that I'd known her all my life. Seen her practically every day since me and Dee were born. She was my best friend's mother, that's all she was to me.

She played the radio a lot. That was a big thing, 'cause the radio was never on in our house and always on in theirs. And she sang; no matter what the guy put on, she knew all the words. She clipped stuff out of magazines, piles on her kitchen table; I guess they were recipes. I don't know what she did with them after she cut them out.

But mostly what she did was lay out in the sun . . . in a black one-piece bathin' suit with the straps let down in front, on a big gray blanket in the middle of her yard. She'd sprinkle herself from a pot of water that she'd set next to her and turn over from front to back like a chicken on a spit. It didn't matter the temperature; if there was sun out, there she'd be.

It made Dee nuts. He hated that his mother lay out there. I never gave it much thought, but it really made him nuts.

I came out of the bathroom, into the hall. It was her tracks that caught my eye, wet foot-tracks across the hardwood floor. She was sittin' on the edge of the bed brushin' her hair, sittin' on a white bedspread with cotton tufts, like the one my mother had. She was bent at the waist with her head down between her knees, brushin' her hair clear to the floor, long black wavy hair that I'd only seen tied up or pinned.

There was no sound in the house, no radio. Whatever sound there was was really just a hum—kids outside, crickets, maybe a car. She brushed her hair forever while I stood and watched. I know I didn't move; I'm not sure if I breathed.

She was the first naked woman that I had ever seen. She was naked and she was wet. You could see that from the light, the only light on in the house, a little bedside lamp with the shade tilted toward her, amber light on her wet skin. Brown from the sun—her arms, her legs, her face, the parts that I had seen—and then she sat up . . . and the rest of her was white, the parts I hadn't seen. She raised her arms with the brush, and her breasts lifted up, round and big and as white as the bedspread where she sat. That was when she saw me.

"Pete Chickery? What are you doin' out there?"

My eyes flew off her breasts and down to the floor. My big black dirty high-tops with broken laces, glued to the floor.

"Pete?"

"Yes, ma'am," I whispered back.

"What are you doin' out there?"

"Uh . . . I was, uh . . . lookin' for Mark, ma'am."

I don't know why I lied. It didn't make any sense. I could have just said I was usin' her bathroom. Besides, she knew where Dee was, she knew he was with me; we were always together.

"I believe he's playin' ball," she said.

She didn't sound like she was mad. I didn't say anythin'. She was naked and talkin' to me. I didn't move an inch.

"Down to Hargrove's lot," she said.

"Yes, ma'am."

Silence. She stood up. I didn't see her stand because I didn't take my eyes off my shoes, but I felt her stand, I felt her stand up and move. She was movin' toward me; I could hear that. And then she was there. Right in front of me in the doorway to her bedroom, the doorway in that hall. My head was still down, my eyes glued to my shoes, but her bare feet were there, in the corner of my eye. She had red polish on her toes.

And then her hand was on my arm. Right below my elbow, she ran her fingers down my arm, and then she laced her hand in mine. I thought my head was gonna explode.

"You can look up if you want," she said, real soft.

The brown and white of her, the angles, the softness, her legs, the triangle of black hair where they came together, her stomach, her nipples, her breasts, her shoulders, her neck, her face, her brown eyes on mine.

"Yes, ma'am," I said.

She was the most beautiful thing I had ever seen.

She took one step backward, one foot out of her hall and into her bedroom. She took me with her as she moved, holdin' me by the hand. She closed the bedroom door with her other hand and led me to the bed. She never said another word.

She took off my clothes. I don't think I moved; I know I didn't help her. I was struck still as the air. I know when she knelt and untied my high-tops I thought I might pass out. I remember her hand on my belt, the sound of my zipper, the air on my skin, her fingers on my stomach, her eyes on mine, her breath on my face. And I remember every inch of her.

I CROSSED NALL at Ninety-eighth. It was two more blocks to Ellen's house.

I was with Mrs. Dee until we left Tupelo. I was with her every chance I got. I never learned anythin' about her except everythin' about her makin' love. I knew nothin' about what she wanted in life, nothin' about her marriage, nothin' about who she was. Except for being intimate, we were strangers until the end. I never even called her by her first name; she was always Mrs. Dee.

We never got caught; we never even got scared. There were no close calls and nobody ever knew. Only three things changed. I stopped goin' to church, I stopped playin' ball, and I stopped feelin' sad.

I couldn't go to church because I couldn't take confession. Adultery is a mortal sin, and I wasn't about to stop, so that was it with me and church. Everybody thought it had somethin' to do with my daddy dyin', but that wasn't it at all—it was me and Mrs. Dee.

I stopped playin' ball because that was the only time to see her, durin' practice after school. I made sure I didn't make a team for the rest of that year. Dee made 'em all. Everybody was surprised that I lost interest in ball. Before Mrs. Dee, it was all I cared about.

I stopped feelin' sad. It was the first time I was happy since my daddy died.

I saw her nearly every day, and always after school. Never at night again, never Saturdays or Sundays; only after school. And only in her house; we never met anywhere else. And nearly everythin' we did was in that bed where she slept with Mr. Dee.

He'd been out of town for three days to see his sister in Meridian; that's why he hadn't been home that day. On the mornin' he returned, Mr. Dee was standin' on the porch, his hands in his pockets, lookin' at me. I was waitin' outside for Dee.

"How's it goin', son? How are things with you?"

"Just fine, sir," I said, and that was the end of that.

Mrs. Dee and I didn't look at each other funny when anybody else was around. There were no knowin' glances, no touchin' behind people's backs . . . nothing' sneaky or chancy, nothin' at all like that. Everythin' we did was when we were alone, and it was separate from our regular lives. Separate and apart.

And that's how it had always been with me. The women in my life were separate, they weren't attached to anythin'. They had nothin' to do with my love for Jessie; they had only to do with me. No other woman ever touched my love for Jessie, no woman could. I would make her understand.

I turned down Ellen's walk, ran up the steps by her Alberta spruce bushes, and rang her front doorbell.

She had her hair in a ponytail and she didn't have any makeup on. Not that she looked bad; it was just a thing with her, not lettin' anyone see her without her "face." Ellen has pale sandy hair and pale eyebrows, pale hazel eyes with little beige flecks. I guess she isn't what you'd call pretty, but there's a sweetness about her that catches you unawares.

She didn't want to let me in. We had a conversation through the little openin' in her front door. She said Jessie asked her not to let me in, and if there was one thing I knew about Ellen, it was her loyalty when she gave her word. I knew there was no talkin' her out of it, so I broke through her kitchen screen door. I really had no choice. I didn't mean to scare her; I just had to get to Jess. I knew I'd make it okay later on. Ellen disapproved of a lot of my behavior, but we always had been friends.

It was clear that Jess was upstairs. It was on Ellen's face when I asked, and then we could both hear her—Jessie movin' somethin' up there, somethin' big across the floor. Ellen and I both looked up. I left her in the dinin' room and ran up the stairs.

I hadn't been upstairs in their house for a long time, not since Stevie was a baby. I remember we'd been downstairs playin' poker—Tom and Billy, Shapi and me. The girls had gone out to the movies. Tom had practically pushed Ellen out; she'd been cooped up for days while their three boys were passin' around the flu. They'd been gone about an hour when Stevie's fever shot way up, and the doctor said to give him a bath in alcohol and Tom was a wreck with babies, so I gave Stevie an alcohol bath while Tom stood there and watched. That was the last time I was up there. It's a funny thing, you can be best friends for years with people but you're hardly ever upstairs in their house.

Jessie had barricaded herself in their bedroom; there was no lock on the door. If there had been a lock, I never would have gotten in.

I don't know how she got the chest of drawers across the room, but somehow she'd managed to move the damn thing in front of the door. I pushed it out of the way and walked in.

That was the next thing that caught me. Their bedroom was all blue. Light blue—the walls, the drapes, the bedspread. It was just like Jessie's bedroom in her mother's house, where we used to make love when she came home from school. I just stood there for a minute, rememberin'.

It was very quiet up there. I couldn't hear Ellen or the dog anymore. I called Jessie's name, but of course she didn't answer me. I walked across the room and stood in front of the closed closet door.

There was a framed photograph on the wall next to the closet. I moved closer to it to make sure it was the one I thought it was, the one we had a copy of at our house. It was taken at a New Year's Eve party at the club. We're all standin' together, our arms linked around each other's waists. Ellen and Tom are laughin'; George is bendin' his head to Frances, their lips nearly touchin' in a kiss; my sister is frownin' at Neil as if she just realized who he was; Tee is muggin' at Billy, he's grinnin' back; Anne's eyes are closed, she's leanin' up against Joe, her cheek on his tux lapel. I'm smilin' at Jessie and she's smilin' at me. We all look young. And happy.

Jessie's wearin' the red chiffon dress that I bought her Christmas that year. Red dress, red shoes, red underthings—I spent the whole bonus on her. It was my first Christmas with Ship 'n Shore and the first time in our lives that I had a decent job.

I never thought about how I was gonna make a livin' when I was a kid. I wasn't driven like George to be more important than his father, number one at Harvard Law, the senior partner in his firm. I didn't have a plan like Tom to be a pharmacist and own a chain of drugstores with his name on the front. I had no childhood dream like Billy to be a fireman like his brothers and his uncles and his dad. I had nothin', no plan at all.

My daddy was a carpenter; he made tables on the line at Lane's—not headboards, not chairs, just tables; he had no ambition to move on. My grampa—Poppa—had a little grocery store in the front of his house, but mostly what he did was stand outside on the stoop and smoke. None of the men in my family had amounted to much—it didn't seem to be a part of the Chickery code. All I knew was that I wanted a job and I'd work hard to take care of Jessie and the kids. And I had. I always had.

I looked at her smilin' at me in the picture. I would explain to her how much I loved her, I would make her understand.

"Come out of the closet, Jessie," I said, lookin' over at the door. There was no sound from inside.

"Come on out. This is silly. I found you. Let's go home."

I turned the knob and opened the door. There was no lock on that door either. No locks on the doors in Ellen's house.

The light went on in the closet when I opened the door.

"Why are you hidin', honey? Come on . . . let's go home."

I took two steps inside the closet; it was like a little room. A big walk-in closet with hangin' racks on either side—Tom's clothes on the left, Ellen's on the right. At the back were plastic boxes for their shoes. Shoes and Ellen's purses stacked in a plastic row. Very neat and organized, just like Ellen.

"Jessie . . ."

I moved some hangers on Tom's side.

"Let's go home and talk about this. . . ."

I could smell Ellen's perfume, sweet like vanilla. I moved to her side of the closet and pushed a bunch of blouses out of my way.

Jessie was sittin' behind them, sittin' on the floor. I saw her eyes first, big and brown, starin' up at me.

"What are you doin', baby? Come on out of there."

I reached out my hand; she frowned at me.

"Come on, Jess, let's go home."

She tilted her head to the side and then she looked down. That was when I saw the gun.

Her knees were drawn up to her chest and she was holdin' a gun in her hands. She wasn't pointin' it anywhere; it was just poised in her hands, restin' on the tops of her knees. It was Tom's .38.

I remember when he bought it. We took it way out south in Kansas, him and me and Billy, and shot at targets in a field. I don't even know where the hell we were, but I remember that gun. I hadn't seen it since.

"What are you doin', Jess?"

She looked back up at me.

"Jessie, what are you doin' with that gun?"

I took a step toward her, my hand still stretched out in front.

"Give me the gun, Jessie. Come on, baby, I love you, give me the gun."

She didn't say anythin', but she didn't turn away. Her eyes were locked into mine.

"I love you. You know that. Give me the gun, Jessie."

I took another step.

"Don't move," she said softly.

"I love you, honey . . . please."

Her eyes were very bright, dark and bright in her face.

"It's too late," she said in a whisper.

"No, it's not. Put the gun down and we'll talk. Please, honey, put it down for me."

"I can't do this. Don't you see that?"

"Jessie . . ."

"I can't do this anymore. I'm not laughing. Don't you see that, Pete?"

"Jess, I don't know what you're talkin' about."

She raised the gun up off her knees, holdin' it with both her hands, raised it up and pointed it out in front of her, straight at my chest.

"It doesn't matter," she said, lookin' right at me.

And then she lifted the gun up and back, the muzzle raised and tilted, pointin' up into the soft white flesh under her chin.

"No. No, baby, don't do that."

The gun was stickin' into her throat, bruisin' the white skin of Jessie's throat.

Her eyes were on mine.

"Jessie, please don't. I love you."

"But I don't love you," she said softly. "It's over."

She cocked the hammer back with her thumb. It was just a click. A tiny sound.

I lunged forward to grab the gun before it went off in her throat.

I got my hands on it. I pulled it down. And it went off in my face.

The last thing I saw were Jessie's eyes.

I know she didn't mean to shoot me, I know it was an accident.

I know she still loved me, no matter what she said.

And I know I never would have left her, but of course I wasn't countin' on this.

A NOTE ON THE TYPE

The text of this book was set in a digitized version of a typeface called Baskerville. The face itself is a facsimile reproduction of types cast from molds made for John Baskerville (1706–1775) from his designs. Baskerville's original face was one of the forerunners of the type style known to printers as "modern face"—a "modern" of the period A.D. 1800.

Composed by PennSet,
Bloomsburg, Pennsylvania

Printed and bound by R. R. Donnelley & Sons,
Harrisonburg, Virginia

Designed by Cassandra J. Pappas